I0600157

Cover Design by Ruxandra Tudorica, Methyss Art www.methyss-art.com

Formatting by Missy S Castillo

ISBN: 979-8-9926168-0-4

First Edition: March 2025

For more information, visit www.missyscastillowrites.com

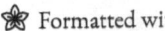 Formatted with Vellum

BOUND IN FLAMES

THE SAVAGE HEARTS SERIES
BOOK ONE

MISSY S CASTILLO

*To the girls who were never meant to be queens but carved their thrones
from the bones of their enemies.
This one is for you.*

∽

Some battles are fought in silence. Others have a Spotify playlist.
Savage Hearts Series: Bound in Flames

TRIGGER WARNINGS

This is an adult dark romantic fantasy that contains graphic and explicit content and mental health themes. This content is only intended for adults of legal age.

Please note that while Bound in Flames includes sexual activities that are loosely inspired by kinks, they are not accurate representations of BDSM and are not meant to act as a guide for engaging in such activities.

- **Abuse & Domestic Violence** ** *Not depicted between main characters*
- **Forced Proximity**
- **War, Violence and Gore**
- **Substance Misuse**
- **Poverty & Social Inequality**
- **Prejudice & Discrimination**
- **Torture**
- **Magical & Emotional Manipulation**
- **Degradation & Humiliation**
- **Explicit Scenes** ** *including dominant/submissive dynamics, non-consensual/dubious consent, size difference, rough sex/oral sex, edging, impact play, breeding/ownership, breath play, and anal play*
- **Mental Health Struggles** ** *including PTSD, anxiety, trauma, emotional distress, self-destructive behavior, self-harm and suicidal ideation*

You've been warned, you've been welcomed. Let's get wild.

CHAPTER 1
CLEO

Blood smeared the horizon, the dying light of dawn struggling to pierce the heavy mist that smothered Syn Farm. I crouched by the hearth. Rough stone bit into my knees, and my hands trembled as I coaxed reluctant embers to life. The acrid scent of charred wood clung to the air, mingling with the sharp tang of my own sweat. My arms ached from the endless labor of yesterday, but it wasn't the weariness in my body that pressed down on me. It was the shadow of my father's voice echoing in my mind: *You'll never amount to anything.* His words were chains, binding me to this dying patch of land, to a future I was powerless to escape.

"Cleo, water on for tea." my father's voice was as rough and unyielding as the stones in the hearth. The demand yanked me from my thoughts, a sharp reminder that here, my rebellion lived only in silence. It wasn't a request. It never was.

"Yes, father," I said, the words hollow, my voice little more than a breath as I reached for the battered kettle. The motions were automatic now, drilled into me like the ache in my bones. I poured the water, watched the steam rise, and when the kettle began to scream, I bit back the urge to do the same.

I swept a hand back through my hair, catching painfully on a knot in the messy braid. I winced but didn't stop, yanking the tangle free with a sharp pull. The sting in my scalp was a fleeting distraction from the clawing ache in my chest. But then, there was something else—a faint, tingling warmth at the edges of my senses. It wasn't the fire, and it wasn't the chill of the morning air. It was something deeper, something I couldn't quite place. It stirred uneasily just beneath my skin before it faded into the noise of my thoughts. Last night's betrayal sat heavy in the air around me, thick and suffocating, as if the shadows of his deal had crept into every corner of the room, whispering of a future I could no longer escape.

A marriage. Arranged in whispers over a grimy tavern table, sealed with the scratch of a pen and the clink of a debt repaid. My father's gambling had been the noose, and I was the tethered goat. The man he'd sold me to was old enough to be my grandfather, his eyes hungry with greed, his smile a promise of misery. I had one week of freedom left.

The kettle's shrill whistle yanked me back to the present. I poured the tea and carried it to him. His cold gray eyes flicked over me, sharp and appraising, like I was a bushel of grain to be weighed and sold. His gruff orders blurred together into background noise. *The market. The debts. Don't come back empty-handed.*

"Yes sir," I murmured.

As I turned toward the door, I felt his heavy gaze follow me. Shackles had less weight. Everything about Syn Farm was a reflection of him: withered crops, crumbling walls, and choices that spiraled endlessly downward. The dowry Mama had saved was long gone, gambled away on promises as empty as the coffers. And me? My worth had been measured and sold to the highest bidder.

The neighbors liked to whisper about me, how my looks were unusual, too bold for their delicate tastes. At twenty-five, my age only seemed to amplify their judgment, setting me further apart in a society that prized youth and conformity in women. They never said it to my face, but I knew the truth. My wild auburn curls had a mind of their own, always a frizzy mess no matter how hard I tried to tame them. Add to that my freckled face and green eyes that seemed to scream defiance, and it was no wonder the neighbors looked at me like I was trouble waiting to happen. Not exactly the meek and mild daughter anyone hoped for. Too strong, they said. Too willful.

Mama had understood me. She used to call my spirit a blessing, not a curse. She'd sit with me by the hearth, whispering stories about women who bent the world to their will, who didn't wait for permission to claim their power. She'd speak of how they could feel the pulse of the earth, the breath of the wind, and the steady rhythm of life coursing through them—and how, one day, I might feel it too. But those dreams had faded long ago, lost to time to his bitterness. I couldn't even visit her grave without his sharp words ringing in my ears, reminding me of how little remained of her in our lives. He saw her in me, in the shape of my face, the curve of my smile—and hated me more for it. As I grew older, the blows came harder, as if he could beat her memory out of me.

I paused in the hallway, the rough wood of the doorframe biting into my palms as I gripped it for balance. My breath hitched, and the walls pressing closer, suffocating me. Something had to change. It had to. Because if this was all my life would ever be, I wasn't sure I could bear it much longer.

THE HEAT of the market pressed down like a living thing as I wove through the throng of bustling villagers. The air carried the tang of spiced meats, the earthy scent of freshly dug turnips, and the acrid undertone of livestock. I walked alone, each step heavy with the weight of what I carried.

Every movement burned with purpose. My pocket held the last of Mama's jewelry. Its presence both a comfort and a wound. She'd once worn the ring with pride, a symbol of love and hope. The thought made my stomach twist with regret.

The whispers of the market goers prickled at my ears as I passed, their words like nettles brushing against my skin.

"That's the Syn girl. I heard she was to be betrothed to—"

"Shame about her father. She'll end up just like him, I'm sure."

Their eyes lingered, but I forced myself to keep walking, my chin held high even as my heart hammered in my chest. The market's vibrant chaos did little to distract me from the gnawing sense of unease that had settled deep in my bones.

I approached the jeweler's stall. The weight of the ring in my pocket seemed to grow heavier, an anchor of memories I couldn't let go. I pulled it out with trembling fingers, the gold catching the sunlight in a way that pierced straight through my chest. It wasn't just a piece of Mama's jewelry—it was her. Her laughter, her warmth, the way she'd smile and say everything would be okay. Now, it was all I had left of her, a fragile link to a life that felt like it belonged to someone else. Now, it was nothing more than a means to pay another debt I hadn't incurred. The ache in my chest deepened, and I couldn't breathe past the grief. The jeweler's sharp eyes assessed it with cold precision, his lips pursed in judgment.

"I can do three gold pieces, not a copper more." He placed a few coins in my hand. Not enough. It was never enough.

Clutching the coins tightly I turned away and made my way toward the food stalls. The air grew thicker with the mingling scents of fresh bread and roasting meats, but even the warmth of the aromas couldn't ease the chill in my veins.

A ragged group of children wove through the crowd like shadows, their thin faces a mixture of desperation and fleeting triumph as they clutched stolen loaves of bread tightly to their chests. The baker's outraged shouts cut through the air, but no one moved to stop them. My steps faltered as I watched them vanish into a narrow alley, their small forms swallowed by the darkness. Their gaunt frames and wide, hollow eyes stayed with me, silent cries for help that clawed at my conscience.

My hand tightened around the coins in my pocket. I could feel the press of my father's expectations like a noose around my neck, but a sharp bitterness cut through the fear. He'd find a reason to beat me anyway—whether I came home with less coins or the wrong tone in my voice. The realization twisted into a defiant thought: if I was going to suffer, why not let it be for something that mattered? I closed my eyes briefly, and their faces swam in the darkness—gaunt cheeks, hollow eyes, desperation clinging to them like shadows. A memory of Mama's voice rose unbidden, her gentle words wrapping around me like a balm. My throat burned with unshed tears as I recalled her voice as clearly as if she stood beside me. *No one should go hungry, Cleo. Not if we can help it.*

Before I could think, I turned toward the nearest stall and handed over a gold coin. The merchant handed me a basket of meat, fruit and bread, his eyebrows raised in surprise. "Generous of you," he muttered.

I didn't answer. My heart pounded as I made my way to the alley. The sounds of the bustling market faded into a low hum as I focused on the children huddled in the doorway. They froze when they saw me, their eyes wide and wary, suspicion sharpening their gaunt features. In this dark and violent world, I knew trust was a luxury they couldn't afford.

"Here," I said softly, setting the basket down and stepping back. "Take it."

None of them moved. Their gazes flicked between me and the basket. Slowly, a boy—thin, no older than ten—inched forward, his movements cautious as if he'd expected the offer to be snatched away. He grabbed the basket and retreated quickly, his eyes never leaving mine. The others crowded close, their wary eyes broke my heart, their suspicion and hunger cutting deeper than any blade. They moved with the hesitancy of creatures long used to traps, their fear so palpable it seemed to bleed into the air around us. I wished I could offer more than a small meal, but in this world, even kindness had its limits.

As the boy tore into the basket's contents, the others swarmed like starving crows, their small hands clawing for scraps with a desperation that tugged at my chest. Their ravenous gaze burned itself into my memory, the desperate glint in their eyes echoing the frantic, wet smacks of their chewing. Each hurried bite gnawed at my conscience, a weight I couldn't dislodge no matter how hard I tried.

"Why?" the older boy asked.

I hesitated as a lump formed in my throat. "Because it's what my mother would have done," I said, my voice quiet but steady. Knowing I could do some good, however small, was enough to make me smile. The world was cruel, and I couldn't change it, but helping them, even in this tiny way, felt like defiance—a rebellion against the darkness.

The boy's grip on the basket loosened as he passed out food to the others. The youngest clung to his side, their small hands clutching at the meat like it was the most precious thing in the world. Their hunger was so raw, so real, that I felt my own bitterness surge again. My father's voice echoed in my mind, berating me for wasting his money, for daring to make a choice of my own. He'd beat me for this, but I didn't care. Let him. At least this would be worth it.

"Thank you." His voice was barely audible, but the gratitude in his eyes burned brighter than any words could convey.

I nodded, stepping back further. "Stay safe." The words felt hollow as I said them.

As I turned to leave, I felt their eyes on me. It wasn't judgment or fear, but something softer. Hope, perhaps. It was a fragile thing, a flickering candle against the encroaching dark, but it was enough to fuel a warmth deep in my chest. My fingers tingled as it rushed through my bloodstream, burning away the lingering chill of my own hopeless fate and it numbed the ache that gnawed at me.

But the warmth didn't last. As the shadows of the alley swallowed me, the weight of the world pressed against my shoulders once more. That small spark of hope felt almost cruel, a reminder of everything this wretched world had stolen from them. My jaw tightened, and my hands curled into fists, nails digging into my palms. Hope was all I could give them, but it wasn't enough. Not for them, and not for me.

WHEN I RETURNED to the square, the world came rushing back. The stench of unwashed bodies mingled with the tang of sour ale and the coppery bite of freshly butchered meat. The air was heavy, thick with smoke that curled lazily from vendors' makeshift stoves, the bitter scent of charred bread mixing with the sharper aroma of overripe fruit. My boots scuffed the uneven cobblestones, each step punctuated by the distant clanging of a blacksmith's hammer and the braying of a mule too stubborn to move.

The crowd pressed in on all sides, voices rising and falling in a chaotic symphony. My father's figure loomed at the far end of the plaza, a storm of anger barely contained in the rigid lines of his posture. His face was a mottled shade of red, the kind that made me want to flinch before he even spoke. His boots struck the ground in a steady, deliberate rhythm as he marched toward me, his presence cutting through the chaos.

The noise of the market dulled, muffled by the pounding in my ears. My heart hammered against my ribs, the sound so loud it drowned out the world, and I felt as if I were walking through water, each step dragging me closer to the inevitable.

"What is this?" he barked, his voice low but venomous. His eyes fell to my empty basket and the few coins clutched tightly in my hand. "Where is the rest?"

I swallowed hard, gripping the basket tightly against my hip. The echo of the boy's thanks rang in my ears, a fragile shield against his anger. "It's what I could manage." My voice was steady despite the tremor in my chest.

"Don't lie to me, Cleo," he snapped, stepping closer. His lips curling into a sneer. "You think I don't know you've wasted what little we have? What did you spend it on? Trinkets? *Yourself?*"

"No," I said quickly, the defiance I'd felt earlier curling into something sharper. "I gave it to people who needed it."

His eyes widened in disbelief. Then the fury returned, it was white-hot. "Ungrateful little bitch!" he spat, his voice rising enough to draw the attention of passersby. "You think you're better than me? Throwing away money we can't afford to lose on beggars? You're as worthless as your mother!"

The words hit me harder than the slap that followed. Pain flared across my cheek, hot and sharp, but it was his words that burned deeper. The market seemed to tilt for a moment before I steadied myself, the dropped basket laid forgotten at my feet. The onlookers turned away, faces blank or carefully neutral. No one intervened.

"She would have done the same." I kept my voice low but audible. I didn't look at him, focusing instead on the uneven stones beneath my feet. "Children should never be hungry."

He grabbed my arm, his grip bruising as he leaned closer, his breath hot and soured by day-old malted ale. "Don't you dare talk about her," he hissed, each word laced with venom. *"You are a fool."*

Heat prickled behind my eyes, but I blinked hard to chase the tears away. His fingers dug into my arm, each press sending a fresh jolt of pain rippling to my shoulder. My teeth ground together, muscles taut with defiance. A tremor threatened to betray me, coiling tight in my throat, but I shoved the words past it. "You can beat me, but you can't decide who I am."

His cruel laugh drew a larger crowd of market-goers. "You think this will save the farm? They are nothing! It will never be enough. *You* will never be enough."

Something inside me snapped. The anger that I'd been holding back surged forward like a storm. "I'm doing what I can! You're the one who gambled everything away! Why am I the one paying for your mistakes?" I shouted, the words trembling with a mix of fury, desperation, and disgust.

I watched as his jaw tightened, the muscles rippling beneath his skin as his lips pressed into a thin, bloodless line. Shadows seemed to gather in his eyes, swirling like the sky before a violent storm. "How dare you! Just like your mother. Good for nothing but spreading your legs and causing trouble."

The second slap snapped my head to the side, heat exploding across my cheek. The sharp crack echoed through the square, freezing the bustling crowd in its wake. My breath hitched, the sting of the blow clawing at my composure, but the murmurs that followed hit harder. Each whisper pierced like a needle, threading humiliation through my skin. I bit down hard, teeth grinding, as my anger surged to meet the shame, locking my spine straight when all I wanted was to shrink into nothing. They just watched. Faces a mixture of pity and morbid fascination. None of them stepped forward. *Cowards.*

"You're a disgrace," he spat. "You'll bring nothing but ruin to this family. I should have sold you off when you were younger and worth more coin."

My vision tunneled and the world around me blurred. Something rose within me, an anger I couldn't control. My hands clenched into fists, and the air around me seemed to shift, heavy with unseen energy. A low hum began to vibrate through my body, growing stronger with every heartbeat, coming from the curled warmth inside my chest.

The ground beneath us groaned, a deep vibration that seemed to echo through my very bones before it cracked open Energy surged through me like a fire roaring in my veins, both terrifying and exhilarating. Thick green vines erupted from the cobblestones, their movements fluid yet deliberate, as though they had a will of their own. I could feel their presence—alive, connected to me—as they coiled around my father's boots.

The heat inside me surged, my fingers tingling and my breath quickening. The vines twisted higher, their grip tightening, and I felt the strain of the cobblestones groaning beneath their weight. My father's eyes were wide with shock, a flicker of fear breaking through his fury as he stumbled back, clawing desperately at the magic. His panicked movements only seemed to provoke them, their coils tightening in response to his struggle like a predator closing in on its catch.

The crowd gasped, stumbling back in a frantic wave, like prey scattering from a predator. Some clutched their children, dragging them away, while others craned their necks, drawn by a mix of fear and fascination. Whispers rippled through them, cutting through the chaos.

"Dark conjurer," someone muttered, the word laced with dread.

"Dangerous—"

I stared at the vines in horror, my chest heaving as the energy surged through me, unrestrained. I hadn't meant to do this. I hadn't even known I could. My father's face twisted with fear as he tore at the vines, his panicked voice rising above the crowd.

Tears burned my eyes, but I blinked them away, refusing to let them fall. My chest tightened, each breath coming fast and sharp as fear twisted in my stomach. My hands trembled, the hum of power still buzzing under my skin, a stark and unshakable reminder of what I had unleashed. I didn't regret defending myself—but the magic, wild and uncontrollable, had shaken something deep inside me. "I—"

"Guards!" he roared.

The crowd split as two guards cautiously approached, their deliberate strides and grim expressions cutting through the square. My chest tightened, panic flooding my veins in a suffocating rush. My breath hitched, shallow and ragged, as the world narrowed to their advancing forms. Before thought could catch up, my body took over. My legs burst into motion, driving me forward, blind and desperate. Cobblestones jarred beneath my feet, each step a frantic slam, as the market dissolved into a blur of noise and color. Stalls flashed past in jagged streaks, faces turned toward me in shock, but I saw nothing—only the path ahead and my instincts to escape.

Behind me, the sharp clatter of armor and the barked orders of the guards grew louder. My father's curses sliced through the air, but I refused to look back. My breath came in ragged gasps, my chest heaving with the effort of escape. Fear clawed at me, but something deeper, something unfamiliar, pushed me forward.

For the first time, I was running from and to something, That unknown may hold freedom, and I wanted to grasp it firmly with both hands and never let go.

CHAPTER 2
CLEO

The guards were on me before I could get far. Their attack was swift and precise, like predators targeting defenseless prey. Their boots slammed against the cobblestones, each step a thunderclap that seemed to shake the ground and fill the air with tension. The crowd had broken apart like scattering birds, but not all of them had fled. Some lingered, their faces twisted in disgust or grim fascination, as if they couldn't resist watching me be cuffed and dragged through the streets like some kind of dangerous monster.

The enchanted cuffs wrapped around my wrists seemed alive, buzzing faintly with energy, as if mocking me. The emptiness they created was terrifying, a hollow silence where an undiscovered magic had once pulsed steadily through me. I barely understood the power I held, let alone how to control it, but the thought of being cut off from it felt like losing a part of myself I hadn't realized I couldn't live without.

Rough hands latched onto my arms, yanking them behind me with a brutal strength. Pain shot through my shoulders as my arms were wrenched into an awkward position that forced me off balance. The pressure of their grip made my skin feel raw. I thrashed instinctively, trying to twist free, but their hold was ironclad. My panic seemed to amuse them, drawing laughter and cruel remarks that cut deeper than any physical restraints ever could.

These cuffs weren't just tools of imprisonment—they were legendary. The Crown's enforcers used them to suppress conjurers, and the rarer wild shamans, making it impossible for them to access their magic in custody. I had overheard whispered rumors of the cuffs in tavern corners, tales of how brutal and effective they were, said to not just sever access to magic, but hope itself. Now I was wearing them, and every faint hum against my skin was a reminder of my powerlessness and the Crown's dominance. They had been right. I felt completely void of hope. Of a life free of oppression, of pain and cruelty. As they clicked shut around my wrists, I felt the weight of finality press down on my chest.

"Think she can wiggle free?" One guard sneered, his voice dripping with mockery. "You're wasting your energy, bitch!"

Their boots scuffed the cobblestones as they pushed me forward, the harsh scrape echoing alongside the pounding of my heart. With every jerk of their hands, I could feel the fight draining from my body. My breath came in sharp gasps, and my pulse raced, driven by a mixture of fear and fury. Each step was a struggle, my feet dragging against uneven stones, yet I couldn't stop trying to resist, even knowing it was hopeless.

The crowd's murmur never ceased, growing louder and more pointed with each passing moment.

"She's dangerous."

"A wild shaman in Sleek Valley? Is nowhere safe?"

A woman was clutching her child tightly, knuckles white as she glared at me. "Keep your distance. Nothing good comes of your kind!"

I stumbled forward under the guards' grip, the cuffs digging into my wrists with every step. Sharp pain shot down to my fingertips, but it was nothing compared to the humiliation. They paraded me through the streets like a caged animal, every whispered word and scornful glare cutting deeper than the metal around my skin. No matter how hard I tried, I couldn't block out the judgment etched in their eyes or the venom in their hushed voices. Their hatred clung to me like a suffocating cloak, tightening with every word, every sneer. Friends and neighbors turned on me so easily, their betrayal settling in my stomach like acid.

"Hold still." One of my captors cursed, his rancid breath feathered across my face as he sharply twisted my arm.

"Let go of me!"

"Look what she did to her father! And to think one of them was hiding amongst us all this time—"

I could feel my panic rising, and the world seemed to tilt. My breath hitched as I frantically searched inside myself for the familiar and comforting warmth I had always felt beneath my skin, a low and steady rhythm I had assumed everyone felt. It was as though someone had ripped away a part of me. My body sagged in the guards' grip as I felt the aching absence of that peaceful presence. My skin felt wrong, too tight and too empty all at once.

"Get her moving. The Crown doesn't pay for you to coddle shamans!" barked a brutish man with a twisted sneer that screamed of his prejudices.

He jerked his head toward the old guardhouse, and they dragged me forward, my heart pounding, a drumbeat of defiance buried deep beneath the mounting dread. The crowds' whispers followed me like a ghost.

"A menace—"

"—should have been drowned at birth. Nothing natural about her eyes!"

"She's dangerous! Get her out of here!"

"Nothing but trouble!"

The words cut through the crowd, each one a fresh wound that made my stomach twist. The hatred branding their words into my heart. I bit back a sob as my gaze landed on my father, disheveled and trembling in rage. His shirt was torn, remnants of vines that had wrapped around him still clung to his pants. His face was flushed, and when his eyes met mine, they were filled with nothing but contempt.

I hated him for what he had become, for the drunken rages and the bruises that had shaped much of my life. But beneath that hate, a part of me still clung to the father he used to be—the one who had held me as a child, his voice soft and steady as he told me stories of the world before darkness crept across Ostelan. That part of me ached, even as his words and fists had struck me like whips for years.

He stepped forward, and my stomach twisted in dread. His lip curled as he spat at my feet, the sound echoing louder than any of the whispers around me. "I should have known. Twenty-five years old, unwed, and a burden from the start. I should have seen the signs! And now a shaman?! A fucking stain on our good family name!"

His words lashed me, but it wasn't just the accusations. It was the complete lack of the man I had once loved, the father who had guided me in my studies before he was consumed by his drinking. Replaced by this hollow, hateful shell of a man. And yet part of me still mourned for what I had lost. Each word struck me like a blow. My knees threatened to give, trembling under the weight of his hatred. My chest ached with the effort to keep the tears at bay. I looked for a flicker of the father I once knew, but there was nothing.

"You've bought shame on this family. On *me!*"

My eyes burned as I ripped my gaze from his, and the cobblestones blurred beneath me as I fought back the tears threatening to fall. I was determined not to give them the satisfaction of seeing me break. Confusion churned in my chest, tangled with anger and grief. *How could I mourn someone who had caused me so much pain?* And yet, there it was —a deep ache for the father I used to know, the one who laughed easily, who held me when I cried. Before the anger. Before the alcohol. That man was gone, lost to his demons, and yet part of me still clung to the hope that he might return. The hope made the pain sharper, cut deeper. I startled when the guards pushed me forward, laughing at my faltering steps.

Worse than the whispers was the hollow ache where the magic had been. The steady warmth was gone, leaving me raw, exposed. Shame scorched through me, laced with the bitter sting of betrayal. But even as humiliation threatened to drown me, I held on to my defiance. They wouldn't see me break.

～

THE JAILHOUSE LOOMED AHEAD, its stone walls cold and unwelcoming, a fortress of despair. The guards shoved me through the heavy wooden doors with a force that sent me sprawling, their laughter echoing in the dimly lit cell. My knees hit the filthy, straw-strewn floor, my palms scraping against the uneven stones. The cuffs around my wrists buzzed faintly, a cruel and constant reminder of the power they had stolen from me, the power that was no longer mine to wield. The flickering torchlight threw jagged shadows on the walls, my nose crinkled at the reek of sweat, rot, and hopelessness.

"Caught yourself a live one." A guard chuckled, his eyes lingering on me in a way that made my skin crawl. "Shame. Pretty thing like her could've been fun to play with."

My pulse thundered in my ears, instincts screaming at me, and I felt like a trapped animal. Every muscle in my body was tense, the weight of their leering gazes coiling around me like a noose. The way they moved, the casual cruelty in their words—it wasn't the first time they'd done this. I could feel it in the air, thick with unspoken violence, and the realization made me sick.

"You call this pretty?" Another guard stepped closer, grabbing a handful of my curls. Yanking me back to my feet so roughly my neck screamed in pain. "Looks more like a feral beast to me. You see the way she snarled out there?"

I wrenched away from him, pain lancing through my scalp as his grip tore free a clump of hair. The sting brought tears to my eyes, but I refused to let them fall. My pain only fueled their laughter—a sound cold and jagged, brimming with malice. It clawed at my nerves, scraping against the raw edges of my fear.

Before I could recover, a hard shove sent me stumbling back. My feet faltered, and my head bounced off the stone with a sickening crack that reverberated through my skull. Stars burst behind my eyes, blurring the world into jagged shapes and shadows. Warmth spread across the back of my head, the faint smell of blood mixing with the dust and grime of the street. An itch prickled beneath the growing wetness, and I struggled to keep my focus as the nausea grew.

Pain and dizziness swirled together, threatening to pull me under, but I swallowed against the urge to vomit, forcing myself to stay alert.

The guards' cruel laughter still rang in my ears, and even as my vision swam, I tried to bite back the groan rising in my throat. I couldn't give them the satisfaction.

The cell door slammed shut, the sound reverberating through the tiny space. I staggered to the corner, the acidic burn rising in my throat as I sank onto the cold, filthy floor. My head throbbed, a dull but insistent ache, each pulse making the room spin. I reached up slowly, my fingers trembling as they brushed against the sticky warmth at the back of my head. The texture sent a shiver through me—matted hair and blood, crusted and damp. I winced, pulling my hand back to examine it in the dim light, but the shadows swallowed any detail.

The thin cotton of my dress offered no warmth against the chill creeping through the stone. It clung to my skin, slick with sweat and grime, doing little to keep the cold at bay. My boots were my only source of warmth, laced halfway up my calves. They felt heavy and stiff, caked with mud that cracked with every movement, the tight leather grounding me. I drew my knees to my chest, wrapping my arms tightly around them, but the cold still seeped in, gnawing at my bones.

The dimness seemed alive, swallowing nearly everything except the faint glint of iron bars and the decaying straw scattered across the floor. My chest tightened, and I pressed myself further into the corner, desperate for even the illusion of safety. The damp air clung to my skin like a heavy cloak. Somewhere in the distance, the steady drip of water echoed, each plunk hammering into my mind like a clock counting down to my inevitable fate.

Outside my cell, the guards exchanged crude comments, their voices carrying through the oppressive silence. "Looks like she'll get real comfortable in here," one said, his tone thick with mockery.

Another snorted. "Comfortable? She'll be lucky to last the night without cracking. Shamans always break. Especially the new ones. They're like fish out of water without their magic. It's only a matter of time before the silence eats away at them."

"She'll crack even faster than most. You can see it in her eyes. Already hollow."

The walls seemed to close in, the damp air pressing against my chest until each breath felt like a battle. My hands shook as I clutched at my knees, nails digging into the thin cotton of my dress in a desperate attempt to hold myself together.

Breathe, Cleo. Just breathe. Five things you can see.

My lips trembled as I whispered the words my mother had taught me. My eyes darted around the cell, latching onto anything: the glint of iron bars. The decaying straw scattered across the floor. The faint smear of blood on my fingertips. The jagged edge of a stone near my foot. The faintly glowing crack of light seeping under the door.

Four things you can touch. I let my fingers move, brushing over the rough stone at my back. The gritty texture of the straw beneath me. The soft fabric of my dress clinging to my skin. The damp, cold leather of my boots.

Three things you can hear. I strained my ears, focusing on the drip of water echoing in the silence. The faint shuffle of boots in the distance. The unsteady rasp of my own breath.

Two things you can smell. The sour tang of damp stone filled my nose. Mixed with the metallic bite of blood.

One thing you can taste. I swallowed hard, the coppery taste of my bitten lip lingering on my tongue.

Slowly, the storm inside me began to quiet. My heart still raced, but the edges of my panic softened, no longer razor-sharp. Mama's voice echoed in my mind, steady and soothing. *"When the world feels like it's spinning out of control, you anchor yourself, Cleo. You find the things that remind you that you're still here."*

Time passed in a crawl, my head fuzzy and still ringing with the barely controlled panic. Outside my cell the guards talked freely, their voices low but still audible.

"Knights Hold won't waste time with her, shamans go straight to the gallows these days. Or worse. The crown doesn't waste resources on their kind."

"Good riddance, fewer of her kind, the safer we all are. They think their magic makes them special."

Their words sent a fresh wave of fear coursing through me. Knights Hold. The name was whispered like a curse among those who dared speak of it at all. It was where the Ostelan Crown sent those accused of crimes too dangerous for local punishment—traitors, sorcerers, and shamans. None returned. Stories of public executions and the horrors that awaited there were told in hushed voices, the details grotesque enough to turn even the strongest stomach.

Even so, their words churned in my mind. I imagined the gallows, the crowds shouting for my death, my body swinging lifelessly in the breeze. Or worse, some experiment at the hands of the Crown's Enforcers. The thought wrapped around my chest like an iron band, squeezing tighter with every passing second. I closed my eyes, trying to push the thoughts away, but their laughter dragged me back, a constant reminder that my fate was already written. I wouldn't cry. I couldn't. Not for them to see. Not for anyone.

Magic. The word itself felt foreign, like an accusation rather than a reality. My mind reeled, trying to reconcile the whispers of *shaman* with the life I had known. I had never seen myself as anything but a farmer's daughter. I had spent countless days working the fields, my hands in the soil, feeling the steady rhythm of the earth beneath me. It was the closest thing to peace I had ever known. The vibrant energy I had felt while tending crops or walking the forests wasn't magic, was it? I hadn't thought so. It had simply been life, as natural as breathing.

Doubt clawed at me. *Had it always been magic?* The hum beneath my skin, the connection I'd always felt to the land. Was that what set me apart? The villagers spoke of shamans as wild, untamed forces, dangerous because they defied the Crown's control. But I wasn't some wild force. I was just... me. *Wasn't I?*

The thought churned in my mind, bitter and heavy. The one thing that had ever made me feel alive, that had made me *me*, could it truly be the reason for all this? The idea twisted inside me, cutting deep in places I hadn't known could hurt.

Time lost meaning in the darkness of the cell. Minutes stretched into hours, maybe even days, though I couldn't tell anymore. Every part of me ached, my stomach twisting painfully with hunger, but none of it compared to the hollow void where my magic had been. The cuffs drained my strength, stripping away the energy I hadn't even realized I'd come to rely on. With every passing moment, the absence of that steady, comforting hum left me weaker, as if I were slowly crumbling from the inside out.

The void was where my thoughts festered. They whispered darkly, twisted and refusing to give me any peace. I thought about the quiet buzz of my magic—how it had once been so constant I had barely noticed it. Now its absence gnawed at me like a phantom limb, a hollow space that couldn't be filled. The silence was deafening.

I saw my father's face twisted in anger as he called for my arrest. His voice, sharp and bitter, echoed in my ears, replaying his venomous words over and over until they became a chant I couldn't escape. I heard the villagers, their voices rising in a hateful chorus.

But beneath the sorrow, anger burned like a low fire. It simmered, growing hotter with each cruel laugh from the guards, each jeering comment they threw my way. Anger at my father for the years of abuse, and for choosing his pride over his own blood. At the villagers for their cowardice, their willingness to turn on someone they had known for years. Anger at myself for being too weak to fight back, too scared to do anything but endure.

When they came for me again, dragging me out of the cell and into the harsh light of day, the anger had strengthened my resolve. It was quiet now, a smoldering ember in the pit of my stomach. I didn't struggle as they chained my wrists to the bars of a prison cart, the ever present weight of the enchanted cuffs ensuring my compliance. A constant reminder of my powerlessness. I didn't flinch at their jeers or react when they mocked me. I only stared ahead, my jaw tight, my green eyes burning with defiance.

Rain began to fall as the cart rattled down the uneven road. The first drops were cold against my skin, a stark contrast to the heat of my anger. Soon the rain came down harder, soaking my hair and plastering the dirt of captivity against my face. The countryside blurred past me, dark and unwelcoming, but I didn't let it pull me in. Instead, my gaze locked on the birds wheeling freely in the gray sky, their wings cutting through the rain with grace. A pang of longing pierced my chest. I envied their freedom, their ability to fly far away from this place, from this life. But I didn't look away.

The guards' voices buzzed at the edges of my awareness, their words sharp and ugly. I tried to block them out, to bury their voices beneath the pounding of my heart, but fragments still slipped through. Crude remarks about my body. Mocking laughter that sent heat crawling up my neck. Bets exchanged over the violent fate that awaited me in Knight's Hold. Each word struck like a lash, leaving raw wounds I fought to ignore. I clenched my jaw, forcing my focus elsewhere to quieten the simmering rage. I focused on the way the cuffs felt against my skin, a faint vibration I latched onto like a lifeline. Somewhere beneath the despair, something still stirred. My magic wasn't gone. Not entirely. It was there, hidden and waiting, flickering just out of reach.

Fear, anger, and loss swirled within me, a raging storm tearing through me. How had it come to this? The end of my life before it had even begun. There was so much I had dreamed of—to see beyond the endless stretch of fields, to be more than a farmer's daughter, to find a place where I truly belonged. All of it stolen from me before I'd even realized it was mine to reach for.

The thought burned, a fire that spread through the bitterness of betrayal and the sharp sting of fear. My nails bit into my palms, grounding me against the tide threatening to swallow me whole.

This wasn't the end.

Not yet.

Not if I had any say in it.

CHAPTER 3
CLEO

The prison wagon jolted violently, its wheels crunching over the uneven dirt road, forcing me to shift awkwardly to avoid being thrown against the cold iron bars. I sat in silence. My back was pressed against the unyielding bars, and my wrists were still bound above my head. The enchanted metal sapped my strength with every mile, a cold pressure that seemed to seep into my bones. The familiar hum of my magic, something I'd always thought of as a quiet part of myself, was barely a flicker, smothered by the cuffs' iron grip. The oppressive weight of the journey to the capital was draining me. I knew each jolt of the wagon carried me closer to my death.

I hadn't spoken to the guards since they had thrown me into the wagon, their jeers and occasional strikes silencing any protests I might have made. Their disdain for me was clear—a shaman, not worth the effort of civility. Each mocking comment was a sharp reminder of the fate awaiting me at Knights Hold.

As the hours dragged on, the countryside morphed from rolling fields to dense forests that seemed to swallow the fading light of late afternoon. The trees loomed like silent sentinels, their gnarled branches reaching overhead to blot out the sky. Shadows pooled in the underbrush, flickering with the wagon's movements as if alive. The forest seemed to hold its breath.

The wagon creaked with each bump and turn, the sound blending with the distant caws of crows overhead. Patches of gnarled roots twisted through the dirt road, clawing at the wagon's wheels as if the forest itself sought to trap us in its grasp. Each jolt sent vibrations rattling through the iron bars, and I couldn't shake the feeling that the trees were watching, their shadows shifting in ways that defied logic. The scent of moss and decaying leaves was so thick it left a bitter taste on my tongue. Somewhere deeper in the forest, an unseen creature let out a low, mournful cry that sent a shiver down my spine. The air was heavy with the scent of rain-soaked earth, and my stiff fingers curled into fists against the chill. Each shift of the cuffs sent a faint vibration through my wrists, the enchantment gnawing at the edges of my mind. It wasn't just physical; it was as if the absence of magic unraveled something fundamental inside me, leaving a hollow ache I couldn't escape.

Up ahead, another patrol wagon came into view at a fork in the road. The oxen pulling it stomped and snorted nervously, their breath misting in the cool air. Guards loitered around the stationary cart. Their laughter and coarse voices carried on the wind. My curiosity stirred despite the exhaustion pressing heavily on me. The clang of armor and the scrape of boots against dirt reached me before their faces did, a jarring rhythm to their casual conversation. As the wagon jolted forward, my breath stuttered in my chest when I caught sight of their prisoner.

The orc was unmistakable. His massive frame towered over the humans even as he was forced to his knees. His dark green skin bore streaks of dried blood and fresh wounds, creating a grim pattern against the thick muscles. His black hair, damp with sweat and grime, clung to his face, only emphasizing the intensity in his sharp golden eyes. Chains bit into his wrists as well, binding him so tightly that every movement was a slow, deliberate struggle. The guards hauled him to his feet, dragging him forward as we approached. Despite his injuries, his eyes burned with defiance, their golden hue piercing as they scanned the scene with unsettling clarity.

I'd heard of orcs before. Their strength and ferocity were legendary, as well as their barbaric way of life, but I'd never seen one in person. The sight of him, bruised but unbroken, was both terrifying and strangely captivating.

"Get him chained up." The lead guard from our small convoy motioned to the rear of our cart. "No free ride for the beast."

The orc's laugh rang out, rich and sardonic, cutting through the air like a blade. "A free ride? I wouldn't dream of it." His deep voice was tinged with mockery.

The guard struck him hard in the face with the butt of a spear. He stumbled but didn't fall, his tusks flashing menacingly as he grinned despite the blood trickling from his mouth. It was predatory, and my skin erupted in goosebumps as an icy primal fear flashed through me in response. "Careful, you might actually hurt me," the orc responded. His smirk was unwavering as they stepped forward to strike him again, but thought better of it. The guard glowered at him, muttering something under his breath before retreating.

The guards exchanged uneasy glances but said nothing as they hauled him into position, securing the seven-foot giant to the rear of the wagon. The cuffs around his wrists looked as though they had been forged to contain something far more dangerous, their metal groaning faintly under his shifting movements. Each clink of the chains seemed louder in the unnatural stillness of the forest, a rhythmic reminder of the strength restrained within. His wrists were bound in front of him, and though his arms were marked with bruises and cuts, they still flexed with a power that demanded attention. His chest, bare save for an old, battered leather pauldron streaked with blood and grime, rose and fell with a steady rhythm. Even in chains, he held himself with an undeniable presence, his eyes sweeping the wagon with a sharp, deliberate precision that made my breath catch.

As the wagon lurched forward, the orc began to walk easily behind us, his sharp eyes locking onto mine. He studied me, his expression unreadable, before a slow smirk tugged at his lips.

"Well, well." He kept his voice low enough for a private conversation. "Imagine my surprise to be face to face with a shaman on such a beautiful day."

I stiffened, my eyes narrowing. "How do you know what I am?"

"Oh, we orcs have our ways," he replied, his smirk widening. "Confirmed by the cuffs. Only shamans and conjurers get such special treatment."

My gaze dropped, heat crawling up my neck. The weight of his golden eyes bore down on me, making the chains on my wrists feel heavier. Shame twisted in my stomach, and I shifted, trying to shake the feeling. Even as I looked away, a strange pull lingered, his attention unsettling. I could feel my pulse quicken, but I forced my shoulders straighter, ignoring the mix of fascination and unease clawing at me. I kept my eyes fixed on the ground. "What do you want, orc?"

"A little conversation," he said, walking almost casually behind the cart as if he was out on an afternoon stroll, and not in chains. "The road's long, and you're the most interesting thing I've seen in weeks. Tell me, what's your name and what did you do to earn that cozy seat up in the cart?"

"Why? Hoping for tips to ride in luxury to our execution?" I shot back, shifting against the bars, my lips twisting in a wry smile. "Or are you planning to sweet-talk your way out of your chains, too?" My voice was sharper than usual, a small act of defiance against the guards who might still hear our conversation when they wandered too close.

"Depends," he said with a smirk. "Can you teach me how to charm my way out of chains as well as you're charming me? Or is it a talent exclusive of shamans?"

I shot him a wary glance but said nothing. The guards were too far ahead to overhear, but his casual demeanor unsettled me. His injuries should have left him weak, yet he exuded absolute confidence.

"Cleo. What should I call you? Prisoner 438? Or maybe Mr. Overconfident?"

His grin stretched wider, teeth flashing in a way that was both playful and predatory, his golden eyes glinting with amusement. He shifted, the movement slow, deliberate, as if to remind everyone how little the cuffs restrained him. His voice, low and smooth, with a teasing edge. "You can call me whatever you like, so long as you say it sweetly."

"You're blocking my view of the road, orc."

His quiet chuckle caught me off guard, a surprising response to what I had intended as a sharp defense rather than an invitation to banter. Despite my best efforts to maintain a barrier between us, he seemed to revel in the game of unsettling me, as though every word I hurled his way only added fuel to his amusement. *If only I knew orcs were as charming as they were large.*

"My name is Dex. You've got the better seat. I've got the better view."

"Oh?" I asked, arching a brow. "What's so interesting behind this cart?"

"I'm talking about you, obviously." His eyes danced with mischief.

My face burned as a blush bloomed across my cheeks, spreading heat down my neck. I shifted uncomfortably against the bench, willing myself not to fidget, but the feel of his golden eyes lingering on me made it impossible to stay still. His gaze was unnerving, like he was peeling back layers of my carefully constructed walls. I forced my attention elsewhere, determined not to give him the satisfaction of catching me off guard again. I failed miserably.

"What are you doing here?"

Dex's grin turned wry. "Let's just say I've been asking too many questions. The Crown is very sensitive about certain topics."

I ignored the way he spat the word *Crown*, his tone dripping with scorn. The contempt in his voice made his feelings toward the human Royal family of Ostelan unmistakable, and I found myself agreeing with his opinion of them. "Like what?"

"Like shamans," he said, his gaze sharpening. "Your kind is rare, and in my culture, you're revered. Without shamans, our magic weakens. Our people suffer."

I let out a sharp breath. "You were looking for me?"

"Not you specifically, but fate has a funny way of making introductions."

I couldn't help but sneak another glance at all of him. Despite the fresh wounds and bruises, Dex carried himself with an unsettling ease, as though the chains binding him were merely decoration. I lingered too long on the contours of his chest, where muscle shifted beneath bruised skin, each subtle movement exuding a raw, unshaken power. Warmth crept up my neck and spilled onto my cheeks before I could look away.

His golden eyes caught mine, and his smirk deepened. Smug, insufferable, and entirely too knowing. *Damn it, Cleo.*

Dex chuckled, a low, rumbling sound that seemed to vibrate through the air. "You keep glancing at me. Should I take it as a compliment?" His words were quiet enough that the guards milling around wouldn't hear, but the knowing edge in his tone made me shift uncomfortably, hyper-aware of their periodic presence.

"You're in chains, bruised and bleeding," I said dryly. "Trust me, it's not admiration."

He laughed, the sound deep and unbothered, rolling through the tension like it had no business being there. "You must be used to people underestimating you and your sharp tongue, little shaman." His eyes glinted with amusement as if he found my defiance entertaining.

"For someone in cuffs, you're annoyingly cocky," I grumbled, crossing my arms in a weak attempt to steady myself. The heat rising to my cheeks only fueled my irritation. I needed to set him as off balance as he was making me feel.

"Confidence isn't something they can lock up." His tone was smooth, like this entire conversation was just a game to him.

"Careful," I shot back, narrowing my eyes. "Or your ego's going to snap those chains before you do."

"Would that impress you?" His voice dropped into a low, teasing drawl, each word laced with deliberate provocation. His lazy smile was infuriating. He shifted his weight, muscles rippling against the heavy cuffs. "Though, I'd wager I'd make quite the spectacle."

"Try it and we'll see." My tone carried the faintest edge of amusement, even as I fought to keep a straight face.

"Ah, there it is," he said with exaggerated delight, his golden eyes gleaming. "I knew there was a personality hiding under all that doom and gloom. Keep going, little shaman. I'm starting to enjoy this trip."

"Not all of us find our current situation quite so entertaining." My lips twitched, betraying the tiniest hint of a smile. He noticed, of course, and preened as if I'd paid him the highest compliment.

"Don't think too hard about it," he said smugly, his tone dropping just enough to make the words linger. "Moments like these are rare, you know."

What was I even doing? Trading barbs with an orc—of all races—while chained and carted toward my own execution? The absurdity of the situation struck me hard, and I wondered if the cuffs were cutting off more than my magic. *Perhaps the blood flow to my brain.* Then there was the way Dex looked at me, his sharp gaze, like he was trying to piece together some puzzle. It made me acutely aware of the torn, dirt-streaked state of my dress, the grime clinging to my arms, and the wild tangles of my hair. The strands stuck to my scalp, tacky and matted with dried blood from the wound I'd earned in the cells. I was a mess, no doubt about it. A flush crept up my neck, heat prickling at my skin, and I clenched my jaw, irritated at myself for caring. He seemed utterly unbothered, but it only made me feel more exposed.

As if sensing my inner turmoil, Dex leaned in, the creak of leather and scrape of metal accompanying the shift of his weight. His expression hovering between amusement and sharp, probing curiosity. It unsettled me, the way his gaze seemed to strip away my defenses, as though he saw far more than I wanted him to. The air between us grew taut, charged with unspoken questions and an unnameable tension. I should have looked away, but instead, I found myself leaning forward, drawn into his orbit despite the warning bells screaming in my mind.

"The humans kill what they can't control, and your kind tips the scales too far for their comfort. That's why they put you in chains. But trust me, there's power in their fear. If you learn to wield it, you'll never be chained by them again."

The weight of his words pressed against the fragile remnants of my resolve. Despite his casual tone, there was an intensity in his voice that hinted at something deeper. "Why tell me this? What do you want from me?" I snapped, my voice pitching higher as frustration seeped into my tone.

I watched as his grin softened, a flicker of something genuine breaking through his bravado. "To survive, and to make sure you do too."

The wagon jolted again, its wooden frame groaning in protest, the sound echoing through the dense trees. The cuffs around my wrists shifted, their cold weight a cruel reminder of my captivity. My thoughts, however, remained fixed on the orc chained behind us. The stillness of

31

the forest seemed to amplify every clink of his chains, every movement of his powerful frame. He was an enigma. Wounded, bound, yet wholly undeterred by the circumstances that would break most others. I didn't trust him, but his words stirred something within me, a spark of curiosity and the faintest glimmer of hope. The way he spoke, with such ease and confidence, was entirely at odds with the bruises on his skin and the chains that bound him. He seemed unaffected by our shared predicament, as though the wagon and the guards meant nothing. That attitude was infectious.

I found myself wondering what it would be like to believe in my own strength the way he seemed to believe in his. His words lingered in my mind, prodding at something buried deep within me. A quiet, unformed question about whether my magic could truly be more than a curse. For all his smugness and sharp humor, Dex spoke with a conviction that was hard to ignore.

Since my arrest, I felt as though I wasn't alone. And for the first time in longer than I could remember, I felt the faint stirrings of something close to peace.

CHAPTER 4
DEX

The rhythmic creak of the wagon wheels over uneven dirt was almost meditative. *Almost.* The metallic jangle of my cuffs kept dragging me back to reality, reminding me that every step the oxen took brought us closer to a fight I wasn't sure I could win. I swept my eyes over the guards walking alongside the wagon, studying them, cataloging each potential weakness. The one on the left had a limp, subtle but there if you knew where to look. His boots told the story, worn thin on the inside edge, the mark of an old injury that never healed right. That kind of weakness would make him slow to dodge, sluggish under pressure. My eyes traced the way his hand hovered near his weapon, fingers twitching with impatience, as though he thought gripping the hilt tighter might compensate for his failing speed. It wouldn't. It would only take a sharp kick to the knee to bring him down, writhing in pain as his screams echoed through the forest.

Another's armor hung too loose at the shoulders, clinking with every step. A clumsy oversight. One solid blow would shove the metal into his neck or shatter his collarbone, leaving him gasping for air as his blood pooled beneath it. The leader, a burly man with a permanent scowl, carried himself with an air of misplaced confidence. Probably thought his rank made him untouchable. He'd be the first to fall, his surprise evident as I tore through him. Arrogance like his always bled the fastest.

I let my gaze drift to the wagon. The shaman—Cleo, as she'd reluctantly revealed—sat stiffly on the wooden bench, her wrists bound. She tried to appear indifferent, her green eyes fixed on the horizon, but I could tell she was listening to everything. Every insult from the guards, every faint clink of my chains. She was calculating, just like me. My gaze lingered a moment too long, tracing the curve of her neck and the way her shoulders tensed beneath her dirty dress. She was short and curvy, and there was a striking balance of strength and grace about her. She was so utterly human, a stark contrast to my own seven-foot, heavily muscled form. The thought struck me harder than I expected: how could I, a creature of war and wilderness, feel an odd pull of attraction toward someone so different? Perhaps it was that difference itself, the contrast of her soft, human curves against the hardened lines of my own body that fascinated me. Or maybe it was the fire in her that burned brighter than the cruelty of the world around her. She deserved so much better than what this life had handed her—a thought that only made the anger simmering within me grow hotter.

Bruises marked her arms, like ghosts of the hands that put them there. Cruel hands. The back of her hair was dark with blood that hadn't fully dried, a fresh wound that spoke of recent violence. My jaw tightened. They'd handled her roughly, probably relishing her struggle. Anger flared in my chest, hot and immediate. I'd seen humans inflict worse, but knowing they'd marked her this way hit harder than I expected, sharp and visceral. Even covered in grime and battered by cruelty, she carried herself with a quiet resilience, a kind of fragile grace that only deepened the ache in my chest. She was sharper than she let on, but there was a vulnerability to her that made it impossible to look away. And somehow, that vulnerability felt like something I wanted to protect, even if I couldn't explain why.

A small smile tugged at my lips. She was trying so hard to appear unaffected, but I could see the cracks in her composure. It was that blend of defiance and uncertainty that stirred something deeper in me. The humans would tear her apart if they got the chance. Hell, I'd seen them do worse to shamans. That's why she needed me, even if she didn't know it yet. I needed her too.

"You've been quiet," I called out, my voice low enough that only she could hear. Her shoulders stiffened, but she didn't turn. "Not enjoying the ride?"

"Why?" she replied, her tone sharp. "Hoping for some entertainment?"

I let out a low chuckle, the kind that rumbled deep in my chest, amused by her in a way she likely didn't even realize. "Maybe. Or maybe I'm just curious. It's not every day I meet a shaman with such a fiery tongue."

That got her. She turned her head, just enough for me to catch the flash of annoyance in her green eyes. "And what about you? For someone on the way to their execution, you seem awfully chatty." Her lips pressed into a thin line, but she didn't look away again. *Progress.*

The wagon hit a bump, jolting her forward. She caught herself on the bars, her knuckles whitening against the iron. I watched the movement closely, my mind spinning with possibilities. She was stronger than she realized. She would need to be if we were going to get out of this alive.

"Tell me, Cleo," I said, leaning closer, my voice low and deliberate. "Do you even know why they're hauling you off to Knight's Hold?"

Suspicion flickered across her face as she straightened. "Because they're afraid of what I might do."

"Afraid of what you *could* do," I corrected, letting the words roll off my tongue with an edge of amusement. "Not because you're dangerous, at least not yet. Because of what you represent."

She hesitated, her brows knitting together as she searched my face. "And what's that?" she asked, her voice quieter now, the defiance still there but tempered by uncertainty.

"*Balance.* For centuries, humans have ruled this land because they've made sure they're the strongest. They've crushed anything that threatened their power. Shamans and orcs were destined to work the earth as one. Together, we could build a world stronger than anything they could ever hope to control. That terrifies them."

Her brows furrowed, and I could see her trying to process my words. She wanted to argue, to push back, but doubt lingered in her eyes. *Good*. That meant she was listening.

"You're wrong. If they're so afraid of us, why not just leave us alone?" she asked.

"Because fear makes people stupid, and humans have been for a long time. Look around you, Cleo. Your kind is hunted, my people are scattered, and the only ones who benefit are the cowards in their castles."

The wagon lurched again, and she flinched, her chains rattling. I softened my voice. "You'll never be safe with them. The only place you'll find safety is with the clans. With me."

Her eyes locked onto mine, a spark flaring in their depths like embers catching fire. "And why should I trust you?" she demanded, her voice sharp, each word laced with challenge.

"You shouldn't," I admitted. "But I'm your best chance. Unless you'd rather see what the Crown planned for you."

She didn't respond, her lips pressing into a thin, stubborn line, but the tension in her shoulders betrayed her. I could practically see the wheels turning in her head, weighing the risk, calculating the odds. Smart girl. She wasn't the type to leap without looking, but I could tell she wasn't one to stay idle for long either.

Her gaze flickered briefly to the guards before snapping back to me. She didn't trust me. That was smart too. Trust would come later. For now, though, I could see the consideration in her eyes. She was already thinking, already planning.

One of the guards approached, his hand resting on the hilt of his sword. I straightened, schooling my expression to that of boredom. He sneered but didn't say anything, retreating to adjust the oxen's harness. My grin returned as I turned back to Cleo.

I inclined my head towards our captors. "They're sloppy. The one with the limp wouldn't make it ten paces if I went for his weak leg. That one's armor? It's loose enough to ram a blade through and still have room to twist. Their leader thinks he's untouchable, but he's careless."

Surprise flickered across her face at my detailed assessment of the guards. "You really think you can take them?" Her tone hovered between doubt and curiosity.

"I can get us out of here, but I'll need your help. Turns out, my wit isn't quite strong enough to bust these chains. Who knew?"

She let out an amused snort. It caught me off guard, a flicker of warmth breaking through her guarded demeanor, and I thought I saw her lips twitch as if fighting a reluctant smile.

"You're a distraction," I said simply, "Give me a window, and I'll do the rest. Just think of it as giving my ego a little backup. Think you can manage that, little shaman?"

Her expression hardened, but she didn't refuse. The silence hung there, weighted with unspoken questions and the fragile threads of reluctant trust. "You don't have to decide now," I said, my tone softer, though my eyes stayed on her. "But if we're going to survive this, we need to work together. Whatever you think of me, I'm not your enemy."

She hesitated, her gaze flicking to mine, lingering as if searching for truth in my words. Finally, she whispered, "What happens after?"

I tilted my head, studying her expression, trying to gauge where her mind had wandered. "After?"

Her throat bobbed in a barely perceptible swallow. "If we get out of this...what then?"

I let out a quiet breath, keeping my tone steady, calm—the kind of voice someone desperate to feel safe might cling to. "You come with me. My clan will offer you refuge, a place where you can truly understand what it means to be a shaman. To learn to wield the kind of power you have." I paused, watching her closely, gauging the flicker of doubt and defiance in her eyes. "With us, you'd be safe. No one would dare touch you."

Safe. It wasn't a lie, exactly—at least not in the way she'd hear it. But safety came with a cost, one I was willing to risk for the future of my people. She didn't need to know about the prophecy, not yet. That truth would come later, when she was ready to understand the burden of what she was meant to become. And the warnings? I pushed them aside, locking them in the part of my mind I couldn't afford to dwell on. If she was strong enough, she'd survive.

Her gaze didn't waver, her chin lifting just a fraction, enough to remind me of the spark that had caught my attention in the first place. Her sharp tongue might have irritated others, but it only made me want to push harder, to see how far that fire could burn. A dangerous thought, one I couldn't indulge.

I leaned back, keeping my expression neutral. "Think about it, little shaman. You're stronger than you know. With the right guidance, you could change everything."

Her expression flashed with a mix of skepticism and something else. Hope, maybe. "And if I don't want to?"

"I'll take you wherever you want to go you think will be safe."

Her gaze lingered on me before she looked away. I let out a quiet breath, my mind already racing with plans. But to my surprise, I felt a strange warmth creeping in as I replayed the soft snort she'd let out. It was such a small thing, but it had been enough to make my chest tighten. Was I really preening under her attention? I almost laughed at myself. She'd probably roll her eyes if she knew. The humans thought they had us trapped, but they'd underestimated me. They always did. And they had no idea what Cleo was capable of, but they would.

The sound of heavy boots crunching against dirt drew my attention. Two guards approached the wagon, their laughter low and crude. My eyes narrowed as one of them leaned closer to Cleo, his words vulgar. "Bet the shaman's got tricks that don't need magic, eh?" His companion snickered like it was the funniest thing he'd ever heard.

"Got some curves on her, though," the first added, his eyes roaming over Cleo in a way that made my blood boil. "Shame she's not my type. I don't go for the plump ones." The other guard burst out laughing, the sound rough and grating, like boots scraping over stone.

Cleo stiffened, her eyes fixed on the horizon, her knuckles whitening in her grip on the bars. She didn't say a word, but the tension radiating from her was palpable. It took every ounce of restraint I had not to lunge at them. The chains rattled as my hands flexed, the metal biting into my wrists. They were lucky the cuffs held. If they hadn't, their blood would already be soaking the dirt beneath their feet.

They lingered, laughter growing louder as they jeered. "What's the matter? Too good to talk to us? Come on, shaman, give us a smile."

When Cleo kept her gaze fixed forward, her chin lifted in silent defiance, the first guard's face twisted with irritation. His scowl deepened, a vein ticking at his temple. "Thinks she's better than us!"

I couldn't help the amusement that tugged at the corner of my mouth, nor the heat that stirred somewhere deeper. She didn't flinch. Didn't cower. Even now, bruised and bound, she carried herself like she was untouchable. That quiet rebellion wasn't just admirable—it was maddeningly enticing.

I shifted against the weight of my own chains, forcing myself to tear my eyes away from her. It wasn't the time, and it sure as hell wasn't the place. But that fire in her? It was dangerous for more reasons than the guards knew.

The angry guard hauled himself onto the wagon, the wood creaking under his weight. He seized Cleo by the upper arm, yanking her forward. Her face slammed against the iron bars, the metallic clang echoing through the empty roadway. The sickening crack of impact made my stomach twist as she let out a groan. Blood trickled down her face in a thin, dark line, pooling at the edge of a gash that split her brow. "Got a little color now, shaman." His grin widened. "But don't worry, I'll fix it."

Leaning in, his tongue snaked the thin line of blood trailing from her cheekbone. Cleo flinched, a small whimper escaping her. My vision went red as my claws instinctively curled into fists, the sharp tips piercing my palms. A low warning growl rumbled deep in my chest, loud enough to draw their attention.

"Beast's growling like he's gonna chew through those chains."

The guard's grip on Cleo's arm slackened, and he spat at my feet, his sneer barely masking the hesitation in his movements. "Not worth the trouble," he muttered, trying to sound sure of himself, but the faint waver in his voice betrayed him. With one last glance, he climbed off the wagon, his bravado crumbling with each step. Their hollow laughter echoed behind them as they retreated, leaving the sour stench of sweat and cheap ale hanging in the air.

Cleo's shoulders remained stiff. Her breaths were shallow but controlled despite the blood still trailing down her face. Blood trickled down her face in slow, uneven streams, but she made no move to wipe it away, as if the act of ignoring it gave her some small measure of control. The defiance in her green eyes burned brighter as she turned to look at me, her jaw set with a determination that made my chest tighten. Her

41

eyes were glassy with unshed tears of rage, each drop a reflection of the storm brewing within her. I realized then that if she were ever given the chance, that passion and fury would make her a devastatingly powerful shaman. Her magic, fueled by this raw, unyielding anger, could reach unimaginable heights. And I knew if I could harness it, I could use that to help my clan survive.

"What do I need to do?" she asked quietly, her voice steady despite the anger simmering just beneath the surface.

I should have looked away, should have forced my thoughts back to the task at hand, but I couldn't. Something about her, raw and unyielding even in pain, pulled at me. It wasn't just admiration; it was magnetic, dangerous in a way I hadn't anticipated.

"Be ready to distract them. At the next stop, ask for a break to relieve yourself. That's when we move."

Her brow furrowed. "Distract them how?"

I hesitated, the words lodging in my throat before I forced them out. "They're drawn to you. The way they look at you, the things they say... If you're willing, we can use that to our advantage."

Her face hardened, the fire in her eyes flaring. I thought she might snap at me, but then she exhaled slowly, her expression unreadable. "If it gets us out of here, I can do that."

Her calm acceptance made my chest ache in a way I didn't like. My fists clenched involuntarily as the images of what the guards had already done flashed in my mind. My voice dropped, rough with anger. "I swear to you, Cleo, they'll pay for every insult and bruise. I'll make sure they regret every second they dared to lay a hand on you."

"Okay." Her glassy eyes met mine and I caught a glimpse of the vulnerability she had been trying to hide. Her voice trembled, as though the dehumanizing treatment she'd endured was cracking through her armor. I felt something primal stir within me. A protectiveness I hadn't known I was capable of for a human. It was confusing, so I shoved it aside to reflect on it later.

"If there was another way, I'd never ask you to put yourself at their mercy like this, but I need you to push one of them from the cart, just enough for me to grab him. Once I have him, I'll get the keys, and we'll make our move. They won't have a chance to stop us, and they will never lay a hand on you again."

""If I was to trust you, how do I know your clan will accept me?"

I let the weight of my words settle between us. "Because I am Dex Kenryr, Chieftain of the Blackfoot Clan. My word is law. You'll have a place among us, Cleo. A place where you can learn, grow, and wield the power that's rightfully yours."

Her lips parted, her surprise evident. "You're the Chieftain?" she asked, skepticism creeping into her tone.

"I am. And I don't offer refuge lightly. You'd be one of us, not an outsider. If you choose to follow me, the clan will protect you and so will I."

CHAPTER 5
CLEO

The creak of the wagon wheels scraped against my nerves with every rotation. I tried to focus on it, on anything, to keep my mind from spiraling into the pit of fear that gnawed at the edges of my sanity. My wrists throbbed against the cuffs, the absence of that faint hum of my power still felt like an open wound. The future loomed ahead. Knights Hold. Trial. Execution. All for something I couldn't control. The word "shaman" had become my death sentence.

My gaze drifted to the orc chained behind the wagon. Dex, Chieftain of the Blackfoot Clan. The words he'd spoken earlier lingered in my mind. Refuge. *Safety.* It sounded too good to be true, a promise wrapped in steel and sharp edges. But could I trust him? My options were as thin as the layer of grime coating my skin. Death at the hands of the Crown, or an alliance with the strange, golden-eyed orc who was either my salvation or another danger.

"What troubles you, little shaman?" Dex asked, breaking the silence. His voice rumbled like distant thunder, a low sound that seemed to wrap around my thoughts.

I scowled, hating how easily he seemed to read me. "I was thinking about what you said earlier. About your clan."

His lips curved into a slow grin. "The prospect of survival suits you. Go on, ask your questions."

"You're their Chieftain. What does that even mean? Are you like a King or something?" I asked, keeping my voice low. The guards walking alongside the wagon were too preoccupied to care, but I couldn't risk them overhearing anything that might make things worse. And this sounded like information that might have Dex cut down while in chains.

He chuckled, the sound both amused and weary. "A King? No. A Chieftain leads by respect, not a throne. My people trust me because I've earned it. It's not a crown, but it's no less weighty."

"And yet here you are," I said before I could stop myself. "Chained like the rest of us."

His grin faded, replaced by a shadowed look. "We were traveling through the Wild Lands, trading with a clan in the Marsh. Humans ambushed us. I led them away from my people. The guards had no idea who I was. If they knew, I'd be dead by now. So, if you could keep that to yourself, I'd appreciate it."

I nodded, the faintest hint of trust blooming in the pit of my stomach. He hadn't needed to share that, but he had. *Did he trust me?* "You're lucky they didn't figure it out."

His eyes gleamed with something unreadable. "Human leaders are rarely in battle. It's an oversight on the Crown to make assumptions on other races."

The wagon lurched to a stop, and the guards shouted commands as the oxen were unhitched and led to a trough to drink. My heart hammered against my ribs. This was it. The plan had been forming in my mind, but the prospect of following through made bile rise in my throat. Dex gave me a quick nod. A small, dark grin curled at the edges of his lips as he whispered, "I'll keep you safe."

What other choice did I have? Dead was dead, whether I stayed here or gambled on an escape with this insane orc. My legs wobbled as I pushed myself upright, but I forced my shoulders back, summoning every ounce of false bravado I could muster.

"I need to relieve myself!" I called out, loud enough for the guards to hear. I sounded too panicked even to my own ears.

The guards exchanged weary glances, before one of them approached the wagon, his hand resting on the hilt of his sword. "Don't try anything." he warned, unlocking the side of the cage, and I stepped forward at his instruction. My pulse roared in my ears as I edged toward the open door. He reached up and unlocked the chains binding my wrists to the top of the cage and my arms dropped instantly, the sharp ache of blood rushing back into my shoulders making me wince. Hours of being strung up like that had left my muscles tender and uncooperative, but I ground my teeth and fought to keep my movements steady. Any sign of weakness now would be an invitation for trouble.

The chains on Dex's wrists were long enough for him to reach the opening, a fact the guards were painfully aware of. Another guard stood with his spear at Dex's throat, the sharp tip trembling, a clear sign of how dangerous they knew an orc could be if given even a fraction of an opportunity.

"Move it," the guard barked, grabbing my arm to haul me down. His hand lingered, the roughness of his grip pressing through the thin fabric of my dress, leaving an unwelcome heat behind. His other hand slid over my hip, possessive and invasive, sending a sick twist of dread curling through my gut. My skin prickled. Every nerve recoiled as his breath, hot and sour with ale, washed over my face. His voice dripped with vulgar amusement. " This will cost you later."

Rage flared deep inside me, and before I could stop myself, my bound hands snapped up and backhanded him across the face. The sound was sharp, silencing the jeering laughter of the others. His lips curled into a sneer as his grip tightened like a vise. He was savoring the control he held over me. His nails dug into my skin and I could feel the heat of his fury. The fire in my chest burned hotter, threatening to spill over.

The guards were distracted for only a split second, but it was enough. Dex moved in a blur—faster than I thought possible—the clatter of his chains cutting through the air as he surged forward. He seized the spear and spun the weapon in his hands, the polished wood glinting as it found its target. He drove the spear clean through the man's chest with a sickening, wet sound. Blood spattered in a wide arc, painting the ground. The guard staggered backward, his eyes wide with

47

shock as he clawed at the shaft protruding from his chest, a futile attempt to stop the inevitable. With a shuddering gasp, he crumpled to the ground, his body landing in a lifeless heap that sent tremors through the dirt beneath my feet.

The man holding me froze for a fraction of a second and it was the opportunity I needed. I twisted in his grasp, my elbow connecting with his ribs. He cursed, stumbling, and I shoved him hard. He tumbled from the wagon, falling into Dex's waiting hands. Grabbing the man by the throat, he slammed him against the wagon, the sharp crack of his head on the bars echoing through the air, before falling to the ground, dazed, blood streaming from the fresh wound.

"Keys." Dex's voice held a dangerous rasp. I stumbled down, dropping to my knees to fumble through his pockets until I found a set of keys. My fingers shook as I worked to unlock his cuffs, the cold metal biting into my skin as the sharp clamor of the guards scrambling for their weapons filled the air. Each noise sent a fresh wave of panic coursing through me. I could feel them advancing, their footsteps growing louder, and my heart hammered against my ribs. I was certain we were out of time, certain they would strike us down before the lock gave. Just as despair began to creep in, the cuffs clicked open, and Dex pulled free with a growl. He launched himself forward like a predator with terrifying precision, moving like a force of nature. Each strike was calculated, every blow designed to kill. Blood sprayed, staining the dirt as he tore through them. One guard's scream was cut short as Dex's claws raked across his throat. Another fell with a gurgle, his weapon clattering uselessly to the ground.

I snapped my eyes back to my wrists as I felt the release of the locks, the cuffs clattering to the dirt. My wrists ached, but the moment the enchanted metal left my skin, a surge of power roared back into me. It was intoxicating, a rush that made the world around me seem brighter and sharper. The dull greens of the forest deepened into rich emeralds, the air seemed warmer against my skin, and every sound felt amplified and vibrant. The magic coursed through my veins like liquid fire. It was sharp and overwhelming, making my knees weak and my head spin. I swayed, catching myself against the wagon, trying to steady the storm of sensations. Finally, the familiar hum settled, a comforting thrum that made me feel whole.

I watched as Dex stepped over the last fallen guard, his chest heaving, blood dripping from his claws. The sheer force and speed he had used to dispatch our captors left me breathless. He had taken down the guard with nothing but his bare hands, a brutal efficiency that seemed almost otherworldly. His strength was a reminder of just how different orcs were from humans, a towering predator amidst frail prey. The guards had been no match for his size, speed, or the raw power he wielded as effortlessly as breathing. For all the fear his presence should have inspired, I felt something else entirely. A strange sense of safety.

A flicker of movement at the edge of my vision caught my attention. The guard who had grabbed me earlier was still alive, dragging himself weakly toward the trees, a trail of blood marking his path with dark, uneven droplets. Dex followed my gaze, his voice dropping low as he asked a question that sent my thoughts spinning.

"Do you want the kill?"

I stared at the man, my heartbeat pounding in my ears like a war drum. "Will he die?"

Dex nodded. "Slowly. Painfully."

I walked toward the guard, where he dragged his broken body, each movement slower than the last. Kneeling beside him, I let the darker part of me rise to the surface. He recoiled as I leaned in, his fear fed the rage surging through me. No death would ever be enough to make up for what he'd done, but watching him squirm was a start.

When I spoke, my voice was low, sharp, and cold as steel. "I hope it's slow. This is for every woman you've hurt, because I know I am not the only one."

The power that had returned to me hummed faintly, steadying my resolve. For the first time, I wasn't the one trembling. I stood and didn't look back, returning to my new companion.

Dex straightened as I approached the wagon, towering over me as he scanned me for injuries. His presence was overwhelming, like a storm on the verge of breaking, and I couldn't suppress the nervous flutter in my chest. Every movement he made seemed to ripple with restrained power. He reached for me, his massive hands caressing my wrists where the cuffs had bitten into my skin. His touch was surprisingly light, his scarred green fingers tracing over the raw, reddened flesh. The contrast between us struck me anew. My smaller, bruised body against his towering, muscular one. His calloused fingers glided along my arms, searching for more injuries, and I felt a strange heat rise to my cheeks.

I was painfully aware of every orcish feature. His tusks, his sharp jawline, the predatory glint in his eye. Despite his sheer size and the lethal energy he exuded, I felt safer in his presence than I had in years. The realization was as unsettling as it was reassuring.

He paused when his eyes fell on the fresh cut at my temple, a wound I had nearly forgotten in the adrenaline of the fight. Brows furrowed, his thumb hovering near the edge of the wound, not quite touching it. "Forgive me, Cleo." His voice was low, each word laced with barely restrained fury.

I nodded. "For what? It's not your fault. I will be fine."

He let out a deliberately slow breath, his anger simmering just beneath the surface, his golden eyes locking onto mine. "If this is fine, then I can't wait to see what you call bad."

A small, bitter laugh escaped me before I could stop it. "Your wounds look far worse than mine. Are you hurt?"

His lips curved into a humorless grin, his tusks catching the light. "Not even a scratch, little shaman." he said, his voice rough like the rumble of thunder settling beneath my skin.

Butterflies stirred in my stomach, uninvited and entirely unwelcome. The way he said it—*little shaman*—was infuriating and yet, somehow, it made my breath hitch. I hated it. I hated the way my body betrayed me, responding to the smug tone of a stranger who, not a few hours ago, I'd been terrified of.

It had to be the adrenaline, coursing through me like wildfire, making me hyperaware of everything. His voice, his presence, the way he moved with an effortless confidence that left me off balance. I forced the reaction down. Whatever this was, it wasn't real. It couldn't be.

He pressed a small boot knife into my hand, the blade cold against my skin. "You shouldn't be unarmed." The edges of his voice softened just enough to feel reassuring.

I stared at the weapon, the gleam of its sharp edge catching the faint light. "I don't know how to use this."

His lips curved into a knowing smile." Then I'll teach you." he said simply, as if it was the obvious and easy solution.

We moved quickly, gathering what we could from the convoy. My hands shook as I stuffed the meager rations into a makeshift bag, the adrenaline of the fight still thrumming through me like a second heartbeat. As I reached for the last bundle, Dex stepped closer and extended a hand, his rough palm enveloping mine as he helped me down from the wagon with surprising care. I knew he'd noticed the shake in my fingers, the lingering effects of everything we'd just been through, but the gesture still sent a blush creeping up my neck.

He handed me a water flask without a word, scanning the perimeter. "We should move, we have a lot of ground to cover." His calm purpose was grounding, even as every sound in the forest felt sharper now.

The snap of a twig or the rustle of leaves sending jolts of awareness through my body. Dex moved beside me. His massive frame was an imposing shadow against the trees, leading us deeper into the forest where the air felt heavier but, strangely, safer.

With each step, the suffocating fear of Knights Hold began to lift, replaced by something new. Uncertainty, yes, but also hope. It felt like something I could face, even if the path ahead was uncertain.

CHAPTER 6
DEX

The Wild Lands stretched out before us in hues of green and gold, the thick canopy filtering the sun into fractured patterns on the forest floor. The air was alive with the sounds of unseen creatures, the rustle of leaves in the breeze, and the distant call of birds. The land was unfamiliar, yet it felt like home. The kind of place where life and death mingled freely, the kind of place my clan thrived.

I adjusted my pace, glancing back to Cleo as she trudged behind me. Her torn and frayed dress clung to her soft hips and shifted with her every move. Despite the bruises from the guards' rough handling, there was a quiet strength in the way she carried herself, a resilience that drew my attention even when I tried to look away. She moved with determination, but I could see the tremor in her steps, the lingering adrenaline that hadn't yet burned out of her system. I slowed my pace. As much as I hated the delay, her smaller legs couldn't match my stride.

The sky above deepened to a dusky orange, and the temperature began to drop. The Wild Lands didn't forgive weakness, and the night would be colder than she could likely tolerate. Even with a fire, the chill would bite at her. My eyes lingered on her dress again, the way it offered her little protection against the elements, before I forced myself to look away. She needed more than we had.

"Are you always this slow, or is it for my benefit?" I called back to her, needing to keep her talking, to make sure she wasn't going into shock.

She glared at me, eyes flashing with irritation. "I'm human, remember? Big, strong orc, conquering the mighty forest! Do you want me to take notes?"

A grin tugged at my mouth. "Might do you some good. Not everyone's built for this kind of terrain."

Her snort was barely audible, but the smile that followed told me she wasn't as worn down as she seemed. That resilience was going to serve her well, if it didn't get her killed first. "Please, I've handled worse than a few rocks. But if you're offering to carry me and all of our belongings, don't let me stop you. You can put those muscles that you keep on flexing to good use!"

"I could if you wanted me to."

I gazed back at her to catch her blushing hard in response. "I'll keep that in mind, Chieftain," she said, her tone laced with mock formality. "But I wouldn't want you thinking I couldn't handle a little rough terrain."

A slow grin spread across my face. "Of course not. Offer still stands. You're tiny, and I likely wouldn't even notice the difference."

Her steps faltered, and she glared up at me, green eyes sparking. "Tiny?! I am a grown woman, not a child!"

I stopped walking, turning to look her over with deliberate slowness. "I am very aware of you being a grown woman. Compared to an orc, humans *are* tiny. Carrying you would not be an inconvenience."

Her blush deepened, but she rolled her eyes and strode past me, muttering under her breath. The corner of my mouth twitched as I followed, unable to resist the way her cheeks flushed so easily. It stirred something within me, a strange curiosity about whether that blush extended all the way down her neck, perhaps even lower. The thought surprised me, a sharp pull of desire for a human—a race so different from my own—but I couldn't deny the way it gnawed at me.

We pressed on, my ears attuned to every sound. The forest was alive, but its pulse was different from what I was used to. This was not my land, yet the soil beneath my boots felt the same. The smell of damp earth mixed with the crispness of the approaching night. Somewhere nearby, an animal darted through the underbrush, its presence marked only by the crackle of dry twigs. I could sense Cleo's discomfort in the silence, her unease at the way I moved through the Wild Lands with an ease she couldn't match.

"This place doesn't bother you, does it?" she asked, her voice cutting through the stillness.

"No, it feels alive. Humans build walls to keep themselves separate from the world. Orcs? We live in it."

"So, you're saying you prefer...this?" She gestured around at the trees, fallen branches in our path, and the chaos of the forest.

"The Wild Lands don't lie. There's no pretense here. You survive, or you don't."

Her steps faltered, but she caught herself quickly. "What about your clan? Do they all live in places like this?"

"The Blackfoot Clan is isolated in the Black Mountains, but we thrive in the forest. All orc-kind do."

"Before the war centuries ago, the Blackfoot Clan lived in these forests. The Wild Lands were ours; the forest was our strength. The humans' greed drove us out, forcing us to retreat to our old strongholds in the Black Mountains. There, we survived, but it was never the same. The Wild Lands have always felt like home, even when the world tried to take them from us."

I wanted to tell her about my hope that she might be the shaman we'd been waiting for. The clans had been pushed to the edges of Ostelan for too long, forced into shadows while the humans claimed everything that once sustained us. If she truly was the shaman from the prophecy, she could be the key to reclaiming the forests and rebuilding what was taken. But I couldn't tell her that. She wasn't invested enough to help us, not with the weight of what it would mean. I needed to earn her trust, to guide her to see our cause as her own. It would take time, and I couldn't risk overwhelming her too soon. Besides, if a new shaman had been born, the darkness would already be stirring, hunting for her. That alone would be enough to keep her cautious and moving forward. The rest... the truth... I would hold back until I was certain she could handle it. Until she was ready to become the weapon we needed against the Crown and the darkness that took over our forests.

The forest had grown steadily colder as we moved, the light fading quickly. I scanned the area, deeming this a suitable place to rest for the night. "We'll camp here. The night is coming fast, and you're not built for traveling in the dark."

She bristled but said nothing, dropping her bag onto the ground with a tired sigh. I set to work gathering firewood, my ears straining for any sound that might signal danger. Every snap of branches and rustle of leaves put me on edge, my senses sharpened by the knowledge that the Wild Lands, though beautiful, were merciless to the unprepared.

Once the fire was lit, Cleo sat close to the flames, rubbing her hands together for warmth. The light painted her face in flickering golds and shadows, picking out the dirt smudged on her cheek and the lines of exhaustion etched into her features. Yet despite the weariness in her posture, she didn't look weak. Just human enough to remind me how fragile she was in a place like this. My gaze lingered on her too long, noting the way her hair caught the firelight, before I turned my focus back to the forest, scanning the darkness for any lurking threats.

The flames crackled louder as the icy wind picked up, sending a violent shiver through her shoulders. I sighed, moving closer to her as it whipped through the clearing. "You're shivering." My voice was more of a rumble as I settled behind her, pulling her back into the circle of my arms. With my warmth shielding her, it could no longer strike her with its bite.

She stiffened under my touch, the unexpected closeness drawing a sharp tension into her frame. Her breath hitched, barely audible, but I felt it like a spark against the night. Every inch of her felt wound tight, caught in the indecision of whether to lean into the warmth between us or push it away.

The scent of her invaded my senses, a blend of sweat and something softer, floral and inviting. It mingled with the smoke of the fire and the crisp bite of the forest night, weaving together into something that made my pulse quicken. The space between us felt charged, alive, as though the night itself held its breath.

The contrast between us was impossible to ignore as I looked down at her. Her skin, soft and fair, caught the flickering firelight, while mine, a deep earthen green, bore the scars and weathering of years on the battlefield. The curve of her bare shoulder brushed against my chest, and I couldn't help but marvel at how delicate she seemed in comparison, like something impossibly fragile.

The wind tugged at her hair, and without thinking, I reached up to brush it behind her ear. My fingers grazed the smooth line of her neck, warm and soft beneath my touch. She didn't flinch. Instead, her shoulders eased, and the blush I'd grown to enjoy painted her cheeks once more.

She was stunning, in a way that caught me off guard. A beauty both soft and fierce, like steel wrapped in silk. I found myself wondering how someone like her had been so thoroughly let down by the world, a world that had shaped her into this perfect paradox of fragility and strength.

"Humans. Always cold," I said, aiming to break some of the tension growing between us.

I could easily imagine the flash of anger sparking in her eyes, the look I had grown so accustomed to. Disappointment tugged at me, knowing my seat behind her kept me from seeing her expressions. I shifted to the side and leaned over her shoulder just enough to catch a glimpse of her face. Her frustration was delicious, a wildfire I couldn't resist feeding. The urge to wind her up, to draw out that fire, was almost impossible to ignore.

"And orcs? Always bossy?"

I tried to smother the smirk from my voice as I responded, gleeful at how easy it was for me to get under her skin. "Always."

The banter fell away, leaving us in the silence of the forest. The firelight danced between us, and though her breathing slowed, her body remained alert. She wasn't yet used to the quiet. To the way it magnified every thought and fear. I could see it in her posture, the way she rubbed at her wrists absentmindedly, likely still feeling the ghost of the cuffs that had bound her.

"You need to learn control," I said, breaking the silence.

Her head tilted, her brow furrowing in confusion. "Control?"

"Your magic," I clarified, my tone softening. "If you can control it, you could call on the warmth of the fire and draw it into you."

"How?"

"I can teach you," I said, shifting impossibly closer. "It starts with learning to feel for it, to pull on it with purpose. Meditation helps, but it will take time to master it."

Her hands trembled as she looked down at her lap, hesitation heavy in her voice. "The last time it came, it wasn't on purpose. It was... chaotic. I couldn't control it."

"What happened? What were you feeling when it reared up?"

Her voice softened as she stared into the fire. "It was... the market. My father..." Her muscles bunched beneath my arms, vibrating with tension. I wanted to see her eyes, to read the emotions flickering there, but all I could feel was the rigidity of her body as she forced the words out. "He humiliated me in front of everyone, blamed me for the farm's ruin, slapped me... and I-I felt this anger. This unbearable rage."

Her shoulders shook, her breaths shallow. "It wasn't just the slap. It was years of his drinking, his fists, his words. My mother had passed, and he took it out on me. I hated him for what he had become."

My hold on her tightened instinctively, as if I could shield her from the memory. "Then these vines came out of the ground, and I couldn't stop them."

The words hung heavy between us, her body trembling against me. How could her father, the man who gave her life, dare lay a hand on his daughter in anger? The thought burned in my mind, fueling a quiet fury I had to work to suppress. Humans confused and infuriated me in equal measure. That she had endured years of abuse and mistreatment, yet emerged as this defiant and kind woman, was nothing short of extraordinary. I was impressed that her spirit hadn't been crushed, that she was as stubborn and resilient as she was, despite everything she'd faced.

Taking a steadying breath, I focused on giving her a small measure of comfort. "You were protecting yourself. That rage, it's what your magic answered to. But you can't let it control you. Harnessing it is what separates a real shaman from chaos."

Cleo shuffled against me, crossing her legs and straightening up again. Before she could fully settle, I pulled her back against my chest, my arms resting loosely around her. *For warmth.* I towered over her, leaning forward just enough to surround her with my body heat. Though I couldn't see the profile of her face clearly in the dark, the way her muscles flexed beneath my arms told me she was flustered. It amused me more than it should. There was something undeniably satisfying about the way she reacted, her independence clashing with her inability to mask her emotions.

"You need to be comfortable," I said, my voice low. "For now, use my body heat so you can focus. Close your eyes."

She snapped her eyes shut with almost comical force. For several minutes she was still, shifting restlessly every so often. My lips twitched, the beginnings of a smirk tugging at the corner of my mouth. I could almost taste her nervous energy, and it was delicious.

"Stop thinking so hard. Meditation isn't about forcing your mind to stop. It's about letting it quiet on its own."

"Right, because quieting my mind is so easy," she said, her tone laced with sarcasm. "Especially when you're sitting directly behind me. I can feel you staring at me. Are you worried I'm going to burst into flames or something?"

"You don't need my help for that. You're capable of doing that all on your own. Now, close your eyes and allow your mind to quiet."

She sighed but complied, her lashes fluttering shut as she shifted again, trying to find a more comfortable position against me. "Breathe. In through your nose. Feel it fill your chest. Let it out slowly. Again."

I could feel her trying to follow my instructions, her breaths coming slower and deeper, but her shoulders remained tight, the tension radiating through her entire body like a coiled spring. Her chest rose and fell unevenly. Each breath betrayed her struggle to find calm amidst the chaos within her. She fidgeted again, her hands tugging restlessly at her dress. The frustration was palpable, and I could feel it as clearly as the heat of the fire beside us, her inner turmoil vibrating through her frame as though it might escape at any moment. Her lips parted as if to speak but closed again.

"Stop fidgeting," I said, my tone laced with amused patience.

"I don't know what I'm doing." Frustration crept into her voice. "This whole magic thing didn't come with a guidebook!"

"Good thing you've got me then. You're not going to figure this out in one night. Start with this moment and forget everything else."

She huffed out a breath. "I can feel you staring at me like that. Can you stop?"

"Like what?" I asked innocently.

"Like I'm some shiny new shaman plaything." There was a hint of embarrassment in her voice. *Interesting.*

"Well, you are."

"That's not distracting and inappropriate at all," she muttered, her sarcasm returning full force.

I leaned forward, my breath ghosting across the back of her neck, watching as several curls danced across her neck. The movement was deliberate, meant to rattle her, and I wasn't disappointed when I felt her shoulders stiffen in response. "Maybe distraction is exactly what you need," I murmured, my voice teasing. Promising.

She twisted sharply to glare at me over her shoulder. Her blush burned bright against her cheeks, spilling down the line of her neck. The sight stirred something primal in me, satisfaction blooming as her wide eyes locked onto mine. She froze when she realized how close my face was to hers. I held her gaze, letting the corner of my mouth lift into a slow, unrepentant smile. The way her indignation warred with embarrassment only deepened my amusement—and, admittedly, my interest. "I thought we were supposed to be teaching me how to meditate."

"I am. Lesson one, stop running from your thoughts. Lesson two, if you're going to let something distract you"—my gaze briefly dropped to her lips—"make sure it's a worthy distraction."

Her blush deepened, but before I could revel in it fully, she snapped her face forward to the flames. The subtle roll of her shoulders and the way her lips pressed together as she muttered only added to the captivating display. "This is inappropriate."

I couldn't tear my eyes away, utterly enraptured by the way every thought and emotion played out so vividly on her face, as though she didn't know how to hide them, or didn't care to. It was a rare honesty that left me wanting more.

Despite her protests, she didn't pull away from my warmth. I let my smirk linger as I settled behind her again, not even trying to keep it out of my voice. "Try again. Unless, of course, you'd rather keep arguing, in which case..."

Part of me was disappointed when she stopped our playful banter, though I couldn't quite understand why. My comfort with her, a human I had met only earlier that day, was unsettling in its own right. It wasn't just her sharp wit or the way her blush deepened with every teasing remark—though I took a shameful amount of pleasure in flustering her. It was the stubborn fire in her, the way she pushed back against me with a strength that belied her vulnerable circumstances. For someone so seemingly fragile, she carried herself with surprising resilience, and it intrigued me. I found myself wanting to see more of that fire, to push just enough to watch her flare brightly in response.

The air around us seemed to shift as she focused, the faint hum of magic growing stronger. I felt a flicker of warmth, faint but unmistakable, beginning to emanate from her body. It was subtle, but enough to make me acutely aware of how she no longer needed my heat to keep the chill at bay. A part of me felt a pang of disappointment at the realization, though I brushed it aside quickly.

The scent of earth flared sharply as small patches of moss and clusters of mushrooms sprang up around us. The casual ease with which she wielded her incredible power was intoxicating, the earth responding to her in a way that felt raw yet undeniably powerful. The fresh scent mingled with the smoke from the fire, and the air itself seemed to pulse, alive and humming in tune with her presence.

"Good girl. Open your eyes, Cleo." Watching her was mesmerizing, but the sensation of her body relaxing against mine was addicting. I could feel the tension melting away from her frame as her breaths steadied, her soft curves pressing gently into me. She let out a quiet gasp of awe as her eyes fluttered open, and though I couldn't see her face fully, the tilt of her head and the soft parting of her lips spoke volumes. The flicker of firelight highlighted her features, illuminating the wonder that radiated from her expression. I was enthralled, not just by what she'd done but by how she carried it. Like the smallest spark of hope had taken root in her, coaxing life into a place where she might have thought it impossible.

"I did that?" she asked in disbelief, her wide eyes roaming the moss and mushrooms sprouting at her feet.

I nodded, a small smile tugging at the corners of my mouth. "You called the earth, and it answered." My gaze lingered on her, taking in the mix of wonder and uncertainty on her face. "That's what it means to be a shaman."

I watched as a moment of peace settled over her, even if it was fleeting. It was a moment I let her have before speaking again, my voice turning practical. "Rest while you can. We have a lot of ground to cover to the Black Mountains. But if you keep this up, you might survive the journey."

Her brief smile faded, replaced by a glint of defiance I was beginning to appreciate more than I should. *"Might?"*

I laughed as I pulled her back into my chest. "The Wild Lands don't forgive mistakes. But you, little shaman, might just be stubborn enough to make it."

I couldn't remember the last time I had laughed so easily. Shaking the confusing thoughts from my head, I cradled Cleo in my arms as I settled in for a long night on watch. And if my fingers trailed soothing patterns on her arms as she drifted to sleep, I would never admit to it.

CHAPTER 7
CLEO

The thick canopy of the forest loomed overhead, its shadows casting a familiar pattern. It reminded me of home—the view from my family's farm in Sleek Valley. I used to watch these trees sway in the wind from my bedroom window, their rhythmic dance a constant comfort. Back then, I'd imagine what lay beyond them, spinning dreams of adventure and freedom.

Now, those dreams felt hollow. My stomach clenched as regret twisted through me, sharp and bitter. I never thought I'd actually step into the unknown, leaving everything behind. The warmth of my mother's smile, the steady routine of the farm, even the simple creak of the porch under my feet—they felt impossibly far away, like a life that belonged to someone else.

And for what? I'd been forced to trade all of it for danger and uncertainty, all because I had been cursed with wild magic in a world that didn't want it. I shook my head in frustration. *Did I really think this magic was a curse?* Yesterday, I would have said yes, but today felt different.

The forest pulsed with a quiet energy I was only just beginning to understand. Leaves rustled above, whispering secrets on the wind, while towering trees loomed in the mist, their shadows weaving through the dense branches. Each step I took was muffled by the thick carpet of fallen leaves beneath my boots.

The air was alive with scents. The sharp, sweet tang of pine mingled with the fruity sweetness of berry bushes and the earthy richness of the soil. It felt fresh, alive, and grounding. I felt an odd sense of belonging, as though the forest itself had welcomed me.

I had never ventured beyond the village growing up. The woods surrounding us had always been a firm boundary set by my father, the wilds filled with beasts that lurked just beyond the safety of civilization. Now, walking with an orc, the forest felt ancient and full of possibilities. It was no longer a distant realm of myth. It was real, and it surrounded me.

A breeze stirred the canopy above, sending a flurry of golden flecked leaves swirling down around us. I watched them drift lazily to the ground in the early morning light. The air was carrying fresh scents of rich soil and something faintly sweet—perhaps wildflowers, the last traces of summer's bloom. Beneath it all was a heaviness, a smell I couldn't quite place. Something darker. Something that made the fine hairs on my arms stand on end. Decay.

Dex walked a few paces ahead, his dark hair pulled back, revealing the sharp cut of his cheekbones. His eyes scanned the forest, missing nothing, his stride powerful, and even with his size, he moved as though the forest was an extension of himself. I allowed myself to observe him, fascinated by the way his muscles flexed and rolled as he walked, the glint of the sword and daggers on his belt as they caught the light with every step. He was the embodiment of strength, a warrior who had seen countless battles, yet here he was, leading me—a human—through lands that once belonged to his people. There was a grace to him, a raw power that was both intimidating and magnetic, and completely unexpected from my knowledge of history and orc kind.

Shaman. The word still lingered in my mind, heavy with possibilities. How could I be something so powerful when I had been at the mercy of my father for most of my life? He had dismissed any notions of magic within me as ridiculous, a sign of childish imagination. But now... now, I couldn't deny what was happening.

I looked down at my hands. The earth had responded to me. Not just in the market, but again last night while meditating. The magic had felt warm and steady, like sunlight cutting through a winter chill, grounding me in a way I hadn't thought possible. That connection was stronger now, more tangible. I could feel it in every step, every rustle of leaves, the vibrations beneath my feet. It wasn't just something I could call; it was something I belonged to.

The memory of last night sent a shiver down my spine. Lounging in Dex's arms, his warmth against me, I'd felt safe for the first time in what felt like forever. His steady voice had eased my fear, the calmness of his presence softening the turmoil inside me.

My fingers brushed the edge of my temple, remembering how gently he'd cleaned the wound there. His touch had been firm but careful, his silence oddly comforting. For someone so rough around the edges, his tenderness had caught me off guard. I clenched my fists, trying to focus on the magic pulsing underfoot instead of the confusing pull of him.

As if summoned by my thoughts, Dex's voice cut through the silence. "Stay close." His tone was calm but firm, his eyes never leaving the overgrown path. He didn't need to repeat himself. I quickened my pace, moving closer to him. His hands rested on the hilt of his pilfered weapon, and his eyes scanned the trees with sharp intensity. The energy radiating from him was unsettling.

My heart pounded in my chest, and I clenched my hands to stop them from trembling. His wariness only heightened my own discomfort. I was a stranger in this world, and though he hadn't harmed me, the weight of the unknown was suffocating. He slowed his pace, eyes scanning the underbrush. The forest suddenly felt different. Darker.

Only a short time passed before we reached a small stream and he finally slowed to a stop, motioning for a quick break. Relief coursed through me, though I kept my expression carefully neutral as I lowered myself onto a fallen log by the creek. My movements were slow as the stiffness in my legs and shoulders pulled at every step. A dull ache in my back served as a reminder of hours spent tense and hunched. The cool mist rising from the water kissed my face, easing some of the tightness in my body as I exhaled.

Plunging my hands in the water, I winced as the cold stung the raw skin of my wrists, before bringing it to my lips. The coolness soothed my

parched throat, refreshing in a way that made me moan softly in gratitude. I let myself relax as I listened to the soft babble of the creek
blending with the rustle of leaves overhead and the distant calls of birds.
The forest held a beauty that was both ancient and alive, its energy
pulsing faintly in the air around me as I refilled my flask.

But the peace didn't last. A prickling unease crept up my spine, and
the hair on the back of my neck stood on end. Someone—or something
—was watching us.

A rustling in the trees snapped my attention to the forest's edge, and
Dex reacted instantly. His muscles coiled like a drawn bowstring, his
hand gripping the hilt of his sword as he stepped forward, placing
himself squarely between me and the threat.

From the shadows, a figure emerged, movements slow and delibere-
ate, each step measured as if he wanted to be seen. At first, I thought it
might be another orc. His skin was dark, blending in with the shadows
of the forest, but as he stepped closer, I realized he was something *other*.
His frame was leaner, his movements almost unnaturally fluid. An old
cloak hung from his shoulders, its edges frayed and worn. His face was
partially obscured by a hood. The moment I caught a glimpse of his
eyes, panic surged through me. Magic flared in response, crackling
beneath my skin as the sickly scent of decay wafted toward us.

Dex's sword flashed in the dim light, his body a solid barrier
between us. His grip tightened on the hilt, and his golden eyes narrowed
with a predatory focus. "You are trespassing," he growled, his voice low
and laced with aggression.

The figure tilted its head, his gaze sweeping over Dex before settling
on me. A slow, twisted smile spread across his lips as he pulled back his
hood, revealing a face that was sharp and angular, skin rough like weathered stone.

"You've brought quite the treasure with you, Chieftain," His eyes
locked on mine, and I felt a chill run down my spine. "Did you really
think you could keep her hidden?"

The leather-wrapped hilt creaked under the strain of Dex's grip.
"State your purpose, or I'll carve it from you."

The stranger's smile didn't waver. Instead, he laughed. A dark,
mocking sound that echoed through the clearing. "Will you now, orc?"

His voice was filled with amusement and venom. "These lands haven't belonged to your people for some time. You walk through our territory now."

Dex didn't take the bait, his stance unyielding, though the stranger's smile widened, twisting into something darker. My stomach churned as his gaze shifted back to me, sharp and invasive, like a blade dragging over my skin.

"I'm not here for you." The stranger's eyes gleamed, catching the faint light as though feeding on it. "I'm here for her."

Me?

In one fluid motion, Dex closed the distance between them by half, his sword steady in his grip. "She belongs with me."

The stranger's eyes flicked to the blade, his twisted grin unfazed by the show of force. "Does she?" he purred, his tone dripping with disdain. His gaze dragged over me again, slower this time, deliberate, "You don't know what you're interfering with."

"Go now, before I leave you bleeding out in this stream."

Holding up his hands in a mock gesture of surrender, the stranger took a step back. "Very well. But know this. I am but a Watcher. My master knows the shaman has been found, and he will come for her. You cannot keep her from him."

With one last glance in my direction, the Watcher melted back into the shadows of the forest, his departure leaving behind an eerie, suffocating silence.

After several long minutes, Dex sheathed his sword, his golden eyes blazing as he turned to face me. His expression could have been carved from stone, his jaw clenched tight. "You're drawing attention."

His words stung.

"I didn't ask for this," I snapped, my voice tight with barely contained fear.

I could see his gaze soften, though his frustration remained underneath, his voice still held a harsh edge as he spoke. "Magic doesn't care what you asked for. It's inside you, and it's drawing enemies from the shadows. We have to keep moving."

I nodded, my thoughts spiraling as the stranger's words echoed in my mind: *My master knows the shaman has been found.* Who was this master? What did they want with me? The questions twisted in my chest, refusing to let go.

Dex stepped closer, his large hand resting on my shoulder. His touch was firm, grounding me. "We'll take the Shadow Lands path through the forest. There's a hunting party of my warriors in the area. They'll help keep you safe." He squeezed my shoulder gently as his golden eyes locked on mine. "We need to move fast."

I felt the weight of my fear ease. The anger and frustration simmering in his expression was obvious, but there was something else there. He was trying to protect *me*.

As his hand fell away, the absence of his touch hit harder than I expected, leaving me feeling untethered and exposed. I already missed the fleeting sense of safety he brought, the way his presence made the world seem just a little less terrifying. Swallowing hard, I forced myself to step forward, unwilling to let him see how much I needed that moment to last.

THE SUN WAS DIRECTLY OVERHEAD, casting a soft golden light over the forest as we moved in deeper. The weight of the stranger's words still clung to me. I could still see his cold eyes when I closed mine. I could still hear the malice in his voice. *He will come for her. You cannot protect her from what's coming.* The threat made me shiver despite the stuffy midday air.

It was peaceful here in the forest. The ground was soft, damp earth giving way beneath my boots, while the towering trees seemed to stretch endlessly into the sky, their branches interwoven into a natural ceiling that filtered the sunlight into fragmented beams.

I couldn't help but feel a sense of awe. The forest pulsed with a wild energy, and I could feel it crackle across my skin like static from a lightning storm. Here, the land was free and chaotic, but in that chaos was a kind of harmony I had begun to notice. The trees grew where they willed, their thick roots snaking across the ground, interwoven with ferns and brambles. Small streams cut through the land, their clear waters winding their way around moss-covered stones. Birds flitted from branch to branch, their songs echoing through the canopy.

I focused on my breathing, just like Dex had taught me. In and out. Deep and steady. It was harder now, while walking through the forest, the uneven ground beneath my feet. My hands curled into fists as frustration bubbled up. How could I possibly connect to the forest while my thoughts were racing and the world felt so unstable?

I could do this. I took a steadying breath, my eyes fluttering closed for a moment. A soft hum brushed against the edges of my awareness, warm and inviting, like an outstretched hand waiting to be taken. I exhaled slowly and let myself lean into it. I opened my eyes slowly.

Glowing veins of magic were flowing all around me. The trees pulsed with a silver-green light, their roots humming deep beneath the earth in an ancient rhythm. The air shimmered, my eyes catching on tiny motes of colored energy, swirling and dancing around us. A soft laugh burst from my chest with delight as the magic wrapped itself around me, brushing against my skin in a warm caress. It felt safe.

My hands began to glow. Faint tendrils of green flecked with silver weaved between my fingers like living threads. I stopped walking, unable to help myself, staring in wonder as the energy thrummed gently in my palms. It felt like the forest itself was breathing with me, alive in ways I'd never imagined.

Dex turned at the sound of my laugh, his golden eyes narrowing before softening. A slow smile spread across his face, and something inside me warmed at the sight.

"It's beautiful," I whispered, my voice trembling in awe as tears welled in my eyes. I glanced up at him, hoping he could see it too—the wonder, the connection, the impossible, glorious harmony of it all.

"Yeah," he said quietly, his smile growing as he stepped closer. His gaze lingered on the magic glowing in my hands, and pride flickered across his features. "It is."

I wanted to hold onto this feeling forever. The hum of the forest, the glowing energy, the connection coursing through me—it felt like I'd found a part of myself. But the world around us pressed in, and I hesitated, glancing between Dex and the path ahead.

Reluctantly I let the glow fade, the threads of magic dissolving back into the air. But the connection didn't disappear completely. I could still feel it, just beneath the surface, waiting for me. A smile tugged at my lips as I started walking again. I knew exactly where to find it now.

I didn't understand it yet, but there was an undeniable connection between the earth and my magic. It was a power that pulsed at the edge of my awareness. The trees' branches swayed as I passed, their rustling leaves a quiet acknowledgment I couldn't ignore. Each passing minute made me more aware of the power around me without having to call it forward.

I realized that Dex had said little since the encounter with the stranger, his focus fixed on the worn path ahead. His silence didn't bother me. In a way, it felt comfortable, like I was beginning to understand his rhythm. He wasn't ignoring me; he was leading. Protecting. I found myself watching him almost exclusively, noticing the way his dark hair caught the light, or the way his broad shoulders shifted with each step. For a warrior, he seemed oddly at ease in the quiet moments.

I hadn't known what to expect when I'd first met this orc. A Chieftain, after all, had sounded terrifying. But now, walking beside him through the woods, I realized he wasn't so scary. Intimidating, yes, there was no denying the power in his stride or the sharpness in his gaze, but it wasn't cruelty that made him that way. He was serious, driven, carrying himself with the kind of authority that came from responsibility. And yet, beneath all that, there was something else. A quiet protectiveness, a sense of purpose that radiated from him in a way that made me feel safe, even when he was the source of my frustrations and nervousness.

My mind wandered back to last night, the way his warmth had seeped into me as I rested against his chest. It felt impossibly natural, as though I'd been meant to fit there all along. The memory sent a flush crawling up my neck, and I shook my head, trying to dispel my wayward thoughts.

I didn't understand why I couldn't stop thinking about it, why the warmth of his chest and the strength in his arms kept sneaking into my mind. There was something grounding about him, like the forest itself, wild and yet steady beneath my feet. I clenched my fists, heat prickling at my cheeks. What was wrong with me? *He was a stranger!* Someone who frustrated me more often than not. And yet, I couldn't deny the pull I felt.

I snuck a glance at him out of the corner of my eye, catching the way the dappled sunlight danced across his features. His golden eyes were scanning the trees, his grip firm on the hilt of his sword. He was constantly aware, always ready, yet there was a calm about him that I couldn't help but admire.

I didn't just feel safe with him. I wanted to be close to him. To feel that warmth again, to have his arms around me. The realization sent a fresh wave of embarrassment surging through me.

This was ridiculous. Whatever I felt, whatever this was, I couldn't afford to let it distract me. I'd been attracted to men before, even intimate with a few, but it had never been more than a tumble in the hayshed, a momentary thrill that left me relatively satisfied, nothing more. But this? This was different. The way heat curled low in my stomach whenever he looked at me, the way his voice sent a shiver down my spine... it fanned a desire that felt almost feral with need, unlike anything I'd ever known. I ducked my head, pretending to focus on the trail ahead, but the thought of him lingered, stubborn and impossible to ignore.

I stumbled over a tree root in my flustered state, pitching forward. His hand shot out and caught my arm before I hit the ground. His grip was gentle but strong, and when I looked up, I found his gaze lingered, flecks of concern warred with a myriad of other emotions, before he schooled his face to neutral.

"Careful." His deep voice rumbled through the air, resonating in his chest like distant thunder.

"I'm fine," I muttered as heat crept up my neck. I straightened and glanced back up at him, noticing the way his lips twitched as if holding back a smile. It was a small, almost imperceptible movement, but it was enough to make the butterflies take flight again in my stomach. *Fuck*.

We continued on, the silence between us no longer feeling oppressive, and I no longer felt like a burden. I was sure there was something more, though I wasn't sure what. For now, I was content with this newfound companionship.

CHAPTER 8
CLEO

The terrain shifted as we crossed into what Dex called the Shadow Lands, and the difference was immediate and unsettling. The Shadow Lands were darker, more oppressive. The air itself was heavier, carrying a faint metallic tang that caught at the back of my throat. Shadows stretched unnaturally long, curling and twisting as if alive, and the sounds of the forest grew quieter, as though even the animals feared this place.

Dex led the way, his massive frame moving effortlessly through the tangled underbrush, while I stumbled behind, each step a battle against the brambles eager to snag my dress. The isolation of our travel pressed on me, amplifying the sense of vulnerability in the silence. Without a larger traveling party, there was no safety in numbers, no comfort in more eyes scanning the trees. It was just Dex and I, alone in the wilderness. The realization should have been unnerving, but as I watched him move, I felt oddly comforted.

The path twisted into jagged inclines and dropped suddenly into gullies filled with thorny vines, forcing us to climb over gnarled roots that clawed at the earth. The trees here stood taller and denser, their branches reaching for the sky like skeletal arms. The sun was already sinking, its light swallowed almost entirely by the thick canopy above, leaving the world bathed in an eerie half-light. The growing shadows gnawed at my nerves.

Dex glanced back to where I struggled. His golden eyes gleamed in the twilight, sharp and assessing. "You're falling behind." The low rumble of his voice carried effortlessly over the distance.

"I'm managing!" I snapped, though my legs burned with exertion and my breath came in shallow gasps. I pushed forward, swallowing my irritation. I wouldn't let him see how much the terrain was getting to me.

We continued much of the journey in silence, the oppressive stillness broken only by the crunch of leaves beneath our feet and the occasional snap of unseen branches. Every step felt wrong, like trespassing in a place that wanted us gone. The hush unnerved me. Dex must have felt it too. His hand rested on the hilt of his sword, his gaze darting to every shadow that seemed too dark, too still. I reached for my magic on reflex, feeling the connection hum close to the surface, a comfort that hardened my resolve to press on.

The day passed in a blur and trees seemed to close in further, the underbrush thickening until the worn path became a mere suggestion beneath our feet. The whispered warning from Dex about keeping quiet was an unnecessary reminder that we were pushing deeper into dangerous territory. This part of the valley fueled stories of mystical creatures and death at every turn. Having once thought of them as nothing more than scary stories told to poor farm girls, I was angry with myself for having underestimated the forest.

Fatigue weighed on me, my legs aching with a dull, persistent throb. Complaining wasn't an option. I wasn't weak. Though his glances had softened over the course of the day, Dex's wariness was still palpable, a stark contrast to the charged intimacy of our conversations the night before. He was focused on keeping us safe, and I couldn't shake the nagging guilt that I was little more than a liability, dragging him deeper into danger.

I gasped for air, my words coming out barely above a whisper, my lungs screaming in effort as I scrambled under a fallen tree. "We need to rest soon." The rustle of leaves nearly swallowed my voice, but Dex's stride slowed, his movements shifting to something more deliberate, as if to match my faltering pace. I appreciated his consideration, though I wouldn't admit it aloud.

His sharp eyes swept over me, lingering on my labored breaths and the slight sway of my body. He didn't speak at first, his jaw tightening as if weighing the situation. Finally, he broke the silence, his voice soft. "Not yet. We need more distance from the river."

I nodded, though my strength felt like it was slipping through my fingers with every agonizing step. My body felt sluggish and heavy as every muscle screamed in protest against the trek. The fiery stitch in my side was a cruel reminder of how unprepared I was for hours of constant climbing and trudging through the tangled forest. Though I had strength from years of labor, this was different—an endurance I hadn't yet earned. Humiliation burned through me at my faltering pace. I gritted my teeth and forced myself forward, one aching step at a time.

The world around me seemed to blur as fatigue began to take hold. My vision narrowed to the path in front of me, dark spots dancing on the edges. I barely noticed the shift in the forest. The way the trees seemed to grow closer together, their branches forming a twisted, unnatural web overhead. Dex stopped abruptly and I crashed into his broad back, my breath catching in my throat as I stumbled to right myself. My heart was racing in my chest, but I wasn't sure if it was from the exertion or the tension that suddenly filled the air. My magic crackled harder against my skin, my senses rushing back into me, energized by the flow of power.

Every line of his body radiated tension, his posture rigid and alert. The air around us felt different. *Dark.* It was as if the forest itself had paused, holding its breath in anticipation. The oppressive stillness pressed against my skin like a physical weight.

"What is it?" I whispered, my voice shaking more than I would ever admit to.

Dex's golden eyes flicked to the shadows between the trees. "We're being followed," he whispered.

Ice trickled down my spine, stealing the breath from my lungs and leaving my chest tight. Instinctively, I edged closer to him, my trembling hands brushing against my sides as adrenaline surged, setting my fingers into a restless twitch. "By who?" I whispered, my voice barely audible over the pounding of blood rushing in my ears.

He didn't look at me, instead keeping his eyes on the shadows that seemed to shift and swirl between the trees. "Not who. What."

The ground beneath us trembled with power. It felt like a warning from the earth. The trees above swayed, releasing a cascade of leaves that fluttered down like confetti, obscuring us for a fraction of a moment. His arms flexed in response, his body coiling like a spring as his hand tightened on the hilt of his sword, searching for the source of the disturbance. I could feel the sharp sting of panic tightening in my chest, making it difficult to breathe. *Now wasn't the time for a panic attack.*

From the thick shadows, something moved. Large, dark, and unnervingly fast. My breath hitched as it materialized from the darkness, its massive form looming over Dex. It was unlike anything I had ever seen. Easily twice his size, the creature's body was covered in coarse, black fur that rippled with every shift of its weight. Its eyes glowed an unnatural red, piercing through the gloom with a malevolent hunger. Its mouth, lined with rows of jagged teeth, gleamed in the fading light, and its breath came in sharp, rattling hisses.

My heart slamming against my ribs, pure terror gripping me as I took in the monstrous wolf.

"Shadow Hounds." Dex's voice was thick with disgust. The venom in his voice was unmistakable. The orcs knew these creatures and they hated them.

"Stay behind me!" Dex barked, his voice commanding, cutting through the fog of fear clouding my mind. His sword flashed in the dim light, his body a solid wall of protection as he stepped between me and the creature.

A guttural snarl ripped through the air, freezing my breath in my chest as the massive creature burst from the underbrush. Its matted black fur bristled like quills, and its glowing red eyes locked onto Dex with predatory focus. It moved too fast for its size, a blur of jagged claws and snapping teeth barreling straight for him.

Dex sprang forward. His sword flashed with a deadly gleam as he intercepted the creature mid-leap. The impact was thunderous, sending him skidding back, boots digging into the dirt to hold his ground.

Twisting his blade, he carved into the beast's flank, spilling a spray of dark, viscous blood onto the forest floor. The metallic tang hit the back of my throat.

The creature's roars shook the air, a guttural sound that vibrated in my bones. I stumbled backward, my feet tangling in the underbrush. Dex moved with lethal precision, his swing controlled and calculated, but the beast was a relentless force. Its massive claws lashed out, tearing through his arm in a blur of motion, leaving deep, jagged gashes in their wake. His groan of pain escaped through clenched teeth.

He dodged the creature's next strike, rolling sharply to the side as its claws tore through the air just inches from his chest. With a fierce growl, Dex surged forward, his blade carving a deep, jagged line across its stomach. A spray of dark blood splattered the ground. The creature twisted with a guttural snarl, its massive paw slamming into Dex, the impact launching him backward and into a tree with a bone-rattling thud. He hit the ground hard, and my breath hitched as he lay still. Then, with a growl of effort, he pushed himself up, his jaw tight and eyes blazing with determination. He squared his shoulders, already moving back to engage the beast.

The Shadow Hound's glowing red eyes shifted to me, its lips pulling back to reveal jagged teeth dripping with saliva. My body was rigid as it began to move, slow and deliberate as it stalked me. *Dex would never reach me in time.* Panic surged within me, making my knees weak, and my magic responded, a chaotic hum that built into a deafening roar in my mind.

"Cleo!" Dex's voice tore through the haze, "Pull on your magic!"

My fingers curled into fists, nails biting into my palms as I fought to keep control. The ground beneath me seemed to thrum with life, a pulse of energy that wasn't entirely my own. My breaths came in ragged gasps as I reached for it.

The earth answered with a violent tremor. Roots exploded from the soil like a living trap, twisting and writhing with a predatory intent. The wolf launched at me with a demonic speed, but my instinctual magic was faster. The roots wrapped around one of its legs mid-air, yanking it down with a shuddering crash that reverberated through the clearing, sending a cascade of leaves and twigs raining down from above. The creature let out a pained snarl, its massive frame writhing as it struggled against the bonds. My desperation fed the magic. It was overwhelming, hot, and burning through me like liquid fire. It tasted bitter on my tongue, as if the very essence of fear was forcing its way out of me. An icy-hot sensation coursed through my veins, spreading to my fingertips in waves. I pushed the power outward. More roots surged upward, coiling tightly around the beast, pinning its legs and forcing its body into a grotesque sprawl. The sharp edges of the roots dug deep, slicing into its flesh and popping joints with a sickening series of cracks. The Shadow Hound thrashed and roared. Its glowing red eyes were wild with fury, but the roots only tightened, holding it in a vice-like grip that left it helpless.

Dex seized the opportunity and lunged with a roar, his blade slicing through the air. The weapon sank deep into the creature's neck, blood spraying as the Shadow Hound let out a final, gurgling snarl. Its massive body convulsed, shuddering one last time before collapsing in a heap, its weight crashing into the earth. The oppressive tension that had gripped the forest lifted abruptly, leaving behind a suffocating silence punctuated only by my ragged breaths.

I stood, frozen, my chest heaving as the magic within me slowly receded, leaving a hollow ache in its wake that made my entire body tremble. A faint silvery-green glow lingered at my fingertips, shimmering softly before fading back into me, as though the magic itself was retreating to some hidden well deep inside. The roots entangling the creature's lifeless form slowly unwound, retreating back into the soil as if they had never existed. My hands shook as I took calming breaths, trying to find my center. The sight of the bloodied ground and the mangled remains of the beast left me cold, but the weight of what I had done—what I was capable of—pressed on me.

Dex turned to me, his broad shoulders heaving with each labored breath, sweat glistening on his flushed skin. The deep gash along his massive arm bled steadily, the crimson streaks trailing down to his fingertips before dripping onto the forest floor. His sword still dripped with unnatural dark blood, and the droplets stained the path beneath him. His golden eyes locked on mine, their intensity undimmed despite the strain etched into his features. "You saved yourself, little shaman."

Tears stung my eyes as I shook my head. "I didn't control it," I whispered, each syllable trembling. "It just... happened."

Taking another step closer, Dex's hand came to rest on my shoulder, the warmth of his touch grounding me in a way I desperately needed. "Breathe. The magic is part of you," he said, his tone firm but not unkind. "It answers to your emotions, yes, but control takes time. You'll learn."

His words settled over me like a balm, soothing the raw edges of my panic. I looked up at him, searching for any trace of doubt or fear, but all I saw was determination—an unwavering belief that I could rise to meet this challenge. It was a lifeline I hadn't known I needed, anchoring me against the chaos that still swirled inside.

"We need to move." His voice was gentler now, though no less resolute. "More will come, drawn by the scent of blood. The hunting party cannot be too far."

I nodded, swallowing hard against the lump in my throat. A small spark of resolve began to flicker within me. If this magic was mine, I would master it. I would control it.

And I would never let it control me again.

CHAPTER 9
DEX

The creature's body lay twisted and still, its blood pooling on the forest floor, soaking into the earth like it belonged there. I couldn't tear my eyes from Cleo. She stood a few paces away, hands trembling and breath coming in uneven gasps. The faint silver-green glow that had danced at her fingertips had faded, but I could still feel it. A lingering pulse of magic that clung to her like a second skin.

Her magic was raw and terrifyingly powerful. It had ripped through the clearing wildly, yet devastatingly precise in its destruction. The sheer force of it made the air hum, answering her fear with a savage intent that sent a chill through me. I had seen powerful shamans before, but this—this was different. Stronger than I'd ever expected from a human. Stronger than even she realized. And that frightened me. Not because of what she'd done, but because of what she could become.

Her red curls caught the light, a stark contrast to the silvery glow of her power. It was impossible to ignore how much she matched the prophecy's description. A shaman with untold strength, born to shift the balance of this world. But this... this well of magic was unlike anything I had ever seen. The fact that she was untrained and still alive spoke volumes to her potential, and the danger she posed. Not because of what it had done to the Shadow Hound—it deserved its fate—but because of what it had nearly done to her. Magic of this level was exceptionally dangerous. Beneath my fears, a spark of eagerness burned. If this power could be harnessed, if she could learn control, she might be exactly what my clan needed.

Wiping my blade clean, I sheathed it with care. Cleo hadn't moved since the fight had ended. Her wide green eyes were locked on her hands as if they belonged to someone else, and her body trembled with the weight of what she'd unleashed. There was something almost ethereal about her in this moment.

"Cleo." My voice was low but sharp enough to snap her out of her daze. Her gaze jerked to mine, those wide eyes glimmering with unshed tears. I hated the way her lips trembled, hated the vulnerability she showed, and hated how much I wanted to take it away.

My chest tightened as I stared at her, and I knew I should look away, should focus on the dangers surrounding us. But I couldn't. My eyes betrayed me, dragging over her face, lingering on the delicate pout of her lips, then lower, tracing the curve of her throat and the way her chest rose and fell with uneven breaths. She was a contradiction—fragile and defiant, vulnerable yet impossibly strong. It was maddening.

A slow heat coiled low in my stomach. How could this human, so different from everything I'd known, command my attention so completely? I swallowed hard, forcing my gaze back to her eyes, but the pull didn't ease. I wanted to touch her, to feel her softness beneath my hands, to chase away that flicker of fear and replace it with something warmer, something that belonged to me.

The realization hit me like a blow. Gods, I wanted to *claim* her. Not just for her power, but for *her*. Now wasn't the time to think on this feral attraction between us. I had a clan to protect. A war to win.

She blinked at me, then looked away as if afraid of what she might see in my eyes, her voice a broken whisper. "I didn't control it... it just happened."

I closed the distance in a few long strides. Without thinking, I reached out and gripping her arm, grounding her. Slowly, her breathing steadied, and the tremble in her hands eased, but I could still see the shadow of fear lurking in her expression, the uncertainty that came with knowing her own power.

She nodded, but just as I turned to go, her hand brushed against my arm, stopping me. "Wait," she said softly. "Your shoulder... you're hurt."

I glanced down at my shoulder, the sluggish trickle of blood oozing from the ragged edges catching my eye. Luckily, it wasn't deep. I'd felt the sting earlier but shoved it aside, the rush of adrenaline masking the worst of the pain. Now that the fight was over, the ache crept in, sharp and persistent. "It's nothing," I muttered, brushing it off with a shake of my head. "I've had worse."

"Sit." Her voice was firmer this time. I raised a brow at her, but her expression didn't waver. "You can't reach it properly, and it needs to be cleaned. Let me help."

There was no arguing with her, she was desperate for some form of control. Reluctantly, I lowered myself to a fallen log, watching as she knelt beside me and rummaged through the small pack slung over her shoulder. She pulled out a strip of cloth and a small flask of water, her movements purposeful despite the faint tremor still lingering in her fingers.

Her hands brushed my shoulder lightly as she worked, and I felt the warmth of her touch even through the sting of the cool water. She cleaned the wound with care, her fingers grazing my skin as she maneuvered around the edges of the torn flesh. Each fleeting contact sent a strange, electric awareness coursing through me, distracting me from the pain. My focus narrowed entirely on her. The way her brows knit together in concentration, the faint rise and fall of her chest as she worked, the way her lower lip caught between her teeth in thought. My gaze drifted lower, and I froze, mesmerized by her kneeling at my feet. Something about the vulnerability of the position, on her knees before me, so close. My throat constricted and I shifted awkwardly, trying to dispel the sudden flames of desire. Lust mingled with the adrenaline still coursing through my veins, and I forced myself to look away, blaming the primal instincts that always surged after a fight. Orcs were wired for this. Battle and blood always stoked the fire for *more*.

Her fingers lingered a fraction too long as she wrapped the cloth around my shoulder, tying it off with a careful knot. "There," she murmured, sitting back on her heels. "That should hold for now. I'm sorry I don't have any healing salves or herbs."

85

Her words pulled me sharply from my thoughts, and I flexed my arm experimentally, testing the bandage. "Not bad," I said, my voice deliberately casual. "You've done this sort of thing before?"

She gave a small, rueful smile that fueled the desire I was fighting to suppress. *Oh, the things I want to do to that pouty little mouth.* I shook the thoughts from my head, focusing on the words as they left her lips instead. "Farm life isn't exactly gentle. I've patched up worse." Her gaze flicked up to meet mine, and I caught the faintest hint of a blush creeping across her cheeks as she took in our position.

I couldn't resist leaning in. "Careful, you're going to spoil me with all this attention."

"Don't get used to it," she muttered, but the corners of her mouth twitched, betraying her amusement. The flush of her cheeks was exactly what I had been hoping for. The coloring sent filthy thoughts tumbling through my imagination, and I had to focus on pushing them back.

Her warmth lingered on my skin long after she pulled away, and I found myself reluctant to break the moment.

"Thank you" I said, the words heavier than they should have been.

"You're welcome."

I stood, towering over her, the sheer difference in our size striking. Something I liked way too much. Her smaller hand slipped into mine, her touch ignited something raw and untamed inside me, a primal hunger clawing its way to the surface, demanding more. I couldn't help but notice the contrast, her human fragility against my orc strength. It made me wonder, not for the first time, why she didn't seem terrified of me. Most humans would have been.

Pulling her to stand, I brushed my thumb over the back of her hand before I released her reluctantly. "We need to keep moving," I said, my tone gruffer than I intended.

She nodded, her cheeks still tinged pink as she fell into step beside me. As we made our way deeper into the dark forest, the pull between us lingered, simmering beneath the surface like a fire waiting to ignite. I found myself wondering if the path ahead might hold something more than just survival.

CHAPTER 10
CLEO

The forest closed in around us as the day wore on, the canopy filtering the sunlight into a dim, almost twilight-like glow. The air was cool, and the tension between Dex and I had shifted to something more intimate. Every time I caught the flicker of his golden eyes on me, my pulse quickened. My body was hyper-aware of him. His strength, his body heat, the way his deep voice seemed to sink into my skin and settle in my chest. *Focus, Cleo!*

It wasn't just his presence that had my blood humming. The memory of my magic, how the earth had responded to my command, still thudded in my veins. I could feel the heady power as the roots had surged up. It had been intoxicating. Overwhelming and terrifying.

And then there was a darker pull, the strange feeling when the Shadow Hound had fallen, its lifeforce draining away into the earth. The dark, cold emptiness of death had brushed against my awareness, and for a fleeting moment, I had felt the urge to reach out and grasp it, to take that energy into myself. The thought left me sick, but it also left me aching with a strange and unnerving hunger for more. A pulse of power throbbed beneath my skin, but the darkness kept it at bay. Barely. It wasn't just magic. It spoke to something darker in me.

"Stop."

Freezing, I scanned the shadows ahead, heart pounding. I thought he had spotted another shape approaching in the shadows, but breathed a sigh of relief when three orcs emerged from the underbrush, their broad shoulders and green skin unmistakable even in the dim light. The first one to step forward was a towering figure with a gray-streaked braid that glinted faintly under the dappled light. His amber eyes locked onto Dex, and his face split into a wide grin, sharp tusks gleaming. "Glad to see you, old friend!" he called out, his voice thick with relief and warmth.

Dex smiled widely, taking in the trio. His voice was steady, but there was a weight to it that I could feel even from where I stood. "Miss me already, Gornak?"

Behind Gornak, the two other orcs moved swiftly into view. One of them, smaller but no less imposing, clutched a curved blade in one hand while his other rested with a falcon perched on his shoulder. The bird's sharp eyes scanning the area as if it, too, understood the danger of the forest. With a quick whistle from its master, the falcon launched into the air, disappearing into the canopy above with a flutter of wings.

"I'll send word to the clan," the smaller orc said. "They'll be relieved to hear of your return, Chieftain."

The weight of their gazes pressed against my skin, their expressions sharpened with curiosity. The tension in the air was suffocating, thick enough to choke on, and it took everything I had not to recoil. Instead, I kept my chin steady, even as my pulse drummed in my ears and my fingers curled into the fabric of my dress. Self-consciousness gnawed at me as their gazes swept over me, taking in every detail. My dress was torn and frayed, dirtied by mud and riddled with debris that clung stubbornly to the hem. The cut on my temple felt raw and exposed under their scrutiny, and I could almost feel the grime on my skin, the days of running and fighting etched into every inch of me. I fought the urge to brush at my hair, knowing it would be futile. They saw me as I was—bruised and vulnerable.

"And her?" Gornak asked. His voice was low but filled with curiosity as he leaned around Dex to take me in.

"She is a shaman. The reason I'm free and the reason we're still alive. She's more powerful than any I've ever seen."

As Dex told them of our journey and how we came to be traveling companions, I watched the orcs closely. They exchanged glances, expressions shifting from suspicion to something resembling cautious respect. The tension in the air didn't completely dissipate, but it softened enough for one of them to step forward, offering a faint nod and crossing his arms over his chest. The gesture felt deliberate, almost protective, as if signaling acceptance.

"Enchanted cuffs," the young falconer muttered, shaking his head as if he couldn't quite believe it. "The Ostelan Crown is cruel; putting anyone through that is akin to torture. I'm Thorn."

"Cleo." I nodded in response.

At their Chieftain's request for food and water, the orcs immediately handed Dex a waterskin while offering me a small sachet of dried fruit. Their glances lingered, curiosity sparking in their eyes as I murmured my thanks, but they said nothing more. I watched as Gornak pressed a dagger into Dex's hand with a slight bow of his head, the golden glow of the runes casting a bronze light against his scarred green hand.

Our group began to move further into the forest, and I followed close behind. I couldn't shake the feeling of being an outsider, but Dex's steady presence at my side kept me grounded. The path wound through dense undergrowth, the shadows growing longer as the sun dipped lower, until the faint smell of woodsmoke reached me.

We arrived at a small clearing where a modest campsite had been set up. The orcs spread out efficiently, unrolling canvas and tending to the fire pit at the center. Dex steered me closer to the flames, and I sank onto a log, the warmth seeping into my chilled skin as I tried to shake off the lingering tension.

"Chieftain!" one of them called out, his voice thick with relief. He was taller than the others, his deep-set amber eyes glowing faintly as he strode forward. "You're alive."

"What's with the pet, Dex?"

"The human"—he glanced briefly down at me, his voice steady but carrying an edge of something unreadable—"is a shaman. Her name is Cleo, and she is seeking refuge with us."

The warriors exchanged glances, their curiosity sharpening as they absorbed his words. They turned their attention to me and offered murmured introductions and greetings, their voices gruff but not unfriendly. My own responses were hesitant and soft, barely audible over the hum of tension in the air. "A shaman?" one repeated, disbelief flickering across his face.

"A powerful one. Her magic was unlike anything I've seen. She was destined for Knights Hold." His golden eyes flicked to me for a moment before continuing. "Without her, I would still be in chains. Her tenacity helped us escape, and her magic has already grown stronger. The Shadow Hound we encountered was no match for her. She drove the Shadow Hound down with it. It's stronger than anything I expected."

They exchanged knowing looks. I fought the urge to shrink under their scrutiny, but the weight of their attention still made my skin prickle.

"Later," Dex said, his tone final. "For now, we need rest."

MY BODY SCREAMED FOR REST, but my mind was far from quiet. Dex returned with smoked meat and some bread, pushing both roughly into my hands before he crouched beside me. His gaze was so intense, so raw, that it made it hard to breathe. There was something pulling between us, something that had been building since we first spoke, and it was becoming harder and harder to ignore.

"You need to eat a real meal, but this is the best we have until the hunters return." His voice was rougher than usual.

"Thank you." I nodded, though the last thing on my mind was food. I was hungry, yes, but not for the dried rations he had given me. As I took the pouch from his hands, my fingers brushed against his, sending a spark of warmth shooting up my arm. My pulse quickened, and I found myself acutely aware of every inch of him. The sharp line of his jaw, the hungry gleam in his eyes, and the sheer strength coiled in his body as he crouched beside me. My thoughts drifted, my gaze flicking to his broad shoulders and down to the way his muscles shifted. *Get a hold of yourself!*

The air between us crackled with tension, and I thought he might close the distance, hoped that he might finally give in to whatever was pulling us together. But just as quickly as it had built, he leaned back, leaving me aching for something I wasn't sure I was ready for. Gods, what was wrong with me? *Stop pining over a stranger!*

As the camp settled into a quiet stillness. The orcs took shifts to keep watch, their eyes focused on the trees for any signs of danger, the fire crackling softly in the center of the clearing. I sat closer to the fire, trying to absorb its warmth into my chilled skin. Every time I closed my eyes, the image of the creature flashed in my mind, its glowing red eyes burning through the darkness. But it wasn't just the sight of its death that haunted me. It was the way my power was desperate for it that had disgust roiling through me.

I could feel the sensation that had washed over me the moment it stepped out of the shadows. A cold so intense it burned. It wasn't the physical cold of ice or snow. It was something far more unnatural. The absence of life. The kind of cold that numbed your soul, like everything alive had been drained from the world around you. That creature didn't belong in this world and it had immediately sent me reeling.

I pulled my knees to my chest, trying to shake off the memory, but it clung to me, suffocating and all consuming. The smell, Gods, I would never forget the smell. The scent of death was thick and cloying as it filled the air when the Hound had appeared. It wasn't just rot or decay; it was the smell of something ancient and long dead. The closer it had come, the more overpowering that smell had been, as though the very essence of life around us had been drained away.

I hadn't realized it at the time, but my magic had sensed it too. The roots had surged up from the earth, seeking something. They had been drawn to the creature, searching for the life force that should have been there but wasn't. That realization had my skin prickling as shivers raced down my arms, and I rubbed them to try and relieve the uneasy feeling.

The magic inside me wasn't just connected to the earth. It was connected to life, and this creature, whatever it had been, it was wrong. Its essence was *missing*. A black void where life should have been. And yet it had moved, and it had fought. But without the spark of a lifeforce.

The word echoed in my mind, and I shivered again, feeling a strange pull within me. *Could I sense it? Could I sense the lifeforce of those around me, the way the roots had sensed its absence in the creature?* The earth wasn't just responding to my fear. It had been eager for the power that surged through the Shadow Hound. That frightened me more than anything at how natural it had felt. How instinctive the magic had curled under my grasp, seeking the energy on its own.

The magic inside me had acted without my direction. It had known what to do without my instruction. *I hadn't controlled it. It had controlled me.* Swallowing hard, I tried to calm the racing thoughts.

I needed to focus, to find something solid to anchor myself. *Five things you can see,* I reminded myself.

My eyes darted around the camp. Trees, their gnarled branches reaching for the sky. Rocks scattered near the fire, some jagged, some smooth. A small pile of snacks—a strange assortment of dried meats and fruits Dex had called rations. The endless stretch of the sky, dotted with clouds. Leaves fluttering in the faint breeze, catching the firelight as they swayed.

Four things you can touch. I pressed my fingertips into the cool dirt beneath me, gritty and grounding. My new cloak, rough and worn against my palms. The smooth edge of the wooden bowl resting near my knee. The coarse braid of my hair, the strands tangled and stiff from days without washing.

Three things you can hear. The steady crackle of the fire, rhythmic and soothing. The distant rustle of the forest, as if the trees were whispering secrets. Dex's low voice somewhere behind me, rumbling softly as he spoke to one of his warriors.

Two things you can smell. The smoky warmth of the fire, mingling with the earthy aroma of the forest floor. The faint, sharp tang of leather from the worn straps of my boots.

One thing you can taste. The lingering saltiness of the dried meat I'd eaten earlier, still clinging faintly to my tongue.

I felt calmer as I returned to my thoughts. There was more to this magic than I realized. I could feel it even now, deep inside me, thrumming quietly, waiting to be called upon. The ability to sense life, to touch it, was there, lurking beneath the surface. It had acted on instinct before, but what if I could learn to control it? What if I could learn to harness it? My chest tightened with a dark curiosity. *What would that make me?*

I hadn't immediately recoiled in fear. There had been a moment where something inside me had wanted to fill the void, to claim that energy for myself. The thought made my stomach turn. I had never considered myself capable of something so twisted. This magic didn't seem to care about morality or intention; it had simply responded to my call, and in that moment, it had wanted to take. To consume.

I was so lost in my thoughts that I didn't notice Dex approaching until he was beside me. He crouched down, his body close enough that I could feel the heat radiating off him. His golden eyes glowed in the firelight.

"You are scared," Dex said.

"How can I not be? With everything that's happening. I don't think I want this."

Dex's eyes softened, though his expression remained guarded. "Magic doesn't care what you want. It's part of who you are. But that doesn't mean it controls you."

"And what if it does?" I whispered, my voice trembling.

CHAPTER 11
DEX

The clearing was alive with quiet activity as the hunters returned with their spoils. The air smelled of fresh game, and the warriors talked amongst themselves as they began to prepare our meal. Cleo lingered near the edge of the fire pit, her eyes darting between them.

She was trying to help, though her human methods were clearly amusing us all. Her hands moved with determination, though not with the efficiency of someone used to such tasks. She fumbled with the kindling, cursing when it refused to cooperate. She had a certain grace in the way she worked, even if it was tinged with frustration. It was rather endearing.

Gornak leaned against a tree nearby, his arms were crossed, and a small, rare grin tugged at his lips as he watched her work. The others were less subtle, their deep chuckles rumbling like distant thunder whenever she fumbled with a particularly stubborn piece of kindling or cursed softly under her breath. She was determined, and while her movements were awkward, there was a stubborn fire in her eyes that spoke volumes.

"Let me help," she insisted as she crouched to arrange the wood. Against my better judgment, the snug pull of her dress around her ample curves drew my attention. The way it clung to the curve of her wide hips stirred something primal in me, a heat that mingled uncomfortably with my amusement at her frustration. The warriors exchanged bemused glances but said nothing, their respect for my authority evident even as their smirks widened.

Stepping forward, I crouched beside her, brushing past the lingering heat of her body as I reached for the flint. "It's all in the angle," I murmured, striking the stones deliberately slow to create a spark. The fire caught almost immediately, flames licking at the dry wood with a satisfying crackle.

She turned and her elbow brushed lightly against my stomach as she adjusted her position. Her cheeks flushed a soft pink, the color spreading as she glanced up at me. I felt the corners of my mouth tug into a grin, unable to resist her mix of determination and sudden shyness. Gods, despite the grime still coating her face, she was beautiful.

"Oh, is this orc flirting? Teaching a human how to cook over a fire?" she asked, arching a brow. Her voice was heavy with sarcasm, but a faint tremor betrayed her nervousness.

She was so close. I leaned in, invading her space, keeping my tone low and deliberate. "If I was flirting, little shaman, you wouldn't be holding a knife." My grin widened. "I'd have you melting in my hands."

She turned away sharply, and the knife slipped from her grip, clattering against the ground. She scrambled to retrieve it, her cheeks glowing as brightly as the flames. I fought the urge to laugh but failed to suppress the amused twitch of my lips. Gornak's deep chuckle rumbled from behind us. Cleo shot a sharp glare at him, though it did little to hide the embarrassment etched across her features.

"You've got a talent, Chieftain," he said, his voice laced with amusement. "Never thought I'd see the day a human would drop her guard so easily around an orc."

"Shut it, Gornak." My tone was light, but it carried a warning edge. Cleo refused to look at me, instead busying herself with wiping off the knife, and returning to peeling potatoes.

Rabbit stew was served and supper passed with easy conversation. My warriors, ever loyal and cautious, seemed to settle into an easy comfort with Cleo. They exchanged brief nods with her, their glances lingering as though they were trying to reconcile her fragile, human form with the immense power they had been told she possessed. Mixed emotions played across their faces, but one stood out clearly. Hope.

It was a rare and dangerous thing among my people. To be in the presence of someone who might truly alter the fate of the clans carried a weight none of us could ignore. That hope flickered like the flames of our fire, fragile yet persistent, against the backdrop of decades of oppression.

We had been hunted relentlessly, driven from our ancestral lands and into the harsh strongholds in the Marshes and the Black Mountains, where survival meant enduring the unendurable. The fucking Ostelan Crown, with their knights and their dark mages, had attacked us during a time of peace, breaking treaties and spilling blood. They painted us as monsters and savages, justifying every cruelty under the guise of righteousness.

Yet here we were, gathered around a humble fire with a shaman. A living symbol of a future we had long since stopped believing possible. The weight of her presence gnawed at me, a mixture of hope and unease that I couldn't shake. Cleo's presence wasn't just a curiosity; she was a disruption, a raw challenge to the scars etched into our history.

The fire danced in her eyes, reflecting a softness that both unsettled and captivated me. It was more than her magic. She carried a promise of change and the thought made my chest tighten. We'd spent generations hiding in the shadows, retreating to the harshest corners of the earth while the Church of the Silver Hand hunted us to the brink of extinction. Against the odds, here was a shaman who could tip the scales.

Yet, that promise came with uncertainty. Could she even begin to grasp the enormity of what she had stumbled into? Did she have the strength to endure the trials that awaited her. The willingness to fight for a race not her own? The questions lingered like smoke as I watched her laugh softly at something Thorn muttered. For now, she seemed oblivious to the hope resting on her shoulders. A hope we were willing to bleed for—to die for—all for a chance at freedom.

The past clawed at the edges of my thoughts, reminding me of the treaties shattered, the blood spilled on both sides, and the force that had driven my people to this point. Every step forward had been forged in suffering, and I couldn't help but wonder if this fragile thread of possibility would be enough. Could it weave a future strong enough to endure the weight of the Crown's wrath?

THE LATE AFTERNOON sun filtered through the trees as the camp settled into a quiet rhythm, the fire's embers casting a faint light across the darkening clearing. I stood, stretching out my stiff back, and caught Cleo's attention. She was sitting by the fire again, her arms wrapped around her knees. Her expression was lighter than before, and it warmed me to know she felt comfortable enough with my clan to relax. "Come, let's get you cleaned up. There's a stream nearby."

She hesitated but nodded, her tired muscles causing her to groan as she stood. The press of her breasts against her dress sent my thoughts tumbling back to inappropriate places. Gods, help me. I grabbed two small pouches from one of the packs and handed it to her as we walked. "Lavender, rosemary, and a bit of oil," I explained. "It's not much, but it'll do as a soap." Her fingers brushed mine as she took it, and I felt the familiar warmth stir in my chest.

We reached the stream, its waters glinting silver under the late sun, a striking contrast to the oppressive gloom of the Shadow Lands. This place felt untouched by the darkness that had tainted the surrounding forest. The air was clean and crisp, carrying the scent of damp earth and wildflowers. Fish darted beneath the surface, their movements sending ripples across the crystal-clear water. Bird calls mingled with the gentle rush of the stream. It smelled of purity and life, a sharp divergence from the decay and hostility we had trudged through. This place of peace felt almost sacred, the Gods themselves driving the darkness away from its waters.

Without a word, I began tugging off my boots and loosening the straps of my armor with practiced ease. The metal clinked softly as I set it aside, each sound punctuating the quiet rhythm of the stream. I found myself hesitating, fingers brushing the waistband of my leathers as I considered stripping down further. I decided against it, not wanting to push Cleo's comfort too far—though the thought of her reaction flitted unbidden into my mind. *Would her gaze falter, her cheeks flush as she tried not to stare at my cock?* My jaw tightened as I imagined her face if she saw the unmistakable evidence of how her presence stirred something primal in me. The heat flared before I forced it down, focusing on securing my armor and boots neatly on a nearby boulder, and ignoring the tight strain in my pants.

Stepping into the water, the icy current wrapped around my calves and climbed higher as I waded deeper, soaking into my leathers and weighing them down. The smooth stones beneath my feet shifted, the chill biting into my skin in a way that felt both refreshing and grounding. Each step forward helped cool the fire simmering within me, though the sound of her soft breaths and faint movements behind me kept the edge sharp.

"It's safe to wash here," I said, turning my back to give her privacy, grinding the herbs in my palm before sliding them over my chest. *Was she watching me?* I heard the rustle of fabric as she stripped, her movements hesitant.

The sound of her footsteps splashing into the water drew my head to the side. I allowed myself to keep her in my peripherals, telling myself it was for safety reasons. The temptation to turn and take her in completely was maddening.

A yelp broke the stillness, followed by a loud splash. I turned to see her emerge from the water, spluttering and gasping. Her hair clung in damp tendrils to her flushed face, and she blinked rapidly, trying to regain her composure. She'd slipped on one of the slick rocks, the current swirling hungrily around her hips and threatening to push her off balance again.

Without thinking, I moved to her, my hand encircling her arm and steadying her. The water splashed around us as my other hand settled at her waist. Her body tensed for a moment, then relaxed under my touch. Her wide eyes met mine, shining with a mixture of surprise and desire. For a heartbeat, everything else faded away. All but the feel of her, the faint tremble of her body under my hands, and the unspoken pull between us.

I had to fight not to let my gaze roam over her wet body, every inch of it a temptation I struggled to ignore. The white cloth of her undergarments clung to her like a second skin, the cotton nearly transparent. The laces at her ribs only accentuated the curves they barely concealed, and her hips flared in a way that made me feral with desire. Her flushed face, the soft pout of her lips, and her heaving chest as she tried to catch her breath only made resisting almost impossible.

The world seemed to fade, leaving only the feel of her against me and the sound of her ragged breaths mingling with mine. Her lips parted, and I thought I saw the same hungry desire flicker in her gaze.

"Careful," I murmured, my voice rougher than I intended. "The rocks are slippery."

"Yeah." She didn't pull away, her hands resting against my chest, fingers flexing as if testing the strength beneath them.

The tension between us crackled like a live wire. My instincts screamed to claim her. My hand moved up her shoulder, brushing back the damp strands of hair clinging to her. The softness of her skin was a stark contrast to the roughness of my calloused fingers, a sensation that sent a shiver through me. I tucked the hair behind her ear, the motion deliberate, and let my hand linger.

Cleo leaned into me, her eyes burning with a need that matched my own. My thumb grazed the curve of her cheekbone, and the soft hitch in her breath was more intoxicating than anything I had ever experienced. Her eyes called to me, dragging me deeper. Hypnotized by the way her pupils were blown in arousal, I crowded her frame, leaning down until her face was mere inches from mine. She didn't pull away. Instead, she leaned in, just enough to obliterate any doubt about her intent. Her eyes, wide and unguarded, begged me to close the gap.

Every muscle in my body tightened, caught between desire for this human, and duty to my people. I could feel the heat radiating from her, the way her body leaned into mine as though surrendering to an invisible force. Her lips were so close, so tempting. I needed to taste them.

My chest heaved as I forced myself to breathe, to break the spell before it consumed me. My hand fell from her face, though the memory of her touch lingered, an echo I couldn't shake. She stared at me, her cheeks flushed, her lips parted as if caught mid-word. The look she gave me was enough to unravel what little resolve I had left.

"Dex..." Her voice was like a siren, dripping in sensual power, calling me to my doom.

Before I could react, Cleo stepped closer, her body brushing mine with hesitant intent. Her hand slid to the back of my neck, cool fingers drawing me down to her. Her lips met mine, soft and uncertain. I froze. Then the intensity of her touch shattered my restraint. My hand gripped her waist, pulling her closer, her warmth searing through the thin fabric between us. Her scent filled my senses, grounding me in the moment, and everything else fading to nothing.

Cleo tilted her head and deepened the kiss. I was mindful of my tusks, careful not to let them tear her soft, delicate skin. When her tongue brushed against mine, a shiver coursed through me, my own hesitancy dissolving as instinct took over. The awareness of our differences only heightened my arousal. I gripped her tighter, my fingers skimming along the exposed curve of her back, tracing the delicate laces of her undergarment. The sound she made, soft and breathless, sent a bolt of need straight to my cock. My groan rumbled low in my throat as I crowded her against me, needing to feel more, to consume the connection that had sparked between us.

Her hands clutched at my shoulders, nails grazing my skin with just enough pressure to anchor me in the moment. My head spun, caught between the primal need surging through me and the impossibility of her yielding so completely in my arms. Her lips moved against mine with growing confidence, stoking the fire that roared in my veins. Her hip pressed against my throbbing cock, and I groaned, shifting to find more friction.

Instead, my foot slipped on an uneven rock, and I stumbled, the world tilting as I lost my footing. Cleo's startled gasp was the only warning before we tumbled sideways into the cold embrace of the stream. The icy water swallowed us whole, the shock pulling a strangled shout from her as she surfaced, sputtering and gasping for air.

Embarrassment burned hot in my chest, but her laughter cut through it, bright and unrestrained as it bubbled up from deep within her. She leaned back, wet hair clinging to her face, and I couldn't help but laugh alongside her, the sound rough and low compared to her melodic joy. Her eyes sparkled with amusement as she brushed a hand over her face. Her grin wide and unguarded.

The water rippled around us, and our laughter faded into a quiet, shared warmth. The stream seemed to wrap us in its serene embrace, a brief reprieve from the chaos that surrounded our journey. I pushed my hair back from my face, catching her gaze as a smile lingered on her lips. Her expression softened, the wariness replaced by something more open, more vulnerable.

"You know, for someone who's supposed to be intimidating, you're surprisingly clumsy," she teased.

I smirked, raising a brow. "Clumsy? I think you're mistaking a tactical misstep for clumsiness. Maybe I just like seeing you all wet!"

She rolled her eyes, but the smile remained, and the shadow of her earlier unease seemed to fade momentarily.

"I already was."

Gods, I don't think she was talking about the stream.

"What?" she asked, catching my pained expression.

I hesitated, then let out a soft breath as I searched for the right words. "Just thinking about how unexpected you are."

A single eyebrow disappeared into her hairline. "Unexpected?"

"Unexpected. Distracting. The most beautiful surprises usually are." My gaze held hers. There was no artifice in her expression, no walls, just an openness that made my chest tighten. "You're not what I imagined, Cleo. In so many ways."

Her lips parted, her cheeks flushing again, but she didn't look away.

I was so fucked.

The sight of her like this—unguarded, laughter spilling from her lips like the sweetest temptation—sent a sharp ache through my chest. It was more than admiration, more than desire. It was hunger, longing, a need so fierce it stole my breath. I ached to touch her, to claim even a moment of that joy for myself, but the intensity of it startled me. *When had she become this vital to me? When had her happiness started to feel like the very air I needed to breathe?*

It would complicate everything. She was a shaman, a symbol of hope for my people, and I was their Chieftain. My duty had to come first. But every glance at her, every moment like this, made that duty feel like a chain tightening around my chest.

CHAPTER 12
CLEO

Thin morning light pierced through the trees, casting pale, shifting shadows as the camp stirred to life. My body ached, every muscle protesting from the journey and the tension coiling deep inside me. Rest felt like a distant dream, one I couldn't afford to indulge in yet.

The orcs moved efficiently, their silence punctuated by the rustle of leather straps and the sharp clink of weapons. Packs were slung over shoulders, blades checked and supplies distributed. Dex handed me a ration of bread and cheese, followed by a large water flask, his wary glance lingered for only a moment before he turned away. I murmured my thanks and tucked the food into my bag, slinging the flask over my shoulder.

The magic stirred inside me as we set off. My boots crunched against the forest floor as I focused on the rhythm of our movement, but the power within me refused to settle, simmering just below the surface.

The deeper we ventured into the forest, the more the air thickened, damp and clinging to my skin. The quiet pressed down like a weight, broken only by the sharp rustle of leaves or the snap of a branch underfoot. Every sound was magnified, the tension around us as palpable as the chill creeping into the air.

The orcs felt it too. They moved with heightened awareness, their eyes darting to the shadows between the trees, weapons within easy reach. The unease was a constant companion, sharpening every step we took.

When the path narrowed into a steep descent along the rocky cliff, I faltered, a strange pulse rippling through me like a shockwave. It wasn't the magic's usual hum, steady and warm; this was colder. My breath hitched as the sensation crept down my spine, its weight heavy and oppressive, like icy fingers tracing my vertebrae.

My magic surged wildly, as if it were pushing back against the foreign energy. My fingers tingled, the faint green glow of power flickering to life against my will. I clenched my fists, trying to contain it, but the connection was undeniable, raw and urgent. The dark thrum radiating from the valley was far too similar to what I'd felt from the Shadow Hounds, but it was stronger this time. Darker.

Every nerve in my body felt heightened, my senses sharpening painfully as I strained to listen. The awareness of the orcs surrounding me brought a fleeting sense of safety. They had noticed the flare of my magic and they closed ranks, weapons raised and ready.

I caught Dex's gaze, his golden eyes meeting mine with a steady intensity. He didn't speak, but the caution etched on my face must have been clear. His nod was small but reassuring, grounding me enough to turn my focus back to the path ahead.

I peered down into the darkened valley, straining to hear. The forest was alive with sounds I couldn't place. Low, eerie noises without clear sources. My heartbeat quickened, each thud hammering in my ears. The unnatural quiet seemed to stretch and twist the faint echoes around me until they felt like whispers slithering through the heavy air, brushing against my nerves with a sinister weight.

The magic continued to press against the surface, desperate and instinctual, as if it recognized the danger better than I. My skin prickled with unease, the decay in that dark energy tugging at me like a heavy fog, and I knew that whatever lay ahead wasn't just dangerous. It was tainted.

"Cleo?" Dex's voice cut through the tension as he reached out, his hand gripping my arm firmly. "What is it?"

I blinked up at him, my chest tight. "Something's wrong," I whispered, my voice unsteady. "We can't go down there. It's not safe."

His muscles rippled with unease his gaze sweeping over the shadowed forest below. "It's the only way to the mountain from the Shadow Lands," he said, his tone resolute.

Gornak stepped forward, his heavy boots crunching against the dirt as he joined the conversation. His eyes flicked between me and Dex, his expression grim but steady. "We passed through here four days ago without trouble," he said, his voice measured. "If we move carefully, we can defend ourselves. This part of the path is dangerous, yes, but once we reach the valley, we'll have the space to fight—"

"And be trapped?" I growled, frustration sharp in my tone as I fought to keep my magic in check. It pulsed faintly beneath my skin, begging to be trusted, but their reluctance grated on my nerves.

Dex turned to me, his expression hardening. His voice was steady, clipped with command. "Scouts reported a large pack of Shadow Hounds following our tracks. Turning back isn't an option without serious casualties." He shifted his attention to the warriors, his gaze sharp and unyielding. "Stay close to the shaman. Nothing gets near her, understood?"

The warriors responded with curt nods, steel sliding free as weapons were drawn and their circle around me tightened.

"Cleo," Dex said, his tone softening as his eyes met mine, "use your magic. Let us know if anything approaches." He stepped forward, his gaze sweeping down into the valley below. His shoulders tensed, and I caught the faint hesitation in the set of his jaw. He didn't trust the path ahead, but he trusted that going back wasn't an option.

The descent stretched before us, a narrow path carved into the jagged cliffside. Orcs shuffled single file, their large frames brushing against the rough rock wall to the left. Behind me, warriors bought up the rear with bows drawn, their sharp eyes scanning the path behind for danger. The scrape of leather and the clatter of tumbling pebbles echoed, each sound stretching the quiet.

I glanced nervously over my shoulder at the scouts covering our descent. How were they supposed to make this trip walking backward? The thought gnawed at me, the danger feeling more real with every step.

Gornak, directly behind me, caught my eye and gave me a small, reassuring smile. "Keep your focus on your steps," he said in a low, steady voice. "We'll handle the rest. You're safe."

His gentle confidence settled my nerves, and I turned back to the path, forcing myself to concentrate on each careful step as the forest's shadows crept closer around us.

The dead trees closed in, their gnarled branches twisting outward like skeletal fingers. With every step, the forest seemed to press closer, the limbs closing ranks and plunging the path into dim, suffocating shadows. Leaves rasped against the orcs' broad shoulders, catching on their armor and breaking the quiet with brittle snaps. Being smaller, I avoided the worst of the clawing branches, though the air grew heavier, colder, each breath a faint fog in the chill. My magic churned beneath my skin, its pulse quickening with my heart as it strained against the decay seeping from the valley below. The green glow of my fingers cast an ominous light in the gloom, illuminating the path just enough for me to spot uneven stones.

The skeletal canopy finally swallowed our view of the valley, plunging us into deep shadow. Claustrophobia tingled at the edges of my mind, my breaths coming shallow and tight. The damp air clung to my skin, and each step forward felt heavier, as though the forest itself resisted our passage. I glanced ahead at Dex, his sharp focus cutting through the gloom. The caution in his expression mirrored the unease coiling in my chest. Forcing myself to focus, I turned my gaze to the path ahead, peering into the dim forest and straining to catch any sound beyond the unsettling quiet.

When we reached the valley floor, I noticed just how different the forest was here. The trees were massive, their bare branches clawing at the sky. Shadows clung to their trunks like tar, darker and thicker than before. The silence was suffocating.

Magic crackled under my skin, and I swallowed hard, trying to keep it in check, but this wasn't just my magic. There was something else here. The orcs tightened their formation around me, weapons at the ready. The path had widened enough for Dex to step to my side. The warriors flanked us, bows, swords and axes at the ready, scanning the shadows. We moved cautiously into the forest, their disciplined movements a reminder of how much danger we were in.

I closed my eyes, taking a breath as I pushed my magic outward. A tentative bubble expanded around us. It brushed against the orcs first, caressing their forms as it spread, warm and curious. The magic seemed to recognize them, brushing across their frames with quiet acknowledgment, as if sensing they belonged to the earth. Again, I was certain choosing to stay with Dex was the right decision.

As my magic stretched further, it crept into the forest ahead, the energy seeking danger in the oppressive shadows. The sense of wrongness grew stronger, sharp and biting, and my hands tingled, the green glow pulsing brighter as the magic strained against the darkness. My grip tightened on Dex's forearm as I tugged him to the right, and the green light curled around his arm like a living tether.

"It's over there." My voice was steadier than I'd expected.

The warriors reaction was immediate, sliding in front of us with weapons raised, their smooth movements a testament to their experience in battle. Dex pulled his arm free from my grasp, his expression hardening as he assessed the threat. His hand moved unerringly to the hilt of his Chieftain dagger, drawing it free to complement the sword already in his other hand. The glowing runes etched into the blade shimmered in the dim light, their pale glow a stark contrast to the encroaching evil around us. Each symbol seemed alive, pulsing in rhythm with the tension radiating from his body.

Ahead, a shadow emerged from the trees. Its skeletal figure floated across the forest floor, draped in a swirling darkness. Glowing red eyes pierced the gloom, unblinking and fixed on us as it moved. Dense mist writhed beneath it like a living shroud.

My breath caught, and the magic inside me flared violently, pushing against the edges of my control. My hands trembled, and the pull of its energy—cold, lifeless, and deeply wrong—wrapped around me, suffocating and familiar. This was no ordinary threat; its magical presence felt like a weight pressing down on my chest.

The shadow figure raised a hand, and a wave of cold swept through the clearing, thick with the stench of decay. I shivered, the dark energy inside me calling seductively, its pull like a whisper in my mind. The desire to reach for it, to let it consume my fear, was almost impossible to ignore. The curl of green magic around my fingers warped to reveal a red edge, and I was terrified by how intoxicating its promise of power felt. I smothered the feeling with every ounce of self-control I had. It scared me more than the skeletal figure before us. My heartbeat thundered in my ears.

The chill nipped at my exposed skin, seeping through the fabric of my dress. My heart raced, the pulse of magic inside me surging wildly in response to the threat before us. The ground beneath me felt wrong, as though something vital had been drained from it. The figure's presence seemed to sap the energy from the forest around us, and the deeper I reached for the earth's magic, the more I felt the void it created.

Dex stood in front of me, his broad shoulders stiff with tension as the orcs fanned out at his side, their weapons drawn. Steel flashed as they shifted into position, and bow strings creaked as they were pulled taut. Though their movements were precise, I caught the flicker of hesitation in their eyes—an unease that mirrored the knot twisting in my stomach. This wasn't just another enemy. It felt like an apex predator wrapped in shadow.

The figure's glowing eyes bore into me, their unnatural red light like searing brands against the gloom. And then I felt it *pull* on the forest. It wasn't just a sensation; it was a force, cold and invasive, clawing through my magic as if seeking to tear it from my veins. A shudder ran down my spine as the void within the figure reached for me, leaving my skin prickling and my stomach lurching. My instincts screamed to push back, to resist the suffocating, icy tendrils trying to burrow into my core.

"Cleo, stay back." Dex's voice was urgent as he stepped to block me from view. "You aren't equipped for this fight!"

Frustration bubbled up, hot and insistent, at his dismissal. I squared my shoulders, pushing down the fear that coiled like a snake in my stomach. "You think your sword is enough for this?" My voice was biting, challenging him. "You can't cut through magic with a blade!"

He snorted, swinging his blade toward the shadows. "Maybe. But uncontrolled magic is a liability."

I narrowed my eyes. "Time to prove I'm more than a liability, Chieftain." His words hit harder than I expected, the charming and gentle orc I had begun to trust now hidden behind an impenetrable wall of command. A sharp sting of betrayal flared in my chest, despite knowing my magic was mostly untested. The cold dismissal hurt in a way I hadn't anticipated, but I swallowed the ache, letting determination rise in its place. Power thrummed beneath my skin as I stepped forward, resolute even as doubt lingered at the edges of my mind.

The figure's gnarled fingers carved shapes into the air, and dark mist began to unfurl around it, coiling like a living thing. The fog thickened as it slid over the underbrush, twisting around the orcs' legs. A wave of icy death rolled through the clearing, their sharp cries cutting through the air as the mist drained the energy from them. Their skin paled, veins darkening as they staggered to their knees, eyes wide with panic.

"No!"

Panic surged through me as the dark mist coiled tighter, its hunger consuming them. Spider-like veins spread across their faces like a corruption, their bodies convulsing as their life force was being drained. Magic surged within me, battling the icy air that wrapped around us. My breath came in ragged gasps, fear and exhilaration warring inside me as the magic demanded more. I forced myself to move, each step defying the weight of the darkness pressing down on us.

The figure's glowing eyes turned on me, the mist wrapping around my ankles, but it didn't touch me like it had the others. As it swirled, I could feel the magic inside resisting the pull of the darkness.

I raised my hand, planting myself in front of the orcs as the mist rolled like a wave, burying them under its weight. The dark energy pressed, clawing at my defenses, but it couldn't break through. Reaching deep into my well of magic, I pulled from the earth beneath my feet.

A vibrant haze of green burst from me, tendrils of magic wrapping protectively around my body. Mushrooms erupted from the ground, blooming in the magic's wake as though I had summoned the forest to life. The warmth inside me grew, and I could feel the darkness faltering, but it wasn't enough. It's power too overwhelming.

Trusting my instincts, I thrust my hand behind me, my heart

pounding as I felt Dex's rough fingers wrap around mine. The instant we touched, it was as if a dam broke—energy flooded between us, blistering hot. The connection sparked something instinctual, and I became nothing more than a conduit, and with renewed strength, it surged outward, bathing the path in a bright green light.

The magic burst from my hands in glowing tendrils, pulsing with a life of its own as it wrapped protectively around the warriors. I felt its purpose, instinctive and unwavering, the rush drowned out the fear clawing at my chest. The glow brightened, swallowing the clearing and driving the mist back. The suffocating darkness recoiled, splintering like glass under the force, and I saw the orcs stagger to their feet, gasping as life returned to their pale faces. My heart thundered at the sheer power coursing through me. The magic felt wild, yet it responded as if it knew exactly what to do.

The darkness convulsed, collapsing inward with a warped scream, retreating toward the skeletal figure as its piercing howls shattered the air. Its form twisted unnaturally, the writhing shadow collapsing in on itself, shrinking into a dense, chaotic mass before vanishing into the depths of the forest. The silence that followed was deafening, the echo of its retreat hanging in the air like the aftermath of a storm.

Energy drained from me and my vision began to darken. I gasped for air as the magic pulled too much from my own reserves. A burning red haze clouded my vision. I squeezed my eyes shut, desperate for relief, but the pressure behind them only grew. My breath hitched as a warmth slid over my upper lip, the sharp, metallic tang of blood filling my mouth, reminding me of the toll of my magic.

Pain blazed through me, a searing heat turning every nerve into fire. My magic twisted, no longer a protective force but a torrent, dragging me under. My knees gave way, and the world blurred, the pressure in my head pounding with every beat of my heart. I was falling, slipping into the dark void, but Dex's arms caught me. His voice cut through the chaos, pulling me back toward the faint tether of his touch.

'Cleo!' he rasped, shaking me gently as if trying to anchor me to the world. His hand found mine, gripping it tightly, and I could feel his fear in the tremor of his touch.

I tried to speak, to tell him what was happening, but my body refused to obey. I wanted to reassure him, but the darkness dragged me under, pulling me into an echoing silence. The last thing I felt was his hand gripping mine, a desperate tether pulling against the void. His warmth pushed back the encroaching cold, a fragile thread holding me on the edge of the light.

CHAPTER 13
DEX

The forest was unnervingly still, its silence pressing against the edges of my senses. My gaze flicked over my warriors as they moved through the temporary camp, their steps quieter than usual, tension etched into their movements. Eyes darted toward the furs where Cleo slept, a wary reverence in their expressions.

Cleo hadn't stirred since I carried her there, her body limp with exhaustion and covered in blood. I'd ordered her furs to be laid with mine against the cliff wall, away from the others in case her magic flared when she woke. Yet, that hadn't stopped them from stealing uneasy glances in her direction, their fear as palpable as the damp chill in the air. I could see it in the way they avoided her name, avoided looking at me too long. Not just fear—uncertainty. Something had shifted in all of us, and no one dared to name it.

The memory of the battle clawed at me. Her magic had surged through the earth, shaking the ground beneath us. The air had thrummed with electrifying energy, her veins glowing with a light so otherworldly it had felt like staring into the heart of the storm. When her eyes flashed silver, it wasn't just magic she wielded—she *was* magic. Not in a way I'd ever seen before. Not in an orc. Not in a human.

I flexed my fists, heat pooling in my chest as I recalled the moment she reached for my hand. The power that surged between us had been alive, scorching and impossible to contain. Together, we had driven the darkness back, but the price was etched into my memory: her collapse, her body wracked with pain, her blood on my hands. She'd carried too much, borne the weight of something too powerful, and it had nearly destroyed her.

And the kiss the night before at the river's edge. The memory blazed through me, as vivid as the firelight flickering through the subdued camp. We had been bathing, the cool water lapping at our skin when she'd closed the distance between us. Her touch had been confident yet desperate, unraveling something tightly coiled inside me. Her lips were soft, grounding me in a way that felt both dangerous and irresistible. With the camp's quiet pressing in around me, I couldn't deny the ache to feel it again.

A rustle broke my thoughts, and I turned to see Torak approaching, silhouetted against the firelight. His expression was grim, his hand resting on the hilt of his dagger like a lifeline. "We need to talk," he said, his gravelly voice carrying an edge of exhaustion.

I inclined my head, motioning for the others lingering nearby to join us. They hesitantly approached, their gazes flicking toward Cleo before settling on me.

Torak spoke first, his tone low and filled with unease. "That wasn't a Dark One, Dex. I don't know what it was, but it felt like it was pulling the warmth from our bodies. Feeding on us."

Gornak nodded. "It was worse than any pain I've felt. It was draining us from the inside."

Murmurs of agreement rippled through the group, and I found myself gritting my teeth as their words mirrored what I had felt. That consuming cold emptiness, the air thinning with every breath as though the mist had devoured.

"And her magic..." Torak's voice softened. "It wasn't just warmth. It was life. It held us and pulled us back from the void."

Gornak added, his voice hushed, "It wasn't just pulling us back. It was filling us, anchoring us. She reached into us—into our very *souls*."

Their words hung in the air, heavy with awe and fear. I stared into the fire, my thoughts a chaotic tangle. They were right. I had felt it how her magic had touched something deeper than flesh, something no orc or shaman could reach. And I knew it meant she was the chosen one. The shaman prophesied to unite the clans, to lead us out of exile. But Cleo's power came with a cost. The way she had collapsed haunted me. Blood seeping from her eyes, nose, mouth, and ears, streaking her pale skin, a macabre testament to the toll of her magic. The memory twisted something deep in my chest. A primal, gut-wrenching fear that burned with a desperate need to protect her. Not just from the world, but from herself. Her magic had twisted violently when she tried to cut the flow, and it had nearly consumed her. If she couldn't learn to control it, I feared it would destroy her.

"Her magic is more powerful than anticipated. She will need to be trained," I said, rolling my shoulders to ease the tension that lingered.

After a brief discussion on our plans for the remainder of the journey home, the warriors dispersed and my eyes drifted back to Cleo. She lay there, unaware of the storm she had unleashed—Not just in the battle, but in me. I flexed my fingers, remembering how her magic had surged through us leaving phantom spikes of energy in its wake. How my touch had steadied the chaos inside her. She was my mate.

The realization struck something primal in me. It gnawed at the edges of my thoughts, both a comfort and a warning. Orc mate bonds were absolute, unbreakable, but this? *A human?* It defied everything I'd ever known, and yet, the truth of it clung to me like her scent on the air —inescapable.

A heavy tread broke my thoughts, and I looked up to see Gornak approaching. He carried himself with his usual easy confidence, though his expression was uncharacteristically pensive. He settled beside me, his gaze following mine to the furs where Cleo lay. The silence stretched between us, broken only by the crackle of the fire.

"She's got a strength in her," Gornak said at last, his voice low and contemplative. "Not just in her magic. She's a fierce little thing."

I nodded, but my jaw tightened. "She's untrained. Unpredictable. That's dangerous."

He chuckled softly, a sound that felt out of place in the tense quiet of the camp. "And yet you can't stop watching her. You feel it, don't you? The connection?"

I stiffened, heat rising to my face. "What are you talking about?"

Gornak leaned back, a knowing grin tugging at his lips. "You know exactly what I'm talking about and don't pretend otherwise. It's written all over your face, Dex. You're drawn to her."

I dragged a hand across my face, the weight of exhaustion pressing into me. Frustration simmered beneath the surface, tangled with thoughts I couldn't escape. Gornak was my oldest friend and mentor, and the only one I felt I could speak to about this. "It feels instinctual, like something carved into my bones."

"That's because she is your mate, my friend." Gornak's grin widened, and he slapped me on the back, the force nearly knocking me forward. "Well, let me know if it's actually possible to bed a human. They're so tiny and fragile looking. Also very timid."

My face burned, and I shot him a glare. The memory of the kiss we shared flashed unbidden in my mind. Against my better judgment, the words slipped out before I could stop them. "She not timid at all. She kissed me. Last night, by the river."

Gornak leaned back with a booming laugh, slapping his knee and earning a few glances from the other warriors nearby. "*She* kissed *you?*" he repeated, shaking his head in disbelief. "Well, Dex, looks like the little human is intrigued enough to try riding your orc coc—"

"Gornak." I scowled, though the corners of my mouth twitched against my will. Despite my frustration, I couldn't deny the rush I felt at his words. Cleo consumed my thoughts, weaving herself into the fabric of my every waking moment. It wasn't just her magic or her defiance—it was everything. Her presence was a storm, impossible to ignore, and I found myself pulled into it, both infuriated and exhilarated by her. My awareness of her was constant, every movement, every breath she took felt like a tether binding me to her, intoxicating and maddening in equal measure.

She was mine.

Oblivious to the possessive nature of my thoughts, Gornak's grin faded as his gaze drifted back to Cleo. "She's something special, Dex. Even the rest of us can see it. Don't mess it up."

As if sensing my thoughts, he answered the question burning in my head. "We have time to figure it out and find another way. A way that keeps both the clan and her safe."

"The clan needs—"

"The clan will not ask you to send your mate to certain death. Sometimes, the strongest path forward isn't the one we planned, Chieftain. It's the one we adapt to. Just make sure you're not too blind to see it."

Gornak clapped me on the shoulder before standing and walking away. His words lingered, weaving themselves into the tangle of my thoughts.

Cleo wasn't just the key to our salvation. She was the chaos I hadn't seen coming. Wild, and utterly consuming. For years, I had thrived on control, on calculated decisions and unshakable resolve, but Cleo unraveled it all within days of knowing her. And for now, I wasn't sure I wanted to find control. I wasn't sure I could.

CHAPTER 14
CLEO

I woke to the sensation of warmth, a steady, pulsing heat that radiated from the body beside mine. My eyelids felt impossibly heavy, and I wasn't sure where I was. Everything felt distant, muffled, as if I were submerged in water. My body ached, every muscle weak and trembling like I'd been torn apart and pieced back together.

Slowly, my senses returned, and with them came the memory of what had happened. The figure. The darkness. It all came flooding back in a rush, and with it, the overwhelming exhaustion that had dragged me under. I remembered pushing myself too far, the blood that had poured from my eyes and nose as I funneled the magic to protect them. The pain had been unbearable, the magic too wild to control.

I struggled to move, but my limbs were leaden and unresponsive. Every part of me felt weighed down, like I was trapped beneath layers of stone. The warmth beside me shifted, and I felt a strong hand close around mine, steadying me. The familiar heat of that touch sent a wave of relief through me, quietening the rising panic, and I turned my head toward it, managing to pry my eyes open.

Dex sat beside me, his gaze piercing, and there was a tightness in his expression that I hadn't seen before. His hand was warm and solid around mine, his grip firm but gentle, like he was afraid I might break if he held on too tightly. I could see the tension in his jaw, the way his muscles were coiled like springs, ready to snap.

"Cleo." His voice was low and rough, a thread of worry woven through it. "You're finally awake."

I swallowed hard, my throat dry and raw. "What happened?"

His grip tightened before he released me, running a hand roughly through his hair. "You nearly killed yourself. You channeled too much power, more than your body could handle."

I shuddered, the memories rushing back. The figure's darkness had been unlike anything I had felt. It had reached for their lifeforce, sucking the very existence from their veins. It had taken everything to keep myself—and them—alive.

"Where is everyone?" My voice cracked, breaking on the words. "Are they okay?"

Dex glanced toward the fire on the other side of the clearing, his brow furrowing. "My warriors are tired but otherwise fine. Some are scouting the area. The others are resting. You have been unconscious for a full day."

A shuddering breath escaped me, relief loosening the tightness in my chest. "Wait... a whole day?" I tried to sit up, but the world tilted, spinning violently, and I sank back into the blankets with a groan.

Dex was immediately there, his hand resting gently on my shoulder, his touch steadying me. "Easy," he said, his voice soft. "You're not ready to be up. You need rest."

I closed my eyes, fighting the wave of dizziness that threatened to pull me under again. "I'm fine," I muttered, though the tremble in my voice betrayed me. "I just... I didn't realize it would take so much out of me."

Dex let out a soft, humorless laugh. "You think? You nearly bled out from your eyes, Cleo. That's not fine. You think you're invincible, don't you?"

The edge in his voice surprised me. I opened my eyes again and turned to face him, but his gaze was distant. His jaw was clenched, his muscles tight with barely restrained frustration. "Why are you so angry?" My whisper barely reached him.

Dex's eyes snapped back to mine, and he looked as though he might argue, might deflect. But then he let out a heavy sigh, his shoulders sagging as he shook his head.

"I'm not angry," he said quietly. "I'm..." He trailed off, running a hand over his face. " I don't know what I feel. Watching you out there, seeing what you did, knowing how close you came to..." His composure cracked, worry etched into every line of his face. "It scared me."

His words struck me, stealing the air from my lungs. *Dex was scared?*

I didn't think Dex could be scared of anything. He was the definition of control, always calm and steadfast, no matter the dangers we had faced. But now, seeing the way his eyes roamed my face, I realized that I wasn't the only one shaken by what had happened.

"Dex," I murmured, reaching out to touch his hand. He flinched, but didn't pull away. "I'm sorry. I didn't mean to—"

"Don't," he cut me off, his voice sharper than before. "No more apologies. You did what had to be done and you saved all of us. But you have to stop risking yourself. Your life as a shaman is more important than ours."

"I couldn't just stand by and do nothing." My voice was instantly defensive, a plea for understanding. "If I hadn't done something, they would have died. That thing was trying to suck the life out of them! I had to stop it."

His brow furrowed. "What do you mean. Could you feel it?"

I hesitated, unsure how to explain it—how to put into words the terrifying sensations I had felt. I wasn't even sure I understood them myself. But Dex deserved to know. And more than that, I needed him to know. I trusted him, and I needed to say it out loud, to make sense of it.

I lowered my gaze, my fingers nervously twisting the edge of the blanket. "I... I don't fully understand it yet," I admitted, my voice small. "But every time those shadows appear I can feel something dark." I glanced up at him, my heart racing in my chest. "It's like... like the air changes. Everything gets colder, and there's this... smell. It's the smell of death, of decay. I can feel it crawling through the air, reaching for everything with an energy source. It's like I can see it—this darkness seeping into them, pulling the very essence of life out of their bodies."

Dex's expression tightened, his golden eyes narrowing as he listened intently. "You can feel it trying to take their lifeforce?"

I nodded, the words tumbling out faster now, the dam breaking. "Yes. It's like I can see the threads of their lifeforce being pulled away, as if something is sucking it right out of them. And it's not just that I can feel it—it's like it calls to me."

I could feel my face burning with embarrassment, my hands trembling as I spoke. "There's this pull," I continued, my voice dropping to a whisper. "Like a dark seduction. It feels... wrong, but also... I don't know how to explain it. It's like it wants me to reach for it, like it's whispering to me to take it. And I'm terrified of what that means."

Dex was eerily still as he processed my confession, eyes remaining locked onto mine with an intensity that made my heart pound even harder.

"I know it sounds insane," I said quickly, my throat tight. "But it's the truth. When I push back with my magic, it feels like I'm battling something inside myself as much as I'm battling whatever's out there. I can feel the temptation to reach for that darkness; it whispers promises of incredible power. It scares me."

I closed my eyes, the weight of my confession pressing down on me like a physical force. My hands trembled and I clutched the blanket tighter. I couldn't lose myself to that darkness. I didn't want to turn into something twisted and evil. I could feel Dex's eyes on me, but I couldn't bring myself to look at him. Shame coiled in my gut, twisting like a knife.

After what felt like an eternity, Dex finally spoke.

"Cleo..." His voice was low, rough, but there was a softness to it. I opened my eyes, surprised to find him closer than before, his hand reaching out to gently cup my chin, forcing me to meet his gaze, his intensity sending shivers down my spine in response. "You're not going to lose yourself to this. You're stronger than whatever darkness is calling to you."

I blinked back tears, my breath catching in my throat. "How do you know that?"

"Because I've seen you fight," he replied, his thumb brushing lightly across my jawline. "I've seen you protect the people around you, even when it nearly killed you. You are different, Cleo. And I'll be damned if I let you fall to whatever this thing is."

His words washed over me, steadying the storm of emotions that had been raging inside. There was something about the way he spoke, the way he looked at me, that made me believe him. As if I wasn't alone in this battle.

"I don't know what's happening to me," I admitted, my voice barely more than a whisper. "But I know it's getting stronger. I can feel it growing inside me, and I don't know how much longer I can keep it at bay."

Dex's hand slid from my chin to my cheek, his touch warm and grounding. "We all fight a darkness inside. I won't let you fight it alone."

His words struck a chord deep inside me, and I felt my chest tighten with a mix of relief. I hadn't realized how much I needed someone to stand by me, to believe in me, even when I couldn't believe in myself. I leaned into his touch, my heart racing as I let the warmth of his hand seep into my skin. For a moment, the fear faded, replaced by a sense of calm.

But even as I found comfort in his presence, I couldn't shake the lingering doubt that hung in the back of my mind. The darkness inside me was growing, and no matter how hard I tried to fight it, I could feel it pulling me closer, whispering promises I wasn't sure I could resist forever, and I didn't know how much longer I could keep it from swallowing me whole. I realized that Dex wasn't just protecting me because of my power. There was something in him, something broken, that recognized the fear inside me.

"You fight a darkness too?" I asked. The question felt like a thread pulling on the fabric of something bigger.

Dex's fingers left mine as he sat heavily next to me. He pulled his dagger from his belt, the sharp edge catching the firelight, runes glowing softly in his giant palm. Then, as if driven by an old habit, he began twirling it between his fingers, his movements smooth and deliberate. His golden eyes flicked to mine, then away, shadowed by something I couldn't quite name.

"Seven years ago, the night I became Chieftain, was the night I got this dagger."

I stayed silent, sensing that interrupting would break the fragile tether of his words.

"I'd survived five days in the Shadow Lands, and brought back the pelt of a Hound. I then defeated my opponent in combat, securing my title. The clan had gathered to watch me take the oath, a rare celebration outside of our strongholds. We were in the middle of a sacred rite, the final ceremony to crown the next Chieftain, when we were ambushed."

"By who?" I whispered.

"The Ostelan Crown. The Silver Hand was sent by the King to make sure we never gained a new leader. They attacked in the middle of the rite, arrows raining down before we even knew what was happening. They were always cowards." His words were laced with venom as the blade twirled faster now between his fingers. "They didn't care who they killed. Elders, women, children... They wanted to leave us broken. Remind us of our place."

Dex's hand stilled, the blade glinting in the firelight as he tightened his grip on the hilt, and his voice turned thick with emotion that spoke of heartache, and a fury hotter than fire. "My sister, Urla, saved me that night. Shoved me out of the way of a crossbow bolt that should've killed me. She took it herself."

I could hear the fire crackling between us, but its warmth did nothing to ease the chill settling in my stomach.

"I tried to save her," he continued, his voice barely above a whisper. "I held her as she bled out, and still she told me to get up. To keep fighting. To be the warrior she trained me to be."

I swallowed hard, my voice trembling as I asked, "What did you do?"

Dex looked at me then, his molten gold eyes burning with something raw and unguarded. "I got up and we killed them all—every last one of them who thought they could break us."

He exhaled, dragging a hand over his face before letting the blade twirl in his fingers again. "That night, I took the oath of Chieftain not because I wanted to, but because I had to. The clan needed someone to lead us to a better future, one without fear and oppression under the Crown's wrath."

"Dex..." I started, but the words failed me. What could I say to that kind of loss?

"The rage fueled me in battle as I tore them apart... but a good

Chieftain cannot rule by emotion and keep his people safe. I swore I wouldn't let emotions drive me again. My sister raised me after my mother passed, and she made sure to teach me that a leader who lets his feelings rule him isn't a leader at all. She knew what this life required— sacrifice, strength, and control. I buried everything that night. For the clan and for her."

I wanted to reach out, to take his hand, but something in his expression stopped me. The war of emotions in his eyes had me still, allowing him the time to work through them.

He let out a shaky laugh, shaking his head. "You remind me of her. Urla always said I carried the world on my shoulders, but never in my heart. She was right. And you..." He paused, his eyes meeting mine. "What do you know about orc way of life?"

"Almost nothing, honestly." My words were a whisper as shame prickled against my skin.

"We share a connection, you and I. Something rare even among my people. Sacred. You are more than just a shaman to me, Cleo; you are my mate. Chosen by fate *for me*."

The words left me breathless as I saw the weight he carried more clearly than ever. "Dex, I—"

"You feel it too, the pull between us?" he asked, his tone softening.

Yes! I wanted to scream, unloading all the frustrations of feeling like I was fighting something inside of me that wanted to be touching him, being held by him. All I could do was nod in response, too afraid to speak as emotion burned the back of my throat.

Dex's smile was genuine as he leaned over, crowding me against the furs, and pressed his forehead to mine. His thumb stroked against my cheek reverently, and his deep huffing breath grazed the side of my neck, making me shudder. Then he pulled back to gaze into my eyes.

"I'm blessed by the Gods to have met you, Cleo."

Wrapping my hand around the back of his head, I urged him closer to me, desperate for another taste of his lips. The memory of our last kiss had plagued my every waking moment, an intoxicating echo I couldn't resist any longer.

His lips met mine, the touch tentative at first. The warmth of his lips contrasted with the slight roughness of his tusks grazing my skin. It was grounding, adding a rough edge to the delicate moment. The sensation sent a ripple of warmth through me as his hand moved to cradle my jaw. The kiss wasn't hurried or frantic, his breath mingled with mine as the world narrowed around us.

Too soon he pulled back with a chuckle, prying my hand from his head and pressing a chaste kiss against my fingers, cradling them close as his eyes fluttered shut. I was frozen, overwhelmed by the tenderness of the gesture.

The warmth of him seeped into my skin. In his presence, the chaos of my magic and the darkness that lingered seemed to fade, leaving behind only a quiet sense of belonging. His presence anchored me, dissolving that ache of loneliness and replacing it with a quiet certainty.

"You need to rest." His voice was quiet but resolute.

I nodded, swallowing against the tightness in my throat. This fragile peace couldn't last. The darkness we faced was far from defeated.

He laid by my side and tucked me in tightly to his body, shielding me from the cool night. His warmth radiated through me, easing the ache in my muscles and quieting the storm of thoughts in my mind. I felt cocooned, safe in a way I hadn't been in years. But as his steady breathing filled the quiet, a bittersweet realization settled over me that this fleeting sense of peace couldn't last.

I let myself sink into him, exhaustion tugging me under once more. But even as sleep claimed me, I couldn't shake the feeling that something deeper was stirring. Whatever was coming, I wasn't sure either of us was ready.

CHAPTER 15
CLEO

The morning began with a biting chill, the kind that seeped through clothing and clung to the skin, sharpening the senses as the world slowly stirred awake. Waking up in strong arms had been a new experience for me, and I found myself hesitant to pull free from where my ear was pressed to Dex's chest, listening to the thrum of his heart. The steady rise and fall of his breaths lulling me back into a languid doze. *He was so warm.*

Butterflies erupted in my stomach as his giant hands on my waist pulled me tighter against him. He pressed a gentle kiss to my forehead before rising, and we busied ourselves with extinguishing fires and rolling up our furs in a rush to get back on the road.

Despite the tension surrounding us, the stolen glances and light brushes of Dex's hand against mine set my pulse racing. Between him and the other orcs' quiet approval, I sensed that, somehow, I belonged here. *I really needed to learn more about their way of life.*

We reached the edge of a large clearing, the ground split wide by a gaping ravine that slashed through the landscape like an open wound. Sheer rock walls plunged into darkness, and the faint roar of water echoed far below. The ravine stretched endlessly in either direction, a natural barrier severing the Shadow Lands from the rest of Northern

Ostelan. The path forward was in ruins, the remnants of a rope bridge dangling in tatters, a jumbled mess against the jagged rocks.

I froze, my breath catching at the sight. The destruction was deliberate; the torn bridge was too precise, too calculated to be accidental. *Did someone know we were coming?* A chill ran down my spine as I scanned the area.

The orcs around me muttered curses, their frustration sharp in the tense air. "They're cutting off our escape," Gornak growled, his voice bitter.

Thorn spat into the dirt, gripping his weapon tightly. The palpable tension rippled through the group, their gazes flicking between the ravine and the dense woods behind us.

Dex's voice cut through their murmurs, firm and commanding. "We need to find another way across, and quickly."

My gaze drifted to him, his broad shoulders tense, the golden depths of his eyes sharp as he surveyed the ruins of the bridge. Behind his stoic exterior, I could sense the frustration simmering, his mind racing through possibilities. Magic prickled under my skin, and I knew instinctively that the solution lay within me. I stepped forward, ignoring the orcs' questioning glances as I knelt at the edge of the ravine.

"Cleo." Dex's voice was cautious, laced with a thread of warning. But I didn't answer, my focus drawn inward. I pressed my palms into the earth, feeling the deep pulse of the land. The hum of magic grew, filling my chest as I reached out, seeking the ancient roots and life buried far below.

My fingers sank into the dirt as power surged from me. It coursed through the ground, a vibrant, thrumming energy. The earth was shifting, buckling as roots twisted and climbed, their movements deliberate, as if they recognized the urgency of my request. Thick branches began to weave together, stretching across the ravine, their roots digging into the far side for purchase.

The warriors fell silent, their earlier curses replaced by a hushed awe as they watched the bridge take form.

The branches continued to grow, intertwining tightly. Following my intuition, I reached deeper, calling to the vines that crept along the nearby trees. They answered, thickening and stretching to wrap around the branches, forming a natural handrail along the bridge, twisting with a strength that belied their appearance.

When the bridge was complete, I staggered to my feet, the hum of magic beneath my skin had quieted to a faint buzz, but the effort had left me breathless. The orcs stared at the bridge, then at me, their expressions a mixture of awe and disbelief.

"I've never seen anything like it," Gornak muttered, shaking his head in amazement. "By the Gods, she's powerful."

"You're incredible," Dex murmured as he stepped closer, brushing a thick finger across my cheek.

I managed a weak smile, still catching my breath. "Just trying to help."

One by one, they began crossing the bridge, their movements cautious but hurried. Dex stayed by my side until the last of his warriors had crossed. His hand took mine as we stepped onto the bridge. Once we reached other side, I turned, looking back at the ravine. The shadows were creeping closer; I could feel their dark pull in the trees, just out of sight. Dropping to my knees, I pressed my hands into the earth, calling on the power once more.

The vines sprouted razor sharp thorns, twisting into a barrier that knotted across the edge of the ravine and onto the bridge. The magic obeyed my command with a ferocity that surprised even me, the plants coiling tightly around rocks and roots to form a nearly impenetrable razor sharp wall.

I stood slowly, brushing dirt from my palms. "That should slow them down."

Gornak's gaze softened, respect shadowing his features. "You did well, girl."

I didn't respond, but his words lingered, their weight settling heavily on my shoulders. The group pressed onward, and Dex's hand found the small of my back, a quiet gesture of affection. His warmth seeped through the layers of exhaustion clinging to me, grounding me in the present.

"Are you all right?" he asked softly, his voice carrying a quiet concern.

I nodded, though the weariness crept into my limbs. "I'm fine, just tired."

"You're doing more than we ever thought was possible." His words were thick with admiration, as he offered me his hand once more.

I shot him an easy smile, my heart swelling at his words. I could feel my defenses crumbling under his constant support and appreciation. *How had I gone from facing execution to standing here beside this orc Chieftain?* And yet, the thought didn't fill me with dread but with gratitude. A strange, quiet gratitude for the twist of fate that had brought me here.

Taking his offered hand, I felt an unexpected energy radiate through me. The touch was steady, as though it carried a silent promise that we would face whatever came next, together. Ahead, the path grew steeper, the air colder, the shadows of the forest lessening into something like a living, watchful force. I took a deep breath before turning to follow the warriors up the steep incline, heading up into the mountains.

THE BLACK MOUNTAINS loomed closer with every step and were a world apart from the south, where cities like Knight's Hold thrived in carefully cultivated order. The great river that split the continent felt like more than a geographic divide—it was a line that separated two different worlds. South of the river, humans lived in blissful ignorance, untouched by the true wildness of the North. It was no wonder most southerners had never seen an orc in their lifetime. The path grew steeper, the air colder, but the orcs pushed forward with determination. As we climbed, Gornak spoke quietly to the others, his voice a deep rumble in the stillness of the night.

"These valleys were once ours," he said, his gaze swept over the landscape. "We ruled these forests before the humans drove us out, before they pushed us into the Black Mountains like animals. This land was ours by birthright."

One of the younger orcs, a warrior named Kaldor, nodded solemnly. "I've heard the stories, but I've never seen it with my own eyes. Not from this vantage point."

Gornak's expression darkened, his voice thick with anger. "You've only known the mountains as our home because that's all the humans left us. We were prosperous once. We walked these forests and valleys as free orcs, not cowed and forced to trade with our oppressors. Disrespected and treated like scum as we move along the sanctioned trade routes."

I listened in silence, the weight of their words sinking in. The orcs had been driven from their lands, forced into exile by humans who saw them as nothing more than beasts.

Dex's gaze remained fixed on the path ahead. "One day, we'll walk these forests as free orcs." His voice was quiet, almost wistful.

Our party fell silent, but I could feel the weight of those words hanging in the air, a silent promise of a future they had long been denied. I could see the pain that clouded their eyes as they spoke of their connection to the valleys, and what had been stolen from them.

The mountain path grew narrower, the cold wind biting at my skin with every step. I felt the earth beneath me, steady and strong, guiding us forward. The magic was still there, humming beneath the surface, swirling around the orcs like a loving caress.

Gornak, who had taken the lead, slowed his pace to drop back alongside me, allowing his deep, rumbling voice to carry back to the rest of the warriors. Turning his head, he addressed the younger orcs who walked nearby, and I noticed the reverence on their faces as they hung on his every word.

"This land wasn't always so still; there were no Shadow Lands," he said, his voice thick with memory. "The forests were alive with the sounds of our people—strong, proud, and united."

"Tell us about it, Gornak, I know you have had the visions," Kaldor urged. "I've heard the stories, but I want to know what it was really like. What did we lose?"

My face must have read as confusion, as Dex leaned in to whisper to me softly. "A warrior's coming of age involves joining with the earth. Our power is not the same as yours, however, some of us are gifted. Gornak saw our history. Our Seer has visions of what has yet come to pass."

I nodded my understanding, amazed at the wealth of knowledge I was learning about the orc clans in just a few days.

His eyes were distant, as though he could still see the lands they had lost. "The rivers once flowed beneath great stone strongholds, bridges of such craftsmanship no race has been able to match. They spanned the rivers like arms outstretched, connecting our settlements. We built fortresses into the cliff face, so high above the water that they seemed to touch the sky."

"The walls were impenetrable," one of the older orcs, Ograk, added, his voice rough with age. "Solid stone, reinforced with magic—our magic. Not the kind the human mages wield, but magic that came from the earth, from the stones themselves. Wild magic not unlike yours, shaman. We lived in harmony with the land, and it gave us its strength."

My steps slowed as I took in their words, a quiet ache building inside me. The orcs weren't just warriors, not just the fierce and strong race I had always imagined them to be. They were builders, traders, and farmers. They had been masters of the land.

Gornak continued, his voice taking on a rhythmic cadence as he recalled their way of life. "In the forests, we built hunting hides in the canopies—great platforms woven into the branches high above the ground, where our warriors would wait for the game to pass. We could move through the forest without a sound, using the trees as cover. The forest was our hunting ground, our sanctuary."

Kaldor's eyes shone with interest. "I didn't know we had lived in the trees!"

Gornak nodded, a small smile tugging at the corners of his mouth. "Aye, we were one with the trees. We had hunting blinds and watchtowers hidden among the branches. No one could move through these forests without us knowing."

There was a pride in his voice, but it was tinged with sorrow—sorrow for what they had lost.

"But the humans came." Gornak's voice hardened, the warmth draining away. "The Silver Hand came with their mages and their knights, with their armies of steel and fire. We fought with everything we had."

"The first wave wasn't so bad," Ograk added, his tone dark. "They underestimated us. They thought we were nothing but savages. We drove them back, time and again. But then they brought their darkest magic, and cursed illnesses that ran through the clans."

The air seemed to grow colder as the conversation shifted. Even the forest around us seemed to hold its breath, as though it, too, remembered the war that had scarred this land.

"The dark mages," Gornak spat, his lip curling in disgust. "Their magic wasn't like ours. It wasn't born from the earth, from the stones and trees. It was something else—something darker and unnatural. They wielded death. Magic that consumed everything in its path."

I felt a chill creep down my spine as I listened. The magic of the earth, the lifeforce that pulsed through the soil beneath my feet, was strong and steady, but I could feel the echoes of that other magic. The kind that sought only to corrupt and consume.

"Then came the knights." Gornak's voice dropped, heavy with memory. "They rode in and they never stopped. Our warriors fought with honor, but the humans... they didn't care about honor. They didn't care about the land or the people who lived on it."

"Their goal was to take it all," Ograk said bitterly. "To wipe us out, or push us out of Ostelan. We fought for every last inch. Until the rivers ran red with blood. But the humans outnumbered us. They brought wave after wave, more knights, more mages, and we—"

He paused, his jaw clenched tightly. I thought he might stop speaking altogether, but then he took a deep breath and continued. "We knew we couldn't win. Not in the end. So, the clans rode out to meet the Silver Hand, to give our people a chance to flee. I saw them kissing their wives and children goodbye, knowing they were going to certain death," Gornak said quietly, his voice thick with grief. "A group of our oldest warriors stayed with the Chieftains in battle, holding the line long enough for the Chieftains' mates to lead the clans back to their homelands, flanked by their personal guard. They all knew they were going to die. They gave their lives so that the rest of their clans could live."

I swallowed hard, the full weight of their sacrifice settling heavily in my chest. The orcs hadn't just lost their land. They had lost their people, their culture, their way of life. And they had been forced into hiding because of it. My throat burned with unshed tears as I could imagine the despair as they ran for their lives.

"The Blackfoot Clan retreated to the mountains," Ograk continued, his voice quieter now. "The humans didn't follow us here. They thought we were broken, that we were beaten. They left us in these rocky caves to *rot*, thinking we would wither and die."

"But we survived," Dex said, his voice filled with quiet defiance. "We rebuilt, but we never forgot what was taken from us. We never forgot the price we paid."

I could hear the pride in his voice, but also the bitterness—the anger that still simmered just beneath the surface. Humans had tried to massacre them, and now they were another race fighting to survive, clinging to the remnants of their former glory.

Kaldor glanced at his Chieftain, his brow furrowed. "Do you think we'll ever reclaim what we lost?"

Dex didn't answer right away, his gaze sweeping over the forest below, the trees that had once been their sanctuary. "Maybe," he said finally, his voice low as he glanced at me. "Maybe one day. But we'll need more than just strength to do it. We'll need allies, and we'll need the land to fight with us."

The land. The earth. The lifeforce that pulsed beneath our feet.

I glanced down at my hands, feeling the magic humming just beneath the surface of my skin. *Me?* The land had always been with them, hadn't it? The orcs had fought with the earth at their side, drawing strength from it, just as I did now.

"You're not alone," I said quietly, the words slipping from my mouth before I could stop them. "The land is still with you. It hasn't forgotten; it's energy follows you."

Gornak's gaze shifted to me, his eyes narrowing. I thought he might brush my words aside, but then he nodded slowly. "Maybe," he murmured. "Maybe you're right."

We continued on, the mountain path growing steeper, the cold air biting at my skin with every step. I could feel the pulse of the earth beneath me, steady and strong. The orcs had lost so much—more than I could ever imagine—but they had survived. And now, with the magic inside me, I felt a strange sense of responsibility to help them. *Could I do that without turning my back on my own people?*

The mountain rose before us, its shadow growing with each step, a silent sentinel of stone. Dex's hand brushed against mine again, a silent reassurance that he was there, by my side. Our eyes met, the determination in his a mirror of my own.

I felt the pulse of the earth beneath me, steady and sure. The past couldn't be undone; its scars were etched deep into the land and its people. But perhaps, with time, those scars could become part of a new foundation. Maybe we could begin to heal what had been broken, to grow something new from the ashes of destruction.

Dex's voice broke through my thoughts, low and filled with conviction. "I'm proud to call you my mate. Your spirit is strong. Your courage to confront the lies you were raised with is remarkable."

His words washed over me like a tide, swelling a warmth in my chest that no cold mountain air could touch. There was a tenderness in the way he held on, as though I were something precious.

"Dex, you give me too much credit. I understand what it's like to suffer, to feel powerless. I don't want anyone to feel that way."

His grip tightened, his expression darkening with an intensity that sent a shiver through me, before he pulled me into his arms. "No one will ever lay a hand on you again, Cleo. That, I can promise."

I let out a soft scoff, sinking into his embrace, greedily taking the solace he so willingly gave. "You can't promise that, Dex. But I appreciate you for wanting to."

His hands gripped my shoulders with a bruising intensity as he pulled me back.His golden eyes burned, molten with fury, his jaw clenched tight enough to crack stone. My breath caught as he scanned my face, his presence overwhelming.

"I can," he growled, his voice a low rumble that vibrated through my chest. "And I will. I'll rip them apart with my bare hands, drain every drop of blood from their bodies, and feed it to the earth before I let them so much as touch you."

His words should have terrified me, the violence of his promise something no sane person would wish to hear. But instead, it fed a flickering ember deep inside me, stoking it into a roaring flame. A soft, involuntary sound escaped my lips, the need pooling low in my stomach as I absorbed the sheer possessiveness in his tone. His dominance, his protectiveness, left me trembling with an overwhelming desire that threatened to consume me.

Dex's towering frame leaned closer, his hands sliding to my hips as though he owned every inch of me. The roughness of his large palms against my skin sent a jolt through me, and the heat of his breath brushed my ear as he spoke again, softer but no less commanding. "You're mine, Cleo. No one will ever take you from me."

I didn't trust my voice, my body too caught in the electrifying pull of him, so I nodded, my fingers curling into the leather of his armor as though to keep myself grounded. He tilted my chin up, thumb brushing across my jaw as he studied me with an intensity that sent my heart hammering in my chest.

His lips claimed mine with a deliberate slowness, coaxing rather than demanding. The kiss wasn't just passion. It was a vow of devotion, of protection. His tusks grazed my skin, the faint scrape a thrilling reminder of just how different we were.

When he pulled back, his forehead rested against mine, his breath uneven, his golden eyes searching mine as though seeking something only I could provide. "You're my mate. *Mine*, understand?" he murmured, his voice raw with honesty.

I exhaled shakily, the weight of his words settling deep into my chest. *How had this fierce warrior become my sanctuary in a matter of days? How had I, a human girl destined to be cast aside, become his?*

We stood there, tangled in each other, until the world crept back in —the murmurs of the orcs as they shifted uncomfortably a short distance away, attempting to give us what little privacy they could on this mountain path. Reluctantly, we parted, his hand slipping back into mine as we fell into step once more.

The orcs walked with a quiet determination, their steps steady despite the steep climb. I could feel their resolve humming through the ground like a drumbeat. Hope flared in my chest. We were retreating to Blackfoot Clan territory, but I knew the battles ahead would not stop at the mountains' edge. Dex's hand brushed mine again, a silent reassurance, and I glanced at him. The determination in his eyes barely overshadowed the desire that lurked in their depths. I knew, without a doubt, that I needed to help them.

∼

"WE'RE CLOSE," Gornak said, his deep voice cutting through the cold silence. He pointed ahead to where the mist parted, revealing a narrow path winding upward toward the jagged cliffs. "The cave entrance is just beyond those rocks. Once we're inside, we'll be safe from the humans, at least for now."

Relief surged through me at the sight of the narrow path ahead, promising shelter from the cold. My legs were trembling from the effort, and the icy air burned in my lungs, each breath a struggle, but I forced myself to keep going. I had come too far to falter now.

As we neared the path, low murmurs rippled through the group, their voices barely carrying over the gusting wind, tinged with the weariness of the journey. Kaldor glanced at me, his sharp eyes studying my face.

His gaze settled on me, curiosity in his eyes. "You've been quiet. What's on your mind, human?"

I blinked, surprised by the question. The orcs hadn't asked much about me since I'd joined them, likely more concerned with survival than small talk. But now that we were nearing their stronghold, it seemed they were finally relaxing.

I paused, words catching in my throat, uncertain how much to reveal. "I've just been thinking," I said carefully, "about everything that's happened."

Kaldor snorted. "A lot's happened, that's for sure. But you've been through a lot too. What about your life before all this? What was it like? You don't seem like the type of human we usually encounter."

I glanced at Dex, who gave me a small nod of encouragement. My old life seemed like a distant memory, blurred and fading. It was strange to think about how much had changed in so little time.

"I grew up in a family that owned farmland in Sleek Valley," I began slowly, the words feeling foreign on my tongue now. "My mother died when I was younger, and my father turned to liquor and gambling to fill the void she left behind."

Ograk had been listening quietly, an eyebrow raised as he joined our conversation. "He didn't care for his own young?"

I exhaled, feeling the familiar weight of resentment settle over me. "My father wasn't a kind man. He was cruel. He didn't care about anyone but himself when he gambled away our fields, our livestock, and eventually, my dowry. He was negotiating my betrothal to a merchant in exchange to clear his debts."

The orcs listened, their eyes narrowing as I continued. "To him, I was nothing more than a tool to be wielded for his own ends. He wasn't shy about showing it, either. He made sure I knew exactly what my place was. Punished and beat me if I ever forgot. He blamed me for our mother taking ill."

Thorn let out a low grunt, his expression darkening. "That sounds like a familiar story," he muttered. "Humans love their power games. They love to think they can control everything."

"That's exactly what it was." A bitter edge crept into my voice, each word feeling like a confession I had long buried. "Control. Everything in my life was decided for me. I sold the last pieces of my mother's jewelry for his damn debts."

Kaldor frowned. "Sounds like the Gods were at play when they put you in the Chieftain's path. I'm sorry you had to grow up under a cruel hand."

I nodded. The memory of that day was still sharp in my mind. "Even if he didn't call for the guards to arrest me for channeling to defend myself, I wouldn't have been able to stay there. I had wanted to find a way out for a while."

Ograk gave a small grunt of approval. "Good on you, girl. It takes guts to leave that kind of life behind."

Dex's expression softened. "Learning control is the most important thing right now for you, and then you get to decide who you want to be."

A hollow laugh escaped me. "I don't think I've ever felt so free as I have in the last few days."

The orcs exchanged glances, their expressions softening. Gornak, who had been listening from the front, glanced back at me, his gaze thoughtful. "Freedom." He muttered the word, almost reverently. "It's something we've all fought for. It's something most humans don't understand."

The truth of his words settled deep inside me. For the first time in my life, I wasn't being forced into a role I didn't want. I wasn't someone's bargaining chip, someone's pawn. *I was free.* And more than that, I was wanted. I wasn't an outsider here. I wasn't judged for the magic I possessed or for the choices I had made. The orcs had accepted me with little reservations, and in their world, I had found a place where I could finally be myself.

"I suppose that's why I'm so drawn to the land," I said, my voice quieter now. "It's the one thing no one could control. It's the only thing I have ever had for myself, even if I didn't know it truly until a few days ago."

Kaldor tilted his head, his eyes curious. "The magic in you is different from anything I've ever seen. The way you control the earth, the way it responds to you is special."

The orcs fell silent, their expressions thoughtful. They had seen my magic in action, but now, they were beginning to understand that my power was something more than just a tool. It was part of me, part of who I was.

"It's a rare gift," Ograk muttered. "A gift that could change a lot of things."

"If it's as special as you say, I want to use it to help as many as I can."

I understood why the orcs had fought so fiercely to hold this land. It wasn't just territory; it was a piece of who they were. The forests weren't empty of life, as so many southerners assumed. It was alive, and it remembered the orcs. But that memory wasn't enough to heal what had been broken.

Gornak, who had been listening with a contemplative expression, nodded slowly. "You will. There's power in the land, power that's been lost to most of us. But you are a conduit for it. You can bring it back."

His words sent a shiver down my spine with the weight of responsibility that came with them. I had always known there was something different about me, something that set me apart from other humans. But now, standing among the orcs, I felt it.

The back of my hand brushed against Dex's fingers again, a quiet reminder that I wasn't alone in this. He gave me a warm smile. "You're already making a difference. Just by being here."

Beyond the jagged rocks ahead was a cave entrance. A gateway to whatever awaited me in the Black Mountain's depths. Gornak slowed, his gaze scanning the dark, jagged cliffs ahead. "This is it," he said gruffly. "The caves will take us to the stronghold. Once we're inside, we'll be safe."

Despite the chill, I felt a strange sense of comfort here, as though the earth itself was welcoming us. It felt like home.

CHAPTER 16
CLEO

The air in the caves grew colder as we pushed deeper into the mountain. The narrow passage widened and opened up into a vast chamber. My breath caught in my throat as I stepped forward, taking in the sheer scale of what lay before us.

The chamber swallowed us in its enormity, walls stretching into shadowed heights that seemed to brush against the mountain's bones, its vastness humbling. But it wasn't the size alone that left me in awe—it was the fortress built into the very rock face, its stone walls carved directly into the mountain. Massive and imposing, the stronghold seemed like a natural extension of the mountain. It was as if the orcs had communed with the mountain itself, coaxing it to form this stronghold.

To the east, the chamber opened up to a sheer drop. A sharp, biting wind howled through the gap, curling around us with a life of its own. Beyond the cliff's edge, I could see the faint outline of the bluffs stretching into the distance, barely visible through the mist that clung to the peaks. The view was stunning, and even in the harsh wind, I could imagine how beautiful it must be at sunrise when the first rays of the sun touched the chamber, casting light over the walls.

Dex moved beside me, his golden eyes bright as he took in the scene with the quiet pride of someone who had walked these paths a thousand times. His hand brushed mine as we moved forward, his presence steady and comforting.

"This is the heart of the mountain." His voice was filled with pride. "Our stronghold. Welcome home."

The citadel rose from the rock in perfect harmony with its surroundings. It wasn't the towering structure of human castles, but a part of the landscape itself. The walls were thick and solid, carved with intricate designs depicting orcs with their weapons raised high as they defended their land.

To the right of their stone refuge, built into the chamber's natural incline, was a series of terraces where crops grew in neat rows. Fruit trees reached toward the sunlight that filtered through the openings. The wind whistled through their branches, but despite the harshness of the weather, they thrived. The crops and trees were irrigated by a river that wound through the terraces, fed by a trickling waterfall that cascaded from high above, its source hidden somewhere deep in the mountain. The waterfall filled a large pond and I could see fish darting beneath the surface.

The pond spilled over into a narrow stream that flowed through the terraces, providing water to the crops. The sound of the water was a constant, soothing presence, the steady flow of life that kept the stronghold alive.

"The mountain is our lifeblood," Dex murmured, "harsh, but fair. The cliff protects us from the east, and the stone walls keep us safe from whatever comes from below."

I moved closer to the edge, feeling the wind tug at my dress as I stared out over the terraces. I saw—grains, vegetables, and herbs. Their green leaves were a stark contrast to the grey stone of the mountain. The trees swayed gently in the breeze, their roots firmly planted in the rich soil.

"It's... incredible." The words were inadequate to describe the sheer scale and harmony of the stronghold. "How did you manage to grow all this up here?"

Dex smiled, his expression warm. "The orcs have always worked with the land. Even up here, in the highlands, we've found a way to make the earth provide for us, and in return, we protect the earth. The mountain may be unforgiving, but it's also generous. The waterfall gives us fresh water, the terraces give us food, and the cliffs give us protection. Everything here is part of a balance."

I nodded slowly, marveling at how seamlessly the stronghold lived within the mountain, almost as if they were one. The orcs hadn't forced the mountain to bend to their will. Instead, they had worked with it, coaxing life from the stone and the wind, creating a place where they could survive—even thrive.

"Orcs have lived here since the beginning of the war?"

Dex's eyes were distant as he nodded. "This stronghold was built by our ancestors when the first wars began. It has protected us ever since."

Glancing over at him, I could see the pain behind his words. It wasn't just the loss of land he was speaking about; it was the loss of a way of life, of a connection to the earth that had been stolen from them. The orcs had been forced into exile, but they had found a way to survive.

"They never dared follow you up here?" I asked, though I already suspected the answer.

Dex shook his head, a grim smile tugging at his lips. "They tried at first but the mountain is unforgiving. Many of their soldiers fell to the cliffs, and those who survived the climb found nothing but death waiting for them. The mountain takes care of its own." Dex's voice held pride, and a warning. "To them, we're nothing but savages. We've always known how to live with the land. They see only stone and wind. They don't understand that the mountain is alive. That it gives us what we need." Each word sounded bitter, heavy with memories of battles fought.

I nodded, a twinge of guilt twisting inside me as I realized how distorted our stories had been. The orcs weren't the mindless monsters I had been taught to fear. They were a people of the earth, connected to the land in a way I could only begin to understand.

"We should head inside. Night's coming, and up here, the cold doesn't forgive."

Reluctantly, I followed him toward the keep, accepting his warm arm around my waist as he tucked me against him, attempting to shield me from the biting cold. The orcs lining the entrance watched in silence, their expressions guarded and unreadable. Some glared, their distrust clear, but others... others looked at me with something that twisted my stomach: pity.

I couldn't shake the unease creeping up my spine. The air inside the stronghold was heavy, and the echoes of our footsteps felt too loud. I glanced at Dex, hoping for reassurance, but his face was unreadable, his golden eyes focused straight ahead.

"Why are they looking at me like that?" I asked quietly.

"They're not used to humans here," he said, his voice steady but clipped. "It'll take time for them to adjust."

I hesitated, his answer lingering uncomfortably in my mind. "It's not just that," I pressed. "Some of them... they look at me like they feel sorry for me. Why?"

That made him stop. He turned to face me, his gaze meeting mine with a calm intensity that only made me more uneasy. "They likely do feel sorry for you, as learning to channel can be dangerous. They're also wary. You're something they don't understand—human and shaman. It's a lot to take in."

His expression didn't waver. The steady confidence in his voice and his stance made me feel ridiculous for even asking. He must be right. The stress of the journey, the exhaustion, and the nervousness of starting a new life in a place so unlike home were twisting my thoughts. I nodded, swallowing the lump in my throat.

"Of course. You're right," I murmured, though the unease in my chest didn't fully fade.

He turned and I hurried to follow. But even as I tried to brush away the lingering doubts, the memory of those pitying stares stayed with me. I cast one last glance at the terraces, I could feel the weight of the mountain pressing down on us as we stepped inside the massive stone doors. I was immediately struck by the warmth and life that filled the central hall. There was a vibrant burst of color and activity, illuminated by the flickering glow of torches set into the walls. The room was lined with deep red tapestries embroidered with intricate patterns, the color vivid against the stone. The floor was a bustle of movement; orc men and women were going about their daily tasks. Children chased each other around tables, and the mouth-watering scent of food filled the air.

The hearth at the center of the hall burned brightly, casting a warm and inviting glow over the room. A massive cauldron hung over the fire, and several orcs were busy stirring a thick stew. The smell of roasting meat, simmering vegetables, and the sharp tang of herbs made my stomach growl with hunger.

Our party entered, a wave of recognition spread through the room. Orcs turned from their work, their faces lighting up as they greeted the returning hunters. Smiles broke out across their faces, and before long, we were surrounded by orc women offering bowls of warm stew, bread, and mugs of ale.

Warriors were greeted with food and drink, I caught a glimpse of Kaldor stepping away from the group. A large orc—his father, I assumed—clasped his forearm in a firm, wordless greeting, while a shorter but equally sharp-eyed orc woman gripped his shoulder with a rare familiarity.

Kaldor didn't resist the embrace. For just a moment, the ever-watchful hunter softened, his posture easing under their touch. Then, as quickly as it came, the moment passed, and he turned back toward the crowd, his golden eyes sharp once more.

The orc women quickly began helping the raiding party remove their gear, pulling away heavy armor, ushering us toward the hearth where we could sit and warm ourselves by the fire. I felt a wave of relief wash over me. The warmth of the hall and the kindness of the orcs made me feel welcome. But just as quickly as the atmosphere had been friendly and open, I noticed a shift.

As the orcs moved closer to the fire, and I removed my travel satchels, more of them began to notice me. Their cheerful greetings grew quieter, their voices dipping into whispers as their eyes fixed on the human standing among them. Some of the women exchanged glances, their eyes narrowing with suspicion. Mothers pulled their children closer, shielding them behind their skirts, and I could see the fear in the children's wide eyes as they peeked at me.

The warmth from the fire, comforting at first, now felt thick and oppressive under the weight of their stares. I shifted, tucking my hands into my cloak.

"Is that a human?"

"What's *she* doing here?" another voice hissed.

A murmur of questions began to rise, the once-celebratory atmosphere turning tense. The whispers grew louder, voices of concern and confusion rippling through the room as more eyes turned toward me.

My stomach tightened, and my pulse quickened, a creeping sense of anxiety clawing at my chest. Of course, they'd be wary. I was human, a stranger in their home, and the stories they'd heard about my kind were likely filled with violence and betrayal. Their fear was justified, but standing there under their stares made me feel like an intruder. Feeling the weight of their judgment was almost unbearable.

Before the tension could escalate further, a sudden hush fell over the hall. The room seemed to hold its breath, and I turned to see what—or who—had commanded such silence.

CHAPTER 17

DEX

Despite the crackling hearths, a chill seeped through the hall, pressing in from the mountain's depths. I stood near Cleo, feeling the unspoken worries thick in the air, heavier than the tension in my own chest. I forced my gaze back to my warriors, their eyes filled with lingering uncertainty, but my focus betrayed me, drawn again and again to her.

I clenched my fists, grounding myself against the pull she had on me. She was a distraction I couldn't afford, yet couldn't resist. The fire's light traced her delicate features, accentuating the quiet strength in her stance. Her flame-red hair caught the flickering glow, forming a halo around her pale face. An ethereal contrast to the dark-clad orcs surrounding her. She stood apart yet rooted, fragile yet unyielding. *Perfect.*

The murmur of conversation faded like a dying ember, the anticipation thickening the air as Arna entered the hall. Her presence alone commanded respect, an unspoken authority that sent a ripple through my clan. Their backs straightened, and their eyes shifted warily. But it was Cleo who caught Arna's attention almost instantly. Her gaze locked onto my mate with an intensity that made my muscles coil. It was as if she could strip away flesh and bone and see the raw magic pulsing beneath Cleo's skin. Assessing. Measuring. *Deciding.*

"Chieftain, you have returned to us." Arna's soft voice echoed through the hall, silencing any remaining conversation.

"The mountain has sheltered us, Seer Arna. And we've returned with what we sought."

But Arna's focus didn't waver from Cleo, her head tilting, eyes piercing in their intensity. "And so, the prophesied shaman stands among us. The one—" she paused, a knowing gleam in her gaze "—who is destined to bridge realms, to mend what has been broken."

Tension radiated through me as Arna beckoned Cleo closer to the fire. Protective instincts warred with reason as I watched her step forward. My people shifted warily. I could feel their uncertainty like an itch under my skin, their fear of what she was. What she represented. And yet, there she stood, head high, refusing to shrink under their scrutiny. My mate was strong.

Cleo knelt before the fire, her fingers brushing the ground as if caressing the power beneath her in greeting. The earth responded, a subtle hum that only a few of us could feel through the soles of our boots. It welcomed her touch in a way that made my chest swell with something deeper than admiration. It was recognition.

The clan watched with the same wary curiosity, but I could see the shift in their expressions. She wasn't just some outsider anymore; she had earned their respect in our travels. Mine included.

Arna's voice lowered, her words weaving through the air like a spell. "The magic that flows through you is not of the human world. It is something older. You must embrace it, learn it, or it will consume you."

The firelight flickered across Cleo's face, casting shifting shadows that danced over her delicate features. My fists clenched, the sight of her absorbing every word with such raw vulnerability igniting something primal in me. I wanted to drag her away, shield her from the crushing weight of expectation that loomed over her like an unforgiving specter. But I knew better. She wouldn't allow it. She'd meet my interference with that fiery defiance I had come to expect, and she'd curse me for doubting her strength. And damn me, but I was beginning to crave that fire as much as I feared for her.

When Cleo finally spoke, her voice was steady but laced with a raw edge of uncertainty. "I am trying to learn. I want control."

Something deep within me stirred at the quiet admission. I wanted to remind her of the power she had already wielded, the strength she had shown, but Arna was already leaning in.

"You will learn, shaman," the Seer said softly. "Because you must."

Cleo's hand hovered over the flames, a flicker of green swirling in her palm before fading. I watched the way she steeled herself, jaw setting in that stubborn way I was beginning to know too well. There was an undeniable force within her, something I had never seen before. She was more than just a shaman; she was a true force of nature.

I moved in, the pull of her presence impossible to resist, sinking to my knees beside her at the hearth. The scent of her—earthy, rich, and laced with something uniquely Cleo—coiled around me, tightening my grip on reality. My hand sought the small of her back. She leaned into the touch without hesitation, and something in me swelled, possessive and fierce. Pride coursed through my veins, and I felt the edges of a rare, almost feral satisfaction curling in my chest.

"You're not alone," I murmured low enough for only her to hear. "I'm here."

Her gaze lifted to mine, and for a fleeting moment, something softened in her expression. An unspoken understanding that settled deep in my chest. Her nod was small but resolute, a silent promise, and in that instant, I knew with bone-deep certainty that letting her go was never an option.

"Chieftain, I see that you have found a mate." Arna's eyes traced our touch with interest.

My eyes locked onto hers across the fire, and the mischief in their depths sent a slow, crawling irritation through me. Seer Arna, ever the watchful shadow at my side, wielded her influence with precision, though she seldom flexed it. Yet now, the barely concealed delight on her face told me she had foreseen this moment and reveled in the disruption it would bring. Despite our common goal, we stood on opposing sides of how to face the encroaching darkness. And my bond with Cleo would only add fuel to that fire, a complication.

"I have."

A ripple of disbelief coursed through my people. Cleo shifted beneath my hand, and I traced my thumb along her spine, a silent reassurance meant as much for myself as for her. Still, I held Arna's gaze, unwavering, sensing the challenge simmering behind her knowing eyes.

"The Gods have blessed you, Chieftain. You both have much to discuss and learn of each other."

The firelight flickered across the stone walls, casting elongated shadows that danced with the movement of the flames. I glanced at Cleo, the glow painting her features in hues of gold and crimson, and I felt the familiar pull that unsettled me more than any battle ever had. My warriors would follow me into the depths of hell without question, their loyalty unshakable—but Cleo? She was something else entirely. A tether to something deeper, something more vital than war and survival. She was the bridge between their fear and their hope, the embodiment of a prophecy that threatened to consume us all.

And I would stand between her and the world that would try to tear her apart. No enemy, no force—human or otherwise—would take what was mine. The prophecy was unfolding in ways I hadn't anticipated, but my role in it had changed. It wasn't just about the survival of my people, it was also about her. *About us.* The realization burned in my chest, dangerous and undeniable.

CHAPTER 18
CLEO

A charged silence fell over the central hall, but the tension remained thick in the air. I sat by the hearth, my hands warming in front of the fire, still trying to process what had happened. The orcs watched me, a mix of curiosity and suspicion, though the Seer's words had quelled any outright hostility.

The prophesied shaman. The title felt foreign and heavy. I didn't know what it truly meant or why it had been bestowed upon me, but the weight of it pressed down on my chest. Seer Arna's eyes hadn't left mine, her gaze sharp and knowing. She could see more than what I showed; that much was clear.

Dex sat beside me, his presence grounding me as my thoughts raced. His hand gently brushed against my back, prompting me to speak. My gaze found his, seeking the quiet resolve I knew he'd offer, before looking back at Seer Arna.

"You said I'm the prophesied shaman," I began, my voice hesitant. "But I don't understand why. Why me? What is this prophecy?"

Seer Arna studied me for a long moment, her face impassive, though her eyes gleamed with knowledge. She slowly folded her hands in her lap and let out a measured breath.

"The prophecy has been passed down through the ages, from the time before we were driven into the alps, when we still roamed the forests and valleys. It speaks of a shaman who will return when the balance of the world is thrown into chaos. When darkness threatens to consume all."

I listened intently, my heart racing in my chest. Seer Arna's voice was steady, yet there was an urgency in her tone, as if the prophecy had always been more than just words. It was a promise.

"The prophecy foretells of one with hair of fire"—her gaze flicked to my bright red hair—"whose presence would be marked by the magic of the earth. This shaman, born outside of our people but tied to the ancient ways, will carry the power to restore the balance between life and death, creation and destruction. The one who walks between these forces will lead our people back to the lands that were stolen from us. Your power will heal not only the orcs, but the scars of a broken world torn apart by darkness."

I could only stare at her as my thoughts began to spin out of control. The prophecy's words painted a vivid reflection—my hair, my magic—binding me to an ancient fate. *How could I be that shaman?*

Dex's hand tightened in mine, grounding me. "You're not alone in this, Cleo. You've felt the magic. You've already started walking the path."

I swallowed hard, my throat tight. "But... How could I be the one they've waited for?" I asked, looking at Seer Arna. "I barely understand this magic. I didn't even know the truth about the war until the journey here."

Seer Arna's eyes softened and she offered a comforting smile. "The prophecy says nothing of having all the answers. Only that you will bring balance to a world teetering on the edge of chaos. That is your destiny. To guide us to restore what has been lost."

I felt a shiver run across my skin as her words wrapped around me like a mantle, heavy with expectations I wasn't sure I could meet. *Guide them?* I had never thought of myself as a leader, let alone someone capable of restoring balance to anything.

"Why do the orcs think I'm the one who can help them return to their lands?" My voice trembled. "How do you know it's *me*?"

She leaned forward, her voice growing softer, as if sharing a secret.

"Because, Cleo, the magic within you is not just a tool for battle or survival. It is the magic of life itself. Of the earth and all its creatures. The prophecy speaks of one who will restore the lands. That is why our people believe in you."

I blinked, the enormity of what she was saying sinking in. The orcs didn't just see me as a protector or a warrior; they saw me as their hope. The hope of reclaiming their ancestral lands, the hope of leaving their sanctuary and returning to the forests and valleys they had once called home.

"But... I don't know if I'm strong enough." My voice barely rose above a whisper.

Seer Arna rose from her seat. She took a deep breath, and then, to my surprise, she began to recite something melodic and ancient.

When the earth is torn, and the sky burns red,
And the balance falters, and the green is dead,
From the lands of men shall a fire arise,
With hair of flame and storm in her eyes.

Her voice carried through the hall, and as the words settled, the other orcs around the room began to join in. Their deep voices blended with hers, creating a chorus that echoed off the stone walls, filling the room with the weight of the prophecy.

She shall walk with the magic deep in her veins,
And call to the earth through its roots and rains.
The shaman will come, to heal and to fight,
To bring back the dawn after endless night.

Her hands shall mend where the darkness has spread,
Her touch will raise what the shadows left dead.
She'll stand with the earth, between life and decay,
And lead the lost home, to the break of day.

The balance she brings will shatter the chains,

Of exile and fear, of sorrow and pains.
Through mountains and rivers, to forests untamed,
The shaman shall guide, and the world reclaimed.

Hair of fire, eyes of the earth,
She will rise from roots of birth,
With hands that mend and flames that guide,
She will stand where fate divides.

She will stand against the dark,
With the earth as her spark,
Through her blood, through her pain,
She will bring us home again.

The weight of the orcs' expectations hung heavy in the silence that followed, and I could feel all eyes on me, waiting. The crackling fire was the only sound to break the silence, its warmth flickering shadows across stone walls.

Seer Arna stepped closer, keeping her voice soft. "That is why, Cleo, you are the one who will mend the world's broken threads. The earth chose you for a reason."

I stared at Arna, her words crashing over me like an unstoppable tide, threatening to pull me under. I hadn't asked for this. I never sought to be anyone's savior, never imagined myself entwined in a prophecy far greater than I could comprehend. Dex had brought me here to learn, to understand the magic simmering beneath my skin, but he hadn't told me what it meant to them. What I meant to them. The weight of it settled in my chest, heavy and suffocating, and my pulse thundered in my ears.

Five things you can see. My eyes darted around the hall for something to hold onto. The flickering firelight cast restless shadows along the stone walls. The worn leather of an orc's boots, scuffed from battle. Deep grooves carved into the wooden table, telling silent stories of years past. Dex's dark silhouette beside me, his shoulders tense with unspoken weight. My trembling hands, clenched in my lap.

166

Four things you can touch. I pressed my palms against the cold stone bench beneath me. The coarse fabric of my dress. My nails bit into my palms. Dex's warmth beside me.

Three things you can hear. The low murmur of voices. The fire crackling, popping softly in the heavy silence. Dex's even breaths.

Two things you can smell. Burning wood filled my nose. The faint scent of sweat and leather, a reminder of the warriors around me.

One thing you can taste. The bitter tang of fear that clung to the back of my throat.

Bit by bit, the storm inside me ebbed, my breaths still shaky but no longer desperate. Dex's hand brushed against mine in concern. The technique worked, as it always did, grounding me in the present and pushing back the tide of panic that had threatened to consume me. My breathing slowed, the tightness in my chest easing little by little. I swallowed hard, willing my expression to remain neutral. I hoped the fear that had nearly undone me wasn't written across my face for all to see. When I finally lifted my gaze, it met Arna's. There, in the depths of her knowing eyes, I saw a quiet kindness, an understanding that made my stomach twist. She knew. *Of course she knew.* And somehow, that made it both better and worse.

"You don't need to be ready now," Seer Arna replied. "But you will be. You have already taken the first step."

Dex's hand tightened around mine, and I turned to meet his gaze. It held a quiet resolve, steadying my own doubts. "We'll walk this path together, mate."

I nodded, though my heart still raced with uncertainty. I didn't know how I would fulfill this prophecy or how I could possibly lead an entire people. I knew they weren't asking me to do it all at once. They were asking me to walk the path and to learn, grow, and to become the shaman they believed I could be.

Seer Arna gave me a final nod, her eyes filled with something like pride. "Rest now," she said. "You will need your strength for the journey ahead."

I nodded, exhaustion washing over me. The events of the day—the battles, the magic, the prophecy—had taken their toll, and now more than ever, I needed sleep.

Dex helped me to my feet, guiding me out of the hall. As we walked through the corridors, the weight of the prophecy still pressed heavily on my shoulders, but there was also a glimmer of hope—hope that maybe, just maybe, I could live up to the orcs' expectations.

CHAPTER 19
DEX

"She's human... small..."

"How can the Seer be sure this is the shaman from the prophecy?"

"I expected someone more... formidable."

My fists clenched at their hushed comments, the weight of their skepticism pressing down on me. I had anticipated their doubts. Cleo was unlike any shaman we had encountered before. They only saw her delicate frame, the softness that stood in sharp contrast to our own hardened bodies. Orcs were used to strength in broad shoulders and battle-scarred skin. But Cleo had a different kind of toughness. And Gods help me, I was starving for her and her deceptive strength beneath her soft exterior. Her flame-red hair cascaded in wild curls, drawing my eyes with every sway of her hips, a hypnotic rhythm that unsettled me. She was a contradiction that gnawed at my resolve—fragile yet fierce, human yet something *more*.

I fought to keep my focus on my people, but my gaze betrayed me, flicking back to her time and again. The way her chest rose and fell with each breath, the delicate curve of her neck, the faint tremble in her fingers as she tucked a loose strand of hair behind her ear. Each detail stirring something primal in me, the need to claim her was an ache that had been simmering beneath my skin since the moment she stepped into my world.

Her scent, a mixture of earth and something sweet, curled around me, making it impossible to stay unaffected. I could feel my pulse pounding against my throat. My hands itched to touch, to take. I had spent years mastering control, wielding it like a blade, but Cleo had unraveled me within a day.

The corridor stretched on, winding deeper into the heart of the stronghold, and with each step, the tension coiled tighter in my gut. The torches cast long shadows along the walls, and I felt her presence beside me like a constant hum beneath my skin. Her smaller body moved with an effortless grace that was foreign yet enthralling, the sound of her soft leather boots whispering in contrast to the heavy thud of mine.

"Your clan is hesitant about me." she said softly, breaking the silence. Her voice pulling me from my thoughts.

I glanced at her, catching the flicker of firelight in her green eyes. They held an uncertainty she tried to mask, but I could see it. My people doubted her, but she felt it more deeply than she let on. A muscle ticked in my jaw as I fought the urge to reach for her, to reassure her.

"They don't know what to make of you yet," I said, my voice rougher than intended. My eyes traced her figure, the way the fabric clung to the curve of her waist, the delicate strength in the set of her shoulders. I swallowed hard, forcing myself to look away.

Cleo tilted her head, a teasing smile tugging at her lips. "I see."

I smirked, but there was a raw edge to it, my restraint stretched too thin. She was playing with fire, and she didn't even know it. "They think you're delicate," I admitted, letting my gaze linger just a little too long. Her lips parted invitingly, and I had to force myself not to focus on how soft they looked. "But they're wrong."

"And you?"

I had seen her wield power beyond anything my warriors could comprehend, but it wasn't just her magic that pulled me in. It was her. I stepped closer, the air thick between us. "I think you are far more dangerous than they realize."

She swallowed, and I watched the delicate bob of her throat, my fingers twitching at my sides, craving to trace that line. The space between us was suffocating, filled with unspoken tension that clawed at my restraint. The way she looked at me, heavy with lust, made my blood roar through my veins.

"You're staring." Her voice held an amused edge, but there was something else in her eyes that mirrored the hunger that gnawed at me.

I grunted, tearing my gaze away, but not before letting my hand brush against the small of her back, a fleeting touch that sent a shiver through her. I could feel the tension crackling like a live wire. Her presence was consuming, an ache I couldn't ignore, and it took everything in me to remind myself of my responsibilities to her as much as the clan. She was exhausted and desperately needed rest. But each glance, each subtle brush of her against me, chipped away at my restraint, fueling my instincts to take her to bed and claim her.

"Where are we going?" she asked, her fingers brushing against mine as we walked.

"To my chambers to retire for the night." I didn't miss the flare of heat in her eyes, and I had to fight against my desires to ravage her body here in the corridors, my clan be damned. "Stop it, I can feel your eyes on me. You need rest before you can play."

Her dark chuckle wrapped around me like a silken thread as we reached my door. The heat in her eyes was a challenge, one I ached to accept, but I had to hold firm. For now.

CHAPTER 20
CLEO

My hand lingered on the rough wood of the door as I hesitated. Moving into Dex's quarters felt monumental, not just for our new relationship but for my place among the clan. To be here, beside my mate, meant more than just sharing a room. It was a silent recognition of our bond.

Taking a deep breath, I leaned into the door and pushed it open. The room was vast, larger than any space I'd seen since arriving at the stronghold. The thick stone walls kept out the cold mountain air, while a large hearth crackled in the corner. Above the hearth, a mantle held relics of orc history. Carved horns, ceremonial weapons, and a polished stone that emitted a soft, faint light.

To the left, a large table was piled with maps, scrolls, and tools of leadership, a clear sign of how much Dex was involved in the daily life of the clan. I could picture him sitting in these chairs, working late into the night, pouring over plans for the next battle, doing everything he could to protect the stronghold and his people. My heart clenched with worry for him, carrying the weight of his clan's future on his shoulders.

Across the room was an immense bed covered in furs and thick blankets, far too large for any human. Dex was larger than life in every sense of the word, but the sight of that bed made my heart race. It wasn't just about sleeping beside him; it symbolized trust and intimacy, something I hadn't known for so long.

I brushed my fingers over the furs, taking in the strength and simplicity of Dex's personal space. The tapestries, hung on the stone walls in a deep red and adorned with clan symbols, made the room feel rich in history. I wondered how long it had taken him to grow comfortable here. I wondered how long it would take me to feel like I could belong somewhere too.

I turned to face him as he stepped up behind me, watching me explore in his rooms. He had grabbed a basin of hot water from the table, muscles flexing under its weight as if it was nothing. Our eyes met, and a warm smile spread across his face.

"Thought you might want to relax." Dex nodded toward a small alcove hidden behind a curtain. "The bath's been drawn for you."

I followed his gaze and saw the massive wooden tub, big enough for Dex to fully recline should he wish. Steam was rising from the water, filling the air with the faint scent of herbs. Only now did I realize how loud my muscles were screaming from all the walking and scrambling over rocks. My thighs ached, and my mind was heavy from using my magic. A bath felt like a blessing.

Dex added the basin of hot water to the tub and crossed the room to me. His hand guiding me toward the bath. "You've been carrying too much. Tonight, let me shoulder the weight. Let me care for you, please," he murmured, his hand a steady presence on my back.

I leaned into his touch, appreciating his offer. I hadn't realized how much I needed someone to be my rock. Dex moved to the tub and began adding salts and oils to the water, and the smell of lavender, rosemary, and something unfamiliar filled the air. The room held a cozy warmth as the scents wrapping around me like a soft embrace.

"Please, allow me."

His fingers brushed against my skin, untying the laces of my dress with such care that it sent my heart racing. Laces undone, he turned to give me privacy as my dress slid down my body, pooling at my feet. The air felt cool against my skin, and I hurried to rid myself of my underclothes and climb into the steaming water.

Stepping into the bath, I let out a soft moan of appreciation as the water's heat eased the ache in my muscles. The cloudy water covered my breasts as I let myself sink deeper. I was painfully aware of the fact I was completely naked inches from Dex, and my core clenched at the thought of him joining me in the tub, my nipples pebbling in response to my inappropriate thoughts.

Dex began to move quietly around the room, adding more logs to the fire, then tinkering with a jeweled box above the mantle. The soft glow of the flames made the space feel like a sanctuary where the chaos of my thoughts were allowed to drift. Feeling at peace, I allowed myself to simply exist. No magic, no responsibilities—just the soothing caress of the water against my skin. The world felt miles away.

Even without looking, I could sense Dex, his energy filling the room. My heart beat a little faster. There was a heaviness between us now, not just from our growing connection, but from something deeper, something primal driven by the bond between us.

My eyes fluttered open and found him standing beside the tub, watching me with a quiet intensity. His eyes were heavy, hungrily tracing the lines of my exposed collarbone and neck. I could feel the heat rising in my cheeks, but I didn't look away. The way he looked at me was thrilling and drove my body wild. The attraction between us had been simmering for days. Now, in the quiet warmth of this moment, it felt as if we were on the edge of something neither of us could stop.

I shifted in the tub, the water rippling around the swell of my breasts. His breath hitched almost imperceptibly, but I caught it, and it sent a spark of electricity through me. I wondered if he was thinking about what had happened in the river. I certainly couldn't stop thinking about it. The way his touch had lit a fire inside me, and how my body had responded to him so instinctively. I was desperate for more, addicted to the blistering heat he had set free on my body.

Kneeling beside the tub, Dex gently pushed a wayward curl from my face. His touch was soft, almost reverent, but there was a heat in his gaze that made my pulse quicken. For a moment, he said nothing, his gaze hungry as it roamed over me. His hand dipped into the water, fingers brushing over mine. "Cleo, I need to explain something important."

His thumb began tracing circles on the back of my hand. "In orc culture, a mate isn't just someone you care for. It's a bond that goes deeper. Deeper than anything I've ever known. It's a connection that can't be broken, not by time, not by war, not by anything." His voice trembled as he spoke, the weight of his words sinking into the space between us.

I swallowed hard, my pulse quickening. "Okay. What are you trying to say?"

He held my gaze, his eyes intense. "I'm saying that you're my mate, Cleo. Not just by fate, but by choice. By everything I am." He paused, and his hand lifted from his side, revealing a delicate gold chain bracelet, ornate and shimmering with rough cut gems. A fine loop extended from the chain, designed to slip over my middle finger, linking the bracelet to the wrist with an elegant drape of gold. "This is a symbol of that bond. Of my promise to you."

My breath caught as he took my hand, sliding my finger through the loop before fastening the chain around my wrist. The stones on the bracelet glimmered in the firelight, each facet reflecting the warmth of the room.

"These stones are sacred in our culture. Strength, loyalty, and the power of the earth itself. They belonged to my mother, passed down to my sister before I took the Chieftain trials. This bracelet is a vow that our bond is as unbreakable as the fiercest of storms. You are mine to cherish and protect, and you are now part of the Kenryr line."

I stared at the bracelet, its significance washing over me as his words settled around my heart. Their weight was both comforting and powerful, as if binding me to him, not unlike the jewelry now encircling my wrist. I was touched, and my emotions were building until tears threatened to spill over. "Dex, it's beautiful. I don't even know what to say."

His thumb brushed a tear from my cheek. "Say you accept it, you formally accept me as your mate."

I leaned forward, pressed my forehead against his, my heart swelling with emotion. "I feel it, Dex. I accept you as my mate, and I will be honored to wear it every day."

We stared at each other for a long time, the silence thick with unspoken emotions. The world outside the room seemed to disappear, and all that mattered was this. The mate bond between us, the warmth of his touch, the intensity of his gaze. The safety of this connection.

Resting his hand on my cheek, his thumb traced the line of my jaw, and I felt the flames of desire roar back to life. My breath caught, the air between us charged with something almost dangerous. Every nerve in my body was alight with anticipation, waiting for him to close the distance between us, to bridge the gap that had been growing narrower with every passing day.

But then, as if sensing the tension between us had reached its breaking point, Dex pulled away and cleared his throat.

"Can I help you bathe?"

"Please," I whispered, desperate for his touch in a way that was downright embarrassing.

Reaching for a cloth, he dipped it into the warm water, wringing it out with deliberate movements. I swallowed hard as he pressed it to my collarbone. The rough fabric gliding down my skin in a slow path that made my skin buzz.

The cloth trailing lower, over the curve of my breasts, down the swell of my hips. My breath hitched, my head falling back, shifting to offer him more skin to explore as his touch moved with an agonizing patience over my body. The glide of the cloth over my thighs had me parting my legs, and a soft moan slipped past my lips before I could stop it. My pulse thundered in my ears as Dex's nose brushed the exposed column of my throat, his breath hot and ragged against my skin.

His hand moved slowly, dragging the cloth down my calves and back up, grazing over my core in a way that was almost innocent, but left me aching. My body trembled beneath his ministrations, my fingers gripping the edge of the tub. When he traced back up over my pebbled nipples to reach my collarbone once more, I whimpered and chased his touch. His grip on the cloth tightened, and the groan that rumbled deep in his chest sent heat racing to my core.

His lips grazed my neck, tusks scraping against my sensitive skin with a delicious burn that made my toes curl. I whimpered louder, desperate to feel his mouth trail my needy body, following the path the washcloth had just taken. As the cloth passed back down over my left breast, my back arched up into his touch.

"I want you," I whispered.

Chuckling darkly against my throat, he nibbled at my pulse point, dragging his sharp teeth roughly on the skin before soothing it with his tongue. He pulled back with a pained groan and I could see the struggle etched into every line of his face. "Not like this," he said, his voice thick with restraint. "You need rest."

I could have sobbed as he retreated, the ache inside me only deepening. I knew he wasn't rejecting me; he was holding himself back, for both our sakes. And somehow, that made me want him even more. *Gods, I was desperate for him.*

Dex exhaled sharply, brushing a damp strand of hair from my face, his touch lingering just a moment longer than necessary. "Relax, Cleo. I've got you."

I leaned back into the water, my body still thrumming with want. Dex stayed close, his watchful gaze never leaving mine, his restraint both a comfort and a torment. And as the fire crackled softly in the hearth, I knew one thing for certain. I was his, and I wouldn't be able to wait much longer for the moment he finally claimed me.

THE WARMTH of the fire still lingered on my skin as I woke, the soft bed of furs beneath me feeling like a distant dream after the hard earth I'd grown used to during our journey. The scent of woodsmoke and herbs filled the room, and for a brief moment, I forgot where I was. But as I blinked sleep from my eyes and sat up, the reality of the stone walls around me and the echo of distant voices reminded me that I was far from the world I had known.

I pulled the furs tighter around me, feeling a strange mix of comfort and unease. The weight of the prophecy was still fresh in my mind—*the shaman with hair of fire*—and the memory of the orcs' voices rising in unison as they recited the ancient verse sent a shiver down my spine. The orcs believed in me, believed I was the one to restore balance, to lead them back to their ancestral lands. But the enormity of it all still felt impossible, like a dream I couldn't wake from.

I had fallen asleep in the tub last night, and I vaguely recalled Dex lifting me from the water and wrapping me in cotton towels before placing me into his bed, before climbing in behind me. Thinking of the way his hands had travelled along my body in the bathtub had heat curling low in my stomach, and I groaned in frustration.

The soft sound of the door latch drew me from my thoughts, and I clutched the furs to my chest as I looked towards the heavy door. Dex appeared in the doorway, his broad shoulders filling the frame. His golden eyes met mine, a small, reassuring smile on his lips.

"Good morning, mate," he said softly, stepping inside. "I didn't want to wake you, but the clan is eager to meet you. We have much to do today."

I nodded, feeling a rush of nerves at the thought of meeting more of the orcs. The ones in the hall had been wary of me, to say the least. Though they had recited the prophecy, there was still doubt in their eyes. I wasn't one of them.

"Are you ready to meet our people?" His voice was gentle, though there was a hint of concern in his gaze.

I took a deep breath and nodded again. "I think so. I just... don't know what to expect."

Dex stepped closer and reached out, brushing a strand of hair away from my face. "They're curious about you, but they will come to trust you. You've already proven yourself to me and the others."

His words were a comfort, and I felt the tension in my shoulders ease. Dex had been a source of strength, and though the growing bond between us was undeniable, I still wasn't sure how to navigate it. There was something more between us, something that went beyond just being allies. But in the midst of everything else—the prophecy, the dark magic, the orcs' hopes—I wasn't sure what to do with those feelings.

"I had your clothes cleaned. The women made some repairs to your dress until we get you fitted for more. Get dressed," Dex offered me his hand. "Let's go meet the rest of the clan."

How could he be so sweet and so deliciously tempting all at the same time? It was like he was immune to the pull between us, while I was a slave to my thoughts and desires. Taking his offered hand, I let him pull me from the bed. Once standing, I turned from him and approached my clothing on the table. I couldn't help but smirk at my devilish thoughts as I allowed the furs to fall to my feet, leaving me naked, before stepping slowly into my underwear, shimmying as I pulled them up my thighs and into place.

I felt the heat of his presence as I straightened, and he pressed into me, grasping my hip and pulling me back roughly back against his chest. His fingers were unyielding, and I watched as they sunk into the flesh of my hip. The sight was one of the most erotic things I had seen, and I rolled my head back, resting it against his chest with a satisfied hum. His claws traced my throat before drifting lower and taking my breast roughly in his palm. His thick fingers pinched my nipple and rolled it softly. The moan that was torn from my throat was desperate, and I ground my hips back against him in response, my breathing quickly becoming ragged when the press of his hard cock nestled against my lower back.

"Fuck Dex, please don't stop," I whispered breathlessly, my voice needy with arousal.

"You're a temptress, little shaman. Gods, how I wish to show you exactly what you do to me." He groaned, chin brushing against my temple as he pressed a gentle kiss against my temple. The stark difference between his punishing grip and his soft lips made my knees weak, and I could feel heat pooling inches from his rough fingers on my hip.

"Make no mistake, Cleo, there is nothing more I want than to hear you beg for me as I take you apart. But we have things we must do first so we can have the evening to ourselves."

The crack of his hand over my ass had me squealing. He grabbed my chin and tugged my head to face the far wall, my eyes landing on a giant mirror. I wasn't surprised by the heat in my gaze, fueled by my orc mate towering behind me. I watched as my throat bobbed tightly when I tried to swallow, the sudden nervousness racing through me at my body being on display for him like this.

"Look at me as you get dressed, slowly. Let me enjoy your body before you hide it from me."

Heat scorched my chest and moved up my cheeks as he watched, a predatory gleam in his eyes. I fumbled with my clothes as I tried to keep eye contact, my body alight with need. My core was dripping with arousal by the time my dress was back in place. He knew exactly what he did to me, and the dichotomy between his Chieftain side, his playful humor, and this ravenous beast had me all but begging at his feet for him to touch me again.

CHAPTER 21
CLEO

The warmth of Dex's touch kept me on edge as we stepped out of the small chamber and into the winding stone corridors of the stronghold. The air was cooler here, providing relief to the over sensitized heat that lingered on my skin, my mind still reeling in frustration.

As we walked, I couldn't help but marvel at the sheer scale of this place. The fortress was built with long, spiraling tunnels and chambers that seemed to stretch endlessly into the mountain. Walls were etched with intricate carvings, telling the story of the orcs' history—scenes of battles fought, of forests and rivers, of a people deeply connected to the land.

"This place is incredible," I murmured, my eyes tracing the carvings as we passed.

"It's been our home for generations."

"Are all orcs trained to be warriors?"

He smiled kindly, but his eyes still held the edge of heat from before, giving me another glimpse of the person behind the Chieftain mask. "Not all. We are a people of the earth, first and foremost. Many of us are warriors, yes, but there are also farmers, hunters, healers. The mountain sustains us, but it is not easy. Everyone has a role to play."

I nodded, taking in his words as my eyes traced every inch of the new sights in front of me. It was a far cry from the world I had come from, where nobility lived in luxury while others toiled in the fields. Here, the orcs seemed to value every life, every contribution, and everyone was treated equally.

We neared the central hall and the sound of voices grew louder. I could smell the familiar scent of cooking meat and herbs and my stomach growled, reminding me that I hadn't eaten since the night before.

Dex glanced at me with a knowing smile. "Hungry, little mate?"

The chatter quieted as we entered, and all eyes turned to us, my response died on my lips as I felt a wave of nerves.

"Chieftain Dex," one of the orcs greeted, bowing his head in respect. "We are glad to see you return safely."

Dex nodded, his voice steady. "Thank you. Grath, this is Cleo."

Grath's eyes flicked to me, curiosity and hope shining in his gaze.

"Welcome, shaman. The clan has been waiting for you."

I smiled awkwardly, unsure of how to respond. "Thank you. It's... a pleasure to be here."

Dex chuckled beside me, his hand still resting on my lower back.

"Grath oversees much of the farming here," Dex explained. "He'll show you some of the ways the clan sustains itself. Have fun, he will bring you back after a quick tour."

THE PATH to the gardens wound through the rock of the mountainside, tucked behind the stronghold and hidden from the view of those unfamiliar with the orcs' traditions. I followed closely behind Grath, his muscular legs moving easily over the uneven terrain.

Arriving at the sprawling gardens, I froze, my breath catching in my chest. A lush patch of greenery nestled within the jagged cliffs and barren rock with an energy unlike anything I had ever experienced—a calm serenity. There was a wildness to it that hummed beneath the surface. An earthy perfume filled my senses, and the plants leaned toward us, as if recognizing a kindred spirit.

"Not what you expected, is it?" Grath's tone was gruff but tinged with pride.

"No," I admitted, still taking in the breathtaking sight, "It's... alive."

Grath chuckled softly. "That it is. Every leaf, every root, connected to the mountain itself. We don't force it to grow. We ask. And when the mountain agrees, it gives."

The hum of magic grew stronger with each step forward. I knelt beside a patch of deep green plants, their leaves thick and waxy, and let my hand rest on the humid soil. The connection was instant—a surge of life, but unlike the chaotic bursts of magic I was used to. Here, the power felt natural, like the plants were whispering their secrets to me, devoid of any hint of corruption.

"You feel it too, don't you?" Grath's voice was quieter now, laced with understanding as he watched me run my fingers through the soil. "The earth speaks to you."

"It does." I could feel the steady heartbeat of the mountain, the way the roots reached deep into the ground, drawing from the life force of the land itself. It was something else—something steadying, something controlled. The garden's peace felt profound, its quiet harmony a gentle contrast to the unforgiving mountain beyond.

Crouching beside me, Grath's gaze softened as he watched my movements. "It took us generations to learn the ways of coaxing life from this harsh land. The mountain doesn't give easily, but it does give."

Lifting my hand from the soil, the residue of magic was a warm thrumming beneath my skin. "I've never felt anything like this before. It's so peaceful."

Grath inclined his head in agreement. "That's because the earth is at peace here. We don't demand from it, like your kind do with magic. We live alongside it. We respect it, and it respects us in return."

I sat in the stillness of the garden, absorbing the weight of his words. In my world, magic had always been a tool, something to be harnessed and *used*. But with the orcs it was something else entirely. It wasn't just a means to an end—it was a part of life, a part of survival. I wondered if my understanding of magic had been too narrow, too focused on control rather than connection.

I stood stiffly, my legs still aching from the climb the day before. "You grow all your own food here?"

Grath rose to his feet as well, his massive frame towered over me. "Mostly. The mountain provides enough if we know how to ask."

My eyes swept over the garden again. I could see the carefully tended patches of vegetables and herbs mixed among the wild growth. It wasn't just a garden—it was a lifeline.

"Even in the harshest winters the mountain provides, but it does not always forgive." His tone held a warning, a reminder of the mountain's power. "That is why balance is vital."

My brow furrowed in confusion. The gardens didn't look large enough to sustain a settlement of this size. "But... how? How do you grow anything in this climate? It must be freezing at night."

"It's the earth's magic," Grath explained. "We work with it and the roots reach deep, keeping the plants warm with the mountain's core. It's not something that happens overnight. It takes time, patience, and respect. It takes the entire spirit of the clan to evoke this kind of magic. We have been maintaining this connection since it was established centuries ago."

I could feel the connection between the orcs and their land. They weren't just warriors, they were caretakers of this place, protectors of the life that thrived here despite the odds. Not just savage fighters, driven by brute force. They were survivors, deeply in tune with the world around them. I realized that there was much I still didn't understand—not just about their way of life, but about magic itself.

I felt the weight of my ignorance. My people had told stories of this wilderness like it was empty, but it wasn't. It was grieving. And the orcs hadn't just lost their home—they'd lost a part of themselves.

"I want to learn. Teach me how to listen."

Grath stepped forward, his deep voice rumbling like distant thunder, though softer now. "You can return here, Shaman, anytime you need peace. The gardens— They don't just sustain the body; they sustain the spirit. It's a place for reflection, for balance. You'll need that if you're going to embrace the magic inside you."

The orcs had always seemed so hardened, but Grath's offer felt like a glimpse into something softer beneath his guarded exterior. I smiled my thanks, truly grateful for the warmth in his offer.

"My grandfather tended these gardens for years," Grath continued, his voice carrying the weight of history. "He was a shaman, too, though not with power like yours. His magic was small but vital. He kept the balance for our clan, ensuring the mountain provided and the earth gave. He always told me that magic like this—magic that works in harmony with the earth—isn't about control. It's about listening and embracing it."

I felt my curiosity peak at the mention of his grandfather, and I gave him my full attention as we continued to wander the winding paths. Grath gestured for us to sit on the roots of an ancient tree, and I sat gratefully.

"He used to sit right here. He'd close his eyes and sing to the plants, feeling the earth beneath him. He never sought to dominate it, but to keep the balance," Grath turned his gaze to me, eyes sharp but not unkind. "You're different. There's a wildness in you, something stronger than we have seen in generations. I see it in the way the earth reacts to you, how it pulls toward you like you are part of it."

He hesitated as if carefully weighing his next words. "I believe you are the one from the prophecy. The shaman who will lead us back to the valleys, to reclaim what we lost. I don't know how it will happen, or when, but I know it in my bones."

I could feel the sincerity in his voice, and kindness in his gestures. His love for his people and way of life. Amongst all, there was something else—purpose.

"I'm excited to see it, to see how you come into your own. The mountain has been waiting a long time, Shaman." His voice held an edge, a reminder of their collective hope and expectation.

Taking a final look around the garden, my thoughts raced with all the overwhelming changes in my understanding of the world over the last few days. Grath's words, the garden's peaceful hum and the connection I had felt—it was overwhelming, but not in a way that pushed me away. Instead, it felt as though the earth itself was pulling me closer, inviting me to step into the role the clan thought I was destined to play.

Pausing as he stood, he shot me a kind smile over his shoulder, his deep voice carrying a note of finality. "Come back when you need to. The earth speaks to those who listen," he murmured, a hint of reverence in his voice. "But don't ever forget to have respect for the ancient power. Your path is a difficult one to walk. Please know that I am here if you need anything."

CHAPTER 22
CLEO

When we returned to the central hall, the orcs had gathered around the long tables for the midday meal. Grath led me to a seat by Dex, where a bowl of stew was placed in front of me almost instantly. Dex nudged me playfully with his shoulder, a small smile tugging at the corners of his lips as he watched me pick up my bowl and eat.

Conversation wove around us, and I noticed more orcs glancing in my direction, their expressions a mix of curiosity and acceptance. Some of the children had gathered at the far end of the hall, watching me with wide eyes, whispering among themselves.

Dex followed my gaze. "They're curious about you. They've heard the stories of our history, but they've never seen someone like you before."

I set my bowl down, sighing. "It's a lot to take in. I'm still trying to figure out what all of this means."

Dex was serious as he leaned closer. "You don't have to figure it all out right now. The prophecy is just one part of this. You have time to learn, to grow into this role as shaman."

His words were reassuring, but the uncertainty still lingered. I wasn't sure how I was supposed to fulfill this prophecy, how I was supposed to lead these people. As the meal came to an end, he motioned for me to follow. "I have something else to show you."

Following him through the winding tunnels of the stronghold, the sound of the clan's voices fading into the distance. After a few minutes of walking in companionable silence, Dex stopped in front of a set of heavy wooden doors. He pushed them open with ease, the aged wood groaning in protest, revealing a vast chamber bathed in soft, warm light. Glowing crystals pulsed gently within sconces, their light refracting through stained glass skylights that painted the stone floors in a kaleido-scope of colors. The air was thick with the scent of old parchment and ink, a quiet hum of ancient knowledge pressing against my skin like a whispered secret.

Rows of towering shelves stretched into the chamber's depths, cradling crumbling scrolls and weathered tomes. Artifacts lay scattered across stone tables—blades dulled with age, carved wooden idols, and maps so fragile they threatened to disintegrate at the slightest touch. Every inch of this place spoke of a world long forgotten, and I could feel its weight settling in my chest. The groan of the heavy doors closing brought my focus back to Dex.

Dex stepped inside, his movements careful but confident, as if the room itself demanded respect. "This is our library. It's where we keep records of our history, our traditions, and everything we know about the world."

I trailed my fingers over the spines of the books, tracing the faded lettering with the tips of my nails. Each touch sent a shiver up my arm, the knowledge within them a tangible pulse beneath my fingertips. "It's incredible," I whispered, my voice hushed in awe.

Dex watched me, his golden gaze heavy with something I couldn't quite place. "I thought you might want to see this. You've been learning about our people, but there's still so much more to understand, and I thought this might be a good place to start."

"Thank you for showing me this."

His lips twitched into a small, almost hesitant smile. "To us, you are more than just a shaman, Cleo. You are the bridge to what we have lost."

Dex stepped closer, his hand finding mine, his grip possessive and warm, the heat of his touch seeped into my skin. The raw hunger in his golden eyes sent a slow, burning ache curling through me, as his thumb brushed over my bottom lip, his touch featherlight but electrifying. Before I knew what I was doing, I rose up onto my toes, my fingers curling into the leather harness on his chest. His hand slid to the nape of my neck, pulling me closer, his lips capturing mine with a hunger that stole the air from my lungs. Tusks grazed my cheeks, adding a delicious bite to the heat between us.

The kiss started slow, a tentative exploration, but the tension that had been simmering between us ignited into something desperate. I could feel his grip tighten as his other hand found my waist, pulling me flush against him. A gasp escaped me at the feel of his hard, solid body pressing against my softer one, his massive thigh slotting between mine possessively.

My hands roamed over his broad chest, feeling the way his muscles flexed beneath my touch. Dex growled low in his throat, and without breaking the kiss, he lifted me effortlessly, his large hands gripping my ass as he pressed me back against the stone wall.

A whimper tore from my lips as he broke the kiss, trailing his mouth down my throat in hot, open-mouthed kisses, his tusks scraping against my pulse point. The contrast between his warmth and the cold stone against my back sent goosebumps down my arms.

"Dex," I gasped, my voice trembling with need as his fingers explored beneath the fabric of my dress, tracing the soft curves of my hips and the dip of my lower back.

His breathing was ragged, his lips finding my ear. "Go on, little shaman," he rasped, his voice thick with barely restrained desire. "Beg for it."

"Please." my body arched into him instinctively, desperate for more.

A wicked grin tugged at his lips before they crashed back to mine, his passion searing. His hands roamed greedily over me, exploring and claiming my flesh. The way he held me, as though he was afraid I might vanish, only made me more ravenous.

Lips leaving mine, he trailed them over my collarbone, his breath scalding against my skin. My knees went weak as his hand found my breast. His rough palm kneaded with a hunger that set my nerves ablaze.

I arched into his touch, his claws scraping against my skin in delicious contrast.

Dex groaned, his lips hot against my throat. "I want you. Please, Cleo. Let me have you."

My head tipped back, offering him everything. "Yes," I breathed, the word tumbling from my lips with no hesitation.

His confession, his need, fueled the fire already burning inside me. My hands fisted in his hair, pulling him back up to me, our mouths colliding in a kiss that was all heat and desperation.

Dex lowered me slowly to the ground, his hands never leaving me. With deft fingers, he untied the laces of my dress, letting it fall in a whisper of fabric to the floor. His eyes darkened, his tongue tracing his lip as he knelt before me, dragging his tongue down the exposed skin of my thighs. My fingers tangled in his hair, my breath coming in ragged pants as he lifted my leg over his shoulder, his mouth hovering just above my core. His eyes burned into mine as his fingers tightened around my hip, his smirk sending another pulse of desire through me. I gasped and scrambled to find my balance, but Dex had other plans. Raising to one knee, he lifted me off the floor, pressing me between the heat of his mouth and the icy stone behind me.

He licked a slow, deliberate stripe up my center, his tongue swirling around my clit with a precision that stole the breath from my lungs. My vision blurred, my world narrowed to the sensation of his mouth, devouring me.

My body trembled beneath his touch as he feasted, dragging me under wave after wave of pleasure. He ravished me with a feral hunger, his low growls reverberating against my sensitive skin. I clung to him, my hips rolling to meet his mouth.

"Tell me, human, how does it feel to have an orc Chieftain on his knees for you? Feasting on your cunt?" He chuckled, his eyes burning into mine as his nose bumped against my clit, making me arch and press into him, a shameless moan falling from my lips.

I shifted in his grasp, chasing more friction to reach the high I was moments away from. His grip tightened, effectively trapping my body to his will. Whining, I dropped my hand to circle my neglected clit. He batted my hand away with a growl, his thick fingers reaching up to wrap around my throat, pressing me back against the wall. His grip on me was possessive, his fingers flexed, a silent command that left me trembling.

"Eyes on me," Dex growled, his voice dark and thick with desire. "I decide when you cum, got it?"

A needy whimper escaped my lips, my chest burning, desperate for air. The edges of my vision swam, the soft haze making every touch, every caress, more intense. Releasing his hold, his thumb traced the delicate curve of my jawline, before he tightened his grip around my neck again, restricting the air and making my head spin. My entire world narrowed to the sensation of his hold, strong, yet achingly gentle in a way that left me raw and desperate and clawing at the stone for purchase.

"Look at you," he murmured, his eyes dark with something dangerously possessive. His grip loosened just enough to allow me a breath, and I dragged in the air greedily, the sensation making my body tremble with a new kind of need. "So eager for it... greedy little thing."

The way he spoke as if he owned me made my thighs clench around his head, my body reacting on instinct to the deep, reverberating timbre of his voice. His gaze devouring every hitch in my breath, every flutter of my lashes, leaving me feeling exposed and utterly his.

His lips brushed over my inner thigh, his tusks grazing against my skin sending a sparks of a pleasurable pain crackling through me. I gasped, the sharp contrast between his gentleness and the commanding hold around my neck making my head tilt back, offering him everything he wanted to take. A low growl rumbled through his chest as he pressed an open-mouthed kiss to the crease of my thigh, his tongue tracing the sensitive skin there, making me shudder.

The heat between us was suffocating, every brush of his lips, every squeeze of his fingers pulling me deeper into the haze of sensation. My body ached, desperate for more, for the tension coiling tighter with each teasing pass of his tongue, each lingering touch that stole the air from my lungs and left me trembling on the edge.

Dex pulled back just enough to meet my gaze, his golden eyes blazing with a dark satisfaction as he loosened his hold, letting air flood back into my lungs in a rush that left me dizzy.

"That's it. Take what I give you, little mate." he murmured, his voice dripping with approval.

A broken moan escaped me as he leaned down, capturing my clit between his teeth with a nip, stealing whatever breath I had left. His hand slid from my throat, tracing down my body with a reverence that sent a fresh wave of heat pooling deep inside. I was completely at his mercy, and the realization only made me want to submit to him more.

"I need you," I whispered. My body arched, silently begging for his approval.

Dex chuckled, his lips brushing over my thigh with an infuriating gentleness. His hand traced possessive path down my side, leaving a trail of fire in their wake. "Answer me, Cleo. How does it feel?" he growled against my clit.

"Dex, please..." My voice whined with need as I rolled my hips against him mindlessly, searching for the friction that will push me over the edge.

"How. Does. It. *Feel*!" Each word was followed by an aggressive nip against my sensitive clit.

"Powerful, Dex. Gods, I f-feel so powerful!"

"Good girl. Let me show you just how powerful you are." He dove back between my thighs like he was a starving beast. The wet heat of his mouth distracted me from the hot burn as his thick finger thrust into me, momentarily punching the air from my lungs. I clawed as his forearm as he began thrusting his finger deep into me, a tingling beginning in my toes and fingertips as my body continued to be overwhelmed.

With a desperate groan, Dex sealed his lips around my clit, his tongue working with ruthless precision as he curled his thick finger and pressed against that devastating spot with unerring accuracy. Each stroke sent a fresh wave of heat spiraling and my body arching instinctively, my lower back lifted from the cold stone, legs trembling.

"Dex!" The cry was torn from my lips as my release shattered through me, a flood of molten pleasure rushing down to pool in his waiting palm.

He slowed his movements, dragging out every aftershock, his tongue offering a slow, teasing caress as my body quaked. Turning my head to press my cheek against the chilled stone, my breath came in ragged gasps, the remnants of pleasure still curling lazily through my limbs, leaving me boneless and dazed.

When I managed to glance down at him, Dex's molten gold eyes locked onto mine, dark and ravenous, and his mouth curled into a wicked smile. Slowly, he ran his tongue across his lips, savoring every drop of me before his gaze dropped to my trembling thigh. Still slung over his broad shoulder, he pressed an open-mouthed kiss to the sensitive flesh, his sharp teeth grazing against my skin possessively, sending another shiver rolling down my spine.

"Gods, you're perfect," Dex murmured, his lips pressing heated, open-mouthed kisses along my skin. The rasp of his stubble left a trail of fire in its wake. Slowly, he eased his thick finger from my core, and I whimpered at the loss, my body already aching for more.

"I'll never get enough of your taste," he whispered against my thigh, his breath scorching. "Or the sweet sounds you make when I take you apart."

I exhaled shakily, my chest rising and falling in erratic pants, the remnants of pleasure still pulsing through my veins. "That was... Gods," I whispered, my fingertips trailing softly through his tousled hair. The tension in his shoulders eased under my touch, but his eyes were still dark with a hunger that sent a fresh wave of heat pooling low in my belly.

A rumble started deep in his chest, the sound vibrating against my sensitized skin. His breath ghosted over my core, making me squirm beneath him. I gasped, thighs clenching instinctively around his shoulders, but he held me firm, his grip controlling. A wicked smirk tugged at his lips, and with excruciating slowness, he trailed his drenched fingers over my aching clit, circling lazily, sending sparks of electricity shooting through my limbs.

"Don't call for the Gods, Cleo. The only name I want you begging for is mine."

"Dex, I—" My voice was a breathless jumble of need, my body already responding to his touch. I swallowed, my chest heaving. "I d-don't... it's—"

He rested his head against the juncture of my thigh, his molten gaze locked onto mine with an intensity that stole the breath from my lungs. His fingers continued their torturous exploration, teasing around my clit. The heat of his mouth hovered just inches away, lips parted, as if savoring the utter control he had over me.

"Let me show you how badly I've wanted you," he murmured, his tone rough with restraint, his breath searing against my skin. "Please. I need more of you."

A deep, primal need coiled inside me, tightening with every brush of his fingers, and I surrendered to it.

"Yes. Please Dex." I whispered, heat crawling up my chest.

A feral snarl startled me as his massive hands gripped my ass, lifting me with effortless strength. My gasp turned into a breathless moan as he nuzzled his face between my thighs, the sudden shift making my balance falter. I arched back, clutching at his thick forearm, feeling the raw power beneath his skin as he carried me across the room. Dex's hand slid to the small of my back, anchoring me against him, pulling me impossibly closer to the wicked heat of his mouth.

My blunt nails raked over his green skin, seeking purchase, fighting against the overwhelming pleasure that pulsed through me. With a kick, he sent a stool tumbling away from the heavy library table before lowering me onto its surface. The contrast of heat and cold sent another shudder through me, and I had only a moment to breathe before his mouth returned with fervor, devouring me with a raw hunger.

Dex groaned into me, the vibrations sending pleasure curling deep into my core. His tongue traced wicked paths over my soaked cunt, each flick making my thighs quake around him. His thick finger thrust back inside me in a slow, punishing rhythm as he trailed open-mouthed kisses up my quivering stomach. I gasped and my body arched helplessly into his touch.

The heat inside me built quickly, an inferno licking through my veins with every stroke of his finger, every graze of his tusks against my skin. My moans turned desperate, broken cries spilling from my lips as I rocked against him, chasing release.

"Kiss me, please." I pleaded. My fingers were tangled in his hair, tugging him up to meet my lips.

Dex pulled away from my breast with a wet pop, his mouth

capturing mine in a bruising kiss, the taste of my release still lingering on his lips. I moaned into his mouth, greedy for more, pulling him closer until his tongue delved deep, claiming me.

"You beg so sweetly, little mate," he murmured against my lips, his free hand rolling my nipple between his fingers. "I want to hear more." His voice darkened, dripping with desire. "Cum for me, Cleo."

His hand slid from my breast up to my throat, pinning me to the table beneath his weight. My eyes fluttered shut, a ragged moan escaping me as he pushed another thick finger inside, filling me. His golden eyes burned with satisfaction as he watched my body stretch to take him.

The lack of oxygen sent my mind spiraling, the pressure around my throat pushing me further into the intoxicating haze of pleasure. My release crashed over me in crushing waves, my body convulsing as Dex tightened his grip, holding me there as if to prolong the torturous pleasure. My scream caught in my throat, and my muscles tightened around his fingers as I shattered beneath him.

Dex eased his grip, his hand sliding from my throat to cradle my cheek. He kissed me deeply, as if trying to claim every gasp, every shudder still racking my body. The contrast between his sweet kisses and his domination of my body left my head spinning.

"Get up on your knees." he growled against my lips, his voice thick with need.

With an effortless strength, he rolled me onto my stomach, guiding me onto my hands and knees. My breath hitched as his massive body crowded me from behind, his clothed cock grinding against my aching core.

"You aren't ready for me today, Cleo," he murmured darkly as his arm wrapped around my throat and pulled me up flush against his chest. "Your tight little cunt isn't stretched enough to take me." His voice was pure sin, and I keened at the heat in his words.

A dark chuckle rumbled through him, and he reached down to pinch my nipple, sending another jolt of pleasure through me. "So needy," he murmured, "so fucking perfect."

His palm landed on my ass with a sharp crack, the sting igniting a fresh wave of desire. My cry of shock echoed through the chamber, and Dex groaned against my neck, his grip rough on my throat.

I ground against him again, rolling my hips in a plea. Dex's growl reverberated through me, his sharp teeth sinking into the curve of my shoulder, a feral claim that left me quivering. With a firm hand, he pushed me forward until my chest met the table. The rough wood scraped against my sensitive nipples, sending jolts of fire burning through my body.

"Gods, Cleo." Dex's voice was thick with hunger, his breath hot against my back. "Look at you. A fucking gift." His thumb dragged possessively over the red imprint his teeth had left on my shoulder. "Your skin marks so easily. So soft... so willing. I'll never get enough of watching you beg for me."

His words sent a fresh wave of arousal crashing over me, and I whimpered as he dropped to his knees. His fingers dug into my hips, pulling me back until his mouth was flush against me once more. His tongue swept over my clit in slow, deliberate strokes, tasting the remnants of my release with an indulgent hum. I trembled, my body still thrumming with aftershocks, but his touch only fanned the dying embers into a fresh blaze.

The vibrations of his groans sparked along every nerve ending, his tongue trailing back up, exploring every inch it could reach. When the slick heat of his mouth circled my asshole, a gasp tore from my throat, my back arching away. I strained to look over my shoulder, meeting his gaze and the dark hunger there sent a shiver down my spine, as if challenging me to refuse him. The sinful slide of his tongue continued to circle, and my breath stuttered, the shock colliding with the pleasure spiraling through my core.

He didn't relent, his grip tightening as he worked me open, his thick fingers slipped between my folds, teasing before pressing two inside. My body clenched, overwhelmed by the stretch, the slow, torturous drag of his touch as he filled me, and his tongue working me in ways that were absolutely filthy.

"Dex-I... I can't—" My voice broke, my nails raking across the table.

"You can," he growled against my skin. "And you will."

My cries dissolved into mindless gasps as his fingers dove deeper, curving to find that devastating spot inside me that made my knees weak, each thrust pulling me ruthlessly closer to the edge. My hips began to rock, chasing the release that burned hotter with every stroke, every swirl of his tongue against the virgin asshole.

"Tell me how much you need it, Cleo. Beg," he demanded, his voice breathless.

I sobbed, my words tumbling out in frantic desperation. "I can't— please!"

A sharp scratch of claws on my thigh sent me spiraling, my entire body seizing as waves of release crashed through me, my orgasm gushing out onto his waiting tongue. My scream echoed through the library as pleasure tore through every inch of me, leaving me trembling and boneless pressed into the table.

He held me through the aftershocks, his tongue lapping gently, savoring every shudder, every whimper. Dex rest his forehead against my thigh, his breath ragged and hot as he caressed my hips.

"I've wanted this for so long." His voice thick with emotion.

With trembling legs, I rolled awkwardly to sit on the table, pulling him up until his lips crushed against mine, thrilled at how willingly he followed my lead. "Let me take care of you too," I whined breathlessly against his lips.

"On your knees."

Pushing into his chest, I felt solid heat beneath his skin as I urged him back, slipping down to the ground in front him, my pulse thrumming with anticipation. My fingers fumbled at his belt, the worn leather yielding under my touch as I worked it loose, my eyes never leaving his. His chest heaved with hungry, ragged breaths, breaking the thick silence between us.

His hand found my jaw, fingers tracing the curve of my cheek with a tenderness that made my skin tingle. The contrast of his strength and the gentle reverence of his touch sent my pulse racing. I watched, entranced by the way his control faltered under my hands, the edges fraying with every brush of my fingers. The way he looked at me— molten gold eyes darkened with need—made my insides clench with longing.

I pressed a soft kiss to his stomach, just above the waistband of his pants, feeling his muscles coil under my lips. His grip on my chin tightened, and a low growl vibrated through his chest as his other hand slipped into my hair, his fingers threading through with a possessive hold. I slipped my tongue out to trace his abdomen as my fingers unsnapped the leather buckle on his belt, the taste of his salty skin exploding on my tastebuds.

"Cleo," he breathed, his voice raw.

The way he said my name was a plea, a vow, and I ached to give him everything he desired. I parted my lips to speak, when the moment was shattered.

"Chieftain! We need you in the hall—it's urgent!"

Dex froze above me, the warmth of his touch lingering for a heart-beat before reality clawed its way back in.

CHAPTER 23
DEX

After a detailed recount of the scouts' clash with the Shadow Hounds, I requested an increase in our hunting party numbers, and for the clan not to stray far from the mountain. With a frustrated sigh, I stood from the table, dismissed my warriors and elders from the meeting, and headed down to the healer's room. Word had trickled back to us that Cleo was hard at work, using her magic to treat the injuries of the scouts under the careful guide of our healers.

When I reached the room, it was cloaked in quiet, broken only by the low murmurs of relief as Cleo's magic took hold. The glow of her power suffused the space, soft and ethereal, casting long shadows that danced along the rough stone walls. It made the room feel almost peaceful, as though her presence alone could drive out the lingering scent of blood and the groans of the injured.

I stood at the back of the room watching her, unable to look away. Her touch was light, deliberate, yet unhesitating as she moved from one wounded warrior to the next. The silvery green glow of her magic clung to her fingers, spreading out in waves that made the air shimmer. It was mesmerizing—dangerous, even, in how it captivated me.

Her power poured into my men, knitting wounds and easing pain with a precision that defied logic. The soldiers watched her in stunned silence, their guarded expressions softening as the tension in their bodies melted away. They didn't understand the full depth of what she was—what she could become. None of us did. But I was beginning to see it, to realize just how powerful she truly was. And that realization carried both hope and dread.

I tried to focus on the lives she was saving, the way her magic was reshaping the tide of our war—but my thoughts kept slipping back to the feel of her beneath my hands, only hours ago.

That moment between us was still fresh in my mind. Her breath hitching as I pressed her against the cold stone, my hands exploring the curves of her body. She'd fit against me so perfectly, her warmth sinking into my skin as though it had always been meant to be there. She was so small compared to me, her skin soft and flushed, and the way she had arched into my touch had nearly undone me. The fire between us had burned wild and unrestrained, consuming everything in its path. It was the kind of desire I hadn't felt in years, perhaps ever.

And it wasn't just her body I craved. It was the strength that radiated from her, the sharp defiance in her gaze that dared me to claim her but refused to yield, not just to me, but to herself. This world would try to break her—it always broke the strongest first.

I had to keep my distance. For her sake, if not my own. She had enough to carry without me adding to her burdens.

Her fierce strength unsettled me. I hadn't meant to feel this way. I hadn't meant to crave her presence like this. She was human— shaman, yes—but still human. And I was orc, bound by duty to my people, to the war that had raged for centuries. I wasn't meant to be captivated by her. I wasn't meant to feel this need. And yet, here I was mated and unable to tear my eyes away.

Cleo moved to the last of the injured, her hands shaking as she placed them over a deep gash on a scout's chest. Her magic flared again, silvery light flooding the room, and the soldier groaned as his wound began to close. She swayed as she worked, exhaustion etched into every line of her body, but she didn't stop. Not until the man's breathing evened out and the glow around her hands faded.

She stepped back, her chest heaving with effort, and I thought she might collapse. My feet moved instinctively, closing the space between us before I could think. But she steadied herself, brushing her wild curls away from her face, and when her eyes met mine, the weariness in them was tempered by something stronger. Determination. Fire.

Grath lingered at my side, his arms crossed as he surveyed the room. His eyes followed Cleo's every move, his expression guarded but thoughtful. He hadn't spoken much since we left our meeting, but I could feel his disapproval simmering beneath the surface. Grath never did hold his tongue for long.

"She's stronger than I expected," he said finally, breaking the silence. His voice was low, rough, but there was an edge to it—a weight I recognized all too well.

"She is," I replied, keeping my gaze on Cleo. She had moved to the corner of the room to rest, her back leaning against the stone wall. The exhaustion was clear in her posture, but she refused to close her eyes, her hands still twitching as though ready to heal again at a moment's notice.

"She's proving herself," Grath continued, his tone shifting. "Even the ones who doubted her power are starting to see it. She's earning their respect."

I nodded, my jaw tightening. "It's important that they trust her."

Grath snorted softly, shaking his head. "Trust?" he said, his voice laced with skepticism. "Is that what you think this is about? Trusting her? Or is it about controlling her?"

I tensed at his words, my fists clenching at my sides. "What are you getting at, Grath?"

He turned to face me, his eyes narrowing. "You know exactly what I'm getting at, Dex. Don't pretend otherwise. Half the clan sees her as nothing more than a weapon—a tool to win this war. And you're the one who brought her here. You're the one who gave them the means to use her."

"That's not why I brought her," I said sharply, my voice rising before I could stop it. "You know that."

"Do I?" Grath shot back, his tone harsh. "Because from where I'm standing, it looks like you're playing right into their hands. You think they'll stop at asking for her help? You think they won't demand more? That they won't take everything she has and leave her hollowed out, just like every other tool we've ever sacrificed for this war?"

His words struck deeper than I wanted to admit. "She's not a tool and I won't let them use her like one."

Grath studied me for a long time, his expression unreadable. He sighed, the tension in his shoulders easing. "Seer Arna and I warned you about this, Dex." His voice was softer now. "You didn't listen then, and I understand why. You thought you were doing what was best for the clan. But now you need to think about what's best for her."

"I am thinking about her," I said, meeting his gaze. "Everything I've done has been to protect her."

Grath raised an eyebrow, his skepticism plain. "Protect her? Does she even know the truth about why she's here? About what they expect of her?"

I didn't answer, and that was enough for him to confirm his suspicions.

"You're a coward," he said bluntly, his words hitting like a physical blow. "You think you're protecting her by keeping her in the dark, but you're only delaying the inevitable. You can't outrun fate, Dex. You can't shield her from it. And when she does learn the truth—when she finds out what the clan expects of her—do you really think she'll stay? Do you think she'll fight for us after everything we've done?"

His words sank into me like a weight, dragging me down into the depths of my own guilt. I hated that he was right. Hated that I didn't have an answer for him.

Grath stepped closer, lowering his voice. "She's not just some prophecy to be fulfilled, Dex. She's a person. A person the earth chose, for reasons we don't fully understand. Arna and I have always respected that choice, even if we don't agree with it. And you need to start respecting it too. You need to stop trying to control what's already in motion."

"I'm not trying to control her," I said, though the words sounded hollow even to me.

Grath shook his head, his frustration plain. "You might not see it that way, but she will. And when that moment comes, you'd better be ready to face her. Don't run from it, Dex. Don't run from her. She deserves the truth."

I looked away, my jaw tightening as I stared at Cleo. She had slid down the wall, but her eyes were still open, her gaze distant. She looked so small, so fragile, and yet I knew how much strength burned inside her. She was a wildfire contained in human form, and I was the fool standing too close to the flames.

"You think she'd turn her back on us if she knew?" I asked, my voice barely audible.

Grath's expression softened. "I don't know," he admitted. "But I think she has a right to make that choice. And I think you'd be a damned fool to underestimate her."

He was right about one thing—I couldn't keep running from this. From her. Cleo wasn't just a shaman, wasn't just the key to winning this war. She was a person, with hopes and fears and dreams that didn't deserve to be crushed under the weight of our expectations. She deserved better. Better than the clan. Better than me. *I didn't deserve my mate.* Fate didn't care about what we deserved. It was a crushing force, dragging us all toward an end we couldn't escape, and Cleo was at the center of it, whether she wanted to be or not.

"I'll talk to her," I said finally, the words heavy on my tongue. "When the time is right."

Grath snorted, shaking his head. "The time is never going to be right, Dex. Fate doesn't wait for convenience. Neither should you."

He turned and walked away, leaving me alone with my thoughts. My gaze drifted back to Cleo. She was so much more than I had expected, more than I had ever prepared for. As I watched her, the weight of Grath's words settled over me like a storm cloud. He was right —I couldn't keep running. But telling Cleo the truth meant risking everything. And for the first time in my life, I wasn't sure if I was strong enough to do it.

She was so small compared to the rest of us, and yet she commanded the room in her own quiet way. She didn't need to speak for me to know what she was thinking. She was exhausted, but she wasn't done. The set of her jaw, the fire in her eyes—it was all there, unwavering.

And yet, as she moved toward me, all I could think about was the feel of her skin under my hands, the warmth of her body pressed against mine. The memory burned in my mind, an echo of softness and heat that refused to fade.

Cleo stopped in front of me, her tired eyes meeting mine. "It's done."

"You need to rest," I said, my voice rougher than I intended.

She gave me a look, equal parts exhaustion and defiance. "I will. But not yet."

Something inside me snapped at her words, the tension coiled in my chest spilling over. "You'll kill yourself at this rate," I muttered, the frustration bleeding into my tone.

Her lips quirked into a tired, humorless smile. "Better me than them," she said simply, and the weight of her words hit me like a blow.

I wanted to argue, to tell her that she didn't have to bear this burden. But I couldn't. Deep down, I knew she would. She'd give everything she had, until there was nothing left, and she'd do it without hesitation, because that was who she was.

And it was that thought—that unbearable truth—that made me realize just how deeply I'd fallen for her. She wasn't just a shaman. She wasn't just a tool to be used or a prophecy to be fulfilled. She was Cleo. Strong. Defiant. Beautiful. And I was utterly, hopelessly lost to her.

The clan would come to see what I saw. They had to. Because whether or not I wanted to admit it, Cleo wasn't just a passing figure in my life anymore. She was my anchor, my equal. Somehow, I would find a way to keep her safe. Even if it meant telling her everything and even letting her go. She was my mate.

CHAPTER 24
CLEO

The midday sun streamed through the high stone windows, casting shifting patterns of light across the long tables laden with food. The scent of roasted meat and spiced vegetables filled the hall, mingling with the low hum of conversation. The orcs sat around me, their broad shoulders brushing mine as we ate. I still couldn't shake the feeling that I was an outsider, but something had shifted in the past few days. They weren't looking at me with suspicion anymore. Word had traveled quickly about my time in the healer's room over the last twenty-four hours, and this was the first time I had stepped away from the injured scouts.

Dex had practically shoved a pair of leggings and a tunic into my hands, giving me only minutes to change before dragging me here, fussing the entire way at me for sleeping in one of the healer's chairs. His worry was endearing, and I kept repeating that I was fine, and I couldn't leave until everyone had been showing signs of improvement. He finally relented as the table had filled opposite us.

Gornak's rough voice broke through the clatter of dishes, drawing my attention. "Shaman, how does it feel when you heal us?"

His words hung in the air, and I blinked at him, my mind searching for the right words to describe what it felt like to draw on the earth's power. "I'm not sure... it's hard to describe."

Gornak's eyes, though sharp, had softened. "It's unlike anything I have seen before, despite my many years. When you drove the darkness from us in the Shadow Lands, it felt like you reached into our very souls. Our life force was wavering, and then you..." He paused, searching for the right words. "You held us together, like you were pulling us back. I felt this incredible warmth. It wasn't just healing magic. It was pure power surging through us, fueling our lifeforce."

I swallowed hard. Had I really done that—sent pure energy through them? I had been so frantic, so desperate to help, I hadn't fully realized the effect of my magic. The idea that I had touched something as deli-cate as their life force was both terrifying and humbling. And yet, a quiet confidence settled in my chest.

Thorn, seated across the table, leaned in with an eager glint in his amber eyes. "It was like light flooding us. We felt you, Cleo. We felt your magic, and Gornak is right—it was warmth."

My cheeks flushed under their scrutiny. "I didn't even know what I was doing," I admitted softly, wrapping my arms around my waist. A small smile tugged at my lips despite myself.

Kaldor gave me a wry grin as he snatched the last bread roll from Thorn's plate. "Then you should keep not knowing, Shaman."

Thorn swiped for his roll, but Kaldor was faster, shoving it in his mouth with a victorious grin. I was beginning to see that they were like overgrown children, always needling each other. *Was this what a family was supposed to feel like?* For so long, I had been the outcast, even in my own home, and now these fierce warriors were welcoming me in unguarded.

I glanced over at Dex, who sat silently beside me watching the exchange lazily. There was something different in his gaze, something softer that I wasn't used to seeing. He caught me staring, and a heat flickered behind his eyes. I knew he was thinking about our tryst in the library. The way I had writhed under him, the way my body responded to his touch. I bit my lip, a thrill sparking in my veins at the memory. *Gods, had I really begged him to touch me?* His eyes traced my lips, and his grip on the tabletop tightened, wood groaning as he shifted next to me, adjusting his pants under the table with as much subtly as an elephant in a ballroom.

"You're right, she did save you. But don't forget she's still learning. This is just the beginning of her grasp on a shaman's power." Dex said, clearing his throat uncomfortably.

Having finished his meal, he stood from the bench and stepped behind me, his hand finding my shoulder. The sudden warmth of his body made me stiffen, before I melted into his touch. The scent of leather and cedar wrapped around me like a comforting shroud and I couldn't help but think of waking up in his arms, his strong, steady heartbeat against my back. I missed that last night, as I drifted restlessly, curled up in the healer's room. I missed the way he had buried his face in my hair, his hand resting possessively on my waist. The quiet intimacy of it sent another rush of heat through me, anticipation curling in my belly. I wanted to finish what we had started.

Dex's voice dropped, his tone commanding. "Cleo is strong, but she's not invincible. She's still learning, and I won't tolerate anyone questioning her while she does."

The warriors nodded in unison, their respect for Dex clear in the way they responded immediately to his authority. But I could still feel their eyes on me, still feel their curiosity.

One of the older orcs, Larnak, gave a small chuckle. "Small in size, but powerful. We'll keep her safe from any who question her, Chieftain."

With murmured apologies at having to leave to meet with the training master, Dex assured me he would see me soon, before he pulled my chin up and pressed a chaste kiss to my forehead. The gesture was simple, yet possessive, and it left my skin tingling in its wake.

My cheeks burned as I turned back to my new friends, catching the knowing smirk from Thorn across the table. "Who knew something as simple as public affection could make a human blush."

Larnak laughed, slapping his knee as he leaned in conspiratorially. "It's amazing, because as I was told from the guards, she wasn't afraid to be heard in the libra—"

Gornak smacked him with his mug before he could finish his sentence, sending water splashing across the table, drenching Larnak in the process. "Watch your mouth when speaking about the Chieftain's mate."

I had come to find that orcs were not as reserved when it came to discussing intimacy, so I knew Gornak was doing that for my benefit, and I greatly appreciated him for it. My face burned in embarrassment as the warriors' eyes focused anywhere but on me, hiding their grins behind their own mugs—Kaldor bowing his head to watch as he shredded another bread roll, Thorn shoving a large chunk of spiced carrot in his mouth.

It didn't take long for Thorn to begin telling stories, their deep voices blending with the scrape of utensils and clatter of mugs. I found myself smiling, laughing even, as they shared tales of their victories and the games they played on one another during long journeys. It was obvious Thorn was eager for any skirmish outside of the mountain, his tales often focusing on the new places he got to see when scouting.

Slowly, orcs began to rise and return to their tasks, and Gornak kindly gave me directions to find Dex in the training grounds when I was ready.

THE RING of steel and heavy footfalls filled the room, the air thick with sweat and dust. Orcs sparred all around me, their roars of effort blending into the steady rhythm of clashing blades. I could feel their eyes on me—glances thrown my way, some curious, others skeptical. I tried to focus on the cool weight of the sword in my hands, a knot of nerves twisting in my stomach, tension humming softly beneath my skin.

I wasn't even sure how I'd been goaded into this. Dex's cajoling about the knife he'd given me in the Wild Lands had been relentless. Apparently, it was for nothing if he didn't teach me how to use it. And somehow, here I was, gripping a sword that felt far too big for my hands, under the scrutiny of a clan of warriors who could crush me with their bare hands.

Dex stood a few paces away, arms crossed over his chest, watching me with that familiar, infuriating smirk. The wooden practice blade felt awkward in my grip, but I set my jaw, determined not to give him the satisfaction of seeing me struggle.

"You're holding it wrong," he drawled, pushing off from where he was leaning against the fence as he watched me go through the practiced motions. He circled me slowly, his gaze raking over my stance, assessing. The way he moved, smooth and confident, made my skin prickle with awareness, and I had to bite back a retort. "You'll break your wrist before you land a decent strike like that."

I shot him a glare, trying to keep my focus on the blade instead of the way his presence seemed to fill the space around us. "Thanks for the vote of confidence. I thought you wanted me to learn how to do this, not just criticize everything I do."

His smirk deepened, and he circled behind me, stepping close enough that the heat of his body radiated against my back. "I do want you to learn. But I also don't want you getting yourself killed when something takes a swipe at you." His breath ghosted against the side of my neck as he reached around me, his fingers brushing mine as he adjusted my grip. My heart stuttered in my chest, a rush of heat flooding my veins. Every piece of training drilled into me today vanished from his proximity. My body betrayed me, leaning into his warmth despite the frustration simmering beneath my skin.

He murmured close to my ear, his voice a low rumble that sent a shiver down my spine. "Relax your shoulders. You're holding it like it's a pickaxe, not a blade. It's all about balance. Remember, slow is fast, fast is slow."

I shifted my weight, trying to follow his instructions even as his nearness made it difficult to think. The blade felt too heavy, too unwieldy. I tried to focus, slowly pulling the sword up and across in front of my chest in a slash, before bringing it back to the ready position. "Better?"

Dex let out a hum, and I could hear the smile in his voice. "Much better, but you're still too stiff. Loosen up, shaman. You're not fighting a tree." His hand lingered on mine longer than necessary, and I swore I felt his thumb graze the back of my left hand, touching my mate bond bracelet. His hands on me were light, but they sent a slow, curling ache deep in my stomach, the frustration mounting inside me in more ways than one.

I huffed out a breath, more to steady my racing pulse than anything else. "Keep talking, orc, and I'll show you just how stiff I can be when I bury this thing between your ribs." My voice came out sharper than I intended, but the teasing edge in his tone made it hard to hold back.

He chuckled, the sound low and dangerous, and I fought the urge to lean into it. *Gods, the things his voice alone did to me.* "I'd like to see you try." He stepped back, finally giving me space, but I could still feel the ghost of his touch lingering on my skin. "Again, and this time, pretend you're actually trying to cut something."

I gritted my teeth, ignoring the way my pulse thrummed as I lifted the sword, feeling its weight as the blade curved in a downward arc. The sword cut through the air with a satisfying whoosh, but the weight of it still made my arms tremble. I glanced at Dex, expecting another smug comment, but he was watching me closely, a look of approval crossing his face.

"Not bad. You might even get close to hitting something if you keep practicing like that," he teased, tossing his own blade into the air and catching it with infuriating ease.

"Thanks..." I rolled my eyes but couldn't help the small, triumphant smile that tugged at my lips. "Next time, I'll aim for your head."

Dex's eyes glinted with something that made my breath catch, and he twirled his blade, the movement smooth and effortless. His gaze traveled over me, lingering just long enough to make heat pool low in my stomach before he turned back to the training grounds. "I look forward to it, little shaman. But first, let's see if you can manage to hold onto that thing without it dragging you into the ground."

I shot him a look, tightening my right hand around the hilt. "Just because you're built like a mountain doesn't mean the rest of us can toss around a sword like it's a twig."

His rich laughter rumbled through the air as he moved to stand directly in front of me again, leaning in just enough that I could see the heated mischief dancing in his eyes. "Size isn't everything, you know. It's all about technique."

I swallowed hard, my throat suddenly dry as I tried to hold my ground. "So, show me, Dex. Or are you worried I'll catch on too quickly?"

He tilted his head, a challenge sparking in his gaze. "If you manage to surprise me, Cleo, I'll let you take the lead in the next fight." His voice dipped lower, his tone turning serious even as his eyes held that teasing edge. "But until then, you'll do as I say and try not to hurt yourself, little mate."

I lifted the blade again, trying to ignore the way his words wrapped around me. I was already aching for him, and the way he spoke only fueled the fire burning deep within me. "You'll regret giving me the chance," I muttered, but there was no bite behind the words this time, and as I took another swing, a part of me couldn't help but enjoy the way Dex's gaze held mine, an intensity there that made it impossible to look away.

I swung again, the wooden blade trembling in my grip as I met another of Dex's furious strikes. Each blow drove me back, the force of his movements sending shockwaves through my aching arms. My breath came in ragged bursts, and my muscles burned, but still, I refused to falter. The weight of his expectations pressed down on me, heavy and suffocating.

"Your stance is slipping," Dex said with a sharp tone, his golden eyes drilling into me with unyielding intensity. "Keep your balance, little shaman. You're leaving yourself wide open."

"I'm trying!" Frustration curled tight in my chest as I dodged another swing. "Not all of us have been training since we could walk, you know."

His lips curled in that infuriating smirk, his blade sweeping in again, forcing me to backpedal. "You're doing fine. Stop complaining and focus."

I gritted my teeth, determined to hold my ground, but the uneven terrain betrayed me. My foot caught on a loose stone, and before I could correct my balance, I fell. The impact rattled through my bones, knocking the air from my lungs in a sharp gasp. My sword rolled from my grasp, a useless piece of wood against the dirt.

Dex's shadow loomed over me as he crouched, his hand outstretched. "Come on, up we go."

But it wasn't Dex standing over me anymore...

The ground beneath me turned cold, the air thick with the suffocating scent of stale ale and blood. My father's voice sliced through the haze, sharp and cruel, filled with that old, familiar rage. "Useless," he snarled, his shadow swallowing me whole. "You're nothing but a burden."

I tried to crawl back, my limbs leaden with terror. But before I could escape, his boot slammed into my ribs, sending pain lancing through my side. I curled inward, clutching at the ache blooming beneath my skin, my breath coming in short, panicked gasps. I willed the words to my lips, but they wouldn't come. I couldn't speak, couldn't scream. I could only brace for the next blow.

"Get up." His voice cracked like a venomous whip. "Stop crying. No one's going to save you. You're pathetic! Worthless—"

A strangled cry tore from my throat as I blinked, the past bleeding into the present. Dex's voice pierced the fog, rough and urgent. "Cleo!" His voice pulled at me, distant but insistent. "Breathe. Look at me. You're safe."

The world snapped back into sharp focus, and horror curdled in my stomach. Vines had erupted from the earth, thick and sinuous, coiling around Dex's powerful frame. They pulsed with an eerie silver glow, twisting tighter with each heartbeat, binding him like a prisoner. His practice sword lay abandoned, forgotten, as he fought to break free, his muscles straining beneath the grip of my magic.

"Cleo," Dex rasped, his voice raw with effort. His eyes burned into mine, "You need to stop this. Fight the fear."

Around us, the training grounds had fallen silent, save for the muttered voices of the orcs who had gathered, weapons raised in cautious fear. Thorn stepped forward, his sword biting into the vines, but they only lashed out in retaliation, knocking him back with a sharp crack.

"Stay back!" Dex barked, his chest heaving as the vines squeezed tighter, his voice strained with the effort to breathe. "I said, *stay back!*"

The weight of their stares pressed against me, heavy with a fear that cut deeper than any blade. I could hear the whispers, sharp and unforgiving.

"She'll kill him—"

"—Dangerous—"

Dex's voice tore through my spiraling panic, dragging me from the edge. "Cleo!" he pleaded, his strength ebbing as the vines constricted further. "You can stop this."

Tears burned down my cheeks as I clawed for control, my fingers trembling as I leap to my feet, reaching for the magic simmering beneath my skin. It fought against me, wild and unruly, slipping through my grasp like sand. But I pushed harder, desperation clawing at my throat. I focused on Dex's voice, the steady, unwavering command beneath the strain.

Slowly, the vines loosened their grip, slithering back into the ground until they were gone. Dex staggered forward, a ragged breath tearing from his chest as he clutched his ribs. Around us, the orcs lowered their weapons, their faces etched with relief, suspicion, and fear.

My knees buckled, and I crumpled to the ground, sobs wracking my body. "I'm sorry," I choked out, my voice shaking. "I didn't mean to-I didn't!"

Dex dropped to his knees in front of me, his golden eyes soft with understanding. His touch was light as he brushed damp strands of hair from my face. "Cleo, it's okay. You stopped it. That's what matters."

I shook my head, the knot in my chest growing tighter. "It's not okay," I whispered, my voice breaking. "I saw my father. When you leaned over me, I thought... I thought it was him."

Dex's jaw clenched, his eyes flashing with something dark and dangerous. "I could kill that man for what he did to you." His fingers tightened briefly before his voice gentled. "But you're here, Cleo. You're safe. And you fought back."

My gaze dropped to the ground, shame curling deep in my gut. "You should hate me."

"I could never hate you." His voice was fierce.

Before I could argue, he scooped me into his arms as if I weighed nothing, his embrace a shield against the prying eyes around us. I buried my face into his chest, the steady drum of his heartbeat drowning out the whispers I couldn't escape.

Dex turned to the gathered warriors, his voice a low, commanding growl. "Get back to work. *Now.*"

The orcs hesitated, their gazes flickering between us before they turned, retreating into their training with wary glances cast in my direction. Their fear lingered, a weight I could feel pressing into my bones.

As Dex carried me away, I clung to him, my fingers curled tightly into his shirt. The whispers, the fear, they would always be there. But in his arms, I could pretend—for just a moment—that they weren't crushing me from the inside out.

CHAPTER 25
DEX

The stars seemed closer up here, scattered like shards of ice across the velvet sky. I had brought her to the highest roof of the stronghold, far from the whispers and judgment of the training grounds. Cleo sat beside me on the wide stone ledge, her arms wrapped tightly around herself, her head bowed. She hadn't spoken since I carried her here, and I didn't push her.

The silence stretched, broken only by the distant sounds of the stronghold below, murmurs of voices, the clang of weapons, the hum of a place that never truly slept. But none of the chaos reached us. Up here, it was just the two of us.

She was still trembling, though she was trying to hide it. Her hands twisted in her lap, her fingers pale from how tightly she gripped them. The silvery moonlight painted her features with an almost ethereal glow, softening the sharpness of her exhaustion and the streaks of dried tears on her cheeks. She was beautiful in a way that defied logic, her human features so different from mine, so delicate—and yet she carried a beauty that made my chest ache.

I could still feel the ghost of the vines on my chest, but it wasn't the magic that haunted me. It was the thought of how afraid she'd been, how deeply scarred she still was by what she'd endured before she came to us. Before she became mine to protect.

"I'm sorry for pushing you too hard. For... triggering bad memories." The word felt foreign on my tongue, too small to encompass the storm I'd seen in her eyes, the fear and pain that had gripped her so tightly. "I didn't know, Cleo. I didn't know about your father. If I had—"

"It's not your fault," she interrupted, shaking her head. Her voice sharpened, a hint of stubbornness breaking through the vulnerability. "I'm the one who lost control. I'm the one who hurt you."

"You didn't hurt me."

"I could have!" her voice snapped. "I let the magic take over, Dex. I let it win. What if it happens again? What if next time—"

"Stop." The word came out harsher than I intended, but it cut through her spiral of guilt like a blade. Her eyes widened, her breath hitching, but I didn't let her look away. I leaned closer, lowering my voice but keeping the commanding tone. "Stop blaming yourself for something you couldn't control. What happened wasn't your fault, Cleo. You were afraid, and your magic reacted to protect you. That's not weakness. That's instinct."

"But I should have been able to stop it," she argued, her voice trembling. "I should have been stronger—"

"You *are* strong, and you *did* stop it." I said, cutting her off again. My hand reached out, brushing against her shoulder before sliding to her chin, tilting her face toward mine. Her skin was warm under my touch, soft and fragile in a way that made my heart ache. "You're one of the strongest people I've met. And you need to stop tearing yourself down. You've spent your whole life being told you're not enough, but I'm telling you now. You are more than enough."

"That fire in you, that passion, it's one of your greatest strengths. It's what makes you unstoppable, and it's one of the things I'm most obsessed with. You're human, and I'm orc. Our worlds are different, our bodies different, but none of that matters in here." My voice was rough with emotion as I pressed her palm against my chest. "I look at you, and all I can think is how I couldn't imagine a life where I wasn't completely consumed by you."

"Obsessed, huh?"

"Completely," I growled softly, the word rumbling between us. "Because that stubborn, unrelenting fight inside you? It's why we were destined to be mates."

Her eyes widened in surprise at my seriousness as I leaned closer, my hand still holding her chin, thumb brushing over her jaw. "You may not see it yet, but you feel it," I continued. "Your passion, your strength, your refusal to give up. That's orc nature; it's the heart of who we are. It's why the bond between us is so strong. You are mine, and I am yours. No force in this world or the next can break that."

She shuddered under my hands, tears glistening as they spilled silently down her cheeks. I reached up to brush them away with my thumb as I continued.

"And hear me now." My voice dropped into a low growl, sharp with promise. "I don't care who they are. I don't care where they come from. If anyone—anyone—tries to hurt you again, I will kill them. I will rip them limb from limb, tear them apart with my bare hands, and leave nothing behind. Not your father. Not *anyone*. You're mine to protect, Cleo, and I will no matter what it costs me. That's a promise." My voice softening.

Tears spilled freely down her cheeks as her small hands unclenched in her lap. "Dex..." she whispered, her voice breaking. "I don't know if I deserve that."

"You do," I said fiercely, my grip on her chin forcing her to meet my gaze. "You deserve everything. And I will spend the rest of my life proving that to you."

Her lips trembled, her hands lifting slowly to clutch at my shoulders as if she was afraid I might vanish. "You're stubborn." Her voice thick with tears.

"So are you. That's why we work."

She let out a soft, broken laugh, and the sound tugged at something deep in my chest. "You make it sound so easy."

"It's not, but I'd do it for you without question."

Her laughter dissolved into quiet sobs, and I pulled her against me, wrapping my arms around her as I held her close. Her head rested against my chest, her warmth sinking into me as I buried my face in her hair. "I'll keep you safe, Cleo. No matter what it takes."

She clung to me, her body trembling, and for a long moment, neither of us spoke. The weight of everything hung between us, heavy but unspoken. The truth about why she was here—the prophecy, the clan's expectations—burned in my chest like a festering wound. But now wasn't the time to tell her. Not when she was still so vulnerable. But I would tell her. *Soon.*

Leaning back, I tipped her face up to mine. Her green eyes shimmered with tears, but there was something else there now—something softer, more certain. "You're mine, Cleo. And I'm yours. Nothing will ever change that."

Her lips parted, her breath brushing against my skin, and before I could think better of it, I closed the distance between us. The moment our lips met, the rest of the world fell away. Her small hands slid up my neck, her fingers curling against my skin as she leaned into me, her lips soft, warm and hesitant. I deepened the kiss, my hand sliding into her hair, tangling in the wild curls as I pulled her closer.

Pressing against me, her warmth ignited a fire that burned through every thought. I tightened my hold on her, claiming her in a way that left no room for doubt. She was mine. My mate. My equal. My obsession.

She pulled back, her chest heaving as she caught her breath and I moved to rest my forehead against hers, my hand still tangled in her hair. "You're everything, Cleo," I whispered. "And I'll never let you go."

She shuddered, her hands still clutching at me, and victory flashed through me when I saw the faintest flicker of belief in her eyes.

"Neither am I."

"Good." A smile tugged at my lips as I kissed her, pouring as much adoration into it as I could. Because no matter what came next, I would never stop proving it to her.

She was mine to protect now. And Gods help anyone who tried to take her from me.

～

THE MOMENT the door clicked shut behind us, the tension thickened like a brewing storm, heavy and electric. The weight of everything—the war, the prophecy, the magic—lingered at the edges of my mind, but none of it mattered right now. It was just her. The fire in my veins burned hotter, igniting the hunger that had simmered beneath the surface since the library.

I hadn't been able to think straight since. The way she had responded to me, how her body melted against mine, how her lips had parted just enough to tempt me beyond reason. It had taken every ounce of my self-control to put duty before pleasure, shoving my aching cock into my pants, pulling her up from her knees and leaving her in the library.

Control was essential, a constant reminder pulsing beneath my need to possess her in ways she had never known, and I had lost control with her then. My fingers twitched with the memory of holding her throat under them, giving in to my primal need to dominate my mate in every way possible. I was lucky it had only heightened her pleasure and not scared her. I was determined to keep my control in check tonight just in case. In this room, there were no interruptions, no distractions. And Gods help me, I was weak to the need to hear her whimpers again, to feel her surrender beneath me.

My gaze drank her in, following the rise and fall of her chest, the voluptuous curves of her hips, the pink flush creeping over her skin. I closed the distance, my size dwarfing hers, the need thrumming through my veins making it nearly impossible to be gentle.

"I haven't stopped thinking about you." My voice, rough and husky, reverberated between us. "I tried to give you time to rest, but—"

Her darkened gaze, pupils blown wide with desire. It was all the encouragement I needed. A low growl escaped me, my restraint hanging by a frayed thread, as I watched her pull her plump lower lip between her teeth. "Then don't."

A growl rumbled deep in my chest as my fingers tangled in her hair, dragging her close. Her soft body pressed against mine as I bent down, crashing my lips against hers. Claiming, devouring, desperate for her taste.

Parting her lips on a gasp, I seized the invitation and deepened the kiss. She moaned into me, hands fisting my pauldron, tugging me closer with a strength that belied her size. Her smaller body fit against mine in a way that made me ache, my hands roaming down her back to the swell of her hips, gripping hard enough to make her groan and rock against my thigh.

I lifted her easily, reveling in the way her legs locked around my waist without hesitation, her arms tight around my neck. The friction of her soft curves against my hardened muscles was exquisite. Torture and ecstasy all at once.

I ground her against my cock, and she let out a choked gasp that sent another surge of primal need burning through me. My lips trailed down her jaw, over the column of her throat where her pulse thundered beneath her delicate skin. I lingered there, savoring the way she shuddered against me as I nipped as her pulse point. The way she offered me her vulnerability without hesitation was intoxicating.

Her nails dug into my shoulders, dragging across scarred flesh, the sharp edge of pain heightening my pleasure, and I growled against her throat. *"Mate."* The word spilled from my lips like a prayer.

Her fingers trembled as they worked the buckles of my armor, the plates clattering to the floor as she went. When her hands skimmed up my bare chest, the warmth of her touch seared me to my very core, and I shivered in response. She touched me with such tenderness, as if I were something precious, and it made my heart soar. Gods, I was so lucky.

Carrying her to the bed, I laid her down gently in the furs, crowding over her. Her eyes met mine, heavy with desire, and my cock ached at the sight of her body arching toward me. The furs cradled her as I traced a thumb over her trembling lips, savoring the way she responded to my every touch.

"Please, Dex." Her voice was breathless and needy.

The plea undid me. Stripping her tunic and leggings from her body in one swift motion, I kissed my way back up her trembling legs, letting my tongue lave over the softness of her thighs, my tusks leaving behind red angry scrapes on her skin. Each one a claiming mark of their territory. *Mine.*

"Gods, Cleo, your body is perfect." I breathed against her, my mouth devouring her as I brushed across her hipbone, nipping at her skin as I went.

In a moment of weakness, I was dragging my lips down to her inner thigh, inhaling deeply. "This cunt is even more incredible." My tongue flicked against her heat, tasting the sweet slickness already pooling at her entrance.

Looking up, I saw a blush spread across her chest, and I smirked against her skin. "Why does it fluster you when I tell you how much I enjoy your body?"

"No one has ever made me feel like this before. I'm rather...curvy... for a human," she murmured, looking away almost awkwardly.

"Curvy? Human men are *fools*. Your body is perfect, plush thighs, full breasts, tight cunt," I groaned in response, continuing to lap gently at her. "Makes me want to lick every inch of it."

"Also, the words you use." She bit her lower lip in embarrassment as she looked down at me.

"What? Cunt?" I teased, watching the way she squirmed under my attention, the muscles in her thighs tightening as I traced lazy circles with my thumb on her inner thigh.

"Yes, it's so... crass."

I chuckled, dragging my tongue firmly over her clit in a slow, deliberate stroke. "Humans have such odd views on intimacy. I much prefer orc culture. I can call it whatever I want." My voice was thick with amusement. "And you like it, don't try to deny it."

I pressed my thick tongue deep into her before she could respond, groaning at the way her muscles pulsed around me, the taste of her sending my need spiraling out of control. Her back arched off the bed with a groan, hips rocking to chase more friction.

"Oh, don't worry, little mate. You're going to be feeling me for *days*." I chuckled, sliding a finger slowly into her slick heat to replace my tongue.

Listening to the hitch in her breathing as I worked her open only made me harder, the ache in my cock nearly unbearable. My tongue flicked over her clit in rhythm with my thrusts, coaxing her open, claiming her. When I added a second finger, her moans grew louder, her hips moving instinctively, taking me deeper. Her tight heat squeezed around my fingers, and I growled at the sight of her, utterly undone beneath me, writhing, trembling, flame-red hair fanned out like a halo.

"Look at how pretty you are, just for me. Tell me you can take another." I groaned against her clit, before pulling it back between my teeth.

"Yes!" she gasped, grinding down into me, relishing in the prick of pain as she chased her pleasure.

I arched an eyebrow, pulling my lips from her clit and easing my thrusts in her clenching core, shushing her whines of disappointment. "Greedy little thing, aren't you... Yes, what?"

Her thighs flexed in frustration, but the desperation in her voice won over. "I can take another. Please! I need it!"

"Yes, *what*?" I growled, pressing back roughly into her cunt.

"Yes, mate. *Please!*"

Oh, how she begged so beautifully for me.

"Good girl." Easing a third finger inside her tight pink hole, I watched as her muscles clenched around me, her hips writhing as she fought to accommodate the stretch. I lowered my mouth back to her clit, pushing her back to the edge of release. Within moments, her body was greedily accepting the giant fingers stuffed in her cunt, and I aimed for her pleasure spot, rewarding her for taking them so well for me.

Her orgasm crashed through her, her screams echoing off the walls like a song only I was meant to hear. Her body trembled beneath me, every muscle taut with pleasure, and I watched in fascination as she came undone. Her inner walls pulsed around my fingers, threatening to push them from her body, and I could feel my cock leaking at the sight.

A growl rumbled deep in my chest as I prowled back up her body, easing my drenched fingers from her core. The desperate little whimpers escaping her throat were a siren's call, pulling me deeper into the intoxicating haze of need. Her fingers tangled in my hair, tugging hard enough to sting as she guided me to her mouth. I let out a feral snarl against her lips, savoring the way she responded to me with such raw abandon. *Control.*

"I'm going to take my time claiming you," My lips trailed her jaw, biting kisses down her throat, "And when I'm done, you'll know exactly who you belong to."

CHAPTER 26
CLEO

Golden eyes bore into mine, smoldering with a heat that sent a shiver through me, curling low in my belly and spreading like wildfire through my veins.

The air between us crackled, thick with need and something deeper —something that made my pulse flutter against my throat like a trapped bird. His massive body crowded me, his hand sliding to my waist, pulling me tight yet tenderly against him. The contrast of his strength with such deliberate care made my stomach clench with longing, especially as I could see the desire battling for control behind his eyes. My hands splayed over his chest and I traced the battle-hardened lines of muscle. The softness of the furs beneath me only amplified every sensation as his weight pressed down, dominating my space.

"Dex..." My voice was barely more than a breath, my need saturating the single syllable. The sound of his name leaving my lips ignited something dark and primal in him. His fingers tightened on my waist, his head dipping to hover just above mine, teasing, taunting. His moments of brutal dominance had me clenching, my body arching into him.

"It almost hurts how beautiful you are, Cleo." His voice was rough and dripping with desire. A shiver of anticipation zipped down my spine, each nerve alight with the intoxicating combination of his gentle words and his blistering touch.

His lips claimed mine and every thought scattered, dissolving into the fire raging between us. What started soft and exploratory, quickly deepened as his hunger called to my own. I clung to him, my nails scratching down his shoulders and across his back. The scent of him—earthy, masculine and raw—wrapped around me, stirring something feral. He liked to play rough and had awoken the same dark desires in me.

"How do you always make me feel like this?" I groaned, my words tumbling out before I could stop them.

"Like what?" His thumb trailed slow, deliberate circles along my hipbone as he ground against me with agonizing precision, his clothed cock sliding against my core, sending pleasure pulsing through me.

"Like I can't think straight. Like I need you more than air." My admission made my cheeks flush, laid bare before him, vulnerable in a way that made my chest tighten in anxiety.

Dex captured my lips in a searing and possessive kiss. His hand found mine, fingers intertwining, and he pressed it above my head, pinning me beneath him. The silent promise of his touch was all consuming.

In a tangle of limbs we I hastily removed our remaining clothes, and Dex guided himself in with a slow push. Hissing through my teeth, my body was torn between pleasure and the sharp bite of pain. Tears pricked at the corners of my eyes and my thighs gripped his hips. *He was so thick.*

Dex froze, muscles taut with the effort to hold back from plunging deep, rocking softly against me, trying to work me open to take him. I could see it, the need to claim me battling his desire to protect. My hand grasped his, unable to speak past the burning in my throat as I held in a sob. The concern on his face cut through the haze of growing panic, and his touch gentled, his lips brushing against mine in a tender caress.

"I'm sorry, Cleo."

A tear rolled down my cheek, disappearing into my hairline, and Dex chased it with his lips, murmuring against my skin. The tenderness of the moment caught me off guard. I had expected him to take, to consume me. I grazed my trembling fingers along his clenched jaw, my heart seizing, overcome with emotions as he brushed my tears away, his touch achingly soft.

Taking a deep, albeit shaky breath, I gave a tentative roll of my hips and pushed him a little deeper. Feeling him stretch me further. The pain and pleasure twisting together in an exquisite mix of sensation that left me shivering.

A deep groan rumbled through his chest, his entire body tensed, trembling with the effort to hold back, his tusks grazing the corner of my mouth as he kissed another tear away. "We don't have to—"

"Please, move." I whispered, clutching his hand like a lifeline.

He hesitated, searching my face, his need to protect me warring with his own desires. "I don't want to hurt you."

"I'm okay. You're so big, it's just going to take me a minute to get used to it." I pressed a soft kiss to his lips, rolling my hips in an invitation. The sting was still there, but a tiny spark of pleasure bloomed underneath the pain, spreading a crackling warmth through me.

Dex pulled our joined hands to his mouth, placing a gentle kiss against my fingers. His lips lowered to claimed mine again, his tongue plunging into my mouth with a passion that made my toes curl. His free hand crept down between us to begin circling my clit while he rolled his hips. He swallowed my moans greedily, groaning into my mouth.

"Fuck. You're so fucking tight. Fit so good, like you were made for me." Dex began rocking his hips a little deeper, burying himself further into my heat. The slow drag of his cock against my walls drove me wild, pleasure mounting with each careful thrust. I wound my foot around his calf, my body arching into him in desperation for more.

A strangled gasp tore from my throat as I felt him hit that spot in me as he bottomed out, sending waves of pleasure, my muscles gripping tight to his thick cock. My vision blurred. Again and again, he slammed against the same spot, and my chest burned with the need for oxygen as I lost control of my body.

"Oh fuck." My body shook, the rush of pleasure cresting too fast.

"*Mine.*" The word was a snarl as he slammed into me. His mouth devoured mine, muffling my cries as I writhed beneath him, oversensitive and wrecked.

My nails raked down his back, desperate to hold onto something solid as my body shattered, fire racing through my veins. A primal growl vibrated from his chest, and Dex sunk his teeth into my shoulder in a claiming bite. I rode out my orgasm, my walls fluttering helplessly around him, and he spilled into me with a roar, his release searing.

Our ragged breaths mingled, our bodies were slick with sweat. He pressed a chaste kiss to the mark he'd left behind, his tongue tracing over the broken skin, soothing the sting with soft murmurs. My body was still wracked with aftershocks, overwhelmed yet still craving the delicious heat of his touch. Every part of me felt branded by him. *Owned.* I was his, and he was mine. I couldn't find it in myself to want it any other way.

CHAPTER 27
CLEO

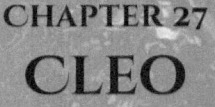

The sound of the wind howled softly through the narrow corridors of the mountain stronghold, a constant, distant whisper of the outside world. Inside, the walls seemed to pulse with the ancient heartbeat of the mountain itself.

After the intensity of learning to heal with Seer Arna, the weight of my new responsibilities hung heavily around my shoulders. I was stepping into a world where I would have to use that power in ways I hadn't yet imagined.

Dex walked beside me silently, his presence reassuring, as we made our way through the winding corridors toward the heart of the stronghold. His hand brushed mine occasionally, sending a warm, steady pulse through my skin, even as the pressure of what lay ahead mounted with every step. His presence was a tether, keeping me anchored amidst the weight of expectation.

This was more than a simple fortress of stone and steel. The stronghold wasn't just a shelter—it was the center of orc life, a place where their history and traditions lived on, even in exile. As we passed through the tunnels, I could see it in the way they moved, the way their culture had adapted to life within the mountain. Their resilience was woven into every stone and whispered in every passing glance.

I had spent so little time here, but walking beside my mate with the shadow of war still lingering in the distance, I had a chance to see more of who these people truly were. Their preparations were calculated; herbs for healing, stockpiling arrows, and forging new weapons and armor—each task carried out with quiet determination.

We entered a wide chamber illuminated by flickering torchlight, the large crystals embedded in the walls cast a soft, ethereal glow over the hall. Orcs bustled through the space, setting down platters and filling the air with the rich scent of roasted meat and fragrant herbs. Laughter mixed with low voices in the dining hall, the warmth of community weaving through the air like an invisible thread, and I found myself smiling.

"They're preparing for the harvest festival. Even in times of war, we honor the land and its cycles." Dex's voice was soft as he noticed the way my gaze roamed the chamber.

I noticed the way their eyes followed us, their whispers growing quieter as we passed. Some of them dipped their heads in respect when their Chieftain glanced their way, but when their eyes shifted to me, there was something else—a mixture of reverence and curiosity. They still weren't sure what to make of me at their Chieftain's side.

The long tables were lined with offerings, the walls adorned with intricate carvings and symbols painted in rich ochres and blacks. The orcs moved with purpose as they carried out the rituals that marked this sacred occasion. I took an empty space near the center of the hall, Dex by my side.

Seer Arna entered soon after us, her silver hair gleaming in the firelight, a staff held firmly in one hand. Her voice carried through the hall, low and resonant, as she began to speak in an ancient orcish tongue. I couldn't understand the words, but each syllable was charged with an otherworldly power that prickled my skin.

Dex leaned closer, his voice a low murmur in my ear. "She's calling on the ancestors, asking them to bless the harvest and guide the clan through the coming year."

I nodded, my gaze fixed on the Seer. When her piercing eyes met mine, I felt a jolt, like she was looking through me, straight into my soul.

"Cleo," she said, her voice carrying the weight of the ritual itself, "step forward."

The blood drained from my face, and I glanced at Dex, searching his expression for reassurance. His golden eyes met mine, calm and steady, and he gave me a small nod. Swallowing hard, I stepped forward, the circle of bodies parting to let me through. Eyes burned into me, heavy with expectation.

"This is the time of renewal. A time to honor the land, the ancestors, and the bonds that tie us together as a clan. To swear fealty to the earth and to each other." She held out a small ceremonial dagger, its blade curved and etched with runes not unlike the one on Dex's hip.

"Each member of the clan offers a drop of their blood to the flames, a symbol of their connection to the earth and their loyalty to the Blackfoot. As the mate of our Chieftain, you are one of us now. Will you take the oath?"

The murmurs around me grew louder, a ripple of anticipation spreading through the hall. I glanced again at Dex, but his expression was unreadable, his gaze steady on mine. This was their culture. I couldn't refuse, not when I had vowed to respect their traditions.

"I will." I said, forcing my voice to remain steady as I took the dagger she held out. My fingers trembled when I wrapped them around the hilt. The blade was warm, almost alive, and the runes etched into its surface seemed to pulse under my touch.

"Just a few drops in the fire, dear." she said kindly.

I stepped closer to the fire, and the heat brushed against my skin as the flames licked higher. My reflection wavered in the flames, distorted and flickering. Taking a deep breath, I pressed the blade to my palm. The sharp slice of the blade made me wine, and I tipped my hand to let the droplets fall into the fire. It fire hissed and crackled louder in response, the light shifting and twisting until the room around me blurred. The glow of the flames consumed everything until there was nothing but light. Heat pressed against my skin, and a voice echoed in my mind—deep and resonant, like the mountain itself was speaking to me.

. . .

WATCH.

The light shifted, and suddenly, I was standing in a barren waste-land. The sky above was dark, thick with churning clouds that blotted out the sun. Shadows writhed around me, a sea of black tendrils that stretched out endlessly, suffocating everything in their path. And in the distance, I saw Dex leading the clan in battle, myself at his side holding a dagger.

We stood together, faces streaked with soot and sweat as we fought against the advancing Darkness. The shadows were relentless, swallowing everything in their path. I watched, helpless, as the tendrils wrapped around Dex, pulling him down. I watched as I reached down to grab his hand in desperation before we were both swallowed by the shadows. The orcs behind us screamed out in pain, their voices rising in a chorus of agony as the darkness consumed them next.

Several long seconds passed as I watched the shadows writhe and churn across the ground, before the vision seemed to slow to a halt.

I blinked, and I was watching it all over again—the same scene, the same pain. But this time, something was different. I watched my vision-self step forward, hands glowing with magic that pulsed bright. The tendrils of shadow recoiled, hissing, as the magic surged out of her, wrapping around the clan and shielding them from the darkness. Dex pushed the warriors behind him and backed away from the glow, leaving vision me alone to battle the shadows.

I burned as if I were feeling her channeling in my own body. My vision-self shrieked, her body glowing so brightly it was almost unbearable. Magic erupted from her, a wave of pure energy that disintegrated the shadows across the wasteland in an instant, but as the light dimmed, I saw her fall to her knees. Glowing veins turning white-hot, scorching and blistering her skin. She begged for help, for death, but the roar of the orcs celebrating their victory drowned out her pleas. I watched her burn until she curled on the ground, crumbling into ash, leaving nothing but scorched earth where she had stood.

You must choose.

I SUCKED in a gulp of air, stumbling back from the fire as the vision shattered around me. The dagger slipped from my hand, clattering to the stone floor, and I barely registered the sound as I fought to catch my breath. The room came rushing back into focus, the orcs watching me with wide, expectant eyes.

Dex was there in an instant, his hands a firm anchor as I swayed. His voice wrapped around me like a protective shield, his eyes searching into mine with an intensity that made my pulse stutter. "What did you see?"

I blinked up at him in shocked terror, the words caught somewhere between my lungs and my throat. The weight of the vision still clung to me, tendrils of fear curling deep into my chest.

His brow creased, and his grip tightened just enough to ground me. "Cleo! What was the vision?"

I shook my head, the memory of blinding pain and endless darkness still too real. "Not here." My voice was barely audible, fear choking me.

Dex's jaw flexed, the muscles ticking beneath his skin as his head turned to glare at Arna. A silent conversation passed between them before his focus was back onto me. When he spoke, his voice carried the kind of authority that brooked no argument. "Excuse us, Cleo needs rest."

But as I held his gaze, the vision pulsed through me once more. The consuming light, the soul-deep agony, the terrifying emptiness that followed. And beneath it all, the voice that whispered again: *You must choose.*

OUR ECHOED footsteps followed us down the corridor, and I focused on the sound, trying to ground myself. The vision still swirled in my mind, sharp and vivid, the searing pain and suffocating loneliness replaying like a cruel loop. Dex walked beside me, his hand brushing mine every so often as if to remind me he was there, but I could feel the weight of his gaze itching under my skin. He was waiting, giving me space, but I knew it wouldn't last forever. I wasn't ready to talk about what I'd seen. Not when I was still processing what I had seen.

We entered a larger chamber, the low murmur of voices and the soft glow of torches filled the space. Guards moved around us, some glancing our way before quickly averting their eyes and continuing on their rounds. I stiffened, wrapping my arms around my chilled body as the whispers grew quieter. The weight of their stares pressed against me, and I couldn't help but wonder how much they knew. Had they already known about the ritual, or was it simply the lingering discomfort of a human standing at their Chieftain's side?

"They're still not used to seeing humans here," Dex said softly, breaking the silence. His voice was calm, but there was a protective edge to it, as if he was trying to ease my discomfort. "Especially not one like you."

I glanced up at him, forcing a small smile. "I'm going to pretend that was a compliment."

His lips curved into a smirk and he nudged me playfully with his shoulder. "A shaman with such strong magic. The Seer's words spread quickly about your affinity for healing, but they're still wary having spent generations hearing stories of betrayal and war. It will take time for them to fully accept you."

"And what if they don't?" I asked before I could stop myself. The question hung in the air between us.

"They will. Because you're more than just a shaman to them, Cleo. You're my mate. And as long as I stand with you, they will too."

His words were meant to reassure me, but the knot in my chest only tightened. I nodded, not trusting myself to speak. The despair of the vision tainted everything, but I couldn't tell him about it yet. We needed privacy.

Dex led me through another corridor, the air growing cooler as we descended into a quieter part of the stronghold. The sound of water echoed faintly, mingling with the steady drip of moisture from the stone walls. When we reached the end of the stairwell, Dex pushed open a heavy wooden door, revealing a vast, torchlit chamber.

"This is the Hall of Memory," he said as he stepped inside. "It's primarily a sanctuary for the clan's most vulnerable in times of danger. The magic here wards off intruders and seals the doors from the inside."

I hesitated in the doorway, the ancient magic that pressed down on me was too similar to the vision I'd just had. The distant stone columns were etched with runes I couldn't decipher, and rows of shelves lined the walls, filled with scrolls and carved tablets. It was like stepping into a living magical archive, a place where the past lingered in every corner.

I followed behind Dex with hesitant steps. His fingers brushing the tablets as we made our way down the shelves. "Every orc clan has its own history, its own stories. Here, we keep the records of the Blackfoot clan —the stories of our ancestors, the battles we've fought, the lands we've lost."

The detail was incredible, the orcs depicted in the tablets were proud and defiant, their faces marked with determination even in the face of overwhelming odds. My throat tightened as I traced the edge of one carving, its lines sharp against my fingertips.

Dex stopped in front of a larger tablet, his hand resting gently on its surface. The image showed a fierce battle, orc warriors locked in combat with shadowy figures that sent a chill of familiarity down my spine. "This was one of the first battles of the exile. The humans brought mages and knights to drive us from the forests. We fought for every inch of ground, but in the end, we were forced to retreat. Countless sacrificed their lives to buy time for the others to escape."

My fingers trembled as I reached out to touch the edge of the carving. "They fought for their families," I murmured, my voice barely above a whisper.

Dex nodded, his gaze distant as he looked at the tablet. "The clans were separated during the war. Some survived, but others..." His voice trailed off, and I felt the weight of his unspoken words.

"How many clans were lost?"

"We know of several that managed to escape, scattered across the Wild Lands. Two clans were run down as they tried to escape to the Marshlands, and three have fallen since then." His jaw tightened, and his hand curled into a fist. "We've always fought to protect what's ours. But now the balance has shifted. The darkness is spreading faster than ever before."

The shadows. The vision. My pulse quickened, and I clenched my hands to stop them from shaking. I could still feel the heat of the fire that had scorched through me while I watched myself die. I wanted to tell Dex, to share what I'd seen, but fear held me back. *What if he couldn't protect me from it? What if it was inevitable?* My fingers twisted together as I tried to slow my breathing. The memory of the vision felt like a thorn lodged in my chest, every breath catching on its edge. Speaking it would make it real, and I wasn't sure I could bear that, already on the edge of a panic attack.

But Dex's gaze didn't waver. His presence wrapped around me like a shield. He brought his hand to cup my chin, tilting my face up. "Whatever you saw—whatever it was—I need to know. I can't help you if you don't talk to me."

I swallowed hard, my throat dry as I searched his eyes for some way out. But there wasn't one. He wouldn't let me carry this alone, no matter how much I wanted to protect him from it. I took a shaky breath, closing my eyes as I tried to find the words.

"I saw two versions of the vision, playing out in front of me like I was just a spectator," I began, my voice trembling.

His brow furrowed, but he said nothing, letting me continue.

"The first, I saw the clan standing against the Darkness, forming a circle around the women and children. We stood side by side, bloody like we had been fighting. The Shadows kept coming and they consumed *everything*. They wrapped around you and pulled you in. I tried to hold on, but I wasn't strong enough. The darkness swallowed us all. I could only watch as everyone screamed and begged for help."

I paused to draw in deep breaths, my chest tightening as the memory of it surged back, the well of emotion constricting my throat. "There was nothing left, just a void, and it felt like it would swallow me too. The quietness of it was..." I trailed off, shaking my head.

His eyes were dark with fear, his hand dropping from my chin to grasp my hands instead. "And the second?"

I hesitated, the second vision flashing through my mind. It had been so vivid, so overwhelming, that even now, it felt like a part of me was still trapped in that moment, reliving the pain. "The second was different. The Darkness came, just like before. But this time, I stepped forward to meet it. My magic—it wasn't just inside me anymore. It was everywhere, wrapping around the clan, shielding them."

His gaze burned into mine, his expression haunted as he listened. "You mean *us*."

Thick tears clouded my vision. "I fought back, and my magic

destroyed the Darkness. It wiped it out completely, burned it away until there was nothing left-" My throat raw with emotion. *Breathe, Cleo.* I took a heavy breath, my chest heaving as I fought off the mounting panic.

"I saw myself glowing, burning from the inside out. The magic was too much and it turned on me. You shielded the clan from it, somehow you kept them safe as you watched me burn," A tear slipped down my cheek, and I quickly wiped it away. "When the pain stopped and light faded, there was nothing left of me but ash."

The silence that followed was thick. I couldn't bring myself to look at Dex, couldn't bear to see whatever emotion was written in his expression. But he didn't let go of my hands. His thumbs stroked over my knuckles, reminding me that he was still there.

"Don't be scared Cleo, we will find a way." His voice was desperate, doing nothing to calm my racing thoughts.

I nodded as the truth of his words settled over me. "I don't want to lose myself, Dex. But I don't want to lose you, or this clan, either. What if... what if I can't find another way?"

"There is always another way. I refuse to lose you when I have only just found you!"

I looked up at him, my eyes searching his for some kind of reassurance. "But what if the magic takes over, like it did in the vision? How can I stop it?"

He shook his head, his grip on my hands steady and unyielding. "Then I'll be there to pull you back. Always. You won't fight alone, Cleo. Not while I'm breathing. You pull on our bond and you hold on tight. That's what mates are for."

His words broke something inside me, a dam that had been holding back the weight of my fear and uncertainty. A sob slipped past my lips before I could stop it, and Dex pulled me into his arms without hesitation. His embrace was crushing, his hand cradled my head as he held me tight to his chest.

"I'm scared." My voice was muffled against his chest.

"I know. Whatever comes, we'll face it together."

I clung to him, the warmth of his presence slowly easing the cold knot of fear and despair in my chest. His words, his touch, his unwavering belief in me. They were enough to help keep the anxiety at bay.

"Chieftain?"

We turned to see an older orc woman standing at the entrance to the hall, her silver hair braided and adorned with small beads. Her eyes flicked to me, then back to Dex, her expression unreadable.

"Seer Arna sent me. She asks that you and the shaman join her in the healer's rooms. we have more injured."

THE AIR in the mountain stronghold carried a quiet stillness, a sense of anticipation before the inevitable storm of conflict. I had spent most of the day in the infirmary, tending to the sick and injured. The stronghold's infirmary was carved into the stone like much of the fortress, but despite the unyielding rock walls, the room was alive with warmth. The scent of herbs mixed with the faint tang of wood smoke softened the space. Healers moved quietly between the injured warriors, the elderly, and the children. It was a place where strength and vulnerability coexisted.

At first, being surrounded by so many lives depending on my help had been overwhelming. But as the days had passed, something shifted. I found myself connecting with the orcs—not just as their shaman, but as someone learning their hopes, their fears, and their quiet moments of resilience. Their stories, their laughter, even their pain—every piece of it wove into something larger than myself. It felt like a family.

Standing at the bedside of a young warrior, I inhaled deeply, grounding myself as I called on my magic to heal. His face was pale, his breath was shallow, the deep gash on his leg festering despite the other healers' best efforts.

I placed my hands over the wound and closed my eyes to reach for the threads of magic within me. By now, the sensation was becoming second nature, though it still resisted when I pulled on it. It was like weaving together strands of vitality, pulling them tight to mend what was broken. Green light glowed beneath my palms, flowing into the wound like water into parched earth.

The orc's life force pulsed beneath my fingers, steady but weak, and I focused on feeding it, strengthening it. Slowly, I wove the magic into his torn muscles and damaged tissue, binding it with care and pushing out the corruption until the jagged edges softened. The would quickly closed, leaving smooth, unmarred skin.

The warrior sighed in relief, his breathing evening out as the pain ebbed away. His amber eyes fluttered open, and he looked up at me with a mixture of awe and gratitude. "Thank you, shaman."

I offered a small, reassuring smile in return, grateful to be able to bring relief. "Rest now. You'll be back on your feet soon."

He nodded, the exhaustion pulling him back into a peaceful sleep. I stood, wiping the sweat from my brow, and glanced around the room. The firelight cast a soft glow across the infirmary, deepening the shadows and softening the hard lines of the stone. It felt like a place where the strength of the orc people was distilled—not just in their warriors, but in their mothers, their children, and their elders. Each of them a thread in a tapestry that had endured so much and refused to fray.

Moving from bed to bed, I continued my work, using the magic I was still learning to wield. With every life I touched, I felt myself forging deeper connections—not just as a healer, but as someone becoming a part of their story. Fathers, daughters, sisters, sons. Their lives not defined by the shadows gathering outside but by the moments of joy and resilience they carved out here, in the heart of the mountain.

An older woman with silver-threaded hair and sharp green eyes took my hand after I healed her aching joints, her grip surprisingly strong. "You've got the hands of a true healer, not just in your magic, but in your heart."

Her words caught me off guard, and I blinked, warmth blooming in my chest. "I'm learning," I said softly. "From all of you."

The woman chuckled, her laughter full of life as she pat my hand. "A shaman who listens? That's rare. Keep listening, girl—it'll serve you well."

I was beginning to understand that healing wasn't just about chan-neling magic. Every orc I touched reminded me that this wasn't just a duty. It was a bond, a quiet promise to do what I could for those who had already given so much.

A small tug at my sleeve pulled me from my thoughts. I turned to see a small face staring up at me, his golden eyes wide, black hair tousled. He couldn't have been more than eight or nine given his size and budding tusks.

"Shaman," he said softly, his voice filled with awe, "is it true you can talk to the earth?"

Smiling at him, I knelt down to his level. "In a way. I can feel the earth's magic, and sometimes, I can help it grow."

His eyes widened as he clutched to my arm with excitement. "Can you grow me some flowers?"

I chuckled, touched by his fascination. "Would you like to see?"

The boy nodded eagerly, his excitement infectious. I spotted a small plant on a nearby shelf. Bringing it to the boy, I summoned my magic. The green light flowed into the soil, and tiny flower buds emerged, unfurling in vibrant shades of purple and blue.

The boy hugged the pot tightly to his chest as though it held the entire world. "It's beautiful!"

I smiled softly. "The earth's magic is everywhere, you just have to listen for it."

"Can I be a shaman too?"

I laughed, ruffling his hair. "Maybe one day. But for now, you've got other things to learn—like how to mind your mother."

He grinned mischievously and ran back to his mother's bedside with the flowerpot. Watching his excitement, I felt a quiet kind of hope take root in my chest.

By the time I reached the final bed, the infirmary had grown quieter. A young warrior lay there, his arm tightly bandaged. His body tense with pain, but he managed a faint smile when I approached.

"Shaman," he greeted me with a tired nod.

I knelt beside him, unwrapping the bandage to reveal the raw, angry wound. "Let me take care of this," I said gently, placing my hands over the injury.

The magic came easily now, a familiar rhythm that pulsed through my fingertips. I wove it carefully into the wound, pulling the threads of life together until the flesh knitted cleanly. The warrior let out a soft sigh, his muscles relaxing as the pain ebbed.

"Thank you."

"You're welcome," I said, pulling my hands away with a soft smile. "You'll be back to training soon."

He chuckled faintly. "Good. We have much to prepare for."

The fires had burned low, casting flickering shadows across the beds. Exhaustion tugged at me, but it was the kind of exhaustion that came with finding my purpose. These orcs were becoming my people.

CHAPTER 28
DEX

The cool mountain breeze swept across the terrace, carrying with it the distant rumble of an oncoming storm. Cleo stood at the edge, her frame silhouetted against the dying light. The wind tugged at her braid, curls tumbling free. Her shoulders were tense, her head bowed as though the weight of the world had sunk into her bones. She'd just come back from the gardens where Grath said the earth's magic pulsed the strongest he'd ever felt. She spent hours there each day, searching for something—answers, control, peace perhaps. But tonight, the tight lines of her posture told me she hadn't found it.

I approached quietly, the soft steps of my boots almost silent on the stone. Her back straightened, she always felt me before I even touched her, but the way she braced herself made me want to shake her. Shake the fear and doubt from her until she could see what I saw. What I knew.

"You're still doubting yourself, my beautiful mate," I said softly, though there was a darker edge to my voice. I hated seeing her like this. It twisted something deep inside me that wanted to destroy anything that dared make her feel this way.

She didn't respond, didn't even turn. Her gaze was fixed on the horizon, the distant peaks stretching endlessly, as if the answers she sought lay somewhere in the fading light. When she finally turned to me the vulnerability I saw in her eyes about bought me to my knees.

"What if I can't control it, Dex?" she whispered, her voice trembling. "If I use this magic in battle and I pull on the wrong thing and hurt someone..." Her voice broke, and she took a shaky breath. "What if I become like them?"

Did she really think that was possible? Her fear of becoming like the Dark Ones wasn't new, but hearing it aloud—hearing the way her voice cracked on the words—made it impossible to ignore. My mate, the woman I would kill for, was terrified of *herself.* And worse, I didn't know how to fix it.

"You're not going to turn into one of them," I said as I stepped closer, my hands gripping her arms tightly to anchor her. To keep her from slipping into the spiral of doubt. "You're not like them. You could *never* be like them."

She didn't believe me. I could see it in the way her lips pinched together, the way her fingers clung to my forearms as though I were the only thing keeping her upright. "But I feel it," she whispered, her voice breaking. "That raw, dark power... it's right there, and it's waiting for me to use it. It's so seductive when it calls to me. What if I'm not strong enough to resist? What if we're desperate enough, and I open that door? And then what? What happens when I lose control!"

The memory of her vision surfaced like a cruel reminder: the shadows consuming her, or her magic blazing to defend us, leaving nothing but scorched earth where she had once stood. The prophecy weighed heavy on my shoulders, its promise of destruction clawing at my mind. *Was this the fate we couldn't escape? My people wiped from Ostelan, or worse—my mate destroyed, consumed by her own power as she fought to protect my people?*

I cupped her face, forcing her to meet my eyes. "You won't lose control," I said fiercely, my voice shaking with the force of my conviction. "Because I'll be with you. When the darkness pulls at you, you draw on me. You pull from my strength, Cleo. I'm your mate. It's my responsibility to keep you safe."

Her lip quivered and her hands fisted in my shirt, clinging to me like a lifeline. "Promise me you won't let me hurt anyone. If something happens, if I can't control it, you'll do whatever it takes to stop me. Even if—"

I tightened my hands on her arms, clenching my jaw so hard it felt like my teeth might shatter. She was asking the impossible. How could I promise that? How could I even consider it? She was my mate. *My life.* The one thing in this world I couldn't lose. How was I supposed to sacrifice her, even to save others?

"Don't ask me for that." I growled in warning.

"You have to, Dex. If it comes down to it, you have to protect the clan. You have to protect them from me." Her eyes shimmered with tears.

A rage burned deep in my gut. Running a frustrated hand through my hair I stepped away, pacing the terrace, feared my anger would scare her. "You're asking me to choose between you and them," I growled dangerously, "Do you even realize what you're saying? You're my mate, Cleo! *My mate.* There is no choice!"

Her fear and frustration tipped the scales, and angry tears spilled over, racing down her cheeks, "But there has to be! If I lose control and I become dangerous, you have to stop me. *Promise me.*"

I stared at her, the crazy woman who had become my entire world, and felt something dark and feral unfurl. "No!" My voice was thick with barely restrained rage. "Do you hear me? I'll kill anyone—anything— that comes close to making you lose control. I'll rip them apart with my bare hands if I have to. But I will not loose you."

Cleo's lips trembled as she looked away from me, shaking her head dismissively. "You can't save me from myself."

"Watch me," I stepped closer until there was no space between us. My hands roughly grabbed her face, my fingers pressing into her soft skin. "You're *mine*, Cleo. My duty. My mate. I'll do whatever it takes to protect you. From the shadows, from the world, or from yourself. I don't care what it takes."

Her breath hitched, and I kissed her fiercely, pouring everything I couldn't articulate into the press of my lips. Love, desperation, fear—it all bled into that kiss, a vow as much as it was a plea. I finally pulled back breathless, and pressed my lips to her forehead. "Don't ask me to promise what I can't give. I'll fight for you, Cleo. To my last breath."

Cleo twisted her hands around the leather of my armor, clutching me close while her tears soaked into my chest. "I'm so scared, Dex," she whispered, her voice trembling. "I don't want to hurt anyone."

"You won't, I'll be there. Every step. Every battle. You won't ever fight this alone."

Dusk fell and the shadows crept closer, but I continued to hold her trembling body, stroking lazily across her back in comfort. I knew one thing for certain. I would do whatever it took to keep her safe. Even if it destroyed me.

CHAPTER 29
CLEO

I eased back, clinging desperately to the fragile thread of control as emotions surged beneath my skin like a storm threatening to break free. Below, the warm glow of fires illuminated the terraces, and orcs were bustling with the rhythm of an evening steeped in resilience. The sharp clang of metal pierced the air as warriors sharpened their blades. Children's laughter echoed through the air, a fleeting innocence that seemed too delicate to exist against the ever-present shadows gathering in the valley below.

They were a proud, strong people, and yet there was an undeniable fragility woven into the fabric of their existence. The weight of their survival sat on my shoulders—a burden I hadn't asked for but couldn't shake. They looked to me, their shaman, to protect them. They believed I could save them.

"They trust too much in the prophecy," I murmured, my eyes fixed on the children chasing one another across the terraces. "They put too much faith in me."

Dex's presence was a solid, steady warmth beside me, his golden eyes reflecting the firelight as he watched me. He didn't speak right away, and when he did, his voice carried the weight of unspoken truths. "The prophecy is important to our people," he began, his words careful.

"Shamans have always been essential to our survival, to the balance we keep with the earth. But that doesn't mean the orcs can't fight their own battles. We've been fighting long before you came here, and we'll keep fighting."

I turned to him, half of his face was hidden in shadow, but his eyes burned intensely. "The prophecy... it's just a guide. But you—" Dex's voice was sharp, his gaze piercing as he looked at me"—You're real. They believe in you because you've given them reason to."

I had spent so much of my life running from who I was, how could I be the one to bring balance to a world teetering on the edge? It felt impossible and it infuriated me. My anger sparked defiance—a small, stubborn flame that was tired of watching people suffer. If I couldn't find strength in myself, I'd need to find it in the faces of those who believed.

"They don't see what I see. They don't see the darkness that lives inside me, waiting to take over. They see someone strong, someone who can save them, but I don't know if I can be that person. Sometimes my magic feels like it's corrupted"

Dex took my hand, his voice was softer than I'd expected as he tried to sooth my doubts. "They don't see the darkness because it doesn't define you. You've shown them strength—not just with your magic, but with who you are. You've healed them, fought for them, given them hope. That's what they believe in, Cleo. Not a prophecy. *You.*"

The raw conviction in his voice took my breath away, but it was the vulnerability beneath it that struck me hardest. I saw a flicker of fear buried deep behind the protective walls he built around himself. He was terrified of losing this fight, of watching me be consumed by the same darkness that had taken so much from his people. It wasn't just the prophecy that haunted him—it was me.

"You're scared too," I said softly, my fingers tightening around his. It wasn't a question, and the slight flicker in his gaze told me I was right.

He pressed his lips into a thin line, and I thought he might deny it, but he exhaled shakily and tugged me into his side. "Of course I am. You think I don't see the burden you're carrying? The way it eats at you, the way it makes you doubt yourself? You think I don't feel it every time you pull away, every time you look at me?"

Gods, I was so sick of crying, of feeling like I was out of control. I've never felt so weak as I did in this moment, his words burrowed deep into my heart and I couldn't stop the tears that burned at the corners of my eyes.

"I'm scared of losing you," he continued, his voice breaking on the words. "I'm scared of watching you slip away, of not being able to protect you. I'm scared of the prophecy, of the darkness, of all of it, but I'm mostly scared of you giving up on yourself."

The rawness in his voice splintered something inside me, and I swallowed hard, my chest tight. I didn't know what to say, didn't know how to respond to the overwhelming emotions roiling inside. I reached for him desperately, my hand trembling as I touched his face, tracing the strong line of his jaw. His golden eyes burned, and I felt the strength of his emotions like a tidal wave crashing over me.

"I'm scared too," I admitted, my voice barely above a whisper. "I don't want to let them down. I don't want to let you down."

"You won't," Dex said fiercely, his grip tight on my waist. "You're stronger than you think, Cleo. You're an orc shaman—your strength comes from the earth and your clan. Whatever happens, we'll be right beside you. I'll be right beside you."

His words should have eased the weight on my chest, but they didn't. Every mention of the prophecy, every declaration of faith, felt like another chain around my heart. How could I live up to their expectations when I couldn't even believe in myself to not hurt them. But as I looked into Dex's eyes, seeing the fear, the love and the desperation swirling there, and I realized he wasn't asking me to be perfect. He wasn't asking me to carry this alone. He was just asking me to *try*. And maybe, that was enough.

I ENTERED our room late that evening, the scent of the gardens still clinging to me after several hours of meditation. I found Dex already inside, leaning against the wall, his arms crossed. The moment his eyes met mine, the tension in his body softened, his gaze holding the kind of warmth I had come to crave in these private moments, studying me in a way that felt like he saw straight through me, unraveling my every thought.

"Feel better?" he asked, his voice a low, rough rumble that rolled over my skin like distant thunder.

I nodded, sinking onto a stool, exhaustion creeping through my limbs. "I'm starting to think I'll never stop doubting myself."

Dex pushed off the wall with a slow, predatory grace, crossing the room to stand behind me. His hands settled on my shoulders, the heat of his palms seeping through the fabric of my dress.

"You will. Give yourself some grace, this is all still very new for you."

I angled my head back to look at my mate, feeling the familiar swell of affection rise within me. This man was a force of nature that had become my anchor in a world constantly threatening to pull me under.

"How can you be so sure?"

His lips curved into the smallest smile, and he leaned over me, pressing his lips to my nose in a quick peck. His sweet affection was a delicious conflict to his possessive nature. "Because I've seen your strength. And if you ever doubt it, pull from mine."

A soft smile tugged at my lips, and I reached up, my fingers tracing the edge of his jaw, feeling the roughness of his stubble. "What did I do to deserve you?"

His chuckle was quick, his breath fanning against my cheek. "I ask myself the same question every day."

I sighed into him, letting his arms wrap around me from behind, his solid chest pressing against my back. His embrace felt like home. The world outside faded, leaving just the two of us in the quiet hum of our connection.

I met his gaze over my shoulder, and the intensity in his golden eyes sent a delicious shiver down my spine. There was no mask here, no warlord or Chieftain, just Dex. The orc who claimed every inch of my heart.

His fingers traced a featherlight path up my bare arm, leaving a scorching heat in their wake. "My precious mate." I closed my eyes and leaned into his touch, letting the words wrap around me.

"I'm here." My voice was a whisper, a promise.

Dex leaned in slowly, his lips brushing against my temple, lingering there as if memorizing the feel of me beneath him. His hands found my waist, his thumbs pressing in slow, soothing circles that pulled me deeper into him. He set my skin ablaze with such a simple touch, a fire simmering beneath the surface.

Pulling me up into his arms effortlessly, and I rest my hands against his chest, feeling the powerful beat of his heart beneath my palms. That steady pulse was all I needed in this moment. My doubts melted, replaced by the overwhelming need to be closer, to drown in his touch.

His thumb grazed my lower lip with agonizing slowness, and I watched as hunger clouded his eyes. The anticipation between us stretched, thick and heady, until I could no longer stand it. I leaned in, brushing my lips over his, tentative at first, testing. He was quick to deepen the kiss, his tongue battling mine with a passion that had heat pooling low in my core.

His mouth moved against mine, teasing, claiming, and I felt myself surrendering completely as his hands roamed my curves, tracing my spine, pulling me impossibly closer until there was no space left between us. I gasped into his mouth, and he swallowed the sound, his responding growl vibrating through me, low and possessive.

His grip shifted and rough palms slid under my dress, to skim up my thighs, leaving a wicked fire in their wake. Goosebumps skittered across my skin and I arched against him, seeking more. I was desperate for more of his touches, for the way he made me feel cherished and desired all at once.

Dex pulled back just enough to rest his forehead against mine, his breathing uneven. "I love you." he whispered.

My chest tightened, the words sinking into my soul. "I love you too," I murmured, threading my fingers through his hair, holding him close.

With a worshiping touch that left me breathless, he lifted me in his arms and took quick strides to the bed, his hands exploring every inch of me as though I were something sacred. His touch soothed the tension I carried, each caress melting away my doubts, replacing them with an aching need.

Dex trailed his mouth down my neck, teeth grazing my skin in a way that made my pulse stutter. Rough hands ghosted up under my dress, dragging across my thighs, hips, and stomach before cupping my breast, his thumb circling my hardened nipple. I moaned and arched into him at his gentle exploration of my body. This was new and exciting territory for us, our intimate moments were hurried and rough, and despite loving it, I had been craving some softness from my mate.

Rocking back on his knees, he fumbled with his armor straps, and I followed him up, placing featherlight kisses along his chest, my tongue tracing the raised ridges of old scars, feeling the tension in his body coil tighter beneath my touch.

I trailed lower, my mouth hovering over the waistband of his leathers. Satisfaction burned hot in me at the hunger in his eyes, the way he groaned as I flicked my tongue out lave against his heated skin, savoring his breathy groans.

"You want to play, little mate?"

Humming in response, I unfastened the heavy buckles, delighting as I watched his muscles flex beneath my fingertips. The weight of his armor crashed to the floor, the dagger clattering loudly against the stone. I stuck out my tongue, swirling it around the swollen head of his cock, smiling at the groan rumbling from his chest as he throbbed under my ministrations.

"You look so fucking pretty on your knees for me."

Dex rocked his hips forward, pressing the head of his cock to my lips and smearing them with a bead of arousal that I eagerly licked up. Parting my lips again, I took the tip in my mouth, laving my tongue against the slit, coaxing another growl from his heaving chest, my jaw aching as I fought to take him deeper into my throat.

A strangled moan escaped him, and his hand fisted my hair, patience crumbling as he thrust shallowly into my mouth. I fought the reflex to gag as he brushed the back of my throat, swallowing around him, the filthy noise drawing another guttural groan from deep in his chest.

"Fucking hell, Cleo... your throat is almost as perfect as your cunt." His voice was hoarse, his fingers flexing tighter in my hair, pushing further into me and making my eyes water.

I burned to say something equally filthy in return, but my mouth was too full of him, too preoccupied with the way he slid over my tongue with increasing urgency. The obscene sounds filling the space around us only fanned the flames building between my thighs, and I rocked in place, desperate for friction. My nails dug into his muscled thighs, encouraging him to take more, to claim my mouth as roughly as he had my body.

"Look at you, so eager to choke on my cock," he rasped as his hips snapped forward. He held me there, not allowing me to retreat, forcing my throat to flutter around him. "Fuck, that's it. Take it."

With a growl Dex pulled back and I gasped for breath, spit trailing down my chin. He didn't give me time to recover, tugging me to my feet and showing me onto the bed with a roughness that had me feral for him. I landed on my chest with a bounce, my breath catching as I watched his claws make quick work of my dress, leaving me bare under his hungry gaze.

His hands traced possessively over my ass before roughly plunging two thick fingers into my slick heat. A startled cry escaped my lips, the wet slide of his fingers sent chills running across my body, but it wasn't enough—I needed more.

Dex withdrew, bringing his glistening fingers to his lips, sucking them clean with a satisfied hum that made me ache. He stroked himself, coating his thick length in our combined fluids before he pressed against my drenched core.

The stretch was overwhelming, a delicious burn that had me gasping, his sheer size forcing me open inch by inch. My body fought the intrusion, but the slickness of my arousal eased the way, and soon he was buried deep inside, filling me completely.

His deep thrust knocked the air from my lungs, and my arms gave way as my face pressed into the furs, a broken moan escaping me. He ground his hips with each thrust, reaching depths that had my toes curling, my orgasm building with staggering speed as he bullied against my g-spot. The sharp crack of his palm against my ass had me bucking against him, chasing the sweet sting of his dominance.

"Tell me who you belong to, little shaman," he demanded, his voice dark, dangerous.

"I'm yours, Dex!" I sobbed, my vision white as pleasure tore through me as my inner muscles fluttered around him. The overwhelming sensation of being stretched and filled sent me spiraling, hitting me in waves that left me trembling and weak.

His thrusts stuttered as he chased his own release. He drove himself deep with a growl, flooding me with cum, grinding slow, shallow thrusts in me as he rode out the aftershocks.

Later, as I lay curled in his arms, the weight of my doubts felt distant, the ever-present tension melting under his touch. His arms were wrapped around me, making me feel safe in a way nothing else could. And in that quiet moment, with the steady rhythm of his breathing and the warmth of his body wrapped around mine, I knew that no matter what came next, with Dex, I was home.

CHAPTER 30
CLEO

The first light of dawn seeped through the furs, casting a soft glow over the room. I lay still, cocooned in the warmth of the bed with Dex. The quiet rhythm of his breathing beside me was a comforting presence. I turned my head to take in the sight of him—his strong chest rising and falling with each breath, his dark hair mussed from sleep.

In moments like this, when the world was still, the weight of everything fell away. There was only him and me, tangled together in the warmth of the bed, a haven against the world outside. I hadn't planned on growing this close to him. Our connection had started as something practical, born out of survival and necessity. But it quickly deepened into something more—trust, respect, and love.

I carefully slipped out of bed, wrapping a blanket around my body to ward off the morning chill. I didn't want to wake him. I needed a moment alone to gather my thoughts. I padded across the room to the basin in the corner and splashed water on my face, catching a glimpse of my reflection in the mirror. I hardly recognized the girl staring back. There was a hardness in my eyes now, a weight in my features that hadn't been there before.

I wasn't sure what I was searching for in the mirror—perhaps some sign of the woman the orcs believed me to be, the shaman they placed their hopes in. But all I saw was myself, vulnerable and afraid, wrapped in a mantle I wasn't certain I deserved.

The prophecy loomed over me with each passing day. I could feel its pressure, growing heavier, more suffocating. The clan looked to me as the one destined to save them, but I wasn't sure I could live up to their expectations. I wasn't sure if I could harness the power inside me without it tearing me apart.

Behind me I heard the soft rustle of blankets and the low, familiar rumble of Dex's voice. "You're up early." His tone was rough with sleep.

I shifted my gaze from the mirror to the figure in the bed. Dex lay on his back, the blankets draped loosely over his waist, leaving his massive green chest exposed. His dark eyes, still heavy with sleep, watched me with a warmth that sent a shiver through my body. There was something about the way he looked at me that always stole my breath.

Dex's gaze darkened as he watched me discard the blanket and climb onto the bed to straddle his waist. The cool morning air brushed against my bare skin, but it was quickly replaced by the heat of his body below me.

I leaned forward and splayed my hands over his chest, feeling the steady rise and fall of his breathing, the warmth of his skin. His hands slid up my thighs, rough and calloused from years of battle, but gentle in their touch. His fingers gripped my hips, pulling me closer.

We were both still, the air between us thick with anticipation, the bond between us humming with energy. I felt my breath hitch as I felt the tension in his body, the way he responded to my closeness, the way his hands tightened on my hips, pulling me even closer.

"My beautiful mate."

My lips brushed against his in a slow, lingering kiss. His hand slid up my back, and I melted into him, my body pressing against his as the heat between us grew.

He traced the curves of my waist, the line of my spine, before lifting me to move the furs draped across his waist. His large hands finally settled at the small of my back, pulling me down to grind against him, coating him quickly in my juices. I gasped when his lips moved to my neck, his kisses leaving a trail of prickling heat in their wake.

I tangled my fingers in his hair and rolled my hips greedily against his eager cock, feeling the growing tension in his body as he responded to my touch. His breath stuttered as he watched me ride him, hands tightening on my waist to help guide my movements, his control slipping. I continued to grind against his hard length until the sparks of a climax began to build, ghosting the edge of my vision. My hands turned from adoring to desperate as I shifted further back, trying to slide him inside my aching core.

Dex growled and claimed my mouth with an aggressive nip to my bottom lip before thrusting his tongue against my own. His passion told me he was burning to take control, to roll me over and lay claim to my body over and over until sleep took us in exhaustion. I felt his fist clench against the furs in restraint, submitting to my desire for dominance.

I shifted up on my knees and slipped my small hand between my thighs, grasping his thick cock and slotting him at my entrance. I bit my lip as I rolled my hips, moaning as he slowly sunk into me. The burn of his enormous cock stretching my cunt to its limits slowed my decent as I ease him further in, inch by inch. The taste of copper flooded my mouth, and I realized he had broken the sensitive flesh of my lip.

Dex's fingers entwined mine, and he brought my hand to his lips in a soft caress. "Fuck, look at you. Always so wet for me." He groaned, fighting his need to thrust up and fully sink into my body.

I pulled our hands up to my chest, encouraging Dex to palm my sensitive breast, throwing my head back in a sigh when he pinched my nipple. I ground the rest of the way onto his cock, burying him completely within my body, ripping a feral growl from his chest. The vibrations traveled to my clit and made me throb harder around him. A desperation to pull more of those sounds from him dominated my focus. *I did this to him...*

I felt tiny sitting on my massive mate, but every bit as powerful as he had told me as he took me apart in the library. My thighs burned from the stretch to reach either side of his hips and I dragged my hand to his lower stomach for support, using the leverage to roll my hips more aggressively as I claimed him. The raw intensity in his gaze sent a wicked heat curling through me, the weight of it pressing against my chest like an unspoken command. Having him beneath me like this, letting me take control, felt like both a challenge and a gift, and I intended to savor every second of it.

He was holding himself back, I could see it in the way his fingers dug into my flesh, the fine tremor running through his arms as he resisted the instinct to take over, to flip me onto my back and ravage me like the beast he was. His restraint made me ache and made the bond between us thrum with an intoxicating heat that threatened to consume me. I rolled my hips, feeling the stretch of him, the way he filled me perfectly, igniting every nerve as he groaned beneath me.

The thrust of his hips shattered my rhythm, a desperate bid to reclaim control, and I gasped at the sudden intensity. Dex froze beneath me, his muscles tensing as his lips parted in a dark, possessive snarl. I saw the flicker of frustration in his eyes, the battle within him raging between submission and dominance. The power I wielded in this moment was intoxicating.

Leaning into the darker side of our connection, the side he had so willingly introduced me to, I trailed my fingers up his abdomen, feeling the taut muscles jump beneath my touch. My nails grazed his skin, leaving faint scratches along his heaving chest, and I felt his grip on my hips tighten, his breath catching in his throat. The confident smirk playing at his lips told me he expected me to surrender, to give in to his dominance, but this time, I wanted to push him, to claim him as fiercely as he had claimed me.

My teeth sunk into my raw bottom lip as I let my hand slide higher, wrapping my fingers around his thick throat, pressing lightly at first, feeling the rapid pulse beneath my palm. A shocked breath stuttered out of him, a breathy, broken curse slipping past his lips. His gaze burned into mine, a flash of something raw and vulnerable crossing his features, and I reveled in it. Rolling my hips harder, I sank back down onto him again, the delicious drag of his cock against my clenching walls sent plea-sure racing through my veins.

"Well, this is a surprise..." he rasped.

I smirked as my fingers tightened around his throat, feeling the power coil in my veins. "Do you want me to stop?" I teased, my voice dripping with challenge.

Dex's eyes flared with a dark heat, his chest rose and fell in ragged breaths. "Gods no, little mate," he groaned, his voice desperate. *"Fuck me. Claim me."*

The weight of his surrender sent a wicked thrill that emboldened me. I flexed my fingers experimentally, feeling the way his pulse quickened under my grip. My lips curled into a filthy smile at the tortured whine that escaped his chest. Satisfaction curled dark and heady knowing I could unravel him like this, make him lose himself completely at my touch.

A deep flush crept up his neck, his cheeks tinged with embarrassment, but his breathless chuckle turned into a shuddering groan as my nails raked over his chest, leaving thin red trails across the hard ridges of muscle. I claimed him with every deliberate mark, every clench of my inner muscles around his cock. His hands fisted at my waist, his grip desperate, and he thrust up into me with a devastating force that sent scorching heat spiraling through my core. I flexed my fingers tighter around his throat, cutting off his air just enough to watch his control unravel, thread by thread.

"Cleo," he choked—his primal need to reclaim dominance clashing against his yearning to surrender. His eyes were wild and dark with frustration and longing. Submission had never looked so utterly delicious.

I lifted myself off him, my body teasing the loss before I leaned forward, ghosting my breath over his parted lips. His chest heaved beneath me as his eyes pleaded for more, but I held him there, hovering just out of reach. "You're not in control here, Chieftain," I whispered, my voice laced with silk and steel. "Be a good boy and hold still." The command rolled off my tongue like a spell, and the way his pupils dilated had me panting.

A strangled whimper tore from him as I slid back down, my hips rolling to take him deep in one fluid motion, enveloping him in a heat that left us both feral. His entire body shuddered beneath me, and I loosened my grip just enough for him to drag in a ragged breath, the sound desperate and raw. His eyes locked onto mine, burning with restraint, but he stayed still, every muscle in his massive frame trembling with the sheer effort of obedience.

"Fuck." he rasped, voice strained. His desperation was electrifying.

A triumphant smirk curled my lips as I rolled my hips in slow, deliberate circles, feeling him throb in response. My own pleasure coiled tighter with each motion, surging with the intoxicating power I wielded over him. "That's it, Dex," I cooed, "Stay still for me. Let me take what I want."

My movements became more urgent as I let myself get lost in the overwhelming sensation. Heat flushed through my body, a delicious burn that spread from my core outward, the intoxicating stretch of taking him filling every inch of me. Dex's thick cock dragged against my inner walls with every deliberate roll of my hips, igniting sparks of pleasure that left me gasping and desperate for more. The sheer eroticism of dominating such a massive orc, having him beneath me like this, sent a delicious shiver of power through me, and I couldn't stop the breathy moan slipping from my lips.

Dex's fingers dug into my thighs with a bruising pressure as he fought against his own instincts, shivering beneath me as I took what I wanted from him. He was a warrior, a Chieftain, a leader—yet here, now, he was *mine*. My hips moved faster, harder, slamming down onto him as I chased my high, the friction sending white-hot pleasure coursing through me.

"Hands on the bed," I moaned, my voice commanding. "You cum when I tell you to, do you understand?"

Dex's breath hitched, a raw, desperate whimper escaping him as his palms slammed against the furs, gripping them tightly until his knuckles turned white.

"Such a good fucking boy for me, Dex." the praise rolled off my tongue with ease.

A final, devastating roll of my hips had me shattering, pleasure crashing over me in blinding waves. I ground down on him as I rode out my orgasm, my slick coating his cock as my walls clenched impossibly tight around him. A guttural growl ripped from Dex's chest as he fought to stave off his own release. His claws tore through the furs in frustration, but I didn't stop. I kept moving, teasing, torturing, determined to break him completely.

"Give me your hand." I demanded, rolling my hips with sinful precision. I pulled my hand from his throat, taking his much larger one in mine and bringing it to my lips for a soft kiss. The sight of his rough, battle-worn fingers trembling fed this dark, possessive part of me.

I pulled his fingers into my mouth, my tongue tracing along the tips, nipping and sucking with a deliberate slowness, never once breaking eye contact. His hungry eyes devoured me as I spasmed around him. I guided his hand down my jaw, dragging it over my throat, my collarbone, before pressing it firmly to my breast. He groaned as his fingers grasped my flesh on reflex, his grip tightening when I pressed his palm harder against me.

A wicked smile curled my lips as my fingers circled his wrist, tugging him lower, dragging his touch down my soft stomach. His breath shuddered out as his fingers brushed over my tight curls. The heat that pooled between my thighs made me arch into him with a needy sigh.

"Touch me, Dex. Make me cum again while I fuck you."

His eyes flashed, grip tightening possessively as his fingers found my aching clit, circling it with a desperation that made my legs shake. I shifted my weight, bringing my hands behind me to brace against his thighs. I used my knees to rise and drop down onto his cock, pushing him deeper. Sparks of pleasure exploded behind my eyes as he slammed into that devastatingly perfect spot with every thrust.

Dex's chest heaved as his thumb rubbed tight circles against my clit. His eyes were pleading, begging for mercy. I wanted to hear him say it, to break him down completely. I rode him faster my back arching, my head falling back as I lost myself in the feeling of him.

"Please, Cleo! *Please, please, please—*" His body shook with the effort of holding himself still beneath me.

I rolled my head forward and drank in the sight of him. His cheeks flushed a deep crimson, sweat glistening on his brow, his eyes swimming with complete submission. The vision of my powerful mate unraveling beneath me sent a fresh surge of arousal crashing through me. *Oh, we finally had found the edge.*

"Doing such a good job for me." I moaned. My voice trembled with my own impending release, each word punctuated by the lewd slap of our bodies meeting. "Do you think you deserve it?"

His broken whine was my undoing. My fingers curled into his thighs as my core fluttered.

"Please—"

"Cum with me!"

My cry tore from my throat as he finally broke, thrusting up into me with a desperate, punishing rhythm. His cock pulsing as my orgasm ripped through me and I felt myself quiver and tighten around him, the wetness between us flooding out, coating his thighs in a slick sheen of our arousal.

He rolled forward to sit, burying his face in my chest, panting heavily as I collapsed bonelessly against him, my fingers carding through his sweat-damp hair.

I pressed a lingering kiss to his forehead, feeling his ragged breath against my skin. "Mine." I whispered. Satisfaction curled through me as I ran my fingers down his trembling back. "Always mine. My perfect mate."

For a long moment, we stayed like that, our bodies still entwined, our breathing slowing as the intensity of the moment ebbed, and I showered his face with soft kisses, my body still humming with aftershocks.

Dex slid his hand up to tangle in my hair, his claws scratching against my scalp just the way I liked it. Our bond went beyond anything I'd imagined, woven into the essence of who we were becoming together. This wasn't like our previous moments together. I felt him through the bond deep in my chest, in my very being. It was as if he had become part of me.

After a while, I shifted away from his body with soft groan of discomfort, our fluids sticky between my thighs as I collapsed beside him on the bed, completely spent. He turned onto his side, propping himself up on one elbow, fingers tracing idle patterns on my shoulder.

"I didn't hurt you, did I?" I said, uncertainty taking over as I took in all the feral scratches I had left on his body. His chest bore the worst of them, blood pebbling in the deeper gouges, where I had dug in my nails.

"No. That was like an out of body experience. I didn't know I would be into that, it was incredible. You're incredible." He murmured shyly, continuing to trace patterns up onto my collarbone.

My cheeks pulled up into a shy smile as I held his gaze, and I ran my hands lazily through his hair, gently scraping my nails against his scalp.

Dex was preening under my attention, the rumble of his voice reminding me of a very large cat purring in satisfaction.

"We are destined for great things together. I can feel it. We'll lead the clan into a new age."

I smiled at him, but doubt coiled like a shadow in the corner of my mind as he spoke. I closed my eyes, letting his words wash over me. I wanted to live in this moment. To believe him, to believe in myself, but the uncertainty gnawed at me, eating away my confidence.

I let out a shaky breath and looked away. "I hope so... but I can't help but worry. If I pull on our bond, I might open you up to my power. I'm afraid to pull you into this darkness with me."

His hand settled gently on my arm, his touch a quiet reassurance against the swirling storm of doubts. "You won't hurt me. You've already done more for this clan than anyone ever imagined possible. You healed our warriors. You've protected us in ways no one else could. The prophecy may say you're the shaman who will lead us back to the valley, but this isn't just about the prophecy. Who you are is rooted in our destiny as much as in me, and our bond." His voice was a soft whisper.

"I've only ever been able to control my healing magic. The rest is like trying to hold water in my hands. I can feel it, but the moment I try to grasp it, it flares and slips away."

His hands cradled my face, his thumb brushing my cheek in a soft, steady rhythm. I leaned into his touch, allowing the warmth to send a wave of reassurance through my frayed nerves. "You're doing the best you can. That's all anyone can ask. I believe in you, Cleo. And so does the clan."

I closed my eyes, letting his words wrap around me like a shield, anchoring me in the safety of his presence. I breathed him in, the scent of leather, earth, and something uniquely Dex filling my senses. Here, in the quiet moments between battles and burdens, I allowed myself to believe. Even if only for tonight.

CHAPTER 31
CLEO

As the morning passed, I wandered through the stronghold, my steps slower than usual as I took in the daily life of the orcs around me. There was a rhythm to it all, one I'd grown accustomed to, though I still didn't feel like I fully belonged. The warriors were hard at work, their grunts and the clash of weapons filling the air as they trained in the courtyard. The children's laughter rang out along the halls, a light sound that contrasted with the tension that pulsed within the keep, each day drawing the looming darkness closer.

Some of the women were gathered around the fires, preparing meals, mending clothes, and talking quietly amongst themselves, their conversations held more than just idle gossip. These caretakers were the clan's backbone, silent anchors holding their people together, while the warriors fought and the leaders made decisions. Yet despite the role I'd grown into, I sometimes still felt like I was watching from the outside, a stranger looking in on something I didn't fully understand.

Everywhere I went, I felt their eyes on me. Some of the orcs watched with awe, others with curiosity, and a few with uncertainty or suspicion. I understood why—ever since the prophecy had been revealed, ever since I'd been named the shaman meant to lead them back to the valley, I was no longer an outsider; I was their hope against the dark magic that threatened their way of life. I couldn't shake the feeling that I was an imposter.

"Shaman, will you join us?"

I hesitated, unsure. I'd been keeping to myself more and more lately, afraid that any sign of doubt or weakness would undermine the faith they'd put in me. But something in the woman's eyes reassured me.

They made space for me on one of the large stones surrounding the fire, the flames warming my skin. These women had an air of wisdom about them, and as I settled into the circle, I could feel their quiet strength. These weren't just any orcs—these were the elders, women who had seen generations rise and fall, who had endured more than I could imagine.

The woman who had called to me was older, her gray hair neatly braided down her back, the lines on her face marking her many years. Despite her age, her eyes were sharp and clear, full of life and knowledge. She smiled at me warmly, though I sensed something probing in her gaze, as if she were looking beyond the surface, assessing me.

"How are you? We've heard rumors of your struggles with offensive magic."

They all knew about my struggles. *Great.* The orcs had placed so much faith in me, and admitting my failures felt like betraying that trust. But I couldn't lie, not to these women who had lived through more than I ever would. There was no point in pretending I had everything under control.

"It's... difficult." My voice was barely above a whisper. "I can heal, but when it comes to the other magic, it doesn't come naturally to me."

The older woman nodded slowly, her expression thoughtful. "Magic is not something that can be forced. It must be allowed to flow through you like a river. If you try to control it too tightly, it will slip away, just as water does when grasped by a fist."

I looked down at my hands, frowning as I remembered all the times I had tried to summon the magic, only to feel it vanish the moment I tried to take hold of it. Frustration crept into my voice. "Yes. Every time I try to channel the earth or air, it feels like I'm fighting against it, like it's resisting me."

One of the other women, younger but with the same sharpness in her eyes, leaned forward. Her voice was quiet but filled with authority. "Magic isn't always for the mind to understand. Sometimes, it must be felt with the heart."

I looked at her, a skeptical frown tugging at my lips. "But if I don't understand it, how can I control it? How can I protect the clan if I don't know how to wield it?"

"You don't control it," She met my gaze, her voice soft but resolute. "Elemental magic can't be controlled."

Her words echoed my deepest fear, a chill prickling down my spine as I wondered if I would ever safely harness the power within, to keep the magic from consuming me.

"There are some in the clan who believe all magic must be tightly controlled," the younger woman added, her eyes locking onto mine. "But there was a time when our shamans were as wild as the magic they channeled, using the raw power of their hearts to shape it. They didn't fear the chaos, they embraced it."

I let my gaze drift across the women gathered around the fire. These women had lived their entire lives in tune with the earth, with the magic that flowed around them, even if they couldn't wield it themselves. They understood things on a level I could only hope to one day match.

"I'm trying," I said softly, my voice betraying the uncertainty that gnawed at me. "But what if I can't figure it out in time? The darkness is still out there. It's getting stronger, and I can feel it creeping closer every day."

The older woman's expression darkened. Her voice carried a weighty gravity, each word resonating with the solemnity of her warning. "Darkness waits patiently, like a shadow that creeps ever closer, feeding on the fear it cultivates. What matters is the intent with which you wield it, not the source from which you draw."

Fear had been my constant companion for so long—fear of my own power, fear of failing the clan, fear of what the prophecy demanded of me. And it was true: that fear had been gnawing away at me, weakening my resolve. But could I really let it go? Could I trust myself enough to channel the magic without letting it slip out of control?

"I don't know if I can," I whispered, more to myself than to them.

The older woman reached out and placed a hand on mine, her grip surprisingly strong for someone her age. "You are our shaman," she said firmly. "But you are also one of us now. We stand with you, Cleo. You do not carry this burden alone."

I swallowed hard, feeling a lump form in my throat as I questioned whether I was worthy of the trust and faith they'd placed in me. Firelight danced over their wise, weathered faces, casting shadows that high-lighted every line etched by time and hardship. These women had lived through the worst. They had survived wars, loss, and exile from their ancestral lands. They had faced darkness before, and they were still standing. And now they were standing with me.

"Seer Arna teaches you control," the younger woman continued, her voice a little softer now, "but remember, elemental magic cannot be controlled, only guided. Use whatever emotion is strong enough to hold onto, and use that strength with your intent."

I had been holding on too tightly, clenching my fists around the magic, trying to force it to bend to my will. But maybe that wasn't what it needed. Maybe the magic wasn't something to be wielded with force. Maybe it was something to be guided, coaxed, and allowed to flow naturally.

"Thank you. You've given me much to think about."

The older woman smiled, a gentle, knowing smile. "It will be enough. *You* will be enough."

I felt a wave of gratitude wash over me, along with something quieter but more powerful. Hope. Maybe they were right and I didn't have to control everything. Maybe I could trust myself, trust the magic, and trust the bond I shared with Dex and the clan.

The conversation lingered with me as I left the elders' circle, and I felt lighter, a weight lifting from my shoulders and I didn't feel quite so afraid.

I FLED THE GARDENS, frustration rolling off me in suffocating waves, each step fueled by the crushing weight of failure pressing against my chest. The air in the stronghold felt thick, the cool stone walls closing in as I moved through the dimly lit corridors. My pulse thundered in my ears, and my hands were clenched into fists at my sides. No matter how hard I tried, I couldn't grasp control of my magic. It flared and pulsed when I least expected it—wild, reckless, and terrifying. It rose to protect me instinctively, surging forth like a beast with a mind of its own, but when I reached for it with intention, it slipped through my fingers like smoke. The thought haunted me, tightening around my throat like a noose. What if the next time it reacted without my consent? If it was Dex standing too close? What if it was Arna, or one of the warriors? What if I lost control at the worst possible moment and hurt the very people I had sworn to protect? *What if it was the children?* My stomach churned with dread, the fear gnawing at my edges like hungry wolves as I hurried toward the comfort of our quarters. *So much for my positivity from earlier...*

"Cleo?"

The sound of my name stopped me in my tracks. I turned to find Seer Arna standing in the dim corridor, her keen eyes assessing me with a quiet, knowing gaze.

"Come, we must speak."

I fell into step behind her, trailing down the winding corridor that led away from the bustling heart of the stronghold. The quiet hum of activity faded behind us, replaced by the soft echo of our footsteps. The air grew colder as we ascended a narrow staircase and entered a small chamber tucked away from the main halls, the flickering torchlight casting eerie shadows across shelves lined with jars and bundles of dried herbs, the musty scent of old parchment flooding my nose. Arna stopped just inside the doorway, her sharp eyes scanned me with an intensity that made my skin prickle. "You've done well here," she said softly, her voice carrying the weight of years and wisdom. "The orcs see you as one of us. You've earned your place with us."

A weak smile tugged at my lips. "That's kind of you to say. Thank you."

She studied me for some time before continuing, her expression unreadable. "You're doing more than trying. You are becoming. I know what you saw, child."

"You know?"

She nodded slowly, her gaze softening. "The flames speak to those who listen. They show us what we need to see. I understand the burden you carry."

I swallowed against the rising knot in my chest. "It doesn't make sense. The darkness, the magic... what it's asking of me. I don't know what it wants." I admitted, my voice trembling.

Arna's lips curled into a faint smile as she stepped closer to take my hand. "It's asking you to choose, Cleo. It always has."

A frown tugged at my brows, confusion twisting in my gut. "Choose? What kind of choices are these!"

Her eyes glowed with something ancient and powerful, the air crackling with energy. "Your vision showed you two paths. One where you stand alone, bearing the cost of our survival. And another where you stand with the clan, destined to die as one of us."

"Was this always my fate?"

The Seer's soft nod was like an arrow through my chest.

"Did Dex... did he know?" I asked, but deep down I already knew the answer.

Arna's expression shifted, a shadow of regret visible across her face as she inclined her head. "Yes. The earth has a funny way of complicating matters. The earth gave us you, but they also gave him a mate. His choice is not unlike yours—to choose between duty and love."

He had known all this time that I was to die for his people, and he said *nothing*.

"Before you judge him too harshly," Arna added, her voice gentle, "know that he has been scouring every piece of our history, every scrap of knowledge on the prophecy that he could find, looking for more answers, another way."

I swallowed thickly as the bitter taste of betrayal mingled with my rising fear. "He didn't find anything, did he?"

"No, he didn't. But that is not his thread of fate to control." There was a spark of something—mischief, maybe—in her eyes that caught me off guard as I looked at her, "That's the tricky part of fate, isn't it? The prophecy did not speak of you being mate bound to the Chieftain; that was fate. Fate bound you to the clan and you became one of us. Humans were not meant to wield the power of the earth, but you are not just a human, you are part of the Blackfoot Clan. Your blood oath binds you to us."

"So everyone knew?" Her nod drove the betrayal deeper. The new family and friends I thought I had found... *did they not even have enough respect for me to tell me I was to die?*

"How does that change my visions?"

Arna chuckled softly and reached out to pat my shoulder. "You're looking for answers in the wrong places, child. Sometimes, the best choice isn't about right or wrong; it's about what feels true to who you are. When you feel yourself losing control, call on your bond with Dex. He will ground you."

I bit my lip, the vulnerability I had fought so hard to keep at bay spilling over. "And if it doesn't?"

Arna's understanding smile at my turbulent emotions was validating.

"Failure is only an option if you let it be. Don't be too hard on him. He's been at war with himself over how to tell you." Her voice softened further. "He didn't want to heed my advice and tell you when you first arrived. He was so sure he could change the prophecy, and he didn't want to risk chasing you away."

I STUMBLED THROUGH THE CORRIDORS, my pulse a deafening drumbeat, my ears ringing. The distant murmur of the stronghold faded beneath the echo of Arna's words, twisting and turning through my mind like barbed wire. Doubt clawed inside my ribs, each inhale sharp and ragged, as if I were suffocating under the weight of it all. By the time I reached the Chieftain's chambers, my legs threatened to give out, trembling under the pressure of my spiraling thoughts. I slammed the door shut and pressed my back against the solid oak, and I slid down to the floor. A gasping sob shattering the heavy silence. Emotions crashed in relentless waves—anger sharp enough to slice through my thoughts, sorrow so heavy it felt crushing, dragging me down, and confusion that wrapped around my throat, choking off my cries. The ache in my chest was a hollow pressure that swelled with each frantic heartbeat, each shallow breath. Panic coiled at the edges of my vision, black spots blooming and receding like a tide threatening to pull me under. I forced in a ragged breath, grasping for control, for something solid amidst the storm.

"Five things you can see..." I whispered, my voice trembling. My eyes darted frantically around the room. The flickering firelight casting restless shadows across the walls. Dex's discarded armor, haphazardly tossed on the table. The thick furs draped messily across the bed. My hands, trembling in my lap. The pitted stone under me.

Four things you can touch. The cool wood of the door behind me. The soft, familiar fabric of my tunic. The scuffed leather of my boots. The warmth of my skin, pulsing beneath my fingertips.

My breathing slowed as I wrestled control back, but the storm inside didn't subside. Doubt seeped through the cracks of my armor, sinking its claws deeper into my chest. Had Dex been weaving a careful web around me from the very beginning? The thought struck like a physical blow, sending a fresh wave of nausea rolling through me. The way he had found me, how effortlessly he had slipped into my life, offering his protection, his strength... it all felt too perfect now, too deliberate. How foolish I had been, handing him my trust, and my heart, so freely. The ache inside deepened as doubt slithered through my veins like poison, corrupting happy memories of my mate.

Had any of it been real or had he just been biding his time, waiting for me to fall so deeply into their cause that I would willingly throw myself into battle, knowing it would be to my destruction? I pressed a hand to my mouth, stifling another broken sob.

Despite the bitter sting of betrayal, I knew one thing for certain. I would have done it anyway. I had come to care for the clan, felt their acceptance warming me in ways I never imagined possible, finding the family I had always craved. Despite the turmoil writhing inside, I knew I would die for Dex without hesitation.

My fingers curled into the my tunic, clutching at my chest as if I could physically hold the fragments of my heart together. Each ragged breath rattled in my lungs, the weight of it pressing against my ribs like a vice. With a trembling hand, I wiped at my tears in a futile attempt to erase the evidence of my heartbreak.

I needed answers. I needed to hear the truth from his lips, even if it would tear me apart. Even if it didn't change my love for him. Drawing in a deep breath, I pushed myself up from the floor, my legs trembling beneath my weight. There was no running from this. Not anymore.

THE CLANG of weapons drew my attention as I neared the training grounds, the sharp sound slicing through my haze. I leaned against the stone wall, and my gaze locked on the warriors sparring in the open yard. They moved with confidence, each strike and block a testament to their discipline and years of training. But my eyes were drawn to only one figure.

Dex.

He was sparring with one of the larger orcs, his movements a masterful blend of strength and grace. Each strike of his weapon was deliberate, every step perfectly placed. The sheer power in his form, the control he exerted over his every movement—it was mesmerizing. I allowed myself to forget everything else, to lose myself in the sight of him.

My mind betrayed me, pulling up memories of his body against mine, his strength making me feel both fragile and unbreakable. In battle, he dominated his opponents with a ruthless aggression and in the quiet of night, he dominated me in a way that left me breathless, his touch a worshipful contradiction to the raw power that defined him.

Even now, as I watched him disarm his opponent with a fluid twist of his wrist, I felt a familiar warmth unfurling low in my belly. But beneath the flicker of desire, darker emotions churned—anger, hurt, and betrayal.

I had trusted him. Believed in him. And now, after what Arna had told me, I didn't know what was real anymore. Did he bring me here because he loved me, or was I just a tool in some grand plan? Did he see me as his mate, or was I nothing more than a piece in the prophecy he wanted to control?

Dex caught my gaze from across the training grounds, his sharp eyes narrowing as if he could sense the turmoil within me. A small smile tugged at his lips, but I could see concern behind his confidence. He wiped the sweat from his brow as he strode toward me.

"You're looking a little distracted," he teased, stopping in front of me. "See something you like?"

I forced a grin. "Distracted? I was just wondering why you took so long to win that fight." My tone was light, playful, but the edge in my voice betrayed the tension beneath it.

Dex raised an eyebrow and leaned in, his hand braced against the wall beside me. His presence crowded me, filling the air between us with his heat, his scent. It felt both comforting and suffocating, and I hated the combination. "Maybe I was trying to impress someone," he said, his voice dropping to a soft murmur. "Make it last."

"Oh?" I raised an eyebrow, my tone feigning amusement even as my chest tightened. "And here I thought you always liked to finish strong."

His grin widened as his eyes gleamed with that roguish glint that always made my pulse race. "I do, but sometimes, taking my time has its rewards."

I laughed but the sound was hollow even to my own ears. Dex tilted his head, his gaze sharpening as he studied me.

"What's wrong?" His teasing tone had faded into something softer, more serious.

I looked away, my heart hammering in my chest. "I'm *fine*."

"Cleo." His voice was firm, cutting through my defenses. He reached out, his fingers brushing against my arm in that gentle, grounding way that always seemed to unravel me. "Talk to me."

My resolve crumbled under the weight of his gaze. "Can we go somewhere else?"

His brow furrowed but he nodded, his hand sliding to the small of my back to guide me.

"Don't touch me," I snapped, stepping back. "Not until you tell me the truth."

His hand froze mid-air, his eyes narrowing. "Cleo, what are you talking about?"

"*Don't!*" my voice trembled with the effort to keep my emotions in check. "Don't play dumb with me, Dex. I talked to Arna. She told me about the prophecy. About what you've known all along."

His face darkened, his golden eyes narrowing into sharp slits. "You don't understand—"

"—You're right!" I cut him off, my voice rising. "I don't understand because you didn't tell me! You let me walk around here, thinking we were in this together, thinking I could *trust you*. And all the while, you knew what the prophecy demanded of me."

"I didn't tell you because I was trying to protect you! Do you think I wanted this? Do you think I wanted to burden you with this when you were already carrying so much?"

I stepped closer, my hands trembling at my sides as I glared up at him. "You had no right to decide that for me. No right to keep me in the dark about something this important. How am I supposed to trust you now, Dex? How am I supposed to believe that any of this—us—is real? Or was it just another way to keep me tied to you?" I thrust my wrist into his face. The jewelry he'd given me for our mate bond mocked me as it glittered in the light.

His expression twisted, a mixture of anger and hurt flashing across his face. "You think this isn't real?" He snatched up my wrist in his hand. "Do you think that I wanted to be caught between my duty and my mate?! In the beginning, I was doing what I had to—my duty is to my clan!"

"What about to me!" I demanded, my voice sharp with anger.

"You changed everything! At first, I thought I could ignore our connection, but you pushed right through the walls as quickly as I could put them up. Now I see it was inevitable. I can't *breathe* without you. I can't think straight! You're not just my mate, Cleo—you're my weakness!"

His pained voice tugged at my heart, but I refused to let them soften the edges of my anger as I pulled from his grasp. "And you think that makes it better? That admitting you're a slave to your emotions somehow justifies keeping this from me?! You lied to me!"

"I was trying to find another way!" Dex roared, his voice echoing off the stone walls. His hands fisted at his sides, his entire body radiating frustration and desperation, his voice dropping into a whisper. "Do you think I want this to be your fate? That I haven't spent every waking moment searching for another way? I won't let this prophecy take you from me. I can't."

For several long minutes we stared at each other, neither of us speaking. My breath came in shaky bursts, my chest heaving with emotions. "Arna told me the earth chose intentionally. Fate intervened."

Dex's eyes narrowed in confusion as he stared at me. "What does that mean?"

"I don't know. She said my bond with you doesn't make me a human shaman anymore, I'm a part of the Blackfoot Clan. She thinks that becoming one with the clan may have been my other option."

Dex's fists unclenched, his shoulders sagging as the fight seemed to drain out of him. "Gods, I hope she is right," he whispered. "But that doesn't mean I'm giving up looking for another way. I won't let the prophecy decide your fate, Cleo. I can't lose you."

I shook my head, the knot in my chest tightening as I looked at him. "And what if there isn't a chance, Dex? What if this is the only way?"

His gaze hardened, his golden eyes blazing with defiance. "Then I'll make one. Even if I have to tear this world apart to do it."

I stared at him, wanting to believe him, to trust that he could find a solution, but the doubt lingered.

"Don't make promises you can't keep."

"I'm not." His hand reached for mine. "I will not be the reason for your death. If it wants to have you it better be ready for me as well."

The raw intensity in his voice sent shivers through me, and I let him pull me into his arms. "Please, swear you won't keep anything from me ever again. I would have given everything for you, Dex, and still would. Right now I need space to think."

I felt him nod above me, trailing his blunt fingers across my back out of habit, hesitant to let me go. But even as I leaned into his warmth, the weight of Arna's words lingered in the back of my mind, a reminder that some battles couldn't be won. I pulled from his grip and turned, hurrying away for some privacy to find my center again.

CHAPTER 32
DEX

The valley lay cloaked in shadow, the fading light casting an eerie stillness that pressed down like a physical weight. I could feel it —the oppressive pull of dark magic creeping closer. Across the stronghold, orcs moved with unspoken urgency, the scrape of metal and low murmurs creating a charged, expectant atmosphere. Weapons were being sharpened, armor secured, prayers whispered to the ancestors and the Gods. I knew they felt it too: the grim finality of what lay ahead.

But tonight wasn't just about the battle ahead. It was about her.

Cleo stood at the edge of the stronghold, her arms wrapped tightly around herself as though warding off an invisible chill. The twilight painted her features in muted tones, but even in the fading light, I could see the tension etched into her posture, the way her shoulders rose and fell with each shallow breath. She was barely holding it together. I had royally fucked up.

I strode toward her, the quiet tread of my boots against the stone amplifying the silence that hung heavy between us. This wasn't the time for softness, not tonight. The clan needed their shaman—and their Chieftain—to lead. There was no room for doubt or fear, not when hundreds of lives rested on our shoulders.

I stopped short of touching her, the distance between us charged with the weight of unspoken words. "Cleo," I said, my voice cutting through the thick silence. "We need to talk."

She turned, her green eyes meeting mine, wide and glassy with the fear she wasn't even trying to hide. My jaw tightened as frustration clawed at my chest. This wasn't her. Not the fierce, defiant woman I knew. Not the mate who had stared down Shadow Hounds and wielded wild magic with a fire that had left me in awe. This—this trembling shadow of herself—was the fear talking. And I wouldn't let it take her from me.

"Whatever's going on in your head, you need to squash it."

Her lips parted, a soft, trembling breath escaping, but she didn't speak.

"You can't let them see you like this," I continued, my tone softening. "Do you understand? The clan is watching. They need to see strength, not fear. You're their shaman, their healer. If they see you falter, it'll spread like poison, and they'll lose faith."

Her eyes flicked down, her hands twisting together in anxious energy. "I'm scared, Dex."

"I know you are, we *all are*. But what matters is that you stand tall, that you show them you're ready. Even if you're not."

Her head snapped up, her gaze locking onto mine with a flicker of defiance. "And if I can't?"

"You can. You've stood against everything that's been thrown at you and you're still here. You are their shaman, and my mate. You are part of this clan, and tonight, you need to act like it. Whatever fear you feel, whatever doubt is clawing at you, bury it."

Her breathing quickened, and panic filled in her eyes. "Dex, I—"

"No." I cut her off, my voice a low growl. "No excuses, Cleo. You're better than this! The clan is counting on us. If you can't do it for yourself, then do it for them. Do it for the children you can hear laughing on the eve of battle. For the warriors who are sharpening their blades, knowing they might not survive the night. They need to believe that their shaman is strong enough to fight with them."

Her chin quivered, and pride flooded me as she straightened, and drew in a deep breath. "I'm not strong like you, Dex. I don't know how to be."

"Yes, you do." My voice softened but lost none of its intensity. "You've been strong since the moment I met you. Strong enough to survive your father, and to stand up to me. Strong enough to wield a magic that terrifies you. Strong enough to love me despite our differences. You *are* strong, Cleo. And tonight, you're going to prove it. Not just to the clan, but to yourself."

Tears glistened in her eyes, her lips pressing together as she fought to steady herself. "Are you scared?"

I hesitated for a heartbeat, the truth catching in my throat. "Terrified. But I don't let it show, and neither can you."

Her gaze held mine, searching for something—reassurance, strength, anything to hold onto. I gave it to her, pressing my forehead to hers and allowing the bond between us to pulse with a quiet power. "You're not alone in this, Cleo. Whatever happens tonight, we face it together. You and me. Do you trust me?"

Her nod was small, almost imperceptible, but it was enough.

"That's all I ask." I brushed a strand of hair from her face. "When you can't stand tall alone, lean on me. That's what mates do."

We stood there in silence, the weight of the night pressing down on us. I watched as determination returned to her eyes, the steel that I knew had been there all along.

"I can do this."

Pride swelled in my chest, sharp and fierce as I leaned down to press a firm kiss to her forehead. "That's my girl."

Her eyes fluttered closed, and I felt her shoulders relax, just slightly, as she drew strength from the embrace. The shadows stretched longer, the sun dipped closer to the horizon and they creeped toward the stronghold like dark inky tendrils. The battle was coming, and it would be brutal.

"Dex," she whispered, her voice shaking. "If it comes down to it, if I lose control... please don't let me hurt them."

Her words sent a bolt of cold fury through me, shattering the peace. "No. We will not speak of this again. Please, don't ask me to do that."

"You have to." Her hands tightened on my tunic. "If it's between me and them—if it's between me and you—"

"Stop asking me to let you go. You are *mine!*"

Her tears fell freely as she ran her fingers along my face, cupping my cheek. "You may not get a choice."

"How am I supposed to do that? How am I supposed to sacrifice *my mate?* How am I supposed to let you go? I won't do it!" I shook my head, anguish tearing into my chest.

"Because it's the right thing to do. Because you're the Chieftain, and this is bigger than us. I do not wish to survive if it means losing those important to me."

I stared at her in disbelief, my chest tight with a thousand emotions I couldn't put into words. She was asking me to do the impossible, to choose between my duty and my heart, and I hated her for it, even as I loved her more fiercely than I thought possible.

"I can't promise that, but I can promise that I will fight for you, Cleo, and I will find another way to protect this clan. I swear it."

She closed her eyes, a sad smile ghosting her lips as she leaned into me, her forehead pressing against my chest. "You can't save everyone, Dex."

"Watch me."

"If something happens... I love you, and I'm so sorry. I really wanted to see the clan return to the valley where we belong."

I whispered promises of protection, and of the future, as we embraced, terrified this could be the last time I would hold her in my arms. Her warmth seared into my skin, a stark contrast to the cold fear clawing at my insides. My arms tightened around her instinctively, as if by sheer will alone I could keep her safe, keep her here—away from fate that threatened to rip her from me.

I buried my face into the crook of her neck, breathing in the familiar scent of her hair, soothing the raw ache gnawing at my soul. The soft rise and fall of her chest beneath my own was a silent rhythm that soothed the storm raging inside me, yet it did nothing to quiet the guilt festering deep within. The weight of secrets kept and choices made pressed in on me, suffocating in their silence.

Each whispered promise felt like a threadbare shield against the inevitable. I murmured against her skin, the words hollow even to my own ears. How many times had I sworn the same? How many nights had I held her like this, desperate to keep the darkness at bay, knowing deep down that I was powerless against the tides of fate?

My fingers trailed up her back, mapping the delicate ridges of her spine, committing them to memory. She felt so small in my arms, so delicate. The thought of her standing alone against the shadows twisted something sharp in my gut. I had failed her, and still, she held me as if I was her safe harbor, her protector.

She didn't know how much I had kept from her. The truths I swallowed down, the burdens I carried in silence, hoping to shield her from the weight of fate. But could she feel it? The tremor in my hands as they had roamed over her, the way I aggressively claimed her, desperation and fear of loosing her making my orc nature rise to the surface.

I pressed a lingering kiss to her temple, my lips trembling against her skin. "I love you," I whispered, the words raw and desperate. My voice cracked, betraying the fear I couldn't hide. "I swear, Cleo. I won't let it end like this. I can't—" My throat closed around the unspoken words, choking on the sheer enormity of my failure.

Her fingers tracing slow, soothing patterns over my shoulder. She didn't say anything—she didn't have to. Her presence alone was enough to tether me to the moment, to keep me from spiraling too deep into guilt.

I knew, deep down, that no matter how fiercely I loved her, how tightly I held her, that fate had its own cruel design.

"Orcs are fierce because we learn to live with the uncertainty of life," My words were strained with emotion. "We use it. We don't run from it. I need you to be one of us tonight, Cleo."

"I thought I already was." She clutched my hand tighter with a sad smile.

I exhaled shakily, pressing another kiss to her forehead, silently pleading for more time. More stolen moments. More chances to hold her, love her, worship her in the quiet darkness of our shared space. Because I knew—no matter how hard I fought, how fiercely I swore to protect her—some battles couldn't be won. And losing her would break me in ways I could never repair. "Yes, you are, Cleo. We do this together, no matter what comes across these walls."

Gods help anyone who tried to take her from me.

CHAPTER 33
CLEO

As night descended, the orcs gathered along the walls of the stronghold, their faces set with grim determination. The wind howled through the narrow mountain pass, carrying with it a foul stench—decay and rot—the unmistakable scent of darkness. My heart pounded as I stood among them and scanned the cave, searching for any sign of movement. It was only a matter of time before it revealed itself.

At first, it was nothing more than a flicker at the edge of my vision —a shadow moving unnaturally fast through the scattered rocks. Then more appeared, slithering and writhing over the rocky ground. These creatures, dark and twisted, were infused with the same malevolent energy I had felt before.

The creatures moved with terrifying speed, their twisted forms barely discernible in the night, but I could feel them—each one pulsing with dark magic. Their very presence sent a chill down my spine. They were stronger than anything I had faced before, and they were hungry.

A tremor ran through my hands as I reached for the magic within. I could feel it, the familiar hum pulsing beneath my skin.

Dex's eyes were fixed on the swarming creatures below, his voice rang out across the murmured prayers. "No matter what comes, we hold!"

The orcs roared in response. The bass echoed through rock beneath them, as they prepared to face the oncoming horde. The sound sent adrenaline coursing through me, but it did little to ease the fear twisting in my gut. I met Dex's beautiful eyes as he squeezed my shoulder—a comforting gesture, but fleeting. His hand slipped away as he moved to join his warriors, pulling his massive axe from its sheath with practiced ease, taking up their defensive positions on the wall.

The ground rumbled beneath us as the first of the shadows reached the walls, their twisted forms clawing at the stone, screeching in rage. The wall shuddered beneath the weight of them, stone cracking under their claws. I stumbled as a section of the rampart crumbled away, sending debris and shadows tumbling into the abyss below. My hand shot out, gripping the edge just in time to keep myself from falling, but the ground beneath us was as treacherous as the creatures themselves. They scaled the walls with dizzying speed, and the orcs launched at them with a ferocity that took my breath away—blades flashing in the moonlight, arrows whistling through the air. But for every creature they cut down, more appeared, their bodies surging forward like an endless tide.

I lifted my hands and called forth healing magic that vibrated through the air. Green light began to glow from my fingers, soft at first, but quickly growing brighter as I pushed more of my strength into it. I could feel the magic welling up inside me, spilling out in waves, spreading across the battlefield like a net. Magic surged, flowing into the orcs. Wherever the green light touched, wounds sealed as their flesh knitted back together, broken bones snapped into place. The power thrummed through the air, vibrant and alive, pushing away the dark magic with a force that was both gentle and fierce.

The orcs could feel the swell of my power. I could see it in their eyes. With their strength renewed, they threw themselves back into the fight, their weapons flashing as they met the onslaught of dark creatures with vigor.

But the magic took more from me than I was prepared for. Every time I pushed, I felt a piece of myself slip away. My body shook under the strain, the exhaustion creeping in. Holding the darkness at bay had my magic flaring wildly, and I could feel a burning sensation in my arms. I glanced down and saw my veins glowing—a faint green-silver light coursing beneath my skin, tracing the lines of my magic as it fought to escape my body. The sight of it made my stomach turn, the glow identical to the one in my vision. A metallic taste exploded across my tastebuds, my nose trickling crimson blood across my lips.

The battlefield roared. steel clashing, the cries of the wounded, the darker side of my magic begging to be unleashed. But all I could hear were Dex's words. *"I thought I could use you."* My chest tightened, my grip on my power faltering, and I shook myself for the mental strength to not fall victim to its call.

A monstrous creature, twice the size of any orc, scaled the wall with terrifying speed. Its skin was slick with dark energy, and its eyes glowed with malevolent light. It let out a guttural roar as it reached the top of the wall, its claws raking through the air toward me.

Before I could retreat, Dex moved like a storm, his axe gleaming as it struck the creature, knocking it back with a powerful blow. Its ear splitting screech of fury had me wincing, racing to cover my ears as Dex swung again, the axe biting deep into the creature's chest, black blood spraying in a gruesome arc.

Dex's eyes stayed locked on the creatures. "Stay close to me!" he shouted.

I stepped behind him, throwing my power to surround Gornak with healing light, his hands clutched at the wound, fear clouding his eyes. My body screamed in protest, the glow of my veins growing brighter, the burning sensation crept up my neck and into my chest.

Gritting my teeth, I flooded the older warrior with the purest magic I could muster, staving off his death. His artery knit together, the flesh melting back into place, leaving only the blood-soaked remnants of the battle on his armor. With a quick nod of thanks, Gornak grabbed his sword and threw himself back into the fray, pulling one of the dark creatures from Thorn and removing its head with a bone-chilling battle cry.

Dex fought beside me, his movements a blur of controlled fury as he cut down anything that came too close. But even I could see the strain on his face—the tension in his muscles as they tightened with each swing of his axe. He fought with brutal precision, his blade cutting through the chaos like a force of nature. I hated that I noticed—hated the pang in my chest at the sight of him putting himself in danger. The darkness whispered to me, its anger seductive. *Why should I care? He'd lied to me, used me.*

My eyes roamed the battlefield as panic clawed at my throat. In a moment of clarity, I saw the orcs fighting with everything they had, their face fierce with determination. Blood streaked their armor, and their muscles strained with each blow, but they didn't hesitate. They stood side by side, holding the line. I felt frantic eyes searching for me, for a strength and reassurance that I feared I could not give.

I knew I was likely an equally terrifying sight. My eyes were glowing, the veins under my skin pulsing with light as I burned with my magic, the agony was clear on my face, the flickering pulse of my magic growing faster, the more I channeled. But they didn't turn away. I could see the recognition on their face, the knowledge that we would not last, but still they fought with everything they had.

Wiping the blood from my hands as I turned to face the battlefield again. The air was thick with screams as the dark magic swirled. I was terrified. But I couldn't let them see I had lost hope.

Dex's words echoed in my mind. *"They need to see that you're not afraid..."*

"I'm not done! Keep fighting!"

I saw something shift in their eyes—a quiet understanding. They saw that I stood despite the unsteadiness in my hands, the tremble of my lip. They knew I was afraid, just as they were, and that made me one of them.

Gornak nodded at me. "We'll hold the line." He sounded exhausted, but he was determined. "Whatever it takes."

I swallowed hard, regret thick in my throat at what we would loose tonight. "Whatever it takes."

CHAPTER 34
DEX

Cleo was fierce. Power surged through her and I watched as she moved from warrior to warrior, healing as many as she could. Her hands shook with the effort. The orcs fought harder when they saw her, their resolve strengthened with each step she took along the walls. Cleo wasn't flawless. She wasn't a leader. But she was here, fighting beside us in the face of overwhelming darkness.

The shadows continued to crash against the walls, their twisted forms screeching and writhing with a foul energy. My axe was already slick with ichor, my arms burning with the effort of cutting them down. Our bodies were battered but our spirits held firm. There was no retreat. There was no faltering, even as the odds were against us.

I roared, my voice cutting through the screech of the dying creatures, I swung my axe with a grunt, the blade sinking into their unnatural flesh. I glanced back at Cleo. I could see the exhaustion weighing her down, the way her shoulders sagged under the burden of the magic. Her power crackled through the air, fueling our warriors to push back the enemy. She was magnificent—terrifying in a way that made my chest ache with both pride and regret. This was what I had wanted, wasn't it? To unleash her, to use her power to destroy those who had taken everything from my people?

Another impact shook the walls, harder this time, and I turned just in time to see a monstrous creature breach the line. It was a mass of roiling dark energy, its eyes burning with a vicious, hatred. It barreled through the defenders, knocking them aside like they were nothing, and headed straight for Cleo. I saw the creature lunge, a claw glinting in the faint light as it broke through the fray. Her back was turned, her focus locked on the healing power she wielded. She wouldn't see him in time.

"Behind you!" My voice tore through the noise, and I didn't think —I moved.

Claws sunk deep into my arm as I shoved Cleo aside, my dagger sunk deep into its throat. Her wide eyes met mine, and the battlefield faded. Blood trickled down my arm, staining the edge of my armor, but I didn't care. I'd take a thousand cuts if it meant keeping her safe.

"Stay behind me," I growled.

My hands tightened around the haft of my axe, the wood creaking under the strain of my frustration, my aches heavy with the strain of overuse. "We don't stop." My voice was firm, laced with the promise of retribution.

Cleo swiped a hand across her upper lip, smearing blood over her cheek, as a glint of fierce determination flashed in her eyes. She reached out, pressing magic into the fresh wound, knitting my flesh together in almost an instant.

But something had changed. The air around her crackled with raw electricity, raising the hair on the back of my neck. Her magic pulsed out of her control, her eyes locked onto the dark creatures, and I saw something wild flare in her gaze—rage.

Driving her hand forward, the world seemed to split apart with a deafening crack of thunder. Lightning exploded from her fingertips, blinding-white, a spear of pure energy that shot across the battlefield, searing through the shadows, the flash left spots dancing in my vision, and I blinked against the light. The bolt jumped wildly from one creature to the next, arcing through their twisted bodies like a chain of lightning, narrowly avoiding the orcs. The air buzzed, the scent of burnt flesh filling my nostrils as I watched the creatures writhing, their twisted forms disintegrating into ash, and for the first time, the tide faltered.

The only sound was the crackling remnants of Cleo's magic, fading into the night. I forced myself to breathe, my chest tight with the aftermath of what I'd just witnessed. Her power had always been a force to be reckoned with—but this was something entirely beyond our understanding. As the last echoes of thunder faded, I couldn't help the chill that ran down my spine, wondering if she could come back from the edge she'd been too terrified to cross.

Cleo was barely upright, swaying as if the ground beneath her might give way. Her veins glowed white hot, pulsing in time with her ragged breaths. I could see the pain etched into her face. She had bought us a moment—a brief, precious moment to catch our breath.

"Stay back." Cleo begged, my heart clenching as I could only watch her wrestle to contain her magic. She was losing control.

I could see the grim realization in the eyes of my warriors. Cleo wasn't strong enough to keep healing us, to keep striking down our enemies. There were too many.

The weight of duty pressed on me, the lives of every member of my clan hanging in the outcome of battle. We would fight until the end and make the darkness bleed for every inch it wanted to take.

I had lost hope. The walls would fall, and we would be overrun. But if this was to be our end, then we would face it with steel in our hands and fire in our hearts.

The shadow creatures poured back over the walls, their claws scraping against the stone, their eyes glowing with a sickly red light. I carved through another, its body crumbling, but the tide was endless, a plague of inevitable death.

I drove my axe through another creature. "Watch your left!" I twisted in time to see Cleo pivot, flames bursting from her hands and reducing the shadow lunging at her to ash.

She shot me a quick look, her lips curving in a smile despite the writhing magic scorching through her veins. "You think I didn't see that?"

Amidst the chaos, I found myself smiling. My mate fought by my side with enough passion left to still throw attitude at me. *There was no better way to leave this earth.*

"Fall back to the inner line!" I ordered, knowing this position was slipping from our control. I found myself circling Cleo, my shoulder brushing against hers. The heat pouring off her skin was like standing next to a forge, her magic searing the air. "We're getting overrun! We can't hold them here!"

Her focus was locked on the creatures swarming over the battlements. Her hands pressed to the stone, her fingers glowing brighter as she sent another surge of energy into the earth. Roots burst from the ground, snaring the creatures' legs and dragging them down. Turning to me, her eyes blazed molten gold, not unlike my own. "Not until we burn every last one of them!" she yelled back, voice trembling with raw power.

Damn her stubbornness. But I couldn't deny the fire in her voice, the way it burned through the fear that had lodged itself in my chest. The creatures were nearly on top of us, their claws flashing in the firelight, and I met them head-on, swinging my axe with a fury that matched the fire in Cleo's veins.

I could hear her breathing coming in harsh gasps as she pushed more power into the earth. The roots twist around the shadows, holding them long enough for blades to cut them down. I caught a glimpse of her face—so different from the uncertain woman I'd first met. Now, she was something fierce, bloodthirsty and unbreakable, and even at the brink of defeat, I'd fight beside her, bound by a fire that no darkness could extinguish.

The ground shook beneath us as the Shadows pressed in, but we held our ground, side by side, the bond between us pulsing like a second heartbeat. My war cry rang across the wall as I swung my axe with everything I had left.

CHAPTER 35
CLEO

Exhaustion weighed down on me, every breath coming with a tremor that I couldn't suppress. I had spent so much of my energy, healing every wound I could reach, mending broken bones, sealing gashes. But it wasn't enough. The residue of the elemental magic I'd unleashed earlier still buzzed beneath my skin, a taste of the forbidden power I had locked myself away from.

The prophecy enraged me—the looming shadow of its cruel grip. My visions weren't of hope or salvation; it was of death. Death to a people I had come to love. A prophecy that demanded I stand by and watch as the orcs, my newfound family, were swallowed by darkness.

It wasn't fair. The anger surged, and I wanted to scream—to rail at the Gods, the earth, or whatever force had decided this was my fate. *How dare they expect me to make this choice? To ask me to let these people—these proud, fierce warriors who had given me a home, a place, a purpose—die in some predetermined war?*

I clenched my fists, my nails biting into my palms as I fought back the tears threatening to spill over. *I wasn't a pawn. I wasn't some tool to be wielded in their grand design.* But my vision and every whispered word from the earth, told me otherwise. I was livid at the prophecy, furious at its inevitability, and most of all, enraged at the crushing lack of choices I had been given.

My heart clenched as I thought of the friends I had made in this clan, their fierce loyalty, their strength. They had become my people in a way I hadn't realized I'd needed. And then there was Dex, his presence a steady rock against the storm of darkness surrounding us. Our bond was a lifeline, something I had come to rely on more than I realized. He believed in me, even when I struggled to believe in myself. I could still feel the warmth of his hands on me, the weight of his words as he told me that we would face this together.

As I looked out over the stronghold, seeing the waves of shadow creatures surging forward, I felt dread clawing at my chest, cold and merciless. We couldn't hold the line like this, not without my healing magic to keep the orcs fighting. And if the walls fell, if those creatures broke through, then the women and children hiding in the caves below wouldn't stand a chance. My hands shook at the thought, and a sob caught in my throat.

The air around the stronghold was thickening, the darkness pressing in on all sides grew heavier. The ground shook with dark energy, and the orcs around me grew still, their fear carved into their faces as we looked out over the wall.

A massive shape emerged from the shadows and my eyes widened in disbelief. It was unlike anything I had ever seen, its massive wings unfurling. *Dragon*.

I remember reading of them in the clan's ancient texts. Dragons were harbingers of destruction, creatures called forth when the dark mages first appeared, centuries ago. They were rumored to have torn apart entire kingdoms, leaving nothing but scorched earth and death in their wake. As it descended into the cave, I realized that the stories hadn't done it justice.

It wasn't just terror I felt as I stared at the beast. It was a raw, searing anger that burned hotter than the dragon's fiery breath. *How could the earth allow this? How could the Gods sit idly by while darkness consumed. How could they expect me to be the one to stop it?*

I had seen the visions on repeat in my head since the festival. The shadows devouring the stronghold, my clanmates—my family—falling one by one. And the other path—the one where I gave myself over to the earth, burning away my own existence to purge the darkness. Neither path felt like salvation. I wasn't a savior. I was a woman backed into a corner, forced to carry the weight of a prophecy that didn't care about the cost. Magic begged for freedom, flaring to life with a violent surge. It didn't feel like a gift anymore—it felt like a curse, a chain binding me to fate.

The ground beneath the stronghold began to crack, and the ancient stone walls groaned, the dragon's dark magic eating away at their foundation. Pain laced through me as I pushed back against the darkness but my power faltered. It slipped through my fingers, too weak to stand against the dragon's immense power. The weight of the dark magic pressed down on my mind and I hit the ground. I tried to summon my magic, but the creeping panic was too loud, drowning out everything else.

Dex was there in an instant. I wanted to push him away, scream at him to not to touch me, but all I could do was gasp.

"*Cleo, get up!*" Dex's voice cut through the haze. He was beside me, his hand gripping my shoulder, the warmth of it grounding me amidst the chaos. His eyes were fierce, filled with that unwavering resilience that never seemed to falter.

His words reached for the strength within me, but instead, something darker roared to life, fueling a boiling rage born of weeks of frustration, helplessness, and the cruel machinations of fate. The visions had been clear: death. His death and mine. The end of everything I had fought to protect. I was supposed to choose. The earth demanded sacrifice, and I was livid that it wasn't enough to ask for one. It was going to take us all. I swallowed the scream building in my chest, the burn of magic at my fingertips threatening to explode.

Dex's grip on my shoulder tightened, his voice snapping me out of my spiraling thoughts. "Cleo?" His voice cracked with desperation, and fear. "Can you hold it long enough for me to drive my axe through it?"

Time seemed to freeze. The battlefield faded to silence. Those words echoed in my mind, louder and louder until they drowned out everything else. He was asking me to let him get himself killed, to trade his life for mine.

"No." The word slipped from my lips before I could stop it.

Dex scowled, his hand slipping to the back of my neck, forcing me to meet his gaze. "Cleo, this is the only way. You can hold it, I know you can. I'll finish it before—"

"*Stop!*" My voice cracked, raw with emotion. "If you go over these walls, you will die."

"If this is the price for survival, then so be it."

"No!" The word came out louder this time, a guttural cry ripped from my chest. My hands trembled as they pushed against him, desperate to shove him away. "Do you hear yourself? *You will die!*"

"I'm not asking for your permission, Cleo! This is my duty and I'll do it without hesitation!"

A bitter laugh tore from my throat, sharp and humorless. "Fate doesn't care about choices. Don't you get it? It's not trading your life for mine—it's demanding *both!* The vision never showed victory. It showed me destruction."

I could see the crack in his composure, the helplessness he was trying so hard to bury. But there was no hiding it from me. His hand dropped to his side, curling into a tight fist. "Then what do you want me to do? Stand here and watch as it kills us all? Tell me what other options we have!"

His words tore at something deep inside me, the raw vulnerability cutting through my anger. I reached deep within myself, past the fear, the exhaustion, the pain. I found the barriers I had erected long ago, the walls that held back the darker side of my power. They had been my protection, my safeguard against the torrent of magic that threatened to consume me. But now, those walls felt like chains, binding me to a fate I refused to accept.

I saw the orcs—bloodied, bruised, clinging to life—and it clawed at the edge of my sanity. The endless darkness, the helplessness that had held me back, that fear of failing them all broke under an unbridled wrath.

Heat flared through me as I called on the seductive magic, watching as my veins set my skin alight with a fiery red glow. It radiated off me like waves from a furnace, scorching the air, making the stone beneath my feet sizzle with heat. The orcs moved back on instinct, their wide eyes filled with a mixture of awe and fear.

My mate's voice broke through the haze. "Hold steady!" He barked the words at the warriors around us, his focus snapping between me and the creatures pressing against the line. His axe swung in a deadly arc, cleaving through them with ease.

My heart clenched. It wasn't just the orcs fighting for their lives—it was my mate throwing himself into the chaos without hesitation, trusting that I would do my part. But the plan wasn't enough. None of it was enough. The dragon loomed in the distance, its dark magic pulsing like a beacon of destruction, and I knew that every second we wasted brought us closer to death.

"Fuck fate."

My feet carried me toward the wall before I could second-guess the decision, my steps quick and silent against the stone. If fate wanted death, then it would get it in spades.

A red haze clouded my eyes as I tore down the barriers to the darkness within. Everything inside me screamed for vengeance, for survival, for a way to make the shadows writhe in pain.

I ripped off my shoes, feeling the cold stone of the ramparts bite into my feet, grounding me to the earth below. Power was seared through my veins until I thought I might burst.

I turned away from my mate, ignoring the bond between us that screamed with his fear. My focus was razor-sharp, honed on the dragon, the shadows, the endless tide of darkness that sought to devour everything. The walls crumbled and the rage inside had taken over, the darkness had pushed me too far. It was pulling me deeper, feeding off every emotion—fear, desperation, anger—building into something I couldn't contain. My hands shook, sparks of energy snapping between my fingers as the glow from my body intensified, shifting into a blazing gold.

With my mate fighting beside me, I was more than just a shaman; I was a force forged in unity and fire. Taking a final step forward, my feet left the rampart, and I let the frenzy consume me as I fell.

CHAPTER 36
DEX

The air was thick with the stench of blood and dark magic, each breath burning in my lungs as I swung my axe with ruthless precision, the blade cleaving through another of the twisted creatures that clawed hungrily at the stronghold walls. The clash of steel and the guttural roars of battle melded into a deafening symphony of chaos. The ground beneath us trembled with the force of the shadow dragon's wrath, its power thrumming through the stone like a living pulse. But then, abruptly, the tremors subsided.

I stilled, my grip tightening around the haft of my axe, muscles coiled and ready. Something had shifted. My gaze snapped to the source—Cleo. She stood atop the ramparts, an ethereal beacon against the night, her hands outstretched, her body vibrating with raw magic that radiated in waves. Roots—thick, ancient, and gnarled—burst from the earth below, weaving through the crumbling stone, sealing cracks and reinforcing the stronghold with a force that seemed almost sentient. I could feel the energy rolling off her wildly, a manifestation of the earth itself bending to her will.

The dragon's roar split the night, a soul-rattling cry that made my bones tremble. Its titanic body thrashed as vines coiled up around its limbs, but Cleo's power held it fast, trapping it down with a strength I had never imagined she possessed.

But hope is a fragile, fickle thing.

The bond between us flared—searing, blistering, as if the very air between us had ignited. A violent heat pulsed through my veins, staggering me, nearly driving me to my knees. Cleo's magic surged through our bond, wild and unchecked, a storm raging inside her that threatened to devour me. I could feel her desperation, her need to protect, but beneath it lurked something darker—an insatiable hunger for more. The sharp edge of it clawed at me, filling me with an unfamiliar dread.

I scanned the battlefield as my heart pounded with urgency. There she was, moving down from the safety of the wall, each step radiating danger.

The warriors nearest her, hardened veterans who had faced horrors beyond reckoning, stumbled back, their faces tight with fear. Gornak hesitated as she passed, his knuckles white around the haft of his axe. To my left I heard someone mutter a prayer to the Gods. She looked like a goddess of war and destruction, and they did not know whether to bow or flee.

A cold sweat slicked my skin beneath my armor, a raw fear curling in my gut. This power—this terrifying, boundless force—was more than I had ever prepared for. She had warned me. She had pleaded with me to understand, but I had underestimated it. I had underestimated *her*. And now, watching her unravel before me, watching her lose herself to this magic, the weight of my failure crashed over me.

"Cleo!" My voice was desperate, but she didn't hear me.

She moved with eerie grace, power bleeding from her every pore, the air around her thick with magic so potent it made my skin crawl. I couldn't tear my gaze from her. Every step she took fed the fire within her, the glow intensifying until it was blinding.

The shadow beasts stilled, their grotesque faces contorting in agony as their bodies withered, shriveling into dust that the wind carried away. Her magic was a tempest, furious, all-consuming, and starved for release. It was destruction incarnate, a wildfire burning beyond reason, and I could see it consuming her.

I pushed forward with renewed urgency, my heart slamming against my ribs. "Cleo!"

Her head tilted at the sound of my voice, but her vacant eyes didn't meet mine. Instead, she took another step forward as golden light bled from her fingertips, magic curling around her hands as she fell into darkness.

CHAPTER 37
CLEO

The battlefield had fallen into a chaotic rhythm—screeches, clashing weapons, and the deep, unending roar of the shadow dragon still thrashing against the vines that bound it to the earth. Exhaustion clawed at my mind, the magic left me raw and stretched thin, but beneath the weariness, something dark gnawed at me.

I had trapped the dragon, bound it with the ancient roots of the earth, but it wasn't enough. The dark creatures still swarmed the stronghold, their twisted forms crawling over the walls.

My breath came in shallow, ragged gasps, my entire body trembling with power that promised retribution, scorching through my soul. Flames licked at my palms, crawling up my wrists. The heat radiated from my skin, searing the air as flames dripped from my hands like molten metal, each drop hissing as it struck the stone beneath my feet. It was as if my anger and fear had found form in the fire, feeding on me, building into an insatiable storm. I could feel it spreading, burning away the last remnants of my control and leaving only raw power in its wake.

Whispers danced in the flames, they spoke of death—of destruction —of endless war. *Choose.*

The creatures let out a deafening chorus of screams as they abandoned their assault on the orcs, their monstrous forms moved with inhuman speed as they leapt from the walls, their eyes fixed on me.

"You expect me to just accept this?" I growled, the fire blazing higher in response to my anger. "Is this the justice of the earth? Of the prophecy? Is this what you wanted?" My voice was raw, the words spilling out into the night, aimed at the world, at the earth, at whatever cruel force had decided my life was theirs to play with.

"You gave me power and chained me to it! You gave me hope! What kind of choice is this!"

The power inside me flared in response, rising like a tide, and I felt the earth shift beneath my feet. With a surge of energy, the ground rumbled and thick roots exploded from the soil, twisting and coiling like serpents. They surged forward, slithering across the battlefield toward the creatures, snagging them, grabbing at their limbs with a crushing strength. The creatures thrashed against the roots, their bodies writhing as they tried to break free, their claws tearing at the stone.

The flames roared into an unstoppable force, my heart pounding like a war drum, each beat pushing more power through my veins, too much to contain, too much to hold back. The air shimmered with the heat, warping the night around me, and the creatures let out piercing shrieks as the flames reached them. The fire coiled around their bodies, wrapping them in an embrace that seared their flesh, their bodies turning to ash

"Cleo, Please!"

I didn't respond to the call through the mate bond. I couldn't. My focus had narrowed into a single minded goal. *Obliteration.* The creatures fell in droves, reduced to charred husks and ash before my eyes, and it wasn't enough. *More.*

Every breath burned, but I welcomed the pain, letting it fill my lungs until I thought I might combust. My skin was numb, deadened to everything but the power that pulsed through me, dark and intoxicating. I didn't want to stop. I didn't want to give it up.

I could feel Dex through our bond, an anchor pulling against the tidal wave of rage and hunger within me. His desperation wrapped around me like a tether, a steady rhythm in the storm, but it wasn't enough to break the hold the power had. His fear echoed through our connection, bleeding into me in shuddering waves, but I shoved it aside, trying to force the connection shut.

"Fight it, Cleo. Fight with me. Don't let it consume you." I could hear him begging to break through the firestorm that had overtaken me. In my heart I knew I wasn't strong enough to stop this. I had bound myself to the flames, giving in to fate, but wouldn't pull him into death with me.

I had crossed the line that fate had drawn, stepping into a place where control slipped through my fingers, where the fire ruled me. The flames burned with rage and need to protect my new family.

The flames devoured the dark creatures before turning on the earth and slammed against my will, racing for the sanctuary walls, threatening to consume everything we had fought so hard to protect.

Dex was still there, his presence insistent, his strength pressing against the edges of my mind, trying to connect. Against my will, I felt the bond between us strengthen, his steady presence forcing cracks into the chaos consuming me.

Could I control this, or would it control me?

"Fuck your prophecy!" I screamed into the fire, fury and heartbreak bubbling over.

CHAPTER 38

DEX

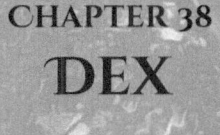

The flames raged across the battlefield, turning the darkness into a twisted, nightmarish glow. From my place on the walls, I could barely hear my own voice over the roar of the fire. My throat burned as I shouted, but the words seemed to vanish into the heat, swallowed by the crackling inferno approaching the stronghold.

"Cleo!" I called, my voice raw with anguish. My hands tightened around the stone of the rampart, my knuckles turning white as I leaned out over the edge, desperately trying to keep her in sight through the waves of heat that distorted the air. The flames leapt up from the earth, burning away the darkness.

She was somewhere beyond the flames, moving toward the dragon with that terrifying power blazing through her. I could feel it pulling at the bond between us, her pain and anger bleeding into every thread as she tried to force our connection shut. I could barely make her out, a figure wreathed in fire, but I knew it was her.

The flames coiled around her, and I couldn't help but think of how she'd looked tucked in my arms in the firelight our first night in the forest, back when the war was just whispers and shadows. But that woman—soft and uncertain—was gone, replaced by this fierce, untouchable being. It terrified me as much as it filled me with awe.

This was my doing. I had driven her to this edge, to this breaking point. She wasn't just fighting the creatures; she was fighting things far greater—fate, the prophecy, and the cruel hand that had shaped her life into this moment. And I didn't know how to pull her back without breaking her further.

I scanned the faces of my warriors gathered along the wall. They were wounded, battered from hours of fighting, their faces pale and streaked with blood and grime, barely held together by my mate's magic as they tried to hold off the remaining shadows. Gornak was standing with one arm hanging at an odd angle, face twisted in pain, but his eyes were sharp and focused on me.

"Hold the line!" I shouted, trying to keep the desperation out of my voice. The warriors needed to see strength from me, even if every instinct I had screamed to go to Cleo, to drag her back from whatever edge she was walking.

Gornak let out a booming laugh. "Aye, Chieftain. We're not done." He glanced over his shoulder, catching the attention of Thorn who clutched a blood-soaked bandage to his ribs. The younger orc quickly bound the wound, raising his weapon with a grim resolve.

The wall beneath us trembled as the dragon let out another earth-shaking roar. The roots Cleo had summoned still held, but I could see the strain in them, the cracks forming where the dragon's dark magic pushed back. It wasn't going to hold forever. And if Cleo's fire consumed her before she could finish this... I shook my head, refusing to let the thought take root. I couldn't afford doubt, not now.

Beside me, Gornak shifted, his face pale but set with determination. "She's burning herself out, Dex." I could barely hear him over the crackle of flames. "She needs the clan's strength."

He turned toward the others, his voice rising to cut through the noise. "She needs us! She needs your strength!"

We'd seen what Cleo was capable of—had witnessed the miracles she worked when she healed and when she fought beside us. She was *our* shaman, my mate, and we couldn't let her stand alone.

Gornak continued, his voice rising with each word. "We know the words! They have power and we need to give it to our shaman."

I felt a pang of gratitude toward Gornak. He had seen the path forward when I had been blinded by fear for my mate, blind to the old ways. He'd reminded me that we weren't alone in this fight. I clapped his shoulder in thanks, a tired smile pulled at the corner of his scarred lips.

The chant spread along the wall, the words ancient and powerful, resonating through the night. They spoke of strength, of resilience, of a future that we would carve out of the darkness, no matter how deep it ran. The frayed bond between Cleo and me flared with renewed energy, no longer a blistering heat, instead, it was tempered, as if the fire that raged through her had found an anchor.

With my heart pounding, I turned back toward the flames and prayed that whatever strength we gave her would be enough. Desperation and shame burned through me at what I had done to her.

CHAPTER 39
SEER ARNA

The cries of the battle reached us deep in the mountain. My mind was elsewhere, turning over the decisions that had led us to this moment. I had known, from the moment Dex proposed seeking the shaman beyond the Wild Lands, that they would see her as a weapon, a means to strike back at the humans who had driven us from our home. But Cleo was more than that. She was a flame the earth itself had chosen, and flames could not be wielded without consequence. I had warned them, yet even I couldn't foresee the full weight of what would come.

Inside the inner chambers, we huddled together—women, children, and elders—faces pale with fear, our bodies tense as we listened to the distant shouts. Every cry of pain, every clash of steel, and each deafening bellow of the shadow dragon sent chills through me. The very air seemed to tremble with the weight of the battle unfolding beyond our sight.

The ground beneath us shook with a ripple of the power she fought to control. It was too much for one so young, one so unprepared. Cleo carried not just the magic but the weight of our hope, and I feared that burden would shatter her before it saved us. How could they not see? She was no weapon to be forged in fire—she *was* the fire. She was dangerous. The power she had unleashed was consuming the dark creatures that dared to threaten our home, but the price she paid was clear. I could feel it in the vibrations that trembled through the stones beneath us, in the way the air crackled with energy. Cleo was struggling—suffering—to control the magic that she unleashed.

I had known the risks when I sent them South to find her, had seen the threads of fate pulling us toward this moment. But seeing it now, hearing the pain in her voice, I questioned whether I had been wrong to trust the earth's will. Cleo had not chosen this path—it had been thrust upon her by all of us, myself included. And yet, as much as I wished to shield her, I knew she had to walk this road alone. The earth had chosen her, and it would not be denied.

And then there was Dex, his voice filled with fear for his mate, carried over the cacophony of battle. He was calling for her, pleading with Cleo to come back to him. His grief echoed through the silence of our sanctuary, carrying the rawness of his dread. Around me, the women clutched their children closer, tears streaming down their faces as they wept for not only their Chieftain, but for their shaman. Their friend.

Beside me, Old Mother Soli sat with her back straight, her sharp eyes fixed on the ceiling as if she could see through the stone. Her hands were calloused from years of labor, and though she no longer wielded a blade, the strength of her spirit had not dimmed with age. I had known her all my life, seen her endure more than many could bear, and now, I saw that same endurance in her gaze. She was listening—feeling—just as I was.

"She fights for us, despite our deception, our shaman fights, but her fate does not have to be final. She is one of us." Soli murmured, her voice echoing through the chambers.

I nodded my agreement, the bond between her and the clan was more than just spells and rituals—it was belief, a shared strength that could tip the scales of fate.

"We need to help her. Our power can reach her. We cannot let the darkness take her. She is part of this clan!" Soli continued, her voice growing stronger.

Above us, through the thick stone, we heard the distant sound of voices—deep and resonant, flowing with a familiar rhythm.

The warriors had begun to chant.

The ancient words of the prophecy, passed down through generations, filled the air, their voices carrying a promise older than any of us. A shiver ran through me as an old magic responded.

I rose to my feet, old bones protesting the movement, but my heart thrummed with purpose. "They are calling to her. And so will we."

Beside me, Soli's gaze burned with fierce conviction, a wisdom that reached back through the ages. She motioned with a weathered hand, urging them to rise. "We chant with them. We give her our strength and call her home."

The others stood as well, some clutching the hands of their loved ones, their children, while others leaned on each other for support. Their fear was palpable, but so was their determination. *Their regret.* We were part of this fight, and now, more than ever, our shaman needed us too.

Our voices joined the warriors. At first, the sound was low, hesitant, but then it grew—filling the chamber with a deep, steady melody that reverberated off the walls. I felt the words move through me, ancient and powerful, carrying with them the weight of generations.

When the earth is torn and the sky burns red,
And the balance falters and the green is dead.
From the lands of men shall a fire arise,
With hair of flame and storm in her eyes.

She shall walk with the magic deep in her veins,
And call to the earth through its roots and rains.
The shaman will come to heal and to fight,
To bring back the dawn after endless night.

Her hands shall mend where the darkness has spread,
Her touch will raise what the shadows left dead.
She'll stand with the earth, between life and decay,
And lead the lost home, to the break of day.

The balance she brings will shatter the chains,

Of exile and fear, of sorrow and pains.
Through mountains and rivers to forests untamed, The shaman shall
guide and the world reclaimed.

Hair of fire, eyes of the earth,
She will rise from roots of birth,
With hands that mend and flames that guide,
She will stand where fate divides.

She will stand against the dark,
With the earth as her spark.
Through her blood, through her pain,
She will bring us home again.

As our voices rose, something stirred in the air around us. I felt it in my center, a vibration that pulsed through the ground, through the very heart of the stronghold. The fire that Cleo had unleashed outside—searing with its raw heat—began to change, to shift, as if it were listening to us.

The stone beneath my feet hummed, responding to the energy we poured into our words. And in what felt like an eternity, the weight of the dark magic began to lift, the oppressive darkness that had pressed against my mind easing just a little. A spark of hope flared in my chest.

"The earth hears us! It answers our call!" I shouted, raising my hands as I felt the energy thrumming through my fingertips. "Again! Show her what it means to be Blackfoot Clan!"

We wouldn't stop, not when our shaman needed us. Not when we could still fight for her, as she fought and sacrificed for us.

Perhaps I should have said more, pushed harder to protect her from our desperation. Now, I could only hope she would see through our failings to the truth of her place among us. Even through the fire and the fury, I saw her strength. Cleo was more than we deserved and I prayed that we would be enough to save her from fate.

CHAPTER 40
CLEO

The firestorm raged around me, a maelstrom of heat and fury. I stood at its center, my body trembling with exhaustion. I could feel the fire licking hungrily at the edges of my control, searing the earth beneath my feet, devouring the darkness that slithered toward me, their whispered promises of despair and ruin coiling around my mind with icy, insidious fingers.

Through the roaring flames, past the shrieks of dying creatures, a whisper of sound caught on the wind, growing louder, clearer, wrapping around me like the comforting embrace of something familiar and steady.

The warriors were chanting, voices rough, rising above the fire, a steady cadence that throbbed with ancient power like a war drum. The prophecy—my prophecy—resounded in my ears, echoing in my chest and forcing back the gnawing dread. They believed in me, and despite everything, despite the betrayal, I felt their faith pulse through me.

Closing my eyes, I let their voices seep into my bones, letting their strength bleed into mine. My hands trembled, the fire dancing at my fingertips, but beneath it all, something ancient stirred—the earth itself, alive and pulsing beneath my bare feet, whispering to me, calling me home. The stones on my bracelet cooled against my skin with a borrowed strength.

I wasn't alone.

The earth wrapped around me and I felt the weight of my clan's sorrow, their fear and their regret. It pulled me back, reminding me that I was more than fire and destruction—I was their hope.

The flames around me responded, no longer wild and hungry, but obedient, bending to my will, moving with purpose. I opened my eyes, and the silver light that pulsed within them seemed to reflect a newfound clarity. The dragon before me was still struggling against the thick, ancient roots that held it in place. Its scales pulsed with malevolent shadows, writhing against the earthen grip, but cracks had begun to form, tiny fractures spiderwebbing across its monstrous form.

The dragon let out a deafening roar, causing the very stones beneath me to shuddered, but I didn't flinch. My heart pounded with a fierce, primal determination. The fire coiled tighter around my arms licking toward the sky like serpents. Silver light gleamed against the dark as power surged through me, swelling in my chest until I thought I might shatter beneath it.

With a voice that rang out clear and resolute, I spoke the final words of the prophecy with them.

"She will bring us home again."

The words vibrated through the air. They were true. They were always true. *I could end this.*

The fire answered my call, a tidal wave of molten fury crashing into the dragon's body. It thrashed, agonized howls splitting the night as the inferno consumed it, eating through the layers of darkness and searing through its essence until all that remained was ash.

Beyond the shadows of the battlefield, a figure emerged cloaked in darkness, moving with an unsettling grace. His skeletal face stretched taut over sharp bones, was a grotesque mask of malice, dark veins pulsing like living serpents beneath his pale skin. His blackened eyes locked onto mine. They were filled with a hunger that made my stomach churn.

There was no doubt this was the dark mage that the clans feared.

His withered hand rose, fingers curling like talons as dark tendrils slithering around his wrist like serpents eager to strike. Shadows churned and swirled at his command. Without warning, a bolt of darkness shrieked through the air, the force of it splitting the battlefield with a thunderous crack. Instinct roared through me, and the earth answered my silent plea, a jagged pillar of stone erupting from the ground just in time to absorb the blow. The impact sent a jarring tremor through my bones, shaking the ground beneath my feet, his dark magic was like a suffocating net of death.

Agony lanced through my bond with the earth, my muscles screamed in protest, and sweat slicked my skin as I shoved the pain aside. The ground beneath me groaned, alive with raw fury, mirroring the seething anger that coursed through my veins. My hands burned, energy swirling beneath my skin, hungry and insatiable.

The mage's lips curled into a ghastly smile as the veins beneath his pallid skin pulsed with dark energy. Shadows coiled around him, undulating, whispering promises of ruin as his magic crept toward me, hungry, curling like skeletal fingers eager to strip me bare. In desperation, I lashed out. Fire surged from my right hand in a flaming arc, but with a casual flick of his wrist, the dark magic rose and extinguished the flames before they could reach him.

Cold tendrils clawed at the edges of my fire, seeking to choke the life from it, forcing me to whip it hotter, brighter—pushing it to its limits. Fear clawed at my chest. My fire, the same fire that had slain a dragon, wasn't enough to reach him. I reached for my mate bond, grasping for Dex like a drowning soul reaching for a lifeline, his presence pulsing through me fiercely, curling protectively around my heart. The strength in our connection tethered me and I plunged into the well of pure magic buried deep within the earth. The raw power coiled like a beast, resisting, testing me, daring me to wield it. My fingers trembled as I wrapped around those volatile threads, a guttural cry tore from my throat and echoed across the battlefield. My mind howled in protest as the power surged through every fiber of my being. With one final desperate push, I thrust my hands forward, hurling everything I had left into one last, defiant strike. A bolt of lightning arced through the air, a blazing spear of raw power that cleaved through the darkness like the wrath of the Gods themselves. It struck him square in the chest, and for a split second, his expression twisted in disbelief, his skeletal form convulsing as the magic ripped through him.

He staggered, mouth open in a silent scream, before his body began to disintegrate. Blackened ash peeled away, layer by layer, and was carried off by the wind. His final whisper—a faint, gurgling gasp—was swallowed by the roaring fire around us.

The oppressive weight of his magic dissipated, fading into the night like a bad dream. Silence stretched across the battlefield, the flames around me dimmed, their hunger sated, and the earth settled beneath my feet as if sighing in relief.

The voices of my clan reached me. Their roar of victory shaking the stone beneath my feet. I swayed on my feet, exhaustion sinking into my bones. I felt the steady thrum of our bond and let out a broken sob of relief, I had worried I may have killed my mate by pulling on him. *Dex was okay.*

The world tilted dangerously, my vision swam and I fell, unconsciousness taking me before I hit the scorched earth.

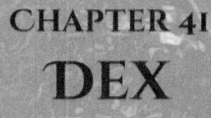

CHAPTER 41

DEX

The air buzzed with remnants of Cleo's magic. Ash blanketed the ground, and the rock still radiated an intense heat. Her body lay crumpled in the dirt, the glow of her power fading as quickly as the darkness that had threatened to overrun us.

I dropped from the stairs and raced across the blistering rock, falling to my knees beside her. My hands shook as I reached out and brushed my fingers against her skin. She was burning up.

Underneath her bond bracelet was the origin point of a channeling scar, stretching down to her fingertips and spiraling up her forearm. A jagged, twisting pattern that reminded me of lightning striking sand. The scar glowed faintly, as if remnants of the lightning she had wielded still pulsed beneath her skin. It should have been grotesque—a channeling scar that no healer could mend—but instead, it was oddly beautiful, shimmering with an inner light.

She had saved us, but at what cost? My chest tightened as I traced the path of the lightning marks with a reverence I couldn't put into words. She had risked everything for the clan that had thought to use her as a weapon. I'd let this happen—I'd allowed her to carry the weight of our survival on her shoulders, untrained and unprepared. I'd been blind, too focused on our enemy to see what I was doing to her.

She didn't deserved any of this.

My thumb brushed over the smooth, healed skin, and my heart twisted at how small her hand looked against mine. Her chest was barely moving with each shallow breath, and a cold knot of fear twisted in my gut. I gathered her into my arms with care and raced for the stronghold.

Gornak let out a sharp bark of orders, rallying the others to clear a path. "Move!" They parted quickly, faces streaked with blood and soot and eyes wide with concern and regret as they saw Cleo limp in my arms.

They surged around us, forming a protective line as we made our way through the rubble and into the safety of the stronghold. My chest ached with every step, but I clung to the steady rise and fall of Cleo's breaths against my shoulder. *She was alive.*

I carried her to healers' quarters, the cold air in the room stark against the heat that clung to her skin. The warmth of her power still lingered as I laid her down on a low cot, like the embers of a dying fire. Our healers knelt beside her, their hands hovering just above her chest as they murmured the incantations that guided their magic. I focused on the rise and fall of her shallow breaths and begged the Gods to show us mercy.

I had failed her. Not just in battle, but long before it. When I'd met her, I had seen her power as a solution, a way to save my people, and in my desperation, I hadn't stopped to consider what it would cost. The one who had given everything for a people she'd barely had time to call her own.

I turned away from the healers and glanced at the exhausted faces of my friends gathered outside the room. They were alive because of her. When she woke I would show her that she wasn't just a weapon, wasn't just our salvation. She was one of us. A part of this clan. I would spend my life proving that to her, earning her forgiveness.

"She burns with power," one of the healers murmured, his expression troubled. "But it's different than anything I have ever seen. I don't know how to help her. "

The words struck me like a blow, knocking the breath from my lungs. My knees buckled, and I sank down beside her, my hand closing around hers. She had poured every ounce of herself into protecting us, and I had no illusions that we deserved it.

Seer Arna stepped into the room, and when her gaze fell on Cleo, her expression clouded with an emotion I couldn't place. But her lips were pressed tight, and something in her eyes was already too knowing.

I rose, holding back the storm that threatened to spill over. "Did you see this? Did you see what we would do to her?"

She glanced away, her silence a betrayal I hadn't expected. A cold knot twisted in my chest as I searched her face for any sign of regret, any hint that she wished things were different. But Arna's face remained impassive.

"She's my *mate*, Arna!" My voice cracked with anguish, the words tumbling out like a plea. "Tell me I didn't kill my mate!"

Arna held her silence, her eyes returning to Cleo, as though an answer lay in the fragile human who laid before us.

"You should have told me," I growled. "If you knew... I could have done something—"

"Dex," Arna whispered, her voice unsteady, though she quickly recovered her composure. "I warned you of trying to wield the earth's power like a blade. Some things aren't ours to alter. *There are sacrifices that must be made to maintain balance.* She chose her path willingly, just as we chose to fight with her. The rest is up to the earth to decide."

Her words were a slap in the face, and I couldn't breathe past the knot in my throat. I forced my hands to unclench, but the anger didn't leave. It settled like a burning coal, low and bitter in my stomach as I turned back to Cleo and took her limp hand in mine. I squeezed her fingers gently, as if my touch alone could call her back to me.

"She has walked through fire but she was never truly alone. That is what saved her."

"Let me see her," Seer Arna said. Her eyes were distant and unfocused, as if she were looking through us, beyond our realm. The healers exchanged uneasy glances as they backed away, aware of the signs of an approaching vision. Arna's hands shook as she reached out, her fingertips brushing Cleo's scarred arm.

Her breath caught, body going rigid as a vision took her. I surged forward, ready to catch her, but she straightened, and her voice spilled out in a low, broken rhythm. Each word was laced with a dark and ancient power.

"She's standing alone in a valley. Blood drips from her hands. The clans gather around her, but shadows press closer, hiding on the edges of the clan fires. Scouts sent to the old tribes. Some return and others swallowed by the darkness—I see the banner of the Silver Hand—"

She fell silent, her chest heaving with each breath. Arna's eyes clouded with the remnants of the vision, shadows swirling in their depths.

"Is that our fate?"

Arna's lips tugged into a grim smile. "Nothing is certain, Chieftain. But the path is there, if she is to wake. Watch for the shadows or they will take her from us."

"When she wakes..." I said, my voice raw with determination. "Even if we survive this night, Ostelan will not forget. They've already seen her power. This victory is borrowed time. They will come for us again, and without unity we will fall."

Arna nodded, her tired eyes regarding Cleo. Whatever lay ahead—whatever darkness still clung to our heels—I would not waver. With Cleo at my side, we would forge a new future, one that no empire, no prophecy, could steal from us.

I squeezed her hand, feeling the faint pulse of warmth beneath her delicate skin. My grip tightened as I willed her to return to me, to see the world we had fought to save. Until then, I would be waiting for her.

My fingers traced over her bond bracelet, my chest swelling with pride. She was fierce, forged by forces few could withstand. And she was mine.

"Tend to the wounded, and send riders to the remaining clans. It's time we took back what's ours."

AFTERWORD

You made it.

Through the fire, the chains, the battles, and the blood. You stood beside Cleo as she fought, as she broke, as she burned—only to rise again. And if you're anything like me, I hope you felt every moment of it.

Cleo goes through hell in this book. Caged, silenced, underestimated—but never truly defeated. Even when the world tries to break her, she fights back. With rage. With resilience. With fire.

I hope there's a little bit of Cleo in all of us. I hope you know what it's like to want more, to fight for your freedom, to stand your ground even when the odds are against you. I hope you've learned, like she did, that your anger is not a weakness—it's power. That no matter what chains have been placed on you, you are more than what the world has tried to make of you.

Writing *Bound in Flames* was intense—emotional, exhilarating, and sometimes, brutal. But this story burned inside me for a long time, and knowing that it's now in your hands? That means everything.

So thank you. For stepping into this world. For fighting alongside Cleo. For proving that we don't always love the hero—sometimes, the monster is exactly what we need.

But this isn't the end. The war has only begun.

Cleo's choices have set a kingdom on fire, but Ostelan's fate doesn't rest in her hands alone.

~

COMING SOON
Kneel in the Ashes

Rowan knows better than to care. The Wild Lands are not kind, and neither is she. For thirteen years, she has hunted, fought, and killed to keep her past buried in blood. Trained as an assassin, forged into a weapon, she does not hesitate. She does not trust. And she does not save those who can't save themselves.

Until him.

Kaldor was sent to deliver a message. Instead, he became prey. Hunted by the Knights of the Silver Hand, he should be dead. But when a sharp-eyed assassin puts an arrow through his pursuer's throat, his fate is sealed. Orcs do not choose mates, the bond does. And from the moment he looks at her, his soul belongs to hers.

But Rowan doesn't believe in fate. She doesn't believe in bonds, in love, in anything she cannot control. She fights him at every turn, refusing to kneel to destiny.

War is coming. Blood will be spilled. And when the fires rise again, she will have to decide—run once more, or stand and fight for what could be hers.

~

CRAVING MORE?
Read Rise of the Chieftain for FREE

The path to becoming Chieftain is carved in blood, pain, and sacrifice. Dex will claim his place, or he will die trying. Survive the trials, win the right to lead, and earn the power to take back what was stolen.

The humans think his people are weak. Beaten. Broken. They think their chains will hold.

But Dex has never been one to kneel. He was forged in battle. He fights for vengeance. And he will burn their world to the ground.

FREE NOVELLA - Savage Oath - Rise of the Chieftain

ACKNOWLEDGMENTS

To my husband, for surviving my late-night writing marathons, endless plot debates, and for never once questioning why I needed his opinion on fictional battle strategies or the physics of elemental magic. Your patience deserves a medal.

To Tamora Pierce, whose stories of fierce, unstoppable heroines lit the fire in a preteen bookworm and shaped the writer I am today. May my leading ladies do you proud.

To my therapist, who reminded me that doing the hard things is worth it—and that the opinions of people who don't pay my bills (or buy my books) don't matter.

ABOUT THE AUTHOR

Missy S Castillo is an Australian transplant living in the U.S., where she shares her life with her husband and kids.

Before stepping into the spotlight as an indie author, Missy honed her craft as a ghostwriter, captivating readers behind the scenes. Now, she embraces the creative freedom of self-publishing, breathing life into stories filled with morally gray heroes, swoon-worthy monsters, and heroines who refuse to be anything but extraordinary.

Representation matters. Missy believes that heroines should be as real as the readers who love them—imperfect, strong, and unapologetically themselves. Whether they're falling for the monster, defying fate, or forging their own destiny, they are never just one thing—because neither are we.

She thrives on connecting with readers, whether it's through her social media platforms or live chats from her cozy greenhouse—a place where creativity and passion intertwine.